nothing

ERIN KINSLEY

HEADLINE

Copyright © 2025 Erin Kinsley

The right of Erin Kinsley to be identified as the Author of
the Work has been asserted by her in accordance with the
Copyright, Designs and Patents Act 1988.

First published in Great Britain in 2025 by
HEADLINE PUBLISHING GROUP

1

Apart from any use permitted under UK copyright law, this publication may only
be reproduced, stored, or transmitted, in any form, or by any means, with prior
permission in writing of the publishers or, in the case of reprographic production,
in accordance with the terms of licences issued by the Copyright Licensing Agency.

All characters in this publication are fictitious and any resemblance
to real persons, living or dead, is purely coincidental.

Cataloguing in Publication Data is available from the British Library

ISBN 978 1 4722 9256 8

Typeset in Adobe Garamond by CC Book Production

Printed and bound in Great Britain by Clays Ltd, Elcograf S.p.A.

Headline's policy is to use papers that are natural, renewable and
recyclable products and made from wood grown in well-managed forests
and other controlled sources. The logging and manufacturing processes
are expected to conform to the environmental regulations
of the country of origin.

MIX
Paper | Supporting
responsible forestry
FSC® C104740
FSC
www.fsc.org

HEADLINE PUBLISHING GROUP
An Hachette UK Company
Carmelite House
50 Victoria Embankment
London EC4Y 0DZ

www.headline.co.uk
www.hachette.co.uk

For Ken, an eagle-eyed marvel

'We must be willing to let go of the life we planned so as to have the life that is waiting for us.'

Joseph Campbell, 1904–1987

PART ONE
Seeds of Disaster

Derbyshire, November 2013

ONE

Wrong place, wrong time.

Tommy Henthorn brakes to a halt at the crossroads just outside the village of Marrop and considers his options. To get home, he could turn right and go through Sledwell, which would save him several miles. But he's in no hurry, and might for a change take the scenic route to enjoy the views over Birdmoor.

A little thing makes up his mind. In the direction of Sledwell, above the hedges lining the lane, he can see the roof of an approaching vehicle, a people carrier or minibus. If he goes that way, he'll likely face the minor inconvenience of having to pull onto the verge so it can pass.

Whereas the lane towards Birdmoor appears clear.

So – believing the choice is insignificant – he heads that way, not yet knowing how many times in years to come he will regret this moment, still oblivious of the consequences of turning left instead of right.

In the cold sunlight, the lane shines copper with fallen leaves. Though it's a while since he was here, he used to come this way often. A few hundred metres ahead is the track leading up to Hagg Side Farm, and the thought comes to him that he could stop and pay a visit. He knows the farm well; as a boy – until he was thirteen or fourteen years old and thought he had better things to do with his time – he used to do odd jobs for the old boy who owned it.

Billy Challiner, recently deceased.

With the benefit of hindsight, he can see now Billy was an introvert, an overtly shy man who never had the confidence to ask a woman out for a drink, never mind find someone to marry him. For years he cared for his frail and elderly mother, who would sometimes appear in the farmhouse doorway while Tommy was hosing down the cow-byre or loading sheep-feed into a barrow. She'd offer him a glass of lemonade or a piece of homemade chocolate cake, which he appreciated regardless of the lemonade often being flat and the cake usually stale. After she died, Billy became moody. People said that out of loneliness he was ruining himself with drink and maybe that was true, but he managed to keep the farm going anyway, right up until the moment of his death.

If not totally unexpected, Billy's death was mercifully sudden. He was found by the postman lying on the muddy yard, one hand stretched out as if he'd fallen flat on his face hailing a taxi. The funeral was well attended, the wake generously funded from a cash-stuffed envelope Billy had years ago left behind the bar at the Cat and Fiddle for that very eventuality, but now legal proceedings were in train. With Billy having no will and no family anyone knows of, searches are underway to find his heirs.

In the meantime, a neighbouring farmer has taken the

ragged livestock down to his fields in the valley. Beyond that, Hagg Side Farm is frozen in time, everything left as it was at the moment Billy dropped dead outside the cow-byre.

And Tommy's thinking there might be one or two items of interest on the property.

Got to be worth a look.

But softly, softly. He'd better not be seen.

When he reaches the farm track, he slows to a stop. The wooden gate that used to be propped open with a rusty anvil is closed, secured by a new-looking chain and padlock, and the *Trespassers will be shot* sign painted in Billy's spidery hand has gone from the post where it was nailed. Tommy drives on a short distance, pulling off the road into the entranceway of the disused quarry that borders Billy's fields. Leaving the Land Rover, he climbs easily over the sturdy aluminium gate barring the quarry entrance, and follows a little-used path to the back of Billy's land, where he scrambles over a dry-stone wall into the sheep pasture.

A bitter wind is blowing from the north.

Lacking gloves, Tommy keeps his hands in his pockets as he follows the downhill slope towards the farm buildings. Underfoot, the animals have trampled much of the grazing to mud, and he wishes he'd changed into the wellingtons he always has with him. Overhead, the flat, grey sky is growing darker, and might even bring snow. Seeing him, a few left-behind sheep stop nibbling the sparse winter grass, and run to gather in a forlorn huddle at the field's furthest corner.

As he walks, he notices what poor repair the wall is in, and wishes he'd made the time to come and see Billy, offered him a hand. The old boy used to be good to him, paid him way over the odds for the work Tommy did. And it was Billy who taught him to rebuild a wall; somewhere here, close by the water trough, is a spot he and Billy repaired together. He finds himself suddenly nostalgic, sad for the old man's passing. Billy was often the butt of jokes, a figure of fun. Now that Tommy's own circumstances have changed and the possibility of a life lived alone is looming, he has more compassion for Billy as a kindred spirit.

When he reaches the bottom of the field, the farmyard lies beyond. Here, too, the gate is closed, though not chained, and he pushes it open just wide enough to squeeze through. In the yard, he listens. All he can hear is the wind rattling the roof panels on the hay barn.

He decides he'll have a look in the outbuildings first, then check out the barn. Depending on what he finds, he might have to come back after dark with some better transport, though there might be small stuff he could take now. What can be passed off as agricultural or architectural antiques – battered buckets, pitchforks and wicker baskets – all sell well on eBay to those wanting rural touches for suburban gardens.

He begins to make his way across the yard, heading for the dairy.

By the time he sees the men standing outside the house – three of them, dressed all wrong for the farmyard in designer Puffa jackets, expensive trainers and jeans – they've already clocked him. One of them he's never seen before; the second he remembers as Dean or maybe Lee.

But the third is someone he used to know well, a man he'd walk to the ends of the earth over hot coals to avoid.

Steven Bull. Who's watching him with those strange, blue eyes.

'Well, look what the cat's dragged in,' Bull calls out to him. 'Slowmo, is that you?'

Tommy considers turning on his heels and walking back the way he's come, but the thing is with Bull, you're always better keeping your cool, facing him down. So he adopts a nonchalant attitude and ambles across the yard, living up to his nickname. Slowmo.

Flashing the gold watch on his wrist, Bull's holding out his hand to be shaken; and even though the idea of touching any part of Bull is repugnant to him, Tommy steels himself and takes it. Best by far just to smile and be nice, though as he expects, Bull's grip is too tight to be friendly and – to remind Tommy who's boss – includes a bone-crushing squeeze before he lets go.

'You know these guys, right?' Bull asks, and when Tommy shakes his head, introduces one of his companions as Donal and the half-remembered other as Lee.

Tommy nods in their direction.

'So what brings you up here, Slowmo?' asks Bull.

Tommy hates that name. He'd thought he'd outgrown it years ago, but somehow of course Bull senses it riles him. Back in the day, Bull's nickname was Headcase, though you'd never dare call him that now. From what Tommy's heard, though, the name's still a good fit: Bull's a crazy, messed-up sadist as likely to chop off your feet as buy you a pint. 'The old man barely cold in his grave and you're up here on the rob?'

'Not really,' Tommy lies. 'Just having a look round for old times' sake. I used to work for him when I was a lad. Anyway, never mind me, what are you doing here? You're a long way off your patch.'

'I suppose we are,' agrees Bull. 'Actually, we're looking at the real estate. A place like this, all nice and quiet, might suit us very well. In the meantime, I think it's our lucky day, bumping into you. We were just saying, weren't we lads, we could do with an extra pair of hands for a little job we need doing. You'd be happy to help out, wouldn't you, Slowmo?'

'Not really.' Tommy dares look Bull in the eye. 'I've got somewhere I need to be.'

'Won't take long.' Bull grins, and Tommy notices he's lost another tooth since he last saw him, gained another ugly, black hole in his malevolent smile. 'You can see we're not really dressed for labouring, whereas you . . .' He runs his pale eyes over Tommy's scruffy jacket and muddied trousers. 'You're all ready to get to work. Donal, find him a shovel.'

TWO

The worst trouble comes on the most ordinary days.

Actually, Adam's thinking today is going better than many. Quite often, he's offered nothing for lunch, but today his mum Gail made fish fingers and the curly chips Adam likes with a big dollop of ketchup, and gave him a pot of Milkybar dessert for pudding. Then she put on the TV and said Adam could watch CBeebies while she went for a nap.

For Adam, time alone with the TV is a treat, even though there's no fire in the lounge and the room is really cold. He wraps himself in a faux-fur blanket and snuggles into the corner of the sofa, pulling the edge of the blanket up over his face to warm his nose, and chooses an episode of *Charlie and Lola*, making sure the volume isn't too loud or Mummy will be annoyed.

After a while, Mummy's phone rings upstairs. It's answered quickly, and Adam can hear the low murmur of her voice, then after a few minutes her footsteps running downstairs. She's combed her hair and put on lipstick and she doesn't look so pale, but she's frowning as she bustles into the lounge and switches off the TV. Crouching, she puts a match to a firelighter in the wood-burner and begins to drop sticks onto the orange flame. At first Adam is pleased because he really hates being cold, but then in her stern voice Mummy tells him to find his coat and wellies and go and play outside in the fresh air.

But Adam doesn't want to.

'It's too cold outside,' he complains. 'Why can't I go to my bedroom instead?'

Mummy isn't listening. Slamming the wood-burner door shut, she runs around the lounge, picking up Adam's lunch plate and all the rubbish that has accumulated over the past couple of days, used coffee mugs and Monster Munch packets and wine glasses with two empty bottles.

'I'm not going outside,' Adam says, sulkily.

'For God's sake! For once, just do as you're told,' snaps Mummy, in that way which means any argument will only bring trouble. 'Why do I have to put up with your whining all the time?'

Adam looks out of the window, where rain threatens. 'Can't I go to Grandma's?'

'No, you can't go to Grandma's.' Mummy's teetering on the edge of shouting. 'She doesn't want you mithering round her any more than I do. Go and get your coat.'

And knowing – even at only four years old – what's good for him, Adam does.

Outside, in the shadow of the hedge, the grass is still silvered with last night's frost. Shivering in his thin jacket, Adam isn't tempted to splash in the yard's dirty puddles or play boats in the waterbutt where a scattering of leaves is trapped in a veneer of clear ice. Instead, he wanders over to the run where his father – even though he doesn't live here any more – still keeps his dogs, but they're snug inside their kennel and no amount of him calling and cajoling will persuade them outside. As he stands holding the wire fence, his hands are becoming too cold to function. Reluctantly, he wanders over to the old forge and pulls open the door.

The forge is long disused, last lit by his grandfather before his death some years ago. The low, stone building is dilapidated and neglected, its windows grimy with coal-dust and smoke, and the unhealthy smell of the place – ashes and dry-rot and rats' piss – always makes Adam reluctant to go inside.

But even if not warm, it is at least better than the caustic cold outside.

Often when he's made to 'play outside', Adam makes use of a Victorian sofa whose horsehair stuffing is all but gone. He settles down there now with his biscuit-tin of Hot Wheels cars and scraps of Lego, and begins to lay the cars out nose-to-tail to see how long a line of them he can make.

Before long, he hears a real car pull up in the yard. The engine is switched off.

Mummy's friend is here.

Adam's seen this friend several times before. Instinctively, he dislikes him.

For a while, he goes back to arranging his cars, but soon grows bored and abandons them. He looks around for other ways to pass the time.

In a corner, there's a sack of cement, though he can't read the blue writing on the sack's paper exterior. Curious what's in there, he tries to tear a hole in the brown paper, but it's tougher than it looks, so instead – out of badness, or boredom – he jumps on it. And again. And again.

On his third jump, the sack bursts. Grey dust billows out, making him cough and stinging his eyes, but the powdery cloud he's created is spectacular, so he decides to jump some more.

Much sooner than he expects, across the yard he hears the front door open. Mummy's friend is leaving. With the sleeve of his jacket, Adam rubs a clear patch on the grimy window and watches the car depart.

Maybe now he'll be allowed back in the house.

But he's in a bit of a mess. Like some hungry ghost, he's grey from head to foot. He's going to need a change of clothes and a bath.

And Mummy is going to be very cross indeed.

THREE

DESPATCHER: *Derbyshire Police, what's your emergency?*
CALLER: *Hello? Well, it's not actually my emergency. I don't know if I should have called really – it's probably not my business . . .*
DESPATCHER: *Can I take your name please, madam?*
CALLER: *My name? Oh. It's Derwent, Barbara Derwent.*
DESPATCHER: *And is this your own number you're calling from?*
CALLER: *Yes, it's my home number, yes.*
DESPATCHER: *And what's the problem there, Barbara?*
CALLER: *It isn't me, it's my next-door neighbour. She's just been round and said her little boy is missing. Well, the child is only four. I said she should call you, but she seemed reluctant. But he's been gone over an hour now, or so Gail says. She does sometimes have a glass of wine in the afternoons so she might have lost track of time.*
DESPATCHER: *So the child might have been gone for longer?*
CALLER: *I think it's possible, yes.*
DESPATCHER: *What's your neighbour's name?*
CALLER: *Gail, Gail Henthorn. You won't tell her it was me that called, will you? I don't want to be a tattle-tale. But Adam's*

only little and it'll be dark soon. You hear such terrible stories, don't you? You of all people know what goes on.

DESPATCHER: *Has the child gone missing before?*

CALLER: *Not that I'm aware of. But he is left by himself quite a lot for one so young. He wanders round here sometimes and I give him a drink and a biscuit. I expect he's off playing somewhere. He might be in one of those old sheds or some place, but as I say, it's getting dark. And obviously Gail is a bit concerned herself or she wouldn't have knocked on my door. I expect she's worried what her husband might say. Ex-husband, as he's soon to be. Anyway, she didn't see any need to bother you. She said he's probably gone to his grandma's down the village but I know he hasn't because I rang his grandma and asked. I wish I hadn't actually because now she's worried sick, as you'd expect.*

DESPATCHER: *What's the address there, Barbara?*

CALLER: *My address?*

DESPATCHER: *Where Adam lives, what's the address there?*

CALLER: *Blacksmith's Cottage, Risedale. It's right at the top of the village, last house on the right-hand side as you go up towards the moor.*

DESPATCHER: *All right, I'm sending someone now.*

CALLER: *You won't mention my name, though, will you? I probably shouldn't have rung.*

DESPATCHER: *You did the right thing calling us, Barbara. We'll take it from here. If we need anything else from you, we'll be in touch.*

FOUR

Well after dark, Tommy drives into the yard of Blacksmith's Cottage. A police car is parked next to Gail's Renault.

Tommy hammers on the cottage door, and is let in by his mother, Lizzie. She looks anxious, close to tears.

'Where on earth have you been? I've been trying to ring you.'

His response is abrupt. 'I've got no battery on my phone. I just bumped into Joan, she said you were up here. What's going on? Where's Adam?'

Lizzie shakes her head, troubled but not yet despairing. 'We don't know. The police are here. I've come to be with Gail. What have you been doing, anyway? Look at the state of you – you're filthy. Take your jacket off, at least.'

Tommy doesn't answer, but glances at the hooks on the wall. One of his outdoor coats still hangs there, Gail having so far refused him permission to collect what remain in the house of his personal belongings since she packed a suitcase for him and left it on the doorstep four months ago. Without removing his jacket, he pushes past his mother and goes into the lounge. Gail is sitting silently with two oversized uniformed policemen, one big-bellied, the other tall. When Tommy and Lizzie both join them, the room feels comically cramped.

Lizzie perches on the arm of the sofa. Skipping any preamble, Tommy fixes his eyes on Gail and demands, 'Where is he?'

Gail's eyes are red from crying. 'I don't know, Tommy, honestly I don't know.'

'Why don't you bloody know? You're his mother, aren't you? It's your job to bloody know. When did you last see him?'

One of the policemen raises his hand. 'Let's all keep calm, Mr Henthorn. We've got no reason to suppose at the moment that this is any more than Adam wandering off and getting himself lost somewhere.'

'Why would he have got himself lost if his mother was taking proper care of him?' Tommy glares at Gail. 'You useless bloody mare. When did you last see him?'

'Gail isn't sure,' puts in Lizzie. 'She thinks it was about half past three.'

'A call came into us around that time,' confirms the policeman.

'So he's been gone over three hours?'

The policeman is placatory. 'Believe me, it's not that long for a child to be missing. They get into all sorts of scrapes and hiding places.'

'He's four years old,' counters Tommy. 'It's been dark for over two hours, and it's freezing cold. Is that not ringing alarm bells with you?'

'Of course it's ringing alarm bells, Tommy,' puts in Lizzie. 'That's why they're here.'

'But not loud enough for them to be out there looking for him?'

'We've always a team standing by,' says the policeman, 'in the event a search becomes necessary.'

'Are you serious?' Tommy shakes his head in disbelief. 'If it becomes necessary, you'll get off your fat arses and go and have a look? Jesus. The state of you.'

'You've a lot of mud on you,' says the second police officer, looking Tommy up and down.

'I've been working outside.'

'What kind of work?'

'Building site.'

'Heavy work after all this rain.'

'Too right. It nearly killed me.' Tommy puts his hand on the doorhandle, plainly intending to leave.

'Where are you going?' asks Lizzie.

'Where do you think I'm going? I'm going to look for my son.'

'You'd be far better letting us do an organised search,' says the police officer. 'No point in you going blundering around in the dark by yourself. We've got a few questions we'd like to ask you, then we can get in touch with the right people and take it from there.'

'What, sit here drinking tea while my son could be at the bottom of a quarry hole? You're out of your mind.'

Tommy goes out into the hall, and moments later Lizzie follows him. 'Where will you look?'

'He can't be far away. I'll take the dogs, see if they can help.'

Back in the lounge, Lizzie apologises for her son's behaviour.

'He's upset, you know. He dotes on that boy, absolutely dotes on him.'

'I told you he's got a temper, didn't I?' says Gail.

As Tommy steps into the yard, a security light comes on. Buster and Nell, the two black Labradors in the wire-fenced run, emerge from their kennel, tails wagging in their delight at seeing him. Letting the dogs out, he crouches beside them and ruffles their heads.

With the dogs in the Land Rover, he drives the short distance to his mother's cottage. This is where he grew up, the place he lived right up to when he married Gail. On his wedding day, he expected to be leaving here for good. Sometimes life takes unexpected turns.

He removes his mud-caked shoes at the back door, and in the kitchen strips off his filthy trousers and jacket and shoves them in the washing machine, adding what he thinks is the right amount of the correct detergent before setting it going.

He washes his hands, then runs up the narrow stairs to the bedroom that's been his all his life to put on clean warm clothes and waterproof over-trousers. Back downstairs, he takes a waterproof coat from the hall stand, pulls on a black beanie and wellingtons and slips gloves and a powerful torch into his pockets.

As he leaves the house again, a frail figure appears on the pathway of the neighbouring house.

'Is that you, Tommy?'

'Yes, it's me, Joan.'

'Is there any news?'

'Not yet. I'm going to look for him now.'

'Have the police come?'

'They're up at Gail's. Mum's still there too.'

'Where do they think he might be?'

'They haven't said.'

'I don't think he'll be far away. And he'll be pleased to know his daddy's coming to find him. You will find him, won't you?'

'If it's the last thing I ever do,' says Tommy.

There's rain in the air, but not enough to give him a soaking. In the glare of a street lamp, a black cat runs across the road.

Tommy pulls up the hood of his coat and lets the dogs out of the Land Rover. With them at his heels, he walks back up the road to where a gap between two houses gives gated access to the field marking the village boundary.

Adam knows this place. Tommy has brought him here many times, carrying a ball to kick about on the cricket pitch at the field's far side.

But Adam's afraid of the dark.

Where Tommy's standing, weak light from the windows of the houses backing onto the field allows him a few metres of visibility. Beyond that, he sees nothing in the blackness but the glint of car headlights where the road runs through the valley and, in the far distance, the lamp-lit windows of isolated hillside farms.

Tommy shines his torch across the field, scanning with the beam to left and right, but sees nothing out of the ordinary. A clever boy like Adam, though, might have learned from observing local sheep, and taken shelter in the lee of a stone wall, or even be out of the weather in the lambing pen on the field's far side.

Tommy's approach is methodical. Starting from where he now stands, he begins to walk the field from one side to the other and back as if he were guiding a plough, the torch all the while lighting his way and shining as a beacon. From time to time he stops and calls out into the night: *'Adam! It's me, Daddy! Adam, son, where are you?'*

One field, and a second. Then the cricket pitch and pavilion. But he finds nothing.

One obvious place remains for him to look.

From a bedroom window, Peter Rains notices a light out on the field behind his cottage.

At first he makes little of it, thinking it's probably Simon playing one of his games.

Until Tessa, coming upstairs, asks, 'Who on earth's doing all that shouting?'

Peter opens the window a crack so they can hear, but the shouter is on the far side of the field and the words are unclear.

Tessa goes for her bath. Peter, though, is intrigued, and continues to watch for the best part of an hour, until the torch beam draws close and he can see who's behind it.

That stocky build is unmistakable.

Tommy walks all the way back up the village, passing Blacksmith's Cottage on his way to Raymond's Wood. Whether or not the police are still there, he can't see.

The night-black wood oozes the dank sweetness of fungal decay. The ground is waterlogged after so much rain, and if he wanders off the path Tommy's boots squelch and slide in glutinous mud.

No child alone could go far here.

The dogs are away after rabbits and badgers, until in the torchlight Tommy sees Buster stop and his ears go up. Then Nell does the same. Buster gives a low growl, and both dogs bound away into the darkness of the footpath ahead.

Tommy whistles them back to heel and, well-trained as they are, the dogs return to his side.

But something – someone – has been disturbed. Some distance ahead a shadow moves, an outline darker than the dark.

He and the dogs are not alone.

FIVE

In Raymond's Wood, first light reveals the outlines of trees behind mist.

The fog which settled overnight is lingering, its murkiness laying traps for careless feet in whips of spreading brambles and roots of ancient oak. Somewhere to the search team's left, the hollow of a medieval drovers' track is camouflaged by fallen leaves; on their right – though they can't see it – lies the treacherous edge of an abandoned quarry. In the grass here and there, rings of buff toadstool umbrellas have sprung up where a child might say the fairies liked to dance.

A child like Adam Henthorn.

The searchers assembled over an hour ago, and spent the time waiting for dawn huddled in vehicles with engines and heaters running, drinking coffee already cold and regretting the leaving of warm beds.

Now they're standing in the lane listening to their instructions, stamping their booted feet to keep the blood flowing. They're keen to start, but are a few bodies short; the manpower they've got is covering three sites. Each of them will have to cover more ground than would be ideal.

The morning's tasks are clearly planned out. A thorough ground search of Raymond's Wood, then on to the next location on the list. If he's honest, DI Ryan Canfield's not expecting to find anything so close to Adam's home. More than anything, this is an exercise in box-ticking.

The team leader takes questions, then supervises an even spread of resources along the western boundary of the wood where it meets the lane. He blows his whistle and the search for Adam begins, slow and methodical. Where the woodland widens, they spread further out, losing sight of one another in the fog.

When a young PC spots an anomaly, it's only a few metres in front of her, but still hard to make out in the gloom.

Is it something, or nothing?

From where she's standing – near the middle of the wood, some way off the public footpath – she can make out . . . what? Is that a ruined building? More likely it's mossed-over spoil and waste from one of the old quarries. Plenty of abandoned workings around here.

But at its base is a mound that doesn't appear natural.

She makes her way forward, and within a few paces she can see clearly what she's found.

Some kind of spring: a stone trough, with water trickling in through a pipe hidden in the rocks behind. The surrounding area is flattened and indented with boot-prints, showing the place is well-visited, and a bench made from rough-sawn timber has been provided for visitors to sit.

A man is sitting there now. Next to him lies a young boy who appears to be sleeping, while the man's hand rests on the child's cheek. At the man's feet are two black dogs, and he seems fixated on the ground, head bent so low that the PC thinks he might be dead.

The tableau is unnerving, unearthly.

'Is everything all right here?'

Slowly, the man lifts his head. His expression is of a soul lost, his eyes swollen with crying.

The PC hurries closer, and gets her first proper view of the boy, his pallid skin, the blueness of his lips.

Life is clearly extinct.

She takes out her whistle to summon help, and blows it hard.

While she waits for a response, she asks, 'What's your name, mate? Do you want to tell me what's happened?'

The man looks at her stupidly, witless from cold and shock.

'What's the boy's name?' she asks.

'He's my Adam,' sobs the man, stroking the boy's hair. 'He was so beautiful. He was my son.'

SIX

Tessa Rains can remember the days when she'd be up and out at 6.30am and run eight miles before breakfast, but that was before Simon was born. Today, it's almost 8am and she's only just downstairs making tea for herself and Peter. The day will no doubt be exhausting enough, bring a raft of challenges that cost way more energy – especially mentally – than any eight-mile run.

A song she used to love comes on the radio. More years ago than she dares count, before she and Peter even met, she used to dance to this track in dark and smoky city-centre clubs now swept away in urban redevelopments. She was a different person then; her dancing days are long gone.

The cat, Marmalade, is yowling as he rubs around her ankles, and she shakes a little dry food into his bowl. Outside, fog is pressing at the kitchen window. She and Peter bought this house for its far-reaching views, but with the village being up in the hills, the views are often obscured by mist or driving rain. And how could they have known there'd be so much snow? Choosing this area because they didn't know anyone – this move north was a fresh start, far away from difficulties of notoriety and embarrassment – meant they had no one to ask about downsides, and the weather's been one of those. Happily, though, as an escape the move's been a success, with none of the old problems resurfacing.

At least, not so far.

The heating hasn't been on long, and the kitchen's still chilly. Tessa pulls her dressing gown tighter round her body, dismayed as she does so at the plump old woman she sees reflected in the kettle. She isn't that fat – is she? – and she really isn't that old. But the levels of stress they've been through would steal the bloom from anyone's cheeks and send you running for the solace only sweet foods can bring. When things go bad, Peter goes the other way and stops eating, but that's not Tessa's metabolism. Carbs equal comfort, all day long. Sometimes she thinks she'd like to take up running again, train for a 10k to begin with, maybe aim for a half-marathon. Sadly, that will never happen in Risedale. To begin with, she'd never let anyone in the village see her puffing and panting along the lanes. And secondly, if she became again the kind of athlete she used to be – if she could get through the pain and find her stride – the temptation to keep on running would be too great. She might not stop until she was a hundred miles from here.

Upstairs, she hears Peter clearing his throat as he climbs heavily from the bed and heads for the bathroom. She makes the tea, adds milk, one sugar for him, a Splenda sweetener for her.

She's wondering about a couple of digestives when she has the sense of being watched.

Thinking it's way too early for the postman, she turns to see who's there.

Standing in front of the half-glazed back door is a man, a tall man all in black. He's big and powerful and, like a creature from every woman's worst nightmare, his head is covered with a full-face balaclava with cut-out holes for eyes and mouth.

Tessa screams.

The man's opening the door. Tessa is turning to run upstairs to Peter, but a voice she knows very well says, 'Mum, relax. It's me.'

Her son, Simon.

She turns back to see him peeling off the balaclava, grinning in delight at her reaction: a gangling sixteen-year-old, his long hair greasy, his skin inflamed with acne, at that unfortunate point of male adolescent development where his overgrown feet and hands make him clumsy. But something about Simon unsettles people – something beyond normal teenage awkwardness and reserve – making it difficult for him to form friendships. Tessa and Peter insist to anyone who'll listen – neighbours, teachers, child psychiatrists – that his problems lie in his being on the spectrum. They explain that mild autism means he struggles with social norms like making eye contact, with empathy and getting along with others. But even his parents know autism doesn't excuse unkindness, even cruelty. He's laughing now at his mother's fear, and Tessa sees no contrition in his eyes, only amusement at her discomfort.

'You stupid bastard,' she says, the expletive coming from anger as much as shock. 'What the blazes are you doing, dressed like that? You near enough gave me a heart attack. And what are you doing out at this time? I thought you were fast asleep upstairs. Where in God's name have you been?'

Peter appears in the kitchen doorway, still in the pyjama

trousers and T-shirt he likes to sleep in. 'What's going on? Tess, what on earth's the matter? Simon, why are you dressed in that ridiculous outfit?' He points at the balaclava. 'What is that . . . face-covering?'

'I got it off eBay.' Simon's still smiling. 'It's for covert ops.'

'Covert ops?' Tessa can feel Peter's anger building, his frustration bubbling up. No one needs this level of drama before they've even had a cup of tea. 'What are you talking about?'

Babbling in the background, the radio DJ introduces the eight o'clock news.

'The police are up in the woods,' says Simon, clearly excited. 'I've been watching them.'

'Police?' asks Tessa. 'What on earth are they doing in our woods?'

'Be quiet a minute.' Peter turns up the volume on the radio. 'Risedale. He just said Risedale.'

'. . . *Four-year-old Adam Henthorn has been missing from his home in the Peak District village since yesterday afternoon and with the weather set to turn wintry, detectives are anxious for his safety. Anyone with information is asked to call Derbyshire Police on . . .*'

'Tommy,' says Peter. 'That's what Tommy was doing in the fields last night. He was looking for Adam.'

Tessa is bewildered. 'All by himself? Why didn't he come and ask for help? That poor boy, lost in the dark . . . We'd have helped if he'd asked, wouldn't we? If only we'd known. Should we go now, see if they need people?'

'You don't need to.' Simon's proud of his inside information. 'They found him.'

'What?' Tessa glances at Peter. 'Where?'

'A policewoman found him, near Druid's Well.'

'What the hell are you talking about?' Peter switches off the radio's prattle. 'Do you mean you've been in the woods while this search was going on? What possible reason could you have for being there?'

'I told you. I was practising covert ops.'

'In the midst of a police operation? Are you completely insane? For God's sake, boy, they'll be thinking you had something to do with him going missing.'

At the word *boy*, Simon bristles. 'It was nothing to do with me. Anyway, nobody saw me.'

'Nobody saw you?' Peter's voice is raised, not far from shouting. 'How do you know nobody saw you? They're trained professionals, so I should think it's far more likely somebody did see you. And you dressed like that.'

'I went behind the field and along the path behind the cricket pitch. They were all lined up along the road. I'm not stupid.'

'Stupid is exactly what you are,' says Peter. 'Stupid beyond all belief.' Picking up his mug, he carries his tea upstairs.

'What about Adam?' asks Tessa. She has scant hope of a happy ending, of the child being safe and well. Life so rarely seems to turn out that way, these days. 'Is he all right?'

'Not really,' says Simon. 'Some policemen took Tommy away with them and they were putting some kind of tent round Adam so I'm pretty sure he's dead. I'm really hungry, actually. Can I make myself some toast?'

SEVEN

The early summons to Risedale has come as a surprise. In his heart, DI Ryan Canfield didn't expect the search team to find anything. If he's honest – as he never would be with the parents – in too many of these cases, missing children are never found at all. They just vanish without trace.

Some might call the Henthorns lucky, though they'll never see it that way, not in a million years.

To many of his colleagues, this task is drawing the short straw, but Canfield accepts visiting bereaved families as one of the most important parts of the job. The way it's handled can make a difference to the investigation's whole path. Do it right, and the family's with you all the way, co-operative and open, realising you're on their side. You become a team.

Get it wrong, and you're plagued with anger and complaints, reprimands and obstruction. Makes it so much harder to get the information everyone needs.

Information isn't the main reason to get it right, obviously. There's only one reason that matters: because if you were in their place, you'd want things handled sensitively, with respect. You have to let them know you really care.

Having daughters of his own, Canfield knows the strength of the parental bond. While he can never fully comprehend the depths of loss Adam's parents will go through, he's witnessed grief often enough to give him a heightened level of empathy.

He'd be the first to say that being present in the early stages never gets any easier. Especially when young children are involved.

They take Canfield's car. In the passenger seat, DS Eamon Pearson – Manny to most that know him – is quiet. Normally he's a talker, especially when there's been a match the previous evening.

'You OK?' asks Canfield, eventually.

Pearson turns his face from the window where he's been watching the passing scenery. Not that there's much worth seeing. They're driving the final mile or two of the city's outskirts before they reach open country, past post-war houses similar to the one in which Canfield grew up, though even those now have price tags that may put them forever out of his own children's reach. The whole world is changing, including these unremarkable suburbs. The pubs – one or two of which he used to drink in – seem all to have become supermarkets, and the once-useful shops – the bakers and hardware stores and newsagents – are barbers and nail-bars, or wear the primary-coloured signage of fast-food chains.

Pearson gives an unconvincing smile. 'Didn't sleep too well, to be honest. Missing kids, they get to you, don't they?'

'Too right,' says Canfield. 'The more of these cases I handle, the more I never want my own kids to set foot outside the house.'

Pearson doesn't reply, but Canfield imagines he's thinking

the obvious, that being close to home didn't help Adam Henthorn.

As they pass the last of the houses and the road begins to run between sheep-grazed fields, Canfield says, 'Thinking ahead, now that we know it's murder, do we have anything on the family?'

'The father's got a nasty temper,' says Pearson. 'Tommy, they call him. We've had a couple of call-outs in the past – domestics, looks like from the file – but the wife, Gail, has never pressed charges.'

'Nothing else?'

'Not until this.'

'Let's see what we shall see, then,' says Canfield, taking the winding B-road in the direction of Risedale.

Buffeted by a chill easterly, from the lane at the top of the village Canfield takes in the lie of the land. A fortuitous break in the usual persistent cloud of the Dales in winter shows a view of rural English splendour in bright sunshine, all the way to the far side of this broad valley where Risedale clings, nothing more than grey stone cottages and narrow back lanes, a post office and a pub. Not an easy place to keep secrets, with the houses so crammed together. The people living here must be in each other's pockets more than they would like.

Behind him, Raymond's Wood looms. Studying the area maps back at the office, Canfield had thought the woodland too close to home to leave such a small body, which could so easily have been taken much further away. That would have made him next to impossible to find.

But somebody had left Adam here.

They must have had their reasons.

The Henthorn house – Blacksmith's Cottage – is the topmost in the village, hidden away behind a high and neglected hedge, which makes Canfield wonder whether it might have deliberately been allowed to grow tall as a barrier to prying eyes.

Does someone have something to hide?

He parks on the road and follows Pearson up a long, narrow driveway. Pearson – sharply dressed as always – is straightening his tie, preoccupied with his appearance as he too often seems to be. Canfield dresses the part, of course, but he's not one to worry about a splash of mud on his shoes. Out of habit, he looks at the ground as he walks, conscious there could be recoverable tyre tracks and, if there are, they'd be better not obliterated by his size elevens.

The driveway opens out into what must once have been a tradesman's yard, paved in stone and generous enough to park several vehicles, likely originating from a time when the only mode of transport was a horse and cart.

The cottage ahead of them is a reasonable size, a two-bedroom probably, of the usual weather-beaten local stone with a slate roof. A blue Renault Clio is parked close by the front door. To one side there's a small garden – no more than a scrap of lawn, a bird bath and a lop-sided swing – and a washing line hung with clothes so sodden they might have been hanging there for days. Canfield's first impression is of lack of care: the house's paintwork is in need of attention; the overgrown hedge is in dire need of a cut. A water butt, full almost to overflowing, catches drips from an unrepaired break in the roofline guttering.

On one side of the yard is a run of low outbuildings whose roofs are beginning to sag in the preliminary stages of collapse. In a wire mesh run, two fit and glossy black Labradors stand watching them, tails wagging uncertainly.

Canfield knows nothing about dogs, but even he can see they're well cared for, anomalies among the property's disrepair, and he wonders on which side of that fence Adam lived, the cared-for or the neglected?

'Those two are well trained,' he says to Pearson. 'I wish our neighbours would train their terrier not to yap every time anyone goes near.'

Pearson appears disinterested. 'That's gun dogs for you – you can train them to do anything. You could probably teach them to eat with a knife and fork if you'd a mind to.'

Outside the front door – carelessly painted blue, so brush-marks had been left on the brass letterbox and doorknob – Canfield pauses, preparing himself.

'You want to go first?' he asks Pearson.

But Pearson pulls a doubtful expression, creasing his good looks. He's never keen on this kind of meeting. 'Prefer not, if it's all the same to you.'

Canfield nods, and raps at the door.

He's relieved when Bethan, the family liaison officer, answers it. Hopefully she'll have been managing emotions as best she can, but when she sees Canfield and Pearson, her face shows the strain of the situation.

They step into a cold hallway gloomy enough to need a light on even at midday. A steep staircase with worn carpet leads up into shadows. On one wall hangs a jumble of coats – a woman's anorak and smart camel-coloured raincoat, a man's knee-length waxed coat, and poignantly a boy's anorak in a Spider-Man pattern which will never be worn again. Scattered on the floor below is a mess of mis-paired shoes and boots. Canfield smells woodsmoke, or maybe it's burnt toast.

Bethan's young, but her outstanding ability to empathise makes Canfield wonder what's happened in her short life that allows her to shine in this most sensitive of roles. He'd never ask so personal a question, but something in the way she holds herself speaks of strength in the face of disaster.

As she closes the front door behind them, in a low voice she says, 'Be ready. She's very emotional, he seems a bit unstable. And they definitely have issues between them. They're in there. I'll go and make some tea.'

Canfield taps gently on the door to his right, and pushes it open. The lounge isn't by any means warm, though its temperature is lifted above the frigidity of the hallway by an ash-choked wood burner smoking sulkily behind sooted-up glass. On a two-seater sofa, Canfield sees a woman who takes care of herself — nails professionally done, her clothes inexpensive but well put together — who'd normally be attractive but who's cried her face to a ruin. This, then, is Adam's mother, Gail. With a balled-up handkerchief in one hand, she looks up at Canfield with empty eyes, glances at Pearson behind him and drops her head.

Tommy Henthorn is sitting on the armchair closest to the fireplace with a blanket round his shoulders, staring at the smoking fire. Broad in the chest and muscled, he's what Canfield would describe as solid, with an untrimmed beard, thick curls of dark hair and a nose whose kink declares it has at some time been broken and left to heal without the benefit of a doctor's attention. Tommy looks the kind who might normally despise tears in anyone, man or woman, but today he's plainly felled by grief, and his eyes are reddened and swollen.

'Mrs Henthorn,' says Canfield. 'Mr Henthorn. I'm DI Ryan Canfield. This is my colleague DS Eamon Pearson. On behalf of the constabulary, please accept our deepest condolences for your loss.'

'Aye, well,' says Tommy. 'You're here now, aren't you, all concerned? Where were you last night, when he was out there by himself? You could have been with me searching for him, and we might have found him sooner. We might have been in time. He might have been saved.'

Canfield has had the pathologist's preliminary report and knows Tommy's accusations are unfounded. Adam had already been dead for fifteen or sixteen hours by the time police arrived on the scene.

But he knows better than to talk logic to a grieving parent.

'And I'll tell you what,' Tommy goes on, 'when I find out who did it, I'll kill him with my own bare hands. I swear on my own life.'

On the sofa, Gail emits an unearthly wail, and eyes closed begins to rock backwards and forwards. Bethan comes hurrying from the kitchen, sits down beside her and puts an arm around her shoulders.

'Where is he?' Gail moans. 'Where's my baby? Where's my boy? I need to see him.'

'All in good time,' says Canfield. 'For now, with circumstances being what they are, we're going to arrange a place for you both to stay for a while. If you prefer, of course you're free to stay with friends or relatives. The choice is yours.'

'I don't want to leave here,' sobs Gail. 'This is his home. I want to stay here.'

'I'm afraid you can't,' says Canfield, gently. 'There are things we need to do.'

'Let's have some tea,' says Bethan. 'We can talk about it after that.'

'I think we'd appreciate it if you could find us somewhere quiet for a day or two,' says Tommy, accepting a mug of tea Bethan has generously sugared. 'Wouldn't we, Gail? Help us start to come to terms with it.'

But Gail looks at him with loathing. 'I'm not going anywhere with you,' she snaps, and turns to Pearson. 'He and I are separated. He doesn't live here any more.'

'Come on, Gail,' pleads Tommy. 'Don't be like that. A time like this, we need each other. He's our son, we're his mum and dad. He'd want us to be together – you know he would – and I don't know how I'll bear it by myself. You could come to stay at Mum's, she'd welcome you. We'd all be together then.'

'I'm not going to your mother's.' Gail looks at Canfield. 'There's my sister. I could go there.'

'I'll ring her for you if you like,' says Bethan, and Gail nods.

'What about me, though?' asks Tommy, tearfully. 'I want to be with you – it's only right. You're still my wife, and we're a family, the three of us. Don't be hard on me, Gail. Not now.'

'You go to your mother's,' says Gail. 'If it's company you're after, she'll have plenty to say.'

'But how can I stay here in the village? They'll all be yapping away, making stuff up and badmouthing.'

'We'll be glad to find somewhere for you,' says Canfield.

Tommy looks pleadingly at Gail. 'I want to be with my

wife. Come on, Gail. Don't do this. If Adam's gone, I only have you.' His tears begin again, and he seems bewildered. 'How can this be happening? What the fuck is going on?'

'We're doing everything we can to move the investigation on quickly,' says Canfield. 'You're our number-one priority. Meanwhile, Bethan is your carer and your conduit. Anything you need, anything you want to know, she'll get straight through to the team.'

'I want to know when I can see my son,' says Tommy. 'I want to know who's taking care of him, because that's my job. Our job.'

Canfield feels a rush of sympathy for Tommy. His child is dead, and the boy's precious remains have been taken away by strangers. 'He's with good, kind, respectful people, Tommy. Bethan will explain to you the arrangements we'll put in place so you can see him.'

'Will it be today?'

'More likely tomorrow. If you don't want to be in Risedale, we'll get you somewhere to stay tonight.'

But Tommy shakes his head. 'I'll stay with Mum. She's as devastated as we are. I can't leave her by herself.'

'All right, then. And you have my word we'll get you to see Adam as soon as humanly possible.'

Canfield and Pearson are on their way out the door when Tommy stops them.

'There's something I want to ask. I want to know if he . . .' He rubs at his eyes with his sleeve. 'Was he assaulted in that way? Interfered with?'

Canfield hesitates, reluctant even himself to contemplate

such a dreadful question. 'I can't answer that at the moment, I'm afraid, Tommy. As soon as we have more information, trust me, you'll be the first to know. We'll know for absolute certain after the post-mortem.'

EIGHT

The snug at Risedale's only pub – the Mason's Arms – is all but empty, though a recently stoked coal fire in the black-leaded grate is giving off a welcoming warmth.

Pearson was keen to get back to town and so declined a drink, begging a lift to the office with one of the forensics team. But Canfield needs a while to centre himself after the harrowing emotions he's just witnessed. Irene really hates it when he brings his work home, especially when 'work' means a saturnine mood. A stop to spend a few minutes alone with his thoughts will help him process what he's seen, restore his equilibrium.

The snug's low ceiling crossed with rough timber beams point to the building's eighteenth-century origins, and it appears to have avoided any modernisation beyond the 1970s. Leatherette benches and terracotta tiles, a wall dedicated to framed photographs of the village cricket team, a dartboard and – best of all – no muzak: at this moment, Canfield could have found no better place to soothe his soul.

The pub's only lunchtime customers – three men seated together at one table – take no notice of him as he walks in.

The woman behind the bar, though, appears glad to close

the magazine she's been reading, and jumps down from her stool with a smile. Canfield sees the glow from the optic lights was being kind to her, and close up she's older than she looks, fifties rather than forties. But with her careful make-up and caramel-coloured hair, in jeans and a pastel blue jumper she's still attractive.

'What can I get you?'

Canfield's tempted by the draft ales, but asks for a pint of lager shandy. As the woman pours his drink, he senses her covertly eyeing him up and down, taking in his out-of-place suit and overcoat. Given what's going on here, he thinks, she won't have to be a genius to figure out who he is.

Still, maybe picking up on his disinclination to talk, she has the good manners to ask him no questions.

Canfield carries his pint to a table near the fire and takes a long, welcome drink. One of the three men drains his glass, slaps both his knees and stands up.

'That's me, then. Better get back or I'll be in trouble.' As he pulls on his coat, his companions mumble their goodbyes, and opening the door, he calls over to the woman. 'I'll see you tomorrow, Tina.'

'See you, Stan.'

When he's gone, the other two men lapse into silence, until the older of the two finishes his drink, stands and carries his glass to the bar. 'One for the road, please, Tina.' He turns round to his companion. 'You having one, Vince?'

'I am if you're buying,' says Vince, finishing his beer. 'You don't get an offer like that every day.'

'Two pints of mild, then, Tina m'duck,' says the man. 'And have one for yourself if you want one.'

'I'll have a gin, if that's all right, Owen,' says Tina.

As Tina fixes the drinks, Owen turns brazenly towards Canfield and asks, 'You here about the lad, then?'

Canfield finds himself too tired to dissemble. 'You mean Adam.'

'Adam, yes. No offence if you aren't, but you've got copper written all over you, even if you weren't drinking shandy. It's a bad business, that is, a very bad business. I've lived in Risedale all my life and never seen anything like it. It'll be someone from outside, mark me. Don't be looking to find anyone in this village who'd do a thing wicked as that. How's Tommy, how's he holding up?'

'Don't be bothering the man, Owen,' interrupts Tina, placing the first pint on the bar. 'He's got enough on his plate without answering your questions. You don't need him to tell you how Tommy will be. He'll be knocked sideways, and who wouldn't be?'

'There'll be a post-mortem, I'm sure, won't there?' persists Owen. 'Someone from outside it'll prove to be, I'll put money on it. Look at those weirdos we had up here on the moor last month, with their drugs and their music, leaving their rubbish everywhere. If you lot would do more to stop the druggies, we wouldn't have these murders and such, would we?'

'They were nothing to do with this,' puts in Vince as Owen hands him a pint. 'This'll be some pervert.'

Tina shudders. 'Don't be saying that. I couldn't bear to think of that little boy ... I can't even bear to say it.' Now she dares address Canfield directly. 'It's come as such a shock, a small place like this. You think you're sheltered from the world, and then the worst possible thing happens. Makes you wonder if the rest of our kids are safe. Should people be keeping them at home?'

Tina, Owen and Vince are all looking at Canfield for an answer he doesn't feel qualified to give.

'To be honest, I don't know,' he says. 'But for the time being, I don't think it would hurt to pay a little extra attention where they're going and who they're seeing. Just to be on the safe side.'

Sobered by his response, they ask him nothing more. The clock behind the bar is telling him it's high time he was on his way back to his desk. He'll be late home again tonight, of course, and he should let Irene know sooner rather than later, save her the time and trouble of another ruined dinner – though his consideration won't dissipate the unspoken tension that's always there, these days, from the moment he opens the front door. Nor will he be able to talk to Irene about Adam Henthorn; she has an understandable horror of this kind of case, so he'll keep it all to himself, lying awake and going over it in his head as the silent night hours tick by.

Who is he kidding? The truth is, except for his girls, home holds little attraction for him because there's somewhere else he'd rather be. Someone else he'd rather be with than his tired, terse wife.

The story's as old as the hills, with no obvious solution.

More rain is blowing in from the east.

As Canfield leaves, he bids the bar's occupants a polite 'Good afternoon'.

NINE

Sometimes, the demands of the job feel overwhelming.

Canfield didn't have to attend Adam's post-mortem – rank gives him the option to delegate the task elsewhere in the team – and yet on this occasion, he felt strongly that he should be there. Not because there was anything specific he wanted to ask – whilst he did have questions, they could have been written down and handed on to someone else – but because he's intent on understanding what provoked the murder of this pitiable child, and the dispassionate medical analysis of exactly what happened to Adam is the first solid data they'll have on the road to identifying his killer. Canfield wanted those details from the mouth of the pathologist as he worked, to hear the exact words of his recorded commentary, to note the points at which the doctor frowned, or hesitated, or found something unexpected.

And as it happened, he was glad he was there, since the official recorded cause of death was not commonplace among cases such as these.

After a morning at the morgue, Canfield remains thoughtful. Grabbing a quick lunch in the Kenton Road canteen he sees

Pearson arrive, chatting to a young woman who's recently started in the press office. She's attractive, and Pearson's body language says he's interested, but she's smiling a little too politely at whatever it is he's saying, and it looks as if he's out of luck. When Canfield calls out to him and beckons him over, the press officer departs Pearson's company without a backward glance.

Pearson gives Canfield a thumbs up, points to the food-service area and wanders over to the uninspiring salad bar. Pearson treats his body like a temple, decaf coffee and a largely vegetarian diet. Usually he looks good on it, but as he approaches Canfield's table with a plate of what appears to be iceberg lettuce and grated Cheddar, a blueberry smoothie and – his Achilles heel – a large Snickers bar, Canfield thinks again he's not looking as fresh-faced as usual. Too many hours on a difficult case – or a troublesome private life – will do that to anyone.

Pearson sits, and immediately asks, 'What's the news?'

'Unexpected,' says Canfield. 'The good news is, there's no sign of any sexual activity. But the cause of death was a surprise. Adam drowned.'

Pearson's eyes grow wide. 'Really?'

'Hundred per cent certainty. His lungs were full of water, poor kid.'

Pearson opens the first of three sachets of salad cream – another Achilles heel – and squirts it over his salad. 'Where, then? How?'

'Well, the how is straightforward. His face at least was immersed in water.'

'What, you mean pushed into it? That makes it difficult. It could have been anywhere.'

'I thought so at first. But there are significant bruises round both ankles, and possible finger marks. So it looks more like he was somehow dangled in water.'

Pearson looks doubtful. 'It would take some strength to do that, though, wouldn't it? He wasn't a two-year-old toddler. And wouldn't he have fought back?'

'I'm sure he tried.' The conversation is a reminder of that room in the mortuary, and Canfield finds his appetite is gone. He lays down his knife and fork, leaving most of his chicken pasta uneaten.

'You OK?' asks Pearson.

'I'll get over it,' says Canfield, though he's by no means certain that he will. That small body, those bruises . . . On days like today, he wants to be anywhere but up to his neck in the minutiae of distress.

Pearson takes his first mouthful of dressing-sodden salad. 'Ten to one he died where he was found, then, at that spring.'

'Probably.'

'If that's the case, Adam fell in that stone trough all by himself, and got the bruises when someone pulled him out?'

'If it happened like that, he must have been alive at the time. Dead bodies don't bruise. And at the scene Tommy said Adam was already dead when he got there, and lying on that bench.'

'Maybe someone tried and failed to resuscitate him with mouth to mouth,' suggests Pearson.

'But why wouldn't they have called an ambulance?'

'Lonely spot and a dead child. They might have thought it would take some explaining. But you have to admit it's a possibility. In which case, we'd be looking at accidental death instead of murder. Big difference.'

Canfield agrees. 'Forensics are still on scene, so it'll be interesting to see what they come up with. And the water samples from Adam's lungs will tell us more. From memory, though, I'm not sure a child his age would get into that trough by himself. I seem to recall it came up to my waist, or at any rate not much lower.'

'Fair point. Do you think the location – the spring – suggests local knowledge?'

'Not necessarily,' says Canfield. 'There must be hundreds of walkers who go through Raymond's Wood in any given summer. Druid's Well is a local landmark, bound to be marked on every ordnance survey map ever published. Don't people say the water's good for your health?'

Pearson pulls a face. 'What, people drink from that trough? I wouldn't be doing that.'

'Why not? No chemicals, straight from the source, probably do you a world of good.'

Pearson's unconvinced. 'Probably give you E. coli.'

'There is one other thing that's occurred to me, though,' Canfield adds, thoughtfully. 'We shouldn't be assuming Adam drowned at Druid's Well. At the Henthorn house, there's a water butt a child would easily fit inside. In the yard there, right outside the front door.'

TEN

Lorna Hitchin has broken a firm promise to herself, that she'd only have two glasses of wine. Now a third is half-empty on the table in front of her, and inevitably Jess is going to move in for the kill.

Looking at the pair of them, no one ever believes she and Jess are sisters. Jess has always been a queen of style, hooked on fashion websites from the age of thirteen, somehow skipping all the early make-up disasters to which Lorna fell prey, moving straight into photoshoot perfection with her first birthday-money Mac lipstick purchase. And here she is, sitting next to Lorna looking gorgeous – black hair impossibly shiny, eyes seductively sultry even without fake lashes or overdone eyeliner, lips still glossed and pouty despite having had several drinks – and way out of the league of every man in the place. Which of course doesn't stop some of them trying.

The bar's getting louder. So they can keep talking, Jess moves a little closer to Lorna on the bench seat, ruffling the air with her scent of roses and patchouli, which Lorna knows on her would smell like something bought at a pound shop.

If Jess wasn't her best friend in the world, Lorna might find herself feeling jealous.

But Lorna feels she's scrubbed up well herself this evening, showing off her legs in a short but not too clingy dress, her hair much lighter than Jess's with its fresh-from-the-hairdresser highlights. She's pretty enough to draw some attention too.

'Come on, then,' says Jess, eagerly. 'Let's hear it. Who is he?'

Even before she's named him, Lorna feels herself blush, though happily the corner they're sitting in is poorly lit enough that Jess doesn't notice. But Lorna's surprised at herself. She didn't realise she'd got it that bad. Blushing at the mention of him, that's a schoolgirl's game.

And Lorna doesn't feel ready to be totally open.

She stalls. 'Who?'

Jess raises her eyes in that give-me-a-break roll she does when she knows someone's bullshitting. 'Don't even think about playing that game, lady. Tell me, right now.'

'He's just some guy.'

'What guy?'

'I met him through work.'

'Oh God. Is he a boring lawyer?'

'Like me, you mean?'

'I save you from being boring. So he is a lawyer?'

'Worse.'

'What could be worse? Wait a minute, no, don't tell me. Is he a policeman?'

Lorna picks up her drink, and takes a sip without answering.

'Oh my God.' Jess does her eye roll again. 'How could you? You know they're all fascists, don't you? And the ones that aren't fascists are more tedious than lawyers. Right, I have a mission here.' She gazes around the room, assessing. 'I'm going to find you someone else, a really hot guy. Him over there, maybe – he's cute. I could never bear the shame of my sister dating a policeman.' She opens and closes her hand over her head. 'Nee naw, nee naw. Lorna, how could you?'

Lorna laughs. 'Stop being an idiot. He isn't that kind of a policeman. He's a detective.'

'What, like murders and shit? Never. Tell me more. Name?'

'Ryan.'

'Age?'

'He's a bit older than me.'

'A bit being . . . ?'

'He's thirty-six.'

'Thirty-six? And you are, let me see . . .' Jess adopts a phony quizzical expression. 'Oh yes, you're twenty-four. Nothing weird about that, is there?'

'It's not weird.' Lorna finds herself defensive. 'You can't help who you fall in love with.'

There it is, the third-glass-of-wine effect. The bombshell is accidentally dropped, a nugget of information she wasn't ready to recognise the truth of herself.

'Oh my God. You're in love with him? No way.'

Lorna's becoming irritated. 'Just leave it, Jess. It's none of your business.'

'Of course it's my business if there are going to be wedding bells any time soon.'

'There aren't going to be wedding bells.' Too late, Lorna realises she's been too firm in this assertion.

Jess pantomime slaps herself on the forehead. 'Silly me. How could I not see it? None of us have ever got to meet him, you see him at odd times, it's so obvious it's dazzling. You're dating a married man.'

Lorna blushes again, ruby red from embarrassment and anger.

'It's none of your business, OK?' She stands up, and pushes past her sister. 'I'm going to the loo.'

Being uncharacteristically tactful, Jess doesn't return to the subject until they're in the taxi on the way home. Lorna can't deny feeling tipsy, though she did have the sense to stop after the third glass. Jess, of course, never drinks too much. She says it's bad for both weight and skin.

'This Ryan,' she says, as they wait at a traffic light. The late-night city streets are empty of traffic, the only sounds the shouts of drunken revellers making their way from pubs to clubs. 'I suppose he's given you all the usual lines.'

'He isn't like that.' At the thought of him, Lorna feels a warm glow, somewhere between affection and desire, and wishes he were here.

'He'll be leaving his wife, then, will he?'

Lorna can hear a rare note of pity in Jess's voice.

'You don't have to worry about me, Jess. We're in love. We'll work it out.'

Jess sighs, and looks out of the window as the taxi moves forward.

'You think I'm a mug, don't you?'

'You've fallen for the oldest trick in the book,' says Jess, still looking out. 'He tells you he loves you, that his wife's some old bitch who doesn't understand him, you think you're going to be wife number two. Does he have kids?'

Lorna thinks about lying, but doesn't. 'Two.'

The admission is hard. Though she wouldn't tell Jess, she does have reservations about the affair. Not in regards to his wife – where adults are concerned, isn't all fair in love and war? – but those two gorgeous, beaming little faces that pop up every time he switches on his phone always bring on a bad bout of guilt. Could she ever really countenance stealing their daddy?

'Oh, Lorna. How could you? You're a beautiful woman. You could have any man you wanted. Why do you have to choose some old bloke who's not even free?'

'Don't you dare tell Mum.'

Jess shakes her head. 'Listen to yourself. You're in a relationship – if you can call it that – you're so proud of, you daren't even tell your own mother. Just do yourself a big, big favour, and tell him never to call you again. He'll break your heart, Lorna, I'm telling you. Don't fall for it. Don't waste any more of your time.'

'I'll introduce you all when the time's right.'

'The time will never be right.' Jess speaks to the taxi-driver. 'Just here on the left is fine, thanks.' She presses a twenty into Lorna's hand, her share of the fare. 'He's a user. You should have more self-respect than to throw yourself away on someone like him.'

As the taxi pulls away, Lorna waves through the rear window.

But Jess is walking away from the cab and doesn't look back.

ELEVEN

Tessa Rains has been like a cat on hot bricks since she took the call yesterday, initially intrigued and – it must be admitted – a little excited. Of course everyone in the village is talking about the murder. It's become the sole topic of conversation, the known – or rumoured – details repeated and rehashed from one household to another, embellished and revised, dissected and debated. Adam's sudden death is so awful that everyone's blindsided by improbability and disbelief, as if they'll wake up from some weird shared psychological experience to find they've all had the same bad dream. And because everyone is talking about it, Tessa assumes everyone is having a visit from the detectives, until she happens to mention it in the post office.

She's buying a couple of items she could have done without – a tin of the Heinz ravioli Simon likes for lunch (which is horribly expensive in the village shop and would have been far better bought from the Co-op in town), and half a dozen farm eggs in case she decides to bake this afternoon – but the shocking news has birthed an irresistible restlessness, an urge to seek out information that Peter calls gossiping and won't indulge. His reaction has been to draw a cloak of silence about himself and retreat. But Tessa wants to understand the what and the why, and has headed to the best place to learn more.

Postmistress and shopkeeper Audrey Staples is picking Tessa's eggs from a straw-filled basket and inspecting them for cracks, when Tessa remarks, 'We've got our police interview this afternoon.'

Audrey pauses, the fifth egg mid-air between basket and recycled eggbox. Owen Luck, who was rifling through the frozen vegetables, immediately loses interest in the price of green beans, closes the door of the humming freezer and gives Tessa his full attention.

'They're interviewing you, are they?' asks Audrey, and Tessa immediately knows she's said the wrong thing.

'I thought they were interviewing everyone.' She hears a defensive note in her own voice. 'I think it's normal that they would in a case like this, to rule people out. Isn't that what they do?'

'They're not interviewing me,' says Owen, picking up a pot of yoghurt from the fridge and squinting at the sell-by date. 'Though I had a young lad in a uniform knock and ask me some questions off a clipboard.'

'We had that too,' agrees Audrey.

'Didn't look old enough to be out of school,' says Owen.

'Who is it who's coming to see you, then?' Audrey asks, placing the fifth egg in the box and choosing number six.

'I don't really know,' Tessa lies. 'But I think it's some detective.'

'A detective, eh?' asks Owen. 'Well now, that is something.'

'Not really, is it?' asks Tessa, shortly. 'It is a murder case.'

'I wonder why they'd be coming to see you, though,' muses Audrey, closing the lid on the eggbox.

But Tessa knows exactly what they're thinking. There's only one reason their household would be singled out for what it seems is a special visit.

Simon.

TWELVE

At Kenton Road police station, Canfield's beginning to feel like he's falling behind. Every time he sits down to tackle the backlog of bureaucracy, his phone rings.

Now he's been called to the deputy chief constable's office, apparently required in a meeting.

Upstairs, DCC Nolan's secretary Ellen – a petite, congenial woman Canfield has always admired for her calm competence, even when situations collapse into crises – greets him with an apologetic smile.

'I'm afraid you'll have to wait a few minutes,' she says. 'I thought they'd be done by now, but they seem to have overrun. Have a seat. I can make coffee if you'd like some.'

Canfield accepts the coffee. He hasn't brought his phone – Nolan is notoriously intolerant of interruptions while he's talking – and it's good to sit a while and clear his mind, get his thoughts straight on what he suspects he's going to be asked.

The door to Nolan's office opens. Canfield knows the two men who leave – a DI and a DCI working on a long-running white-collar case, cash-for-contracts at a local authority. Canfield's heard the case is moving too slowly for the upper echelon's targets, and the DCI's cowed resemblance to a humiliated schoolboy says they've been incentivised with a stick rather than any carrots to improve their results.

As they pass by him, Canfield offers a sympathetic nod. His turn next.

When he walks into the office, his heart sinks. Seated in one of the chairs in front of DCC Nolan's desk is Superintendent Darren Lomas, a man whose over-cautious approach to policing has been a hindrance to Canfield's work more than once.

He wishes the two men good morning, takes the offered seat and waits for the grilling to begin.

'Good to see you, Ryan,' says Nolan, as always taking the lead. At least he'll get to the point quickly, rather than pussyfooting around like Lomas would. 'I've been wondering how the Henthorn case is going, and I thought it best to go straight to the horse's mouth.'

'Well, obviously no arrest has been made as yet,' says Canfield.

'And do you feel you're close?'

Canfield takes a deep breath. 'Honestly, not as close as we'd like. You'll have seen in my written update last week we're looking at a couple of possibilities. The neighbour Simon Rains is one. His name came up several times early on during the door-to-door interviews. He's very young and has no previous, but I'd say he's on the spectrum and there's been some questionable behaviour. No history of violence so far, though. I've got people talking to staff at his current school and his previous ones, and we've got an interview lined up with his parents, though I'm not expecting much from that.

No doubt they'll be cagey at best. The family seems to have moved around a fair bit, though, which may be something or nothing. Hopefully they'll shed some light on that.'

'OK. Who else?'

'The father, Tommy Henthorn. I've got some doubts myself about him being a possible, to be honest, because at interview he came across as truthful and very attached to his son. But there's been a recent marital separation, and as we know, people can go totally off the rails in those situations. And he lacks an alibi.'

Nolan's eyebrows raise. 'Really? Interesting.'

'The thing is,' says Lomas, 'Adam's age and the slightly unusual cause of death are keeping the case in the public eye. The press office is still fielding calls from the nationals, and Channel 4 are making noises about doing some kind of special this week as part of their 7pm news broadcast. Potentially that's a big audience. We don't want their angle to be that Derbyshire Police are busy doing nothing while a child-killer is still at large. We need to look proactive.'

'We are proactive,' says Canfield, defensively. 'As always. If anything's slowing us down, it's the long turnaround times from support teams. And I assume that's not news we'd want to share.'

'So what lines are you actively pursuing?' asks Nolan.

'The usual. We're still waiting for some forensics, particularly an analysis of the water in Adam's lungs. We need to confirm it came from where we think it did.'

'We can help with that, hurry it along,' says Nolan, and Lomas writes himself a note. 'What else?'

'We're doing our best.' Canfield shrugs. 'Everyone's working at capacity. That's all I can say, really.'

'I wonder if we might do a press conference,' suggests Lomas. 'That might take the heat off for a while.'

'Not if we don't have any new information,' says Nolan. 'They'll just say we're dragging our feet. Which we're not, are we, Ryan?'

'Absolutely not, sir,' agrees Canfield.

'We've already authorised overtime,' says Lomas. 'Maybe we could give you a couple more bodies for a week or so?'

Canfield shakes his head. 'I don't think that would help. It takes that long to get anyone up to speed.'

Nolan rubs at the side of his head as if to soothe an ache. 'Look, there's this bash coming up in London in a couple of weeks, one of the royals is the guest of honour and the chief constable's been asked to make a speech. So he's mighty keen to have a national-newsworthy result as a headline. Do you understand what I'm saying?'

Canfield understands perfectly. Either he or the white-collar lads need to make some serious progress before the chief constable sits down at that dinner.

'I'll do my absolute best,' he says.

'Good man,' says Nolan. 'A win on this case is going to look very good on your record when you put in for your promotion. And we have every faith in you, as you know. I've always said, Ryan, you're a safe pair of hands.'

Canfield is back at his desk when Pearson appears in the doorway, pointing to his watch. 'Interview in Risedale with the Rains family,' Pearson reminds him. 'I can handle it by myself if you're busy.'

Canfield glances down at his lengthy hand-scribbled to-do

list. For every item he crosses out, two more seem to get added. 'I could really use the time here, to be honest.'

'I'll leave you to it, then,' says Pearson. 'I'll let you know if there's anything of interest when I get back. Oh, and I almost forgot. The front desk called up. There's a woman downstairs asking for you by name. I offered to go, but apparently she's insisting she'll only speak to you.'

Canfield sighs. 'Speak to me about what?'

Pearson shrugs. 'No idea. If you want, I can speak to her on my way out, tell her you're not in the office.'

Canfield glances at the incomplete MG21 form waiting on his screen, and at his to-do list.

'No, I'll go,' he says, standing up and putting on his jacket. 'A walk up and down stairs is just what I need to clear my head.'

The woman who's asked for Canfield is shepherding a small boy on his precarious journey along a bank of empty chairs. The child is two or three years old, mischievous-looking but with all the charm that suggests he gets away with more than he should. His mother is a harassed-looking woman carelessly dressed, with sallow skin and grey bags under her eyes, her dark hair falling out of a twisted scrunchie. She appears distracted and detached from the boy's antics, but supervising him closely is in her own best interests, since responsibility will fall on her if he suffers any injury.

Canfield wanders over to the front desk and asks for information on who she is. Armed with the background, he approaches her.

'Mrs Jutt?'

She nods, and removes the child from the chair on which he's standing to hold him in a firm and expert grip. Fortunately, he's briefly interested enough in Canfield not to object.

'I'm DI Ryan Canfield.'

She nods again. 'I know you are. I saw you being interviewed on *East Midlands Today* about Adam Henthorn. You organised the search. That's why I asked for you.'

Canfield is too busy to have his time wasted, so he's brusque in his response.

'And can I ask why you want to speak to me?'

The child is quickly becoming impatient to be back on his chair adventure and begins to wriggle, but she is sharp with him – 'Zain, behave yourself in front of the gentleman' – and surprisingly, he becomes still.

'It's about my husband. He's missing.'

Inwardly, Canfield sighs. This will be, he thinks, a familiar scenario, one to which he can personally relate. The wife's let herself go and her focus is all on the kids; the husband has found himself what he thinks is a better option. Maybe he'll come home when he's had his fill of being single again – or at least behaving as if he is – or maybe he's gone for good. Either way, it's highly unlikely to be a police matter, which according to the desk sergeant is exactly what she's been told, yesterday and today.

He's about to tell her so when she says, 'Don't try and fob me off. I'm not an idiot. Of course you look at me and think why wouldn't he leave me, but Faizan wouldn't go voluntarily at this time in his life. He had something going on, and he'd never run away when there was money on the table.' Her eyes show the light of true belief. 'I'm telling you, Mr Canfield, something has happened to my husband.'

Upstairs, Canfield's to-do list is waiting; but Mrs Jutt is very earnest, and her appraisal of her situation is both honest and persuasive.

'All right,' he says at last. 'We'll take some details. Come with me, and we'll get someone to help you report him officially missing.'

THIRTEEN

When the agreed time for the detective's visit arrives, both Tessa and Peter are relieved that Simon is out. Not by arrangement; suggesting to Simon he should be out of the way at the time of the police call would be guaranteed to keep him at home, determined to know first-hand what's going on. But by a stroke of luck, he's had a rare invitation to a friend's house in a neighbouring village, probably so the boy's mother can interrogate Simon regarding what's going on in Risedale. The woman knows Simon has no filters, and will bluntly answer any question she cares to ask.

Of course Tessa has gone to too much trouble, vacuuming the lounge carpet even though it doesn't need it, dusting round with a spritz of Pledge to make sure everywhere smells nice while Peter grumbles at her making such an unnecessary fuss. And he's right; they've seen enough Channel 4 true-crime documentaries to know these people are used to visiting the lowest hovels imaginable, crack houses and squats of unspeakable squalor, and any home in Risedale is a very far cry from that. But in all her forty-two years, Tessa can't recall ever having a visit from this kind of authority. A little preparation seems only right.

The detective is late. Five past four comes and goes, then ten past. The post-sunset gloom fills the room and Peter turns on the light, so the reflection on the window glass obliterates any view outside. Tessa's becoming increasingly agitated but trying not to show it, while Peter's saying he'll give the bloke five more minutes and then he's got an errand to run before the shops close, that if he can't turn up on time he'll have to come back another day.

'Don't be silly,' says Tessa. 'It's the police. You can't just tell them to come back tomorrow.'

The doorbell rings. A look passes between them, saying neither knows quite what.

'Showtime,' says Peter.

The front door opens directly onto Risedale's main street. Outside, Tessa's relieved to see no vehicle easily identifiable as a police car, only a recently washed silver Peugeot, its wheel arches splashed with clay slurry left by the passing quarry traffic.

Of whoever's rung the doorbell there's no immediate sign, until a man steps into view from the house-side where he's obviously been scoping out the property. He's wearing a suit beneath a dark-blue overcoat, and a tie slightly loosened at the collar.

'Mrs Rains?' He holds out his hand, which Tessa takes and finds cold. 'DS Eamon Pearson. Sorry I'm late.'

'No problem.' As Pearson steps into the hall, she wonders if he has Italian blood, maybe Greek or Turkish. He's not tall, but he looks fit, like he works out and would be useful in a fight, which is, she reflects, what you want in a policeman. 'Can I take your coat?'

He hands it to her, and she hangs it on the hooks behind the door where it makes Peter's anorak look shabby.

Pearson straightens his tie, and Tessa catches a scent she likes, some musky, mossy aftershave.

'My husband's in here,' she says. 'Please come through.'

Pearson sits down in an armchair. He takes out a small notebook and a stainless-steel ballpoint, and accepts Tessa's offer of coffee.

While she's absent in the kitchen, Peter attempts small-talk: *Have you driven far? Where are you based? Haven't the roadworks on the ring road made driving a nightmare?* Pearson responds politely with answers that say very little, and Peter's relieved when Tessa returns with a tray which she unloads – coffee mugs, sugar and home-baked shortbread – onto the low table by the sofa.

Pearson takes his time sugaring his coffee, tries a piece of shortbread and compliments Tessa on its flavour. Tessa and Peter sit together on the sofa. Tessa is smiling a little too widely; Peter is a little too relaxed and nonchalant.

'So.' Pearson sits forward in his chair, elbows on his knees, his body language giving him control of the conversation. 'Of course you know why I'm here. It's to do with Adam's unfortunate death.'

'It's a terrible thing,' says Tessa, and she finds herself suddenly tearful, reaching out for a tissue from the box on the table. 'I'm sorry. It's just so awful. He was such a lovely child.'

'I want to talk to you about your son,' Pearson goes on. 'Simon, isn't it?'

'Simon?' Peter sits up straighter, defensive. 'What's it got to do with him?'

'In these situations, we have to follow every possible lead, as I'm sure you understand. As we've been making enquiries in the village, Simon's name has been mentioned as someone who might have information.'

'Who's mentioned him?' demands Peter. 'People gossip here. They've nothing better to do.'

Tessa places a placatory hand on his knee. 'Hold on a minute, darling. People do talk to each other, but under the circumstances you can't blame them. Simon's a bit of a loner, and he has some issues. People find it hard to see past that.'

'What sort of issues, Tessa?'

Pearson's easy use of her first name is a surprise. Tessa blinks. 'Well, he's what you'd call on the spectrum. Autistic.'

'And how does that affect him?'

'He has difficulty making friends,' says Tessa, cautiously. 'Like I said, he's a loner.'

'Hold on a minute.' Peter has become decisive. 'Let's get this out of the way now. This probably isn't news to you, you've no doubt got records you've already checked, so cards on the table. We moved here a couple of years ago because Simon's behaviour was becoming out of control. He develops fascinations with things, things that hold his attention for a few weeks or months and then he drops them, moves on to something new. Where we lived before – it was in the Birmingham area, just in case you don't already know, and I'll happily give you the address – he became obsessed with fire. We caught him a couple of times with matches, and there was an incident at home when the fire service had to be called. No major damage was done, but still. Then there was a fire at a local farm, a barn fire.

Some animals died, and it was thoroughly unpleasant, to be honest. The fire service ruled it as arson, and some of the locals believed Simon was responsible. He wasn't. He'd moved on from that obsession by then – he was all about fighter jets. But it made our lives very difficult. We were ostracised, and Simon was bullied at school. So we moved here. That's all there is to say.'

'If Simon has obsessions, what's his obsession now?' asks Pearson.

Tessa drops her head, waiting for Peter to answer.

'He likes playing soldiers,' says Peter. 'SAS, all that nonsense.'

Pearson glances at his notebook as if he's reading from some list. 'Some people here in Risedale have told us he spies on them. Would you say there's any truth in that?'

'Malice, pure and simple,' says Peter.

'Why do you think people would feel malicious towards him?'

'Because he's different. People want everyone to be the same.'

'He's a good lad,' puts in Tessa. 'He might play at peeping round corners, but he doesn't mean anyone any harm.'

'So you're not aware he has any particular interest in anyone in the village? Anyone he talks about excessively, maybe?'

Tessa is indignant. 'He hasn't been watching anyone, if that's what you're asking. You sound like you're talking about stalking, but he wouldn't do that. He has his night vision goggles, but he only uses them up in the woods. There are badgers up there. He likes to watch them.'

'Did he ever have any direct contact with Adam Henthorn?'

'Adam was a little boy,' says Tessa. 'Why would he have contact with him?'

'Is there any possibility of a sexual interest?'

'No! There's never been anything like that.' Tessa blushes. 'Simon isn't like that.'

'Look, I can see what you're getting at,' interrupts Peter. 'You're trying to suggest Simon's some kind of pervert, but he isn't. He's a gentle soul. When I was a boy, they'd have called him a bit simple, but I don't suppose I'm allowed to say that any more.'

'I'm not suggesting anything,' says Pearson. 'I'm only establishing facts.' He smiles at Tessa. 'I don't want to be cheeky, but can I have another piece of shortbread?'

'Oh. Of course.' She holds out the plate. 'It's my mother's recipe. You're lucky there's any left. If Simon had found it, he'd have wolfed the lot.'

'Look,' says Peter, 'I understand you have to rule things in and out – establish facts, as you say – but we've heard that Tommy . . . Well, frankly, that his arrest is imminent.'

Pearson rubs crumbs from his fingertips. 'Where did you hear that, Peter?'

'On the grapevine.'

'Grapevines are not generally reliable sources of information. Obviously I can't talk about the case, but I can tell you no arrest is imminent. In fact I would say we're a long way from that at the moment. Hence my talking to you. And we may need to speak to Simon, at some point.'

'Are you saying he's a person of interest, or whatever you call it?' asks Peter.

'Again, I can't comment on the case.'

'But we can infer it just from your being here.'

'If or when we do interview Simon, I can assure you as his legal guardians you'll be consulted at every turn.'

Tessa is dismayed. 'But if you do that, we'll be ... We haven't been here very long, and we're just settling in. If anyone gets the idea that Simon had anything to do with ... It would be a disaster for us.'

Pearson seems sympathetic. 'I understand it's difficult, but if Simon's behaviour is innocent as you say, really you have nothing to worry about. It's not very often we get it wrong. But regardless of how he's got there, Simon's on our radar for now, and there's a process we have to go through to eliminate him from our enquiries. You might help him by putting together his alibi. Not in any detail, of course. That's our job. But if you could make an outline list of his movements that day, you'll find that helps if we do have cause to interview him.'

'An alibi?' Tessa looks shocked. 'He doesn't need an alibi. He hasn't done anything.'

Pearson gives her a smile. 'As I say. Chances are there's nothing to worry about.'

'What about Tommy, then?' demands Peter. 'How's his alibi?'

'Well, we don't believe he was in Risedale,' says Pearson. 'At least, no one we've spoken to saw him here.'

'What, no one at all?' asks Tessa.

Pearson shakes his head.

'I might have seen him,' says Peter.

Tessa looks at him. 'Might you?'

'We can see everything from here.' Peter points out the

clear view of the road through the front window. 'Everyone who goes by. He drives that old Land Rover, doesn't he? Noisy old beast. We always hear him coming five minutes before he arrives.'

'And you think you might have seen him last Tuesday afternoon, about 3.30pm?' asks Pearson.

'Well.' Now Peter appears unsure. 'I'd have to check my diary to make sure I'd got the right day.'

'Why don't I leave you my card, then?' Pearson reaches into his pocket. 'And if you can confirm you saw Tommy in the village at that time, please get in touch. That might just be the breakthrough we've been hoping for.'

'What about Simon?' asks Tessa, anxiously. 'Would you still need to speak to him?'

'Unlikely, if we'd already charged someone else. And take it from me, in cases like these, nine times out of ten the guilty party is someone very close to home.'

After Pearson has left, Peter sits at the kitchen table on his laptop. Both he and Tessa have started on this evening's red wine.

Simon slams through the kitchen door the way he always does, bumping into a chair as he heads straight for the fridge and wrenches open the door. 'Got anything to eat?'

'Dinner's ready in a few minutes,' says Tessa. 'You're late. I thought you were catching the 5.30 bus.'

'I did. What is it for dinner? Can we get takeaway pizza?'

'We're having shepherd's pie. The bus went by half an hour ago, Simon. Where have you been till now?'

'I went to have a look at Druid's Well. I wanted to see if I could find any clues the police had missed.'

Tessa stares at him. 'For God's sake, Simon, why can't you understand? You have to stay away from there.'

Simon's taking the wrapper off a packet of cheese slices. 'Why? I might like to be a detective. I wanted to have a practice.'

'Jesus Christ.' Peter rubs his hands over his face, wearily.

'Put those back,' says Tessa, taking the cheese from Simon and returning it to the fridge. 'Go and get changed and wash your hands, then it'll be time to eat.'

'People at school say the police know who killed him,' says Simon over his shoulder as he heads for the stairs. 'They reckon it was his dad.'

'I really don't think Tommy would have done that,' says Tessa. 'He loved that child to bits.'

'He might if he was angry,' Simon replies. 'I sometimes think I'll kill someone when I'm angry.'

And Tessa believes him. As her son's got older, more than once she's felt afraid that he might hurt her.

'What shall we do?' she asks Peter, after she hears Simon's bedroom door slam. 'He's behaving like a total idiot.'

Peter considers for a moment, then opens a new window and clicks a button to compose an email, typing in DS Pearson's address from his card.

'Peter, what are you doing?' asks Tessa. 'What are you going to say?'

'That I saw Tommy in the village last Tuesday.'

'But you didn't.'

'I might have done. I can't remember if I did or not. But I've checked my diary and I was here at home, so it's not impossible.'

'Don't be ridiculous, Peter. You can't go saying things to the police that aren't true.'

Peter hesitates, then nods his agreement. 'You're right. Of course you're right. It'd be mad to do that without being a hundred per cent.'

He closes the laptop lid, and pours them both more wine.

But late that night in bed, both of them are wakeful. Eyes tight closed, Tessa is trying to force herself to sleep when she senses Peter getting up.

She turns on the bedside lamp. 'Are you OK?'

Over his pyjamas, Peter is putting on the awful baggy cardigan he likes to wear around the house. Tessa hates that cardigan, which reminds her of a very similar one her dementia-addled father wore during his last days in the care home. As he puts on his slippers, Peter looks similarly dishevelled and somehow older. Constant worry about Simon is taking its toll on them both.

'Where are you going?'

'I'm going to write to that policeman about Tommy.'

'Peter, don't be ridiculous. It's two in the morning. Come back to bed.'

'Everybody thinks Tommy did it. You heard what Simon said.'

'That's just stupid kids spreading rumours round school. It's not evidence. Tommy doted on Adam. He adored him. Don't you remember the two of them playing football on the field? They were a delight. I don't think he would have hurt him, honestly I don't.'

But Peter isn't listening. 'Look, the more I think about it, the more I think I did see Tommy that day. It was either the

Monday or the Tuesday, so it's fifty–fifty that I did, isn't it? And if it was the Tuesday and I don't come forward, then Tommy might literally get away with murder, and how would we feel then? So I'm going to make a statement in good faith. And if I'm wrong, Tommy will be able prove his innocence in other ways, won't he? No harm done.'

'But you have to swear on the Bible, and you're not sure.'

'I'm eighty percent sure. Maybe ninety. And I'm just going to give them a bit of help in case they need to build their case against Tommy.'

'Peter, you can't. It's against the law. You'll end up in jail yourself.'

'I can, and I'm going to. I have to. Because if they don't have sufficient evidence against Tommy, that policeman pretty much said Simon's next on their list. We have to protect him, Tess. Because hand on heart, are you absolutely sure that he's got nothing to do with what happened to Adam?'

FOURTEEN

As crime rates climb, the CPS's job becomes more demanding.

Lorna's boss is off with some kind of flu, and while she can't make decisions or even really advise in his absence, that doesn't stop people ringing and asking her for help.

So it's just after six when she gets home – almost an hour later than she planned – but though she's tired, she's still upbeat as she puts on music and runs a bath. Actually she's starving hungry, but she won't eat until he gets here. She spent her short lunchbreak buying some expensive treats from a city-centre deli – olives and serrano ham, a goat's cheese tart and chocolate mousses – and wants to wait for him so they can try them together. Just for a moment, she wonders if she's trying too hard. If he's had a long day too, maybe he'd prefer pizza. But if that's the case, no problem. What she's bought will keep for another day.

In the bathroom, she slides gratefully into the perfumed water. A song they once made love to begins to play, and she smiles.

They won't have long together tonight, but the time they do have is going to be very special.

* * *

Cases like Adam's don't come up every day, thank God, but, when they do, they make you take stock, force you to look at the direction your life is taking. Because a case like Adam's reminds you in the most unavoidable way that life is unpredictable, and that you'd better pay attention to what's important, because you never know when the music's going to stop.

Canfield has strayed off the path he expected his life to take, a long way off. On his wedding day, he wholly expected – and wanted – to be one of the lucky ones whose monogamous marriage would last the rest of his life.

Somehow, that changed.

He used to regard as weak the kind of men who messed up their lives getting involved with other women. For years, he was proud to call himself a family man, until family life became difficult, uncongenial. Then it became apparent he was as vulnerable as anyone else to straying, to believing he could have his cake and eat it. The guilt was unexpected, both towards the wife he's deceiving and the woman he's been – he realises – leading on. Flattered that Lorna – somewhat younger than him, and a very attractive girl – is falling in love with him, he's been less than honest about his long-term intentions, wanting their affair to continue. Or maybe he's a little in love with her too? No. He's sure it isn't that. She's somewhere he goes when the real world gets too much, an enthusiastic lover who always greets him with wine and candles, where his wife Irene's default is exhausted and sullen, complaining of being left from morning till midnight with the care of two young children, plainly sick and tired of being married to a policeman whose shifts seem to get longer and longer, and for whom she no longer has any respect. He's fallen into the trap he always promised himself he'd avoid: the temptation of another woman. And this other woman deserves to be so much more than that.

So now he's in a lay-by somewhere off the A6, sitting in the dark, watching the tail lights and headlights of the passing traffic, hearing the swish of tyres on wet tarmac as they pass by, trying to find the courage and the will to do what has to be done. He needs to move on, to go back to valuing his family as he should, to being the honourable man everyone – especially Irene – believes him to be.

He opens his phone: 6.53pm. Only seven minutes until he told her he'd be there, and he knows she'll be waiting for him. She'll have shopped for wine, made an effort to spoil him. She'll try to hide it, but she'll be upset that he's letting her down.

He feels a pang of regret: for the time he won't spend in her company, for the hurt he knows he's going to cause.

That can't be helped.

He's got her in his phone as Lenny Goddard, an old friend of his who Irene knows well. Deviously – when did he become devious? – he's switched Lenny's number to Turner's garage who service Irene's car; Turner's, when he next needs them, he can easily google. But the thought that something could go horribly wrong has been with him since this deception began, and undeniably it will be a relief to have everything safely legitimate again, to not feel panic every time Irene goes near his phone.

All he has to do is touch the name on the screen.

Yet something holds him back. Does it have to be final, be over?

Just do the decent thing, he tells himself. *Just get it done, and get on with your life.*

He connects the call and immediately wishes he hadn't, but her phone's already ringing out. She's going to be angry. He prays she doesn't cry.

'Lorna?'

'Hi.' Her voice is bright and optimistic. Irene, he recalls, used to shine with brightness and optimism, but somewhere along the line of their marriage they've been eradicated, or at least shoved so far into the background of her persona barely a spark remains. In large part, that's probably his fault, and now he's going to trample on those same qualities in a young woman he should never have had anything to do with in the first place, if he'd been the man he'd thought he was.

'Hi. How are you doing?'

'I'm good,' she says, 'waiting for you,' and there's a smile in her voice, a delicious tone of anticipatory sensuality. It isn't too late. He could be there in twenty minutes, not stay too long.

In other words, he could use her.

'Listen,' he says. He closes his eyes, as if that will make it easier. 'I can't make it tonight.'

A short silence. He pictures the smile leaving her face, and knows she'll have to work hard to hide her disappointment.

'Why not?'

He sighs, a heavy exhale of his own unwillingness to say the words, his sadness at their parting and, if he's honest, his sense of loss. Now the moment's here, he's hit with the realisation he's in deeper than he thought.

'We can't do this any more. I'm not what you need, I'm wrong for you. I want to be honest with you. With everyone.'

'You mean her.'

'Yes, her. You're a wonderful woman, Lorna. You deserve so much more.'

'But I want you.' He can hear tears in her voice, and to his surprise he feels his eyes pricking too.

'And I want you – you know I do.'

'But not as much as you want her.'

He shakes his head. 'It isn't like that, it's not as simple as that. There are the kids . . .'

'You weren't bothered about them before.'

'I was always bothered about them.'

'But not as bothered as you were about bedding me.'

'Please, Lorna. Don't be like that. You know I'm very fond of you, fonder than I should be.'

'Fond? You're fond of me?' He can hear her quite justified anger. 'You said you were going to leave her, be with me. My God, what a mug I've been. Oldest line in the book, and I fell for it.'

'Come on. It wasn't a line, and you know it.'

'Do I?'

'I'm sorry. Really, truly sorry.'

'Not as sorry as I am. You've wasted six months of my life.'

'It wasn't a waste. We had some good times, didn't we?'

She ends the call.

He drives a long way home, taking a route that passes near her flat, tempted to stop and ring the doorbell, to try and turn the clock back half an hour.

But as he's waiting at traffic lights his phone pings with a message from 'Lenny Goddard'.

He opens it, and reads. *I hate you you absolute total prick.*

There's no way he's ever coming back from that.

FIFTEEN

Tommy hasn't called ahead, but he knows the chances are he'll find his sister Dawn at home. Dawn's a creature of habit, the kind of person whose schedule never varies. On a Friday, she finishes work at the quarry offices at 2.30, and she's always unlocking the front door before four, even if she stops to deal with the weekend shopping-list she tucked in her handbag as she kissed her husband Jake goodbye that morning, eight o'clock sharp.

Dawn lives in Over Monkton, which isn't exactly Risedale but might as well be, considering it's only a twenty-minute walk from one village boundary to another, and how well most of the inhabitants know each other: their kids go to the same schools, they use the same supermarkets and public services, they drink in the same pubs and join in the same celebrations and festivals.

Her house is on an estate built only a decade ago and immune to the perpetual damp and draughts they both grew up with in a traditional cottage. Dawn's pristine car is on the drive. Tommy parks his dirty Land Rover behind it and rings the front doorbell.

Dawn takes longer than usual to open it, and when she does Tommy sees she's been crying.

'Sorry,' she says. 'I was just having a moment. I've been trying to ring you, where have you been? You look terrible. Come in, I'll put the kettle on. Go and make yourself comfortable. Do you want anything to eat? I can do you a sandwich.'

Tommy declines the sandwich, and wanders into the bright, light living room. Dawn's taste is all Ikea blond wood and simple lines, duck-egg throws and curtains. Their father was a man who liked everything bottle green or navy blue, occasionally allowing a splash of blood red in the tartan lining of his outdoorsman's coats. What he'd have made of this place with its feminine touches, God only knows, but he'd no doubt have complained that Jake was less of a man for letting his wife have her way with the decor.

Tommy was always the one in thrall to their father, tramping across the moors behind him on pheasant shoots from the age of only eight, graduating through the years to drinking at his dad's elbow in the pub, while Dawn was always a homebody who enjoyed her bedroom, her books and her mother's company.

Tommy misses his dad; but at the moment, that's the least of his despairs.

He sits down on the cream-upholstered sofa, quickly stands to check the seat of his trousers is clean and sits again. The silver-framed photo of Dawn and Adam which is usually on the bookshelves – Dawn's love of reading has stayed with her through life – is on the coffee table.

Tommy picks it up. In the picture – how old is Adam here? Two, maybe three – his cheeks are splodged with poster paint smears of blue, yellow and red, his face close to Dawn's as she dabs a red-stained finger on the tip of his nose. Both of them are laughing, and Adam's eyes are alight with mischief. Tommy's never noticed it before, but his sister's face is shining with love. Dawn often said Adam was the son she never had, couldn't have, despite years of trying. The realisation hits Tommy that Dawn will be feeling this almost as much as he is.

How is it possible he'll never see Adam's smile again, hear his laugh?

Tears sting his eyes, even as his conscience pricks: there wasn't much laughter in his life in his last days. For reasons he can't understand, everything in their lives was going to shit. Adam should have been protected from all that.

But you can't turn back time.

Dawn carries in coffee on a tray. There's so much of their mother in Dawn, a caring quality Tommy used to think he himself lacked, though lately he's come to realise he doesn't lack it, he just doesn't know how to or daren't express it. He can't recall a single instance of his father ever making his mother even a cup of tea. Dad took it as his God-given right to wait to be served in his favourite chair, always a proper cup with a biscuit on the saucer, and his father – to his credit – always smilingly grateful for her efforts. And now Dawn seems to emulate her, though with mugs instead of cups and saucers, and slabs of the marble cake Adam always liked to help her make, being allowed to swirl the chocolate mix into the vanilla and lick the spoon clean afterwards as a special treat.

The sight of that cake stabs him in the heart.

'I made it for Adam,' Dawn says. 'Call me mad, but I felt he was there with me while I was doing the stirring.' Placing the tray on a low table, she pulls a tissue from her pocket and dabs at her eyes. 'I'm sorry. I wasn't going to cry, but I miss him so much. Anyway, you'd better eat some now I've made it.'

Tommy's barely eaten for days, but the scent of warm vanilla provokes his appetite. He takes a piece of cake, and eating it quickly, takes another, only to find that the first bite of the second piece makes him nauseous, and he can eat no more.

Dawn sits down heavily in an armchair. 'Any news?'

'A bit,' says Tommy. 'I've just been to the police station.'

Dawn nods. 'I thought that must be on the cards. I suppose they've plenty of questions for you. How did it go?'

'I thought it went all right, but the solicitor says I said too much. I don't know what he means. I've got nothing to hide.'

Dawn frowns. 'You've got a solicitor? Why do you need one of them?'

'Because I've got no alibi. I've told them where I was but they don't believe me because I can't prove it.'

Though she was aware it must be going on, Dawn hasn't brought up the police investigation before because it seemed insensitive. Obviously in a case like this, Tommy's going to be top of the list when it comes to suspects, because aren't most victims of murder killed by someone they know? Personally, she doesn't believe Tommy could have harmed a hair on Adam's head. Didn't he love that boy more than his own life? But he was crazy about Gail too, and beyond devastated at losing her. Was anger part of that devastation, and did anger breed a need for the worst possible revenge, the taking of her child? That makes no sense; the wound has impacted Tommy as deeply as it's cut Gail, possibly deeper. But Tommy's been no angel in the past. Occasionally over the years, Dawn's heard bad things about her brother, locally rumoured incidents people will swear actually happened: a bloody beating in a pub yard after Saturday night closing; key scratches on an expensive car, which cost thousands to remove; a fire set under building-site machinery and a gate smashed to pieces with a sledgehammer. None of these episodes were reported to the police, because people didn't mess with Tommy. Tommy had friends in all the wrong places.

But the moment Gail fell pregnant, he declared himself a reformed character. Adam seemed to be his saviour, the one thing in this world that made Tommy want to be a better man.

'Why can't you prove where you were?' asks Dawn. 'Should be easy enough, surely?'

'I wish to God it was. I was in an out-of-the-way spot, just walking, doing a bit of thinking. No phone signal, no CCTV. They rely on technology for everything these days. If you're not on some camera, they say you weren't there.'

'That sounds like rubbish about your phone. They can track them anywhere, can't they?'

'I had it switched off. I forgot to recharge it.'

'That's really thoughtless, Tommy. That should never happen when you've got kids. Wasn't he your responsibility as much as Gail's?'

'Course he was. It was just one of those things. You think I wouldn't have been home in a second if I'd known something was up with my boy? You think I wouldn't have dropped everything and come running? I don't understand why they don't believe me. It's the only thing anyone would have done. Why do they think I would hurt him? I'm not a monster. I was his dad.'

Tommy seems both heartbroken and wholly sincere, but even though she doesn't want to acknowledge it, a seed of doubt sprouts in Dawn's mind. His story of remote locations and a switched-off phone sounds improbable, and she understands where the police are coming from. *No need to come running if you were already there.*

She considers. 'You can prove it with a negative, though, can't you? If you can't prove you were somewhere else, they still have to prove you were in Risedale. And if you weren't, they can't do that, can they?'

Tommy's expression turns grim. 'Aye well. Seems there's some in the village who don't much like me. People who say I was there. Liars who say they saw me.'

'What people?'

'I don't know, but I'll find out, and when I do find out, they'll regret it.'

'You watch your mouth,' warns Dawn. 'You'll get yourself in a bigger hole than you're in now.'

'Am I in a hole, then?' says Tommy, combatively. 'Is that what you think? I thought you of all people would be on my side.'

'Don't be so touchy. I'm only going on what you've said. No alibi and people lying, I'd say that's a hole. Wouldn't you?'

'I suppose.'

'Look, the police aren't stupid. If there's people telling lies, they'll find out.'

'You reckon? I think they'd like it to be me, quick result, cut and dried.'

'You're probably right.'

'And something else that Gail's said, that faithless, worthless bitch. She's only gone and told them I said I'd hurt Adam if she tried to divorce me. I never said that – I would never say that.' He's becoming tearful. 'She knows I wouldn't have harmed a hair on his head. He was my only joy in life. He *was* my life.'

He begins to cry, but Dawn feels a growing unease. How likely is it that people in the village – from everything she knows, all law-abiding citizens – would actually lie to put Tommy in the frame? Because that in itself is no small thing, and isn't something you'd do out of mere spite.

An awful thought occurs to her.

'Tommy,' she says carefully, 'those guys you used to do business with sometimes, I mean before Adam was born. I know it was a while back, but you never did anything to upset them, did you? I mean, like, *really* upset them?'

Tommy sniffs, and wipes his eyes. 'What do you mean?'

'Well, from what you said, some of them were real hard cases. Could they have had anything to do with – you know, with Adam?'

'No,' he says, shaking his head. 'It's nothing to do with any of those lads. I just need to find out why someone's lying about me. If they weren't lying, I'd be all right.'

'Don't worry too much. Justice will be done – you'll see.' Dawn's platitude is useless, but soft words never hurt. 'Try and eat some more cake, and I'll make you another coffee.'

As Tommy leaves, from the window she watches him climb into the Land Rover, troubled to see the sad, diminished figure he's become. For a while she sits, going over things he's said. Would he be capable of violence? Almost certainly. Isn't it in the human male's DNA? Isn't any man, if really pushed?

But Adam? Could he be capable of that?

Dawn's forced to admit to herself that, actually, she simply doesn't know.

SIXTEEN

People say that the drugs don't work, but for Gail that isn't true.

The little white pills the doctor prescribed induce a merciful blur on everything around her. What's disturbing, though, is that the blur occasionally morphs into hallucinations, a plausible almost-reality where through the window she sees Adam cycling in circles in the yard, his lips moving as he sings to himself. Several times, she's sure she's heard him singing in the house, a song about a train he learned at playgroup and always loved. But the singing is always in a room where Gail isn't, sending her running for the kitchen or Adam's bedroom only to be met by silence the moment she opens the door. Adam himself she feels is very much still here, not yet left and perhaps never intending to go, and Gail prays for him to stay at least until she finds him – if only once – because she has so much she needs to say.

The pills screw with her memory as well as her brain, so for entire moments and minutes she forgets that Adam's gone and regresses to brief oases of normality where she thinks about laundry or what to make for tea, until the underlying truth of her awful new life muscles back in. Every day now is one in a tedious procession of days to come, and Adam's death is an open wound where no healing scab will ever form. Day by day, year by year, the burden will have to be carried.

And today is the day she buries her son.

On the eve of any such occasion, a mother would have lain awake all night thinking about what was to come. Gail, though – having drunk a couple of glasses of wine on top of her medication – fell into deep sleep the moment she lay down in bed, and doesn't wake until her sister Chrissie comes knocking at the bedroom door, bringing strong, sweet tea and toast and honey, but none of the benevolent pills of which she's surreptitiously taken custody for the day.

Chrissie throws open the bedroom curtains, but the morning outside is maudlin grey and the bedroom's gloom remains. She sits down on the bed, exhaling a whiff of alcohol and cigarettes, the alcohol stale from last night, the smokiness fresh from one just put out. Chrissie lets her hand rest on the shape of Gail's hip under the duvet, and for a few quiet moments it's like they were together when they were kids, toughing it out when bad things happened, until Chrissie has to say, 'Time to get dressed, sweetie. They'll soon be here.'

Through the fog of sleep and pills, Gail asks, 'Who?'

Chrissie's reluctant to say the words. 'The undertakers. The hearse will soon be here. We have to get you looking respectable.'

'I don't want to look respectable.' Gail pulls the bedclothes over her head. 'I don't want to go.'

'Don't be daft. Of course you're going. Go on, hop in the shower. I'll help you dry your hair after.'

Chrissie watches her sister stumble from the bed. Of the two of them, Gail has all the looks, though far less obvious now with her blonde hair greasy and her wan, newly haggard face. She looks like a woman living through all the horrors of hell, and for all Chrissie knows, she is.

Water begins to run in the shower at last. Chrissie picks up a piece of her sister's honey-slathered toast and takes a generous bite.

Gail's eventually been persuaded to do what Chrissie insists is the decent thing, to put on a show of family solidarity and walk beside Tommy to the church. By the time Gail's dressed and wearing a slick of lipstick, Tommy's already waiting in the living room, talking to Chrissie's husband Rob and looking halfway handsome in a dark-grey suit and black shirt.

He's clutching a plush blue rabbit, and when Chrissie says how cute it is, Tommy's eyes fill with tears.

'I always said I'd get him a rabbit when he was old enough to look after it.'

Chrissie hands him a box of tissues, and Tommy dries his eyes.

Gail sits on the sofa staring at her black patent shoes as if her feet aren't her own, and says, 'Shall we have a drink before we go?'

'Great idea.' Rob dives into the kitchen and returns moments later with tumblers of whisky, handing one to Tommy and the second to Gail before returning for shots for himself and

Chrissie, who's standing by the window, supposedly looking out for the hearse.

Rob drains his glass and says, 'You can't see the road from there, Chris. I'll go and wait at the end of the drive, show them where to come.'

'I'll come with you,' says Chrissie.

The door slams as they go outside, shutting Tommy and Gail in together with their misery.

If it weren't for the abundance of flowers, the hearse would be overwhelmingly too big for the small white coffin.

Tommy has insisted there's to be no suggestion of charitable donations, that tributes to his beautiful son are very much welcomed. Placed on top of the coffin among sprays of white roses sits the blue rabbit.

The church bell tolls. The hearse begins to move down the village, one of the undertaker's men in a black tailcoat walking ahead of the cortège, Tommy and Gail leading the mourners behind. Outside the church, the crowd of onlookers falls silent as they approach. Tommy's too dazed by grief to take in much, but he notices there's an awful lot of people gathered, most of whom he doesn't know.

Behind him, he hears his mother Lizzie whisper to Chrissie, 'Who are all this lot?'

'People come to pay their respects, I suppose,' replies Chrissie. 'There must be hundreds.'

Only four bearers are needed. In truth, for a coffin so light, two would easily have managed and Tommy even proposed he'd carry his boy alone, until gently dissuaded by the undertakers.

Tommy takes his place at the front on the right. Adam's shared weight feels like nothing at all, no more than a pressure on his shoulder, and yet such a burden of sorrow.

This should not be. How can this be?

As they carry Adam across the church threshold, the congregation stands, but with his eyes on the trestle before the altar, Tommy sees no one. When the coffin is in its place, he's reluctant to leave Adam there, and is only persuaded to take his place in the pew beside Gail when Lizzie takes his arm to lead him away.

Music is played, hymns are sung and the vicar gives an address about God's possible purpose in taking such a short life. His platitudes fill Tommy with such rage he can barely keep his seat.

Then Adam is carried back outside, across the road to the cemetery.

After they lay their son in the ground, after the vicar has said his final few words, offered his most sincere condolences and followed the rest of the gathering away, Gail faces Tommy across the open grave. The blue rabbit lies on Adam's coffin lid where Tommy has thrown it, one soiled ear sticking out of the handfuls of dirt the mourners have thrown. A little distance away, an engraved white marble headstone – an expensive gift from a TV personality Tommy doesn't even like – leans against an ash tree. Once the sexton has done his morbid work, burying Adam deep under the worm-ridden soil, Tommy knows that stone will mark the place where his own heart lies.

'What do we do now?' he asks, bleakly.

Gail shakes her head. Chrissie's allowed her no pills this morning, and with the residue of last night's dose an inadequate cushion, the shock of what's happening is starting to bite.

'I suppose we should go to the pub,' suggests Tommy. 'Have a drink and that.'

Gail really doesn't care, but a place serving alcohol sounds better than most.

Even under these circumstances, Tommy knows better these days than to offer her his hand to hold. Instead, he walks away ahead of her, leaving her to follow him alone.

SEVENTEEN

Now the funeral is over, the future feels barren and unwanted.

Tommy doesn't know how long he's been lying awake in the single bed of his boyhood bedroom, staring at a crack in the ceiling, waiting for time to pass.

At 11.35pm, he hears his mother get up in the bedroom next door and go to the bathroom, then the creak of the stairs as she heads down to the kitchen. A while later, she knocks at his door.

He calls to her to come in. In the lamplight she looks undeniably aged, the dressing gown she's had for years somehow suddenly too big for her, her hands bony and ridged with veins. But she loves him the way she always did, and it brings a lump to his throat to see she's brought him cocoa and digestive biscuits like she used to when he was a boy, always doing what she can to make things better.

She's a mother in a million, his mum.

'I saw the light under your door,' she says.

'I can't sleep.' He pats his bed for her to sit. She places the cocoa and biscuits on the bedside table, and the smell of hot, sweet chocolate brings him brief comfort, a short-lived moment of hope that everything will be fine. When she's close to him, he can see from her eyes she's been crying again.

'What are we going to do?' She pulls a handkerchief from her dressing-gown pocket and dabs at her nose. 'I can't bear to think of him out there, all by himself in that wind and rain. He should be here with us, tucked up where it's warm.'

Tommy reaches out and squeezes her hand.

'I don't know how I can stand it,' Lizzie goes on. 'He was the light of our lives, that lad. The only thing I'm glad for is that your dad's not here to go through it. He thought the world of that child, he did really. Gave him a new lease of life when he came along.'

'Dad'll be with him up there now,' says Tommy. 'And Adam will be driving him nuts asking him questions.'

'Do you think that's true, Tommy, honestly? That wherever they are, they're together?'

Tommy sighs. 'I hope so, Mum. I really do.'

He sips the cocoa, and gives her a smile of appreciation.

'I shan't rest until I know who did it,' says Lizzie. 'Barbara told me at the wake that everyone's saying it was the Rains boy. Do you think it was him?'

'Maybe. There'd better be some news soon from the police, though. It's driving me mad, wondering who it might have been.'

'Whoever could be so wicked, that's the question. Who would do such an evil thing?'

Lizzie draws her dressing gown tighter round her, as if the thought of her grandson's killer has given her physical chills.

'Don't worry,' says Tommy, ominously. 'We'll find out soon enough. And when we do, there'll be no mercy shown, I promise. I swear it on my son's bones.'

EIGHTEEN

At the end of a long day, Canfield's in his Kenton Road office with Pearson and DC Emma Goodwin, debating whether Tommy Henthorn should be charged with his son's murder.

The discussion's been going on a long time, and Canfield's got a banging headache, brought on no doubt by too much snacking on junk food, an overload of instant coffee and poor sleep the previous night – plus a level of stress brought on by the argument between him and his colleagues.

Canfield and Pearson are usually in tune when it comes to making judgements. They often joke about how they share the same guilty-as-hell radar, how they can pick them out of a line-up with their eyes closed. But in this case, that unanimity has fractured. Pearson is convinced of Henthorn's guilt and Goodwin's siding with him, but Canfield has his doubts. All the evidence they have seems to rely on witness statements and the lack of an alibi, which isn't a total surprise. Any forensic evidence showing contact between Adam and his father is completely irrelevant, given that they saw each other often. And Canfield is uneasy about Tommy's willingness to co-operate, and the fact that he's never once reverted to the 'no comment' defence, which seems to be all they hear in interviews these days. Tommy has from the first vehemently insisted he's innocent, and in his gut Canfield feels inclined to at least half-believe him.

But as Pearson says, if not Tommy, then who?

Pearson steps back to the whiteboard and picks up a red pen. 'I'm going to go back to the basics and list what we've got,' he says, wiping away the scribble on the board, so altered and messed around with during the last hour's debate that it's actually lost all meaning.

Canfield glances at Emma, noticing her interest in Pearson's rear view, and wonders, not for the first time, if something's going on there, or if Emma at least would like there to be. If there is something going on, Canfield will be the last to know. The whole department knows how he frowns on office attachments. They cloud people's judgements, take their eyes off the ball. But if Emma's got a crush on Pearson, she won't be the first. And his own disapproval of anyone's relationship with anybody feels like the worst kind of hypocrisy after his entanglement with Lorna.

'Opportunity,' says Pearson, writing the word large on the board. 'Obviously he's got that in spades.' He writes again. 'Alibi. He doesn't have one, just some cock-and-bull story about being in the Buxton area he can't or won't back up. Witness statements, we have Gail Henthorn's statement that Tommy threatened to harm Adam if she wouldn't reconsider filing for divorce, plus we have a history of call-outs for domestic violence incidents at that address in our own records. And we have Peter Rains's statement of seeing Tommy's vehicle in the village during the afternoon in question.'

'Which Tommy denies,' says Canfield.

'Well, he would, wouldn't he?' puts in Emma.

Canfield sighs. 'I just think we have to be very careful not to jump to conclusions because of his character. I'm not saying he's a straight-up all-round good bloke, because he isn't. But did he have it in him to murder his own child? I'm not sure we've got enough to persuade a jury.'

'I think we have to try,' says Pearson. 'Who else have we got?'

'I agree,' says Emma.

Canfield considers. 'Simon Rains. He's a strange character.'

'No forensics,' says Pearson. 'No witnesses.'

'But have we done enough house-to-house?' asks Canfield. 'The village is thirty per cent holiday lets. Have we spoken to everyone who was visiting at the time?'

'It was very off-season, so only a couple were rented,' says Emma. 'Those that were, we spoke to.'

'Someone from outside, then,' suggests Canfield. 'Someone who hasn't yet appeared on our radar.'

'You think we should just sit around and not charge him in case fate throws us a curveball somewhere down the line? Top brass won't like that, will they?'

After his recent meeting with Nolan and Lomas, Canfield's one hundred per cent in agreement there. He glances at his watch. Forty minutes before the CPS phone lines shut down for the day.

'OK,' he says, still with a measure of reluctance. 'Emma, get on to the CPS and tell them what we've got. We'll let them make the decision. If they say yes, then obviously we have to give it a go.'

Pearson's eyebrows raise, and there's the beginnings of a smirk on his lips.

'Don't you want to call the CPS, boss? If you speak to your contact, we'll get a much fairer hearing, clear the hurdle a lot easier.'

Canfield appears to be busy with gathering up his notes from the desk in front of him, and his face is hidden from Pearson as he speaks.

'She's not my contact any more. And I wouldn't want anyone insinuating that I would use any personal relationship I may or may not have had with anyone at the CPS to influence their decision making, which should be and always has been as far as I'm aware completely impartial. Is that clear?'

'As clear as day, boss.' Pearson gives Emma a wink that happily Canfield doesn't see. 'Come on then, Goodwin, don't keep us all waiting. Make that call.'

NINETEEN

Despite what's going on at the office, Canfield has done his best to get home reasonably on time, though little pockets of delay have conspired against him. He was later than he wanted to be leaving the office because of a wait for the CPS call-back and a round of back-slapping and next-steps assignments when their decision was for prosecution. Then, as he was leaving the building, he almost literally bumped into DCC Nolan in the lobby, who quite reasonably asked for an update, though his questions were interrupted by short conversations with others going out and coming into the building, so what should have taken three or four minutes stretched to ten. And then, of course, there were the roadworks on the ring road.

All of which means he's home significantly later than he promised he was going to be and dreading the reception awaiting him. *Please, God*, he thinks, *let it for once be a quiet evening, let Irene put her 'I'm stuck here at home all day' rant to one side, just this once.*

Hungry, thirsty and in need of some space to relax, he can't help thinking of Lorna's calm, welcoming flat. And Lorna's soothing, diverting company.

He pushes the thought of her away.

When he pulls into the driveway and turns off the engine, he hesitates a moment before getting out of the car, putting on the mental armour he might need when he walks into the house. As he puts his key in the lock, there's silence on the other side of the front door: no young feet running to greet him, no excited shouts of 'Daddy!', and he finds himself disappointed.

Instead, Irene is there, not quite smiling but not obviously raging either, which is a good start.

As he moves to close the door, she stops him and peers round it, frowning.

'Who's that?'

Across the road, under a lamp post, a small car has pulled up, its engine running, the vapour from its exhaust like smoke in the cold night air.

Whoever is in the driving seat is looking at them.

Irene is hopeless without her glasses, unable to bring the driver into focus even if she squints.

But Canfield can see the make and model of the car.

He knows someone who drives one of those.

He knows the woman at the wheel.

Lorna.

Caught unawares, he stares at the car a moment too long.

He wants to go to her. He wants to say he's sorry.

But here and now, he has no choice.

'Looks like a delivery driver,' he says. 'Someone's having a takeaway.'

And, with perfectly pretended indifference, he closes the door.

TWENTY

In the wake of Adam's death and in his wife's much-mourned absence, in the evenings Tommy seeks the warming, smoky comfort of Jack Daniels. Its consolations, he has found, are two-fold. Firstly, by the bottom of the first glass, the aching misery that constantly weighs him down begins to disperse. Secondly, by the end of the third or fourth glass, generally depending on how generously he's poured, deep, profound sleep irresistibly overcomes him, and that is the most precious solace he can ask for. Notwithstanding the sometimes troubling dreams which come to him, sleep brings forgetting and oblivion. And sometimes, if he's lucky, a large enough dose of Jack will carry him insensibly through till almost daybreak.

So, by the time he's awake, the disturbance downstairs is well-established. His bedroom is still in darkness, which in these winter days could be any time before 7.30am. Yet he can hear men's voices downstairs, and his mother shouting, which is in itself – since she's normally so mild – an extraordinary event.

Tommy leaps to the obvious conclusion, that the house is being broken into.

In a second he's out of bed, ignoring a strong need to piss as he pulls on the trousers he was wearing yesterday and heads bare-chested and barefoot to the top of the stairs. He's spoiling for a fight. With all that's been going on, nothing would give him more pleasure than to beat the living daylights out of anyone who deserves it – or honestly, even someone who actually doesn't.

At the head of the stairs he stops, disbelieving of what's going on in the hallway, where in her nightdress and slippers Lizzie, God bless her, is blocking the open door with her slight frame, arguing with the frontman of four uniformed police officers demanding admittance to the house. All that's holding them at bay is her vulnerability. None of them wants to force a woman who's no threat out of their way.

But the frontman is losing patience, shouting at Lizzie to step back from the door.

Tommy yells downstairs. 'What the hell do you think you're doing? Leave her alone, you pig!'

His mother looks up at him, her face panicked. 'They've come to take you away, Tommy! I've told them you won't go. I've said they can't come in.'

But with her attention briefly distracted, the frontman seizes his moment, and pushes past her.

Too roughly. With a cry, she stumbles and falls.

'You prick!' Tommy's anger cranks up. 'You leave her alone!'

He and the frontman meet halfway on the stairs, the frontman blocking Tommy's descent. His colleagues have followed him into the house, fanning out into the downstairs rooms. At least one of them has had the decency to attend to Lizzie, crouching beside her to check she's OK.

Facing up to Tommy, the frontman is aggressive. 'Thomas Henthorn, I have a warrant for your arrest. You do not have to say anything, but it may harm your defence if you do not mention when questioned something which you later rely on in court. Anything you do say may be given in evidence.'

'Evidence of what? What are you talking about?'

'I'm arresting you for the murder of Adam Henthorn.'

'Fuck off,' says Tommy, derisively. Aided by a policeman, Lizzie is slowly sitting up, but she's shocked and dazed.

'Mum, are you OK?' Tommy glares at the frontman. 'You lot are brutal, that's what you are. Get out of my way, let me go to her.'

'You need to go back upstairs and put on some clothes,' says the frontman. 'We'll be taking you to Kenton Road police station for processing.'

'You will not,' says Tommy. 'Mum, are you all right?'

'I'm all right, son,' says Lizzie weakly. 'Don't let them take you away, Tommy. I don't want to be left here all by myself.'

Tommy turns smartly round and runs back up the few stairs he's descended, into the bathroom where he slams and locks the door. Immediately, the frontman is there, banging to be let in.

'I'm having a piss,' shouts Tommy. 'I can do that in private, can't I?'

But as he flushes the toilet, he sees he's gained himself an advantage. The bathroom window opens onto the flat roof of the outhouse that his mother uses as a log store. If he gets out through there, he can be across the fields and away. But where to? And how conspicuous will he be, barefoot and half-naked?

He doesn't give a damn. Throwing open the window, he

has one leg over the sill before he notices movement below him, a shadowy figure who shines the bright beam of a torch right in his face.

They've put a man down there to block this route out.

The frontman is still hammering on the bathroom door.

'Open up, Tommy. You're coming with us one way or another. Better for your mum if we don't have to make a mess.'

Realising he's beaten, Tommy slides back the bolt. In a second, the frontman is beside him, grabbing his forearms.

'Let me go,' snarls Tommy. 'I got stuff to do before I can come with you. I have to see to my dogs.'

'You won't be doing that today, son.'

'I'm not your son. And who's going to take care of them? My missus won't do it, not to save her own life.'

'Not my problem, mate. I'm here to execute this warrant.'

'How long will I be gone, then?' demands Tommy. 'I need to speak to my solicitor so we can get this sorted. I have to be home to see to them this afternoon.'

'You're best off asking your mum to make some long-term arrangements,' says the frontman, without sympathy. 'I don't think you'll be coming back home for quite some time.'

TWENTY-ONE

Following Tommy's arrest, Canfield's first priority – according to Superintendent Lomas – is to liaise with PR to get a press conference organised, and prepare a statement he can read out while seated next to the deputy chief constable.

Of course, Lomas tells him, top brass are delighted.

Pearson is all smiles. 'Coming for a drink? I reckon we've earned one. Emma's gone to save a couple of tables over at the Crown.'

Canfield's phone rings. He listens, and says he'll be right down. 'There's someone asking for me at the front desk. You go ahead. I'll see you there.'

'Don't be late,' says Pearson, shrugging on his overcoat. 'I'll get you a pint.'

The woman waiting in reception has a familiar face, though Canfield can't immediately place her. Apparently, though, she recognises him. She's picked up her coat and handbag from the seat beside her and is walking towards him.

Her face is stern. 'You don't remember me, do you?'

Canfield is weary, and skips any social niceties. 'I'm sorry, no, I don't.'

'Laila Jutt. I spoke to you a couple of weeks ago about my missing husband, Faizan.'

Canfield only vaguely recalls a short conversation, and handing this woman over to a PC to take details. Beyond that, it's slipped from his mind, and most likely way down Derbyshire Police's list of priorities.

'No one's been in touch with me,' she says. 'Not even a phone call.'

Ouch. 'I'm sorry about that, Mrs Jutt. Someone should have made contact.'

'Well, they didn't. So I don't suppose there's any point in me asking if you've done anything about finding him?'

Chances are the details have been put on file and not looked at since. 'Off the top of my head, I can't answer that,' Canfield says. 'Have you heard nothing from him?'

'Not a single word.' Her expression changes, her belligerence replaced by sadness, grief. 'Nothing. But I've had a phone call from the police in Buxton. They rang to speak to him. They say they found his car.'

'Well, isn't that good?'

'Not really. They found it burnt out, miles from anywhere.'

'Stolen, then?'

'Maybe, but where from? Faizan loved that car – it was his pride and joy. Now it's turned up burnt out in the back of nowhere. Does that mean he's been not far away all this time? Meanwhile, he hasn't touched a penny in our bank accounts. What's he been living on? And he's never even called to talk to our son. He adores that boy. Why would he just run away and leave us?'

There are a thousand possible reasons, thinks Canfield.

While the money thing could be a red flag, there are plenty of people with secret bank accounts their partners know nothing about. Combined with the burnt-out car, though, Faizan Jutt's disappearance is turning a shade darker than the average scenario of a man abandoning an unwanted domestic set-up.

The pint Pearson's promised him will be getting warm, but Canfield's not that enthused about celebrating Tommy Henthorn's arrest, and the later he arrives, the more his liver will thank him.

Besides, if this turns out to be something rather than nothing, he doesn't want to be the one who dropped the ball.

'All right, Mrs Jutt,' he says, at last. 'Please take a seat, and I'll go and have a look what's going on.'

TWENTY-TWO

A cursory search for Faizan Jutt on the database throws up a surprise. The missing person report is there, unactioned as are so many where there's no clear reason for suspecting that the adult in question has done anything but decide they want a new life.

But there's more.

Whether his wife knows it or not, Faizan has been in trouble more than once, though he's never got as far as the courts system. Certainly he's been dabbling in life's seedier side: intent to supply a controlled substance, and most recently exploitation of prostitution, for which he was arrested. That kind of exploitation is these days often linked to truly nasty crimes like people-trafficking, and to networks run by some disturbing characters. How deeply was Faizan Jutt involved with them?

Canfield knows someone who might be able to answer that question.

He's anticipating finding no one in the office this late and leaving a message, but on the third floor, he finds Tate Fritchley still at his desk.

Tate's what would kindly be called a big man, squeezed into a suit which Canfield might fit into twice. He's sitting staring at a screen, his tie and collar loosened round his massive neck, drumming his fingers on his desk as he watches a grainy video of what looks like a vicious bare-knuckle fight.

'How you doing, Tate?'

Fritchley glances round, and with impressive speed hits a button on his keyboard to blank the screen. Years ago, before numerous re-organisations and re-brandings, Fritchley was a leading light in what used to be called Vice. Canfield doesn't know exactly where he reports in now, but old habits apparently die hard. Vice was always a law unto itself, clandestine and separate, the visible team always working to protect a network of undercover operatives, hidden and vulnerable among the county's depraved and dangerous. Fritchley was a leading player in the war against the lords of that underworld.

'Hello, mate.' Fritchley holds out a damp, soft hand, and Canfield shakes it. 'Long time no see. What brings you up to these giddy heights?'

'The usual,' says Canfield. 'Come to consult the oracle.'

Fritchley smiles at the compliment. 'Pull up a pew.'

Canfield sits. 'Might have something for you, though it's a big might. A few weeks back, a woman came in saying her husband was missing. I didn't think much of it at the time, sounded like a bloke run off with another woman to me. But she's come back in with more info. He's still not been in touch, and there's been no activity in the bank accounts – the ones she knows about, at least. And today, she's had a call from Buxton station saying his car's been found burnt out somewhere in the back of beyond. So I'm wondering whether it could be foul play.'

'You got a name?'

'Faizan Jutt.'

If he wasn't trained to spot the little tells – the involuntary body language that gives real thoughts away – Canfield might have missed Fritchley's double blink.

The name means something to him.

'Come on, Tate, let's have it. What do you know?'

Fritchley nods an acknowledgement. 'OK, yes, I know the name. He was managing a club for Freddy Lowndes for a while – not much of a club, but somewhere to cut his teeth on – but I heard he got a bit greedy and Freddy gave him the push. Word was then that Faizan was trying to run a few girls – East Europeans most likely – but he was treading on toes. That's as much as I know.'

'Could he have trodden on anyone's toes badly enough to draw blood?'

Fritchley pulls a face. 'Not impossible. Nothing's impossible with those people.'

'So what do you think? Could you take a closer look? The car and the bank accounts make me think there could be something there.'

'Yeah, all right. I'll put some feelers out, have a word with Buxton.'

'His wife's not going to like it.'

'Speaking of wives, how's the lovely Irene?'

'She's fine. She's finding it a bit of a challenge being a stay-at-home mum.'

'Tell her I said hello.'

'I will. And thanks. Listen, I'm going over to the Crown, celebratory thing, the Henthorn murder. Come with me, I'll buy you a pint.'

But Fritchley shakes his head, and points to the screen. 'Things to do, mate, too much to do. The city never sleeps, you know?'

'I do,' says Canfield. 'Let me know if you find anything on Faizan Jutt.'

Canfield's arrival at the Crown is so late that the moment he sits down is the time when he should be getting up to leave, heading home to Irene, who is beyond any doubt far more exhausted than him after another day of full-time child care, and arguably more deserving of an evening's drinking with her mates. But the pint in his hand is refreshing, and when it hits his bloodstream he feels better than he has all day. By the time he's finished his second, the world's a far brighter place, and he's totally on board with his colleagues' self-congratulatory euphoria. The third is, of course, a mistake, the fourth a grave error. By the time he's downed the whisky shot someone's shoved into his hand, the nagging feeling he should be somewhere else is coming to the fore.

As he takes a piss in the pub's dubious toilets, he finds he needs the support of a steadying hand on the wall. The rowdy banter and pumped-up music from the bar are muffled here, and as he fumbles with the lock on the toilet door, he knows he has to leave.

The pub management knows its customers. The number of a local taxi firm is pinned on the wall above the wash-basins. Canfield finds his phone and dials the number.

But waiting on the pavement outside the pub and too inebriated to care about the cold, a mad idea takes hold of him.

He takes out his phone again, and in his contacts list finds Lenny Goddard.

Even though he knows it's a terrible mistake, even though he's not so drunk that he doesn't understand what he's doing, he touches the name, and the call connects.

Four, five times the phone rings.

Then the ringing stops. The line sounds dead.

'Lorna? Lorna, are you there?'

The silence persists a few more seconds, until she says, 'What do you want? Bit late for social calls, isn't it?'

He finds his eyes have filled with tears. 'I miss you.'

He hears the softest of sighs. 'You should have thought of that before you dumped me.'

'I made a mistake, Lorna. Can we talk about it? Can I come over?'

'What, now?'

'I know it's late, but there's things I have to say.'

'You're pissed.'

'Maybe a bit. Maybe enough to be honest. Look, I . . .'

He hears a buzzing in his ear: call waiting. He glances at the screen. Irene.

'Lorna, hold on a second. Please don't hang up.'

With difficulty, he switches calls. 'Hiya.'

He can hear the barely contained fury in Irene's voice. 'Where the hell are you?'

'I'm just waiting for a cab.'

'Have you been drinking?'

'I had a couple. We were celebrating the Henthorn case.'

'Well, good for you, Inspector Gadget. Thanks so much for letting me know.'

'I'm sorry. Things got away from me.'

'I'll bet they did. You really are a piece of work, Ryan. Did everyone else forget to call their wives, too?'

Probably not, he thinks. He can't deny that he thinks of Irene's convenience and happiness less and less.

A car pulls up alongside him. The driver winds down the window. 'You call a cab, mate?'

Canfield nods, and opens the rear door. 'I'm coming home now,' he says to Irene.

'You know what,' she hisses, 'don't bloody bother.'

Irene is gone. Canfield slides into the back seat, unsure whether the sinking of his heart is fear of Irene's anger or something else.

Something to do with Lorna.

'Where to, mate?' asks the driver.

Lorna is still there, on the line, waiting.

'I love you,' he says into the phone. Without waiting for a response, he ends the call and gives the driver his home address.

TWENTY-THREE

In the same way he feels responsibility to break bad news to victims of crime, Canfield wants to be there to share good news when they have it – if indeed good news it turns out to be. He's unsure – how could he be otherwise? – how Gail Henthorn is going to react to the news that Tommy's being charged for Adam's murder. His guess is she'll be relieved the killer has been caught, but potentially shocked that the child's own father and the man she married – and presumably loved, at some point – would commit such a heinous crime.

Canfield's decided to visit Blacksmith's Cottage alone. He parks at the end of the driveway, making sure the unmarked pool car is well tucked in on the verge, out of the way of the passing quarry lorries. He locks the vehicle, knowing the locals would no doubt tell him there's no need, that Risedale is safe as houses, no crime to speak of, but Canfield knows plenty about rural crime. Sometimes bad people come through these villages, career criminals from urban centres like Manchester and Sheffield looking for easy pickings, and he'd feel a real idiot if he came back to an empty space where his car should be.

Behind him, Raymond's Wood looms, the muted winter trees sodden from overnight rain. He hears a low rumbling quickly growing louder, and steps sharply onto the muddy grass verge as a quarry truck comes thundering down the hill, a giant slab of stone loaded on its bed, a dribble of clay-coloured water leaking from its tailgate down the centre of the narrow road; and as it passes, Canfield finds himself truly believing in Tommy's guilt. A stranger would surely have hidden Adam's body, and done that very easily somewhere in the huge expanse of the nearby quarry, or dumped it in the depths of the pool at its core, where it might never have been found. Tommy couldn't bring himself to do that. Love got the better of him, Canfield's finally sure.

He begins to walk along the driveway. Even before he's turned the bend where the house will come into view, the dogs start barking in their run. Gail will know someone's coming, and sure enough as he draws closer he sees the net curtain at the front window move, suggesting someone's checking him out.

The two black Labradors are paws up on the fence, their long bodies stretched almost as tall as Canfield. Maybe they're friendly, or maybe they'd rip his arm off if they got the chance. He gives them as wide a berth as possible, and by the time he reaches the front door they've fallen silent and are wandering back inside their covered kennel.

The door's opened before he's even knocked. Gail takes one look at him, says nothing but walks away down the hall and into the lounge, suggesting – he supposes – that he should follow. She drops into a chair, and picks up the cigarette burning in an ashtray on its arm. The air is a fug of smoke from both cigarettes and the wood burner, and Canfield can't repress a cough.

'Have a seat,' says Gail.

In some ways, she looks a different woman to the one he first met. Dark roots show on what he had taken to be natural blonde hair. She was already thin, but she's lost weight, so from her face you might take her for someone starting out on crack or with a fledgling crystal-meth habit. The light in her eyes is all but out.

Murder does that to people. Those left behind slowly wither.

And yet, she's still making an effort. Her clothes are smart – opaque tights and a mid-thigh skirt, a retro twin-set with a heart-shaped locket at her neck. If it weren't for the fluffy slippers, she could be any woman pushing a trolley round Morrison's.

'How are you, Gail?' he asks.

She sucks deeply on the cigarette, exhales more smoke into the fug, then peers at the half-smoked fag as if it tastes bad and stubs it out.

'You've arrested him, then?'

Well, he should have known someone would already have told her. A drama like the one they had arresting Tommy will be the talk of Risedale for days to come.

'Yes.'

'You got enough on him to make it stick?'

'I believe so. Otherwise we wouldn't have made the arrest. The Crown Prosecution Service wouldn't allow it.'

'Where is he now?'

'He's in custody in Derby, being interviewed. We expect to charge him later today.'

'I suppose he's saying he didn't do it.'

'He's denying the charge, yes. His lawyer almost certainly will advise him to do so.'

'I need a drink.' She stands abruptly, knocking the ashtray and its contents onto the carpet, though she seems not to have noticed. 'You want something?'

Canfield shakes his head. While she's in the kitchen – he hears the chink of glasses, the running of the tap, the fridge door open and close – he looks around the room, thinking it's oddly bare, no pictures of Adam anywhere, no mantelpiece shrine with perpetually burning candles he's seen so often in similar situations. That will almost certainly change as time goes on. The wound of Adam's loss must still be open and raw, and some of the bereaved can bear no reminders of what they've lost so early in the process of what – hopefully – will become the road to healing.

But sometimes what you don't see is as interesting as what you do.

Gail doesn't seem to be a big one for tears.

She returns to her chair carrying an alarmingly full glass of white wine, carefully slurping the first couple of centimetres off the top before she sits down.

'Don't judge me,' she says, testily. 'I do what I have to do.'

Canfield raises his hands. 'I don't judge you, not remotely. I won't keep you long, anyway. I just wanted to tell you officially about the charges against Tommy, answer any questions you may have. And there is one other thing. I wonder if I could ask you again about Tommy's motive. I'm sorry to bring this up, but motive is such an important part of persuading a jury of guilt.'

'How the hell should I know what he was thinking? He's got a screw loose, simple as that. Why else would he have done it?'

'You said in your statement that he had threatened to harm Adam on several occasions.'

'He was always saying it. He was eaten by jealousy, thinking I was seeing other men. He thought he could keep me with him by threatening Adam, said he'd kill him first and then himself. Pity he chickened out on the second part. We'd all be better off if he'd gone through with it.'

Her near-dead eyes have come alight with – hatred? Contempt? Revulsion? Are those the only emotions she has left? Have they overwritten even her love for Adam? Certainly he can see no softness in her at all.

'And you've said you know of no specific reason why he chose that day to act on his threats? Nothing to provoke him? He didn't find you with another man, for example, nothing like that?'

'I've told you before, no. I've had enough of blokes like him, and so would you have. He's just a man who likes to throw his weight about, always has been. He did it to get at me, because I wanted to divorce him. He never cared about Adam anyway, not really. He's good at putting on a show, is Tommy. People get taken in.'

Canfield is silent, waiting for her to go on, but she only drinks more wine, looks around for her cigarettes, picks up the packet and then changes her mind.

'Well,' says Canfield when it's obvious she has no more to say. 'If you think of anything else, you've got my number. Just before I go, I know it's a long way off, but I want to explain what part we'll be asking you to play when the case goes to court.'

Gail looks startled. 'Me? Do I have to be there? Haven't I been through enough?'

'You'll be a key witness, Gail. Of course we're going to have to ask you to be in court.'

'What, and give evidence against him? You must be kidding.'

'It'll be key in securing a conviction. Once we have that, he'll be out of your life, for the foreseeable future at least.'

'He's not going to like that, is he?'

'I'm sure he won't. But we'll take care of you, make sure he behaves himself.'

'What if he comes after me when he gets out?'

'That'll be a long time off. You'll be living a different life by then, maybe in a different place. Chances are he'll be different too. Prison changes people. You'd be surprised – often it's for the better. Let's take it one step at a time.'

'When will this be?'

Good question. 'To be honest, with all the delays there are in the courts at the moment, I wouldn't expect it to be any time very soon. Eight months possibly, maybe even a year or more.'

Her eyebrows lift. 'And where will he be all that time?'

'He'll be in jail. On a murder charge, the suspect is always kept in custody.'

'And if he's found not guilty? What if they don't convict him?'

Canfield sees she's becoming abnormally edgy, and he wonders if her weight loss might actually be drug-related, prescription or otherwise.

'Then he'll be free, obviously.'

'That's my worry,' says Gail, darkly. 'That's my worst nightmare. If you're going to put him through this, you'd better make damn sure you make it stick, because otherwise my life won't be worth living. In fact, I most likely won't have a life to live at all.'

Leaving the house, Canfield wonders how Gail is going to find her way back to any kind of normality. Misery seems to be spreading like a cancer all around her, blighting the cottage and condemning it to decline, with her trapped inside like some raddled Sleeping Beauty.

As he steps onto the yard, the dogs come padding out into their pen. Gail yells at them to get back inside their kennel and they meekly obey.

'Bloody animals,' she says. She puts a hand on the door frame to stop herself swaying, and Canfield suspects her glass of Chardonnay was not the first one of the day. 'I'm ready to see the back of them. I can't look after them, not in my state.'

Canfield feels mild regret for the dogs. 'I don't suppose you'll have any trouble finding them a good home. They look like pedigrees.'

Gail gives an unkind laugh. 'Tommy's pride and joy, they are. Thinks more of them than he ever did of me. When the time comes, there's a charity who'll come and take them. What happens to them after that isn't up to me. But I promised Lizzie they could stay here until after he goes to court, long as they're not a trouble to me. After that, they're gone. But don't you dare tell anyone I said so.'

Reaching his car, a word comes to him that describes

Gail perfectly: brittle. She's a woman who's all hard edges. But living in an abusive relationship will do that, shut you down and toughen you up. Gail's no doubt learned crying's a weakness that gets you nowhere.

No wonder she's afraid what will happen if Tommy isn't found guilty.

TWENTY-FOUR

Never in her life did Lizzie expect to see the inside of a prison.

Waiting outside the looming walls to be admitted, she already feels a claustrophobic dread which must, she knows, be so much worse for Tommy. Since he was little, he's craved open spaces and fresh air, oblivious to wind and rain as he trailed behind his father across the Dales uplands. How desperate must he be feeling in a place like this?

At least she's not alone. A small crowd is waiting with her; most are women, and some have brought their children, from babies to near-teenagers. Coming from tranquil Risedale, they're an alien species to Lizzie, with their crude jokes, their brash energy, their cockiness. When prison officers at last appear to let them through the gates, Lizzie's instinct is to stand quietly until her papers have been checked, but the boldest of the others taunt the officers and complain loudly at being kept waiting. To her surprise, the officers don't appear to care, offering banter in return and even addressing some of the women by name.

Not knowing the routine, Lizzie is one of the stragglers at the back as they go inside. The reception area is all protective screens and cameras, and Lizzie, bewildered, takes guidance from watching the obvious old hands as they strip off coats to pass through body scans and pat-downs, offer their handbags to be searched and hand over their mobile phones. The prison officers have become quiet and watchful, intimidating with their batons and bodycams.

One by one, the visitors are beckoned through an airlock. Lizzie's briefly, disturbingly caged between sliding doors of toughened glass, before stepping out and realising she's imprisoned, no longer able to leave without permission. She feels hugely stressed and slightly sick, her nausea increased by the smell of the place, something sharp and sour between carbolic and days-old refuse. The entire wall facing her is covered in mugshots of brutish-looking men – any newspaper would call them thugs – and below the photographs, in large red capitals, is an unambiguous warning: THESE MEN ARE A DANGER TO YOU. And all around there's a dissonance – whistles and shouts, the whine of a floor cleaner, the clatter of boots on iron stairs, the jangle of keys – and a shimmer of pent-up testosterone, while the tension in the air – fed by anger and frustration and nothing-to-lose despair – almost crackles, only waiting for a spark to blow it all up.

Not while I'm in this hellish place, she prays, *and not while Tommy's in here either*.

She and her companions are led through other doors, two officers leading them, two following behind, and every few steps it seems there is another security door, another rattling key to unlock and relock it when they've been counted through. Lizzie's claustrophobia is growing worse.

The group is led to a large, grey room with no windows.

Tables are bolted to the floor, and at each table are two or three scruffy chairs.

Lizzie doesn't want to tread on these women's toes, instinctively understanding they may have pecking orders and protocols, and so hangs back until they're all seated before heading to a vacant table near the back.

The women – even the children – are quiet now, and it occurs to Lizzie that maybe some of them don't want to be here, that the men they're here to see aren't locked up for nothing. This prison isn't low-security: it's a place of punishment for rapists, killers and paedophiles. How many of these families have suffered at their men's hands? Yet here they are, dutifully standing by them when they could stay away, because who knows what routes such men would have to the outside, to other, similar men, who'd knock uncompliant wives back into line?

But not all of them can feel like that. Some of them, like her, must be here out of love.

She has a sense of being watched, and glancing to the far side of the room, sees a woman somewhat older and better dressed than the majority, sitting straight-backed and dignified. For a moment, she holds Lizzie's eye, and seeing the pity in her face Lizzie feels crushed, realising how naïve her hopes are that everything will be fine, how far down the line to a future in prison Tommy actually is, and if that happens, that this dreadful place or others similar will be part of the rest of her life, too.

She wants to cry; but the men are here.

They file in, all wearing the same utilitarian grey tracksuits, some grinning in delight at seeing their visitors, others deadpan as poker players, giving nothing away. Tommy is close to the back of the line, and as soon as she spots him, Lizzie knows how he's feeling. Only a mother would see it, but Tommy is struggling not to cry.

Yet by the time he sits down in front of her, he's all pretended nonchalance and swagger, a performance of care-less no doubt intended for his fellow inmates.

She reaches across the table for his hands, but is stopped by one of the watching officers. 'No touching!'

'There's no f-ing nothing allowed in here,' says Tommy, sullenly. She can tell he's on edge from the way he's bouncing his foot on the floor, a habit he's had since he was small. 'Don't do this, can't do that. Can't even make a phone call or have a shower when you want one.'

She's dismayed to see a new pallor in his face, as if all the light of open country he's absorbed over the years has already drained away. And he's gained a little fat, his fingers are a little plumper. He's missing his exercise, his long dog walks across the moors.

'Are they feeding you well, at least?' Such a banal question, but what else can she ask when every word is being listened to?

'Are they buggery. Everything fried and greasy, or else slops you wouldn't feed to a pig. And you can't sleep nights for all the mad bastards yelling.' For a moment, the bravado slips. He lowers his voice. 'It's a terrible place, Mum. Tell Meacham to hurry up and get me out.'

But Meacham, Tommy's legal representative, has already delivered the blow.

'I spoke to his assistant before I came here,' says Lizzie. 'She said you'll have to stick it out now until your trial.'

Tommy's head drops.

Lizzie leans forward so she won't be overheard. 'You have to be brave, son. It's only a few more weeks.'

From under lowered lids, Tommy gives her a look – *Easy for you to say* – and she wishes the glib words could be taken back. But he sits up straighter and asks about the dogs.

'They're full of beans,' says Lizzie. 'Missing you, of course. But they're eating well, and I've been giving Sam Cooper a pound or two of pocket money to give them a good walk. Not every day, but three or four times a week. And I'm taking them myself when I can, though it's a bit slippy underfoot at the moment.'

'You be careful,' says Tommy. 'Last thing we need is you with a leg in plaster.'

'Oh, I'll be all right. Dawn sends her love. She wanted to come today, but she couldn't get time off work.'

This is a partial lie, and Lizzie hopes Tommy doesn't notice the blush that steals over her face as she says it. Dawn did want to come, but Jake was dead against it, and Dawn deferred to him. Her life wouldn't be worth living if she disobeyed him, was what she said. Why do so many women become so obedient to their men?

A silence falls between them. His foot-tapping stops. The well-dressed woman Lizzie noticed earlier is talking to the oldest man in the room. Well into his sixties, he has the look of a retired professional, a banker or accountant.

'You do know I didn't do it, right?' asks Tommy suddenly. 'You do believe me about that? You know how I loved my little prince? I swear on my own life, Mum, I never harmed a hair on his head. Never, in all my born days.'

Lizzie reaches out again, and touches his fingers before the officer barks, 'No touching!'

'I know you didn't, love. Of course I know it. But Mr Meacham's assistant says part of the problem is they don't have anyone else.'

'I told them who else!' Tommy's anger is evident. 'Why aren't they looking at that weirdo, that Simon? Ten to a penny he's involved somewhere. Always hanging about in the woods, he is. I reckon it was him who was up there the night Adam died. Someone was there. Why isn't he in here instead of me?'

'I don't know, love, I really don't. You'd make life easier for yourself if you could give them some kind of alibi.'

'If I was by myself that afternoon, there's not much I can do about it, is there? But you tell the police to have a better look at that Simon, because I didn't do it. And they want to find out who Gail's been seeing and all. What about him? Who is he?'

'She's always told me she's not seeing anyone.'

'Well, she's a lying, cheating bitch. I'm telling you, she's seeing someone and has been for a while. Why don't you tell them to ask her again, because she knows more than she's letting on. Promise me you'll go and see them – tell them what I said.'

Lizzie's uncertain. 'I'm not sure it's my place to go making a nuisance of myself with the police, Tommy. They'll know I'm biased in your favour, for a start.'

'It's not about bias, Mum – it's about facts, it's about digging deeper. There's more still to be found. There has to be. Please, promise me you'll go. If you won't stand up for me, who will?'

'You know I'll always do that, son, of course I will. All right, I'll go.'

'And soon?'
'First thing tomorrow.'

When Lizzie leaves, Tommy joins the loose line of men waiting to be escorted back to their cells. Lizzie's pretended optimism as they said their goodbyes broke his heart. They were permitted no hug, or kiss, or even the touch of a hand. She was plainly distraught to be abandoning him there, and her poorly concealed distress made his own misery more keen.

He won't cry. Not where he can be seen. He walks the long corridors head down and silent, keeping a respectful distance from the man in front. He learned early on that some people in this place don't appreciate you invading their space.

But someone, he notices, is walking close alongside him, so close his upper arm is almost touching Tommy's. Tommy glances across, and sees a prison officer he doesn't recognise – a short bloke, very fit-looking – who catches Tommy's eye and gives him an unpleasant smile, which makes Tommy realise this might be trouble.

'You're Henthorn, right?'

Tommy keeps his eyes front, and nods.

'You're from my neck of the woods, aren't you, from the Dales? I grew up in Wirksworth.' The officer's familiar accent confirms his origins. 'So you and me got something in common. That your mum who was visiting you today?'

Tommy wants to ask the guy why he's talking to him – if the other prisoners notice, they might take him for a snitch – but something in the officer's attitude persuades him to say nothing.

'Nice to have a family visit, ain't it? Where would we be

without our mums? By the way, something else we got in common, a mutual acquaintance. My old mate Steven Bull. You remember Steven, don't you?'

Headcase. Taken aback, Tommy blinks. How can this guy know someone like Headcase?

'Anyway, Steven sends his regards. He's asked me to give you a message.'

Without thinking, Tommy snaps, 'I don't want any messages from him.'

'Wanted or not, I said I'd deliver it. Steven says to remind you he'll be keeping an eye on your family while you're tucked up in here. Help them avoid any nasty accidents. He's all heart, is Steven.'

The officer claps Tommy on the shoulder. 'Anyway, you mind how you go. I'll tell Steven I saw you. Keep your nose clean, son, and you'll do all right.' And he walks away to the back of the line.

Tommy is left shaken and disturbed. He's afraid of Bull – only an idiot wouldn't fear that psychopath – but it seems he's underestimated the extent of his influence. The tentacles of his little empire can reach him even in here. And Bull is the last person on earth he wants taking an interest in his mum and Dawn.

Because wherever Steven Bull's involved, everything turns rotten.

TWENTY-FIVE

On the way out, by accident or design, Lizzie ends up next to the well-dressed woman. As they wait for the opening of one of the interminable locked doors, the woman speaks.

'First time?' Her accent, as Lizzie suspected, is well-bred: not posh, but not country burr or city dialect either. 'It's tough, isn't it?'

Lizzie's grateful to have someone to talk to. 'It really is.'

'Is that your son?'

'Yes.'

'Blood relatives are so difficult. I'm here to see my husband.'

They're interrupted by the opening of a barred door. Lizzie finds herself hurrying through it, anxious not to be left behind.

As they collect their belongings from the reception area, the woman speaks again.

'I'm Jennifer, by the way.'

'Lizzie.'

'If you're not in a big hurry, maybe we could go somewhere for coffee?'

Jennifer suggests a place on the outskirts of the nearby

town, and Lizzie – not knowing the area at all – is glad to follow her there.

As she turns the key in the car ignition, she sees the orange dashboard warning light that popped up yesterday is lit again. If he were able, Tommy would take care of it. She hopes it's nothing serious, something that can wait until he gets home.

She misses him.

At the café, she follows Jennifer inside to a quiet table. A waitress appears, greeting Jennifer in a familiar way. Jennifer asks for black coffee and a scone. Lizzie's hungry – the drive here was over two hours, and she couldn't face breakfast before she set off – and so orders herself a cappuccino and a sandwich with chips, then feels a pang when she thinks how much Tommy would appreciate being able to eat the same.

'Thank you for bringing me here,' she says, 'for taking pity on me. It's all very new to me, and I'm not from round here.'

'Neither am I,' says Jennifer. 'And the bad news is, they move them, all the time. Robert – my husband – has been here a while, and I'm grateful because it's only an hour or so from home. I gave up visiting when they sent him to Bristol – I really couldn't face the drive, and the train was so expensive.'

The waitress brings their coffees. Lizzie's stomach rumbles at the smell of frying chips.

'Go on, you can ask me,' says Jennifer, spooning brown sugar into her cup. 'You want to know how many years he's been inside, don't you? Seven years and eight weeks. That's quite a long time, wouldn't you say? And here am I, still playing the faithful wife, coming to see him once a month. I used to come once a fortnight, but even I have limits to my devotion. You probably think I'm mad, don't you?'

'No.' Lizzie smiles. 'Maybe a bit.'

'You're thinking I should have moved on. Actually, I have. I found a lovely man who I spend time with discreetly, making sure the neighbours don't know. But on the face of it I'm still faithful and devoted to my husband, and I shall be welcoming him back to our lovely home when he's eventually released. Which may be sooner than I would like. I need to get our marriage over the eighteen-year line so when I divorce him I can be one hundred per cent confident I'll walk away with half of what he's got. I'm hoping for a considerable amount, and no less than I deserve for putting up with a man with his depraved appetites. Believe it or not, he was a doctor, a highly respected surgeon.'

The waitress returns, and Lizzie can't resist starting on her chips.

Jennifer butters her scone, and for a while she's happy to answer Lizzie's questions about what's allowed on visits and what's not allowed, and how to keep herself sane when she's overcome with worry.

'They settle down more quickly than you'd think,' says Jennifer. 'We had a very comfortable lifestyle, and prison was a dramatic change for Robert, a real shock, yet within a couple of months he'd carved himself out a niche, made not friends exactly but allies, and come to terms with it. The trick is to accept it and go with the flow. You should tell your son that.'

'I don't think Tommy will be in that long.' Lizzie drains her coffee. 'They'll never find him guilty.'

Jennifer sighs. 'Oh, my dear. Can I tell you something? When Robert was first arrested, I absolutely could not believe he would have done the terrible things he was accused of. I was completely in denial. He and I were close, we shared all our secrets. Like this, I thought.' She holds up two crossed fingers. 'So when he went to trial and witnesses stood up and told their stories – and some of them were pretty grim, let me tell you – I dismissed their evidence as lies. Who knew him better than me, after all? I swore the oath and spoke up for him loud and clear. I told the press how I would stand by him. I fell out with my dearest and oldest friend when she tried to tell me things I wasn't prepared to hear. The moment he was sent down – and what a terrible moment that was, how I wept – straight away I was talking about travesties of justice. And then, a couple of months after the trial, I was on one of my visits. Initially he was very quiet, not asking after the children as he usually did or saying much of anything, while I gabbled on about making an appeal. And he just came out with it. I remember clear as day what he said. "Jenny, my love, hush now. I am guilty of all they said, and there's an end to it."

'Well, that was certainly the end of my previous life. I felt like the whole world had fallen on my head. I was so ashamed, so embarrassed. Worst of all, I felt like a complete fool for having believed him, for having been so gullible. The children of course were devastated. They've never seen or spoken to him since and we rarely mention him. I didn't visit him for a while after that, until he wrote to me and said if I wanted a divorce, he'd make it easy. I wasn't so gullible then. Make it easy for him to come out of jail to most of his cash left in the bank, is what he meant. That's when I took legal advice. No divorce for me until the eighteen years are up. Two can play at that game, and I can pretend I still love him as long as necessary, make him think everything will be sweetness and light when he's released.' She leans forward across the table. 'All I'm saying is, the police and the courts don't make many mistakes, no matter how much we wish that they did. Every man in that place will tell you he's innocent. Love is blind, Lizzie, and there's no love blinder than a mother's. Open your eyes, and see what's in front of you. Your son's no different to every other man in there. All bad eggs, they are, every last one of them, and if he's been charged with an offence, it's ninety-nine per cent certain that he's guilty.'

TWENTY-SIX

Dawn's been waiting in her car for over an hour, switching on the engine from time to time so she can run the heater and stave off the chill. When Lizzie arrives, by the time she's reversed into a tight parking space, gathered up her handbag and the prescription she's picked up from the doctor's from the passenger seat, Dawn's already standing by Lizzie's back door, arms wrapped round herself against the cold.

'I hope you left the heating on,' she says, as Lizzie walks down the path, keys in hand.

'I did not,' says Lizzie, finding the right key and unlocking the door. 'What do you think I am, made of money? I'm not surprised you're cold in that thin jacket. You want to get yourself a proper coat.'

Immediately the door is open, Dawn hurries into the kitchen and flips the heating switch. Lizzie fills the kettle. From under her jacket, Dawn produces a packet of Hobnobs.

'Emergency supplies. I thought you might be hungry.'

'I am,' says Lizzie, finding mugs and coffee for Dawn, tea for herself. 'They kept me waiting an age before I got to speak to anybody.'

'And did you?'

'Put those biscuits on a plate and let's get this tea made. Then we can talk.'

Outside the kitchen window, the sky is darkening. Bad weather is coming.

Lizzie bites her lip. 'You know what, I ought to go and see to those dogs before it rains.'

'If it rains, I'll take them.'

Lizzie raises her eyebrows. 'Really? Is that a promise?'

'Cross my heart. Stop fussing. Come and sit down, and tell me what they said.'

Lizzie takes a seat at the kitchen table and takes a sip of her tea.

'I can't say they were pleased to see me. Well, why would they be? I said to Tommy they'd know I was just trying to interfere on his behalf.'

'Who did you speak to?'

'A sergeant, DS Preston, something like that? No, Pearson. His name was Pearson. Apparently he's working on Tommy's case. I said I had information that might have a bearing, and he just looked at me. So I said it was well known locally – I embellished a bit, I thought it couldn't hurt – that Gail had been seeing some man, and had the police tracked him down and asked him about his alibi? And he said they were aware and were looking into it. Then I said about Simon Rains and why wasn't he a suspect, that Tommy believed it was him he saw in the woods the night of Adam's death. All he said to that was they were still pursuing a number of lines of enquiry, but of course he wouldn't tell me what they were. And that was all I had really, wasn't it? Except I put in a word for Tommy – a very strong word, actually. I said how much he loved Adam and how he would never have hurt him in a million years, and he said very off-hand like that they have to deal in facts and where the evidence leads, and I said how much Tommy loved Adam is a fact, because it is. Then I let myself down and started crying, and that gave him the excuse to go and get someone to bring me a drink of water, and he went out saying he was sorry, he had another appointment and he never came back. He'd more important business than talking to me, I'm sure.'

Lizzie finds she's crying again now. Dawn reaches across the table, and squeezes her mother's hand.

'You did your best, Mum. We just have to trust them to do their job.'

Lizzie dabs her eyes. 'I suppose so. I don't know what Tommy will say. He won't be very happy.'

'No. I don't suppose he will.'

'You don't think, do you . . .' Lizzie's struggling to find the right words, doesn't want to acknowledge the dangerous seed Jennifer's story has planted. 'You don't think he actually is guilty? Could he be?'

'Mum!' Dawn's shocked. 'How can you say that? He'd never have hurt Adam. What's got into you? You know it and I know it.'

'You're right – I do. It's this fighting the system that gets you down. That place they've got him in, I don't know how he'll stand it much longer.'

'He's strong, and he knows how to look after himself. He'll get through it.'

The first rain patters on the window.

'You'd better go to those dogs,' says Lizzie, 'before this weather really sets in.'

'Can I borrow your boots and your big coat? Save me going home.'

As Dawn wanders into the hall to find them, Lizzie follows.

'There was one other thing I forgot to say. As I was leaving the police station . . . At least, I think it was him. A man, walking across the car park towards the building. He was a little way off and he pretended he hadn't seen me, but I think he had. He stopped to search his pockets as if he'd forgotten something so he wouldn't bump into me.'

Dawn frowns. 'Who did? Who did you see?'

'I didn't have my glasses, so I can't be a hundred per cent sure. But from the distance I was at, it looked an awful lot like Simon Rains's father, Peter.'

TWENTY-SEVEN

Peter is late.

Tessa Rains stands at the window, watching the downpour on the road outside, running as a small river down the hill. Local Facebook pages are talking of flooding on some roads. When she's tried to ring Peter, his phone's switched off.

Can he have been there all this time? Surely what he had to do can't have taken this long?

A car pulls up outside. Finally, it's him.

Yet he doesn't get out of the car. She can see his silhouette through the rain-obscured passenger window, apparently not checking his phone or doing anything at all but looking straight ahead, watching the water running down the road, as she has been doing.

Sensible to wait until it eases somewhat.

Tessa goes back to the sofa and picks up her tablet, but doesn't switch it on.

Twenty slow minutes go by until the door opens, closes again behind him.

Tessa calls out, 'In here!' but he doesn't appear.

Leaving the sofa, she wanders into the kitchen, and finds

him standing just inside the door, as if frozen in the act of coming home.

'Are you all right? You're a very odd colour.'

'I'm OK. Just had a few palpitations, that's all.'

'For God's sake, Peter. Come and sit down. Are you wet? Do you need to change your clothes?'

'I'm fine. I missed the worst of it.'

He follows her into the lounge, and sits down in his favourite chair. 'Where's Simon?'

Tessa shakes her head. 'I don't know. Out somewhere.'

'In this weather?'

'He said he was going to Nick's. He'll be back when he's hungry. What did they say?'

'It wasn't about what *they* said, was it?' Peter's response is snappy, terse. 'It was about what I said.'

'Who did you see?'

'Sergeant Pearson was there, and there was a woman with him, Emma somebody. They wanted me to go through it all again, make sure I was word-perfect for the trial.'

Tessa looks down at her hands. 'Well then.'

'Lizzie was there at the police station.'

'Lizzie?'

'Lizzie Henthorn. That made me feel really bad, worse than I already did.'

'Did she see you?'

'Probably. I think so, yes. She'll be wondering why I was there. It won't be long before she knows I was helping to keep her son behind bars.'

'We've got Simon to think of,' Tessa reminds him.

'Have we? Should we, honestly?'

'How can you ask that? He's our son.'

'And Tommy is Lizzie's son. She looked awful, in case you're interested. Like she was carrying the weight of the whole world. Little does she know that now I'm sharing her burden.'

'Don't be so dramatic, Peter. It's not that big of a deal.'

Peter looks at his wife with something approaching contempt. 'I'll tell you what, then, I'll go and withdraw my statement and you go and make one instead. No? Why not, if it's not that big of a deal?' He stands up. 'I'm going out.'

'Where are you going?'

'To the Mason's.'

'They won't be open at this time.'

'Then I'll find somewhere that is. And don't bother making me any dinner. I won't be home.'

'Peter, come on, we talked about this.'

But Peter has slammed the door on his way out.

TWENTY-EIGHT

Escaping the worst of the rain before she walks the dogs, Dawn is sheltering in the old workshop at Blacksmith's Cottage. A knock at the cottage door has brought no response. No doubt Gail is sleeping. Gail is always sleeping these days, but even if she wasn't, relations between the two sisters-in-law have deteriorated since before Adam's death, when she and Tommy split up. Now Gail seems firmly locked in her own world of alcohol and pain, emerging only to hurl vitriol at Tommy, abuse Dawn can't bear to hear. Gail and Tommy were always a poor match, in Dawn's opinion. Gail has always been vain, self-obsessed, but her brother's a man and no doubt her looks are what kept him bound to her. Because if Tommy had his way, they'd be together still. What drove them apart, Dawn isn't sure. Local rumour is that Tommy knocked her about, which he's always vehemently denied. Dawn would never put it beyond Gail to make up a tale that justified her ending a relationship – even a marriage – she's grown bored with if something better came along. Did something – someone – 'better' come along? Tommy plainly thinks so, but where's the evidence? If Gail's been seeing another man, she's been cleverly discreet.

Inside, the workshop is a mess. The vintage day-bed is damp, the fabric chewed by mice into holes where the horse-hair stuffing pokes out. In one corner, a sack of cement has burst, spreading grey powder everywhere. Adam's bike is propped against a wall, and seeing it there brings a lump to Dawn's throat. The loss of Adam has ripped all the family apart, but if Tommy's convicted of his murder, then their lives will inevitably change for the worse again. Could any of them continue to live in this district after such a scandal?

Not fancying sitting on the mouldering day-bed, Dawn stands at a grimy window watching the rain pound into puddles, and suddenly wants to cry. How can everything have gone so horribly wrong? How have they all ended up in this shocking mess? Somehow, she's wandered into a nightmare from which there's no way to wake, with no morning alarm clock to rouse her back into her old life.

For her mum's sake and Tommy's, she must be strong.

The rain is easing.

Dawn leaves the workshop, and calls to the dogs, who come bounding out of their kennel. They're pleased to see her – to see anyone, probably – and circle her enthusiastically wagging their tails.

'We're not going far,' she warns them as she clips on their leads, 'not in this weather.'

Keen regardless, they pull her along the driveway, knowing the way up to Raymond's Wood.

When they reach the path, she unclips the leads and lets Buster and Nell go. She herself is cautious. The path is treacherously muddy, slippery as ice in places, sucking her boots in over the ankles in others so she fears she'll get stuck.

Tommy wouldn't mind these conditions. Cold, wet, wind, snow never worry him. He sees the beauty in all seasons, even the grey gloom like today.

Then Nell begins to bark.

Dawn stands still. From the overhanging trees, water falls in cold drops on the shoulders of Lizzie's waxed coat, and Dawn shivers. Nell continues to bark, but her barking becomes interspersed with low growling, and she's backing away, hackles up, from whatever it is that's spooked her. If it's a badger, they'd be better leaving quickly; a badger could do either or both dogs serious injury, and vets' visits and bills are definitely something none of them need. And now Buster's joining in, standing like a true hero slightly behind his sister, only ever brave when she's leading the charge.

Something moves. What she's taken as the thick trunk of an oak tree detaches itself, and becomes a male figure in black clothing. Some kind of mask covers his face. The skin round his eyes is pearl white in the gloom.

Dawn's heart beats fast. Who is this guy? Why is he dressed that way?

She doesn't wait to find out. Calling the dogs, she hurries back along the path without checking to see if they're following. Only when she reaches the road does she stop and look back.

The dogs are trotting behind. Of the man who's frightened her, there's no sign. Hastily, she clips on the dogs' leads, mentally apologising to them for the shortness of their outing. She steps onto the road, and as she does so, a small cherry-red car comes into view. She'd know that car anywhere; Barbara Derwent, Gail's next-door neighbour, has been driving it for years, since Dawn was a schoolgirl. She finds herself relieved when Barbara pulls up alongside her.

'I thought it was your mum in that baggy old coat,' she says. 'How are you, Dawn? How are you holding up? Is your mum all right? What about Tommy?'

Dawn gives her an update, and Barbara listens sympathetically.

'I'm sorry for your troubles,' she says, when Dawn finally runs out of things to add. 'It's a bad business all round, a truly bad business, especially with some people behaving as disgracefully as they are.'

'What do you mean?'

'That Peter Rains. I think he's making up stories, telling folks he saw Tommy in the village on the day . . .' She hesitates. 'You know when I mean. I was home all day that day, and let me tell you, if Tommy had been anywhere near my house in that damned Land Rover, I'd have known about it. Noisiest vehicle known to man, that is, and I never heard it. You might suggest he parked it out the way so as not to be seen, and happen he did, but Peter's saying he saw it drive up the village. Well, I don't believe he did. He's just trying to steer people's minds away from that son of his. Haunts these woods, that boy does. He's not right in the head – anyone will tell you that.'

'Oh.' Dawn's mind flashes back to the figure she saw stepping out from behind the tree. 'Maybe that was who I saw just now. He gave me a real fright.'

'That'd be him. Likes to frighten people, he does, but what kind of a person would take pleasure in doing that? We're not all daft in this village, are we, love? Some of us can see what's before our eyes. I hope they let poor Tommy out soon. He'll be pleased to know you're looking after the dogs.'

'Not much fun in this weather.'

'Someone has to do it, though, don't they, and Gail's too off her head these days. What Tommy saw in her I'll never know.'

'The obvious, I suppose.'

'I suppose so. That's men for you, isn't it, always choosing the obvious? Anyway, I best get on. Give my regards to your mum. Tell her to pop in next time she's passing. And send my love to Tommy when you see him.'

'Don't worry,' says Dawn, not knowing when that will be. 'I will.'

TWENTY-NINE

Tesco was a nightmare. Zain played up from the moment Laila walked through the front doors, and was only placated by the purchase of a doughnut from the in-store bakery, which loaded him up with sugar and made him more hyperactive still.

Back at home, she dumps him, sugar-covered and sticky, in front of *Peppa Pig*, and runs outside to bring the shopping in before it begins to rain.

She's weary to the marrow of her bones. Surely life wasn't meant to be this hard?

As she's putting Zain's favourite breakfast cereal in the cupboard – when did it get so expensive? – the doorbell rings.

Running her hand over her lank hair, past caring how she looks, she answers it.

Two men stand in the doorway. One of them is very overweight, the waistband of his suit trousers cutting into his huge belly. The other is younger, fit-looking, but he seems on edge, glancing up and down the road as if he's bothered about being seen.

'Laila Jutt?' The fat man puts his hand in his jacket pocket and pulls out a leather wallet, snaps it open and holds it up to her face. 'Inspector Tate Fritchley, Derbyshire Police. May we come in?'

Laila feels the blood drain from her face.

'What's this about?' Her heart races. 'Is it Faizan? Where is he?'

'If you don't mind, Laila,' says Fritchley, his expression unmistakeably serious, 'I think it would be better if we talked inside.'

Canfield hears the news as he's driving home, a two-sentence item on a local radio bulletin.

'Police are appealing for information in the possible abduction of local businessman Faizan Jutt, who has been missing from his Stockbrook home for several weeks. Officers say they have reason to be concerned for his well-being, and ask anyone with information on Mr Jutt's whereabouts to call them on 101.'

Canfield remembers Laila Jutt. This is bad for her, and probably much worse for Faizan himself. He's pleased he took the time to give Fritchley a heads-up.

Beyond that, he doesn't give the matter another thought.

THIRTY

Nine months after Tommy was charged with Adam's murder and remanded in custody, his case has finally come to trial.

Even though she's been warned it could be days before she's called, Lizzie's been at court since the moment the proceedings began, spending her time between the bench seats outside Court Five and the run-down cafeteria.

Dawn, who's not giving evidence, is allowed in the public gallery and secretly reports back to Lizzie everything that's going on: how Tommy seems, what she thinks of the jurors and the legal teams for defence and prosecution, her opinions on the evidence building against him.

Sometimes, Lizzie's been joined – at a distance – by people she knows. Gail, of course, was an early witness, though Lizzie saw her only briefly, ushered up the stairs by a man with a Derbyshire Police lanyard, straight into the court, and out again a couple of hours later, never even glancing in Lizzie's direction.

Dawn is reluctant to tell Lizzie anything about Gail's evidence, knowing her mother will be upset.

In fact, Dawn's troubled herself.

'I didn't think she had it in her to lie like that,' she says. 'Not brazenly, with Tommy watching. If you could have seen him, Mum, his blood was boiling. If he could have got out from behind those screens, I think he would have killed her.'

'How do you know she was lying?' asks Lizzie. 'What exactly did she say?'

Dawn shakes her head, still disbelieving what she sees as her sister-in-law's treachery. 'She painted Tommy as a man with a violent temper, and said how afraid of him she was, that Adam used to hide from him when he came round.'

Lizzie's shocked. 'That's not true, is it? Adam loved his daddy, adored him.'

'That's not the picture Gail painted. She made Tommy out to be dangerous, Mum. Like someone we've never even met.'

Dawn is fiercely defensive of her brother, but Lizzie spends the following hours and days reflecting on what Gail reportedly told the court. After all, any mother could be in denial about the true character of her son. And how could anyone outside a marriage know what went on behind closed doors? Still, she can't bring herself to believe Tommy could ever have harmed a hair on Adam's head. Might he have threatened Gail, though? That, if she's honest, didn't seem so impossible.

For a long while Peter Rains was here, very smart in a navy suit, sitting arms folded and nervous in an alcove where he must have thought Lizzie couldn't see him.

Lizzie had the strongest urge to go over and ask him what his evidence was, but she resisted. Anyway, it wasn't necessary.

Peter, says Dawn, didn't have much to say in substance, only that he saw Tommy drive through the village in his Land Rover that afternoon, at about three o'clock. Not much by itself, but of course his statement's implications are huge, contradicting Tommy's own that he was nowhere near Risedale. If the jury believe Peter over Tommy, Tommy's fate could be sealed.

On the fifth day, Lizzie hears the usher calling her name. After so much waiting, she's in court barely half an hour, asked only about what she knows of Tommy's movements that day, things he said, how he seemed. She states what she believes to be the truth, that she didn't see him that afternoon but that he definitely wasn't in Risedale, then has to concede after some bullying questioning that there was no way she could know where he was if he wasn't with her at home.

As she leaves the stand, her heart sinks. She can't look at Tommy. Why didn't she lie? She could have given him an alibi, annihilated Peter Rains's statement, or at the very least cast doubt on it. Plenty of others would have done so without a second thought.

She's been stupid. So stupid.

Afterwards, she's allowed to join Dawn in the public gallery.

From that seat, Lizzie has an unobstructed view as her son's life falls apart.

Closing statements are made at last. The prosecution barrister – a highly experienced man in his fifties and hugely persuasive – speaks passionately of a child's life taken, of the effect on his family, particularly his mother, emphasising the tragedy of the case and the cruelty of Adam's killer.

Tommy's defence barrister is a much younger man, who though competent and thorough, doesn't seem to understand the value of an emotional appeal, relying instead on the logic of the case he's constructed to persuade the jury of Tommy's innocence, reminding the jurors of their duty only to convict if the case has been proven beyond reasonable doubt.

The jury retires.

They're out for almost three days.

Dawn and Lizzie spend the time drinking too much coffee in the courthouse cafeteria, persuading themselves such long deliberations can only be a good sign. Then the jury foreman announces they can't reach a unanimous verdict. The judge declares he'll accept a majority, if ten of the twelve agree.

Two hours after that, everyone's called back into court.

Tommy's face is ashen. He sits in the dock with a uniformed man guarding him, handsome in the new suit Dawn and Lizzie bought for him, staring down at his feet.

Dawn is desperate to go and hug him.

Lizzie is doing her best not to be sick.

The judge asks the jury foreman to stand, and he does so. He has a piece of paper in his hand.

The court is completely silent, until the judge asks, 'Have you reached a verdict on which a majority of you are agreed?'

The foreman clears his throat. 'We have.'

'And in the murder of Adam Henthorn, do you find the defendant Thomas Henthorn guilty or not guilty?'

Tommy closes his eyes.

Lizzie finds she can't breathe.

The foreman glances down at the paper in his hand, as if he's forgotten what it says.

Then he lifts his chin, and makes his pronouncement.

'Guilty.'

THIRTY-ONE

A win is always good, but sometimes it's a hollow victory.

Outside the court, the press which has been gathered for days – all the time the jury were deliberating – is preparing for pieces to camera after the announcement of the outcome of Tommy's trial.

Canfield has got his press-office-approved statement ready to go. What he says will be broadcast nationally, and nerves are threatening to get the better of him. He looks around for Pearson to ask if his tie is straight, and at first doesn't see him. Maybe he's still inside the building, chatting to colleagues or others he knows.

Then he spots him, in a huddle with Gail, her sister Chrissie and Bethan from Family Liaison. It would be rude to interrupt. They'll be heading over here in a few moments anyway; Gail and her immediate family will stand at his shoulders as he speaks. Probably Gail's got some legal representative who'll be saying something too. He'll ask Pearson about his tie when he comes over.

As he turns back towards the preparing press, he catches sight of two women making their way down the courtroom steps, staying close to the wall, apparently trying to avoid contact with anyone as they leave. The older of the two women is weeping and appears close to collapse. The younger one is supporting her as they leave.

Tommy's mother and his sister. Of course, it's a terrible day for them.

A killing like Adam's spreads wide ripples. So many people suffer the consequences.

And then he sees Lorna.

She's standing at the bottom of the courthouse steps, looking professional in a camel overcoat and tan boots, her hair up in a style he hasn't seen her wear before.

Unexpectedly, his heart lurches, and a slow blush spreads from his neck to his cheeks.

He's not even sure he wants her to see him. Her back is to him, but before he can even think of where he might hide himself, as if she senses his gaze on her, she turns her head in his direction.

And looks right into his eyes.

This is his chance. He can go over there now, make up some bullshit excuse to speak to her, and tell her the truth: that he thinks of her every day, that he misses everything about her.

But before he can move, apparently as flustered as he feels, Lorna turns back to the man and woman she's with – both in dark suits, no doubt colleagues or work associates. From her body language, she's decided it's time to leave.

'We're ready for you now, sir.' A young police press officer appears at his elbow, keen not to keep her media contacts waiting any longer than necessary. 'Shall we go and join Gail and the family?'

Canfield gives her a nod of acquiescence, but before he follows her, looks over again towards Lorna.

She's walking away, but she isn't alone.

The man in the suit she was talking to – he's tall, Canfield notices, and good-looking enough to be called handsome – is walking with her.

And Lorna's smiling up at him in the way she used to look at him, in those not-so-long-ago days when she might have been his.

THIRTY-TWO

As Tina's dad always used to say, it's an ill wind that blows no one any good.

For sure an ill wind's been blowing through Risedale of late, but as the dust starts to settle and the old rhythms – Christmas, Easter, harvest, Bonfire Night, Christmas again – begin to re-establish themselves, the drama will be slowly forgotten – or at least as forgotten as it can be. Murder is murder after all, and such a thing has never before been seen in this village, nor any of those round about. Even so, as time goes by, people will slip back into their insulated lives, no longer feeling the need to seek out news or gossip in the pub.

But on the evening of the day Tommy Henthorn was found guilty of killing little Adam, Tina's expecting bumper takings. The shelves are all fully stocked with mixers and juices, the wine fridge is fully loaded, and most of the pumps are on new barrels. If things go well, they might do better even than Christmas Eve or New Year.

Keen to protect his regular position of first man through the door, Owen's on the doorstep at ten to seven, and seeing no reason to keep paying customers out, Tina throws back the bolts and turns the old iron key in the lock to let him in.

'You're early,' she says, as he takes his usual bar-stool seat, wriggling himself comfortable, leaning forward on his elbows on the bar-top in obvious anticipation of a good night to come. 'Pint, is it?'

She's picking a glass off the shelf when Terry and Joe Wade come in: a father and son both currently unmarried, Terry having been widowed some years ago and Joe, in Tina's opinion, still likely to be a virgin at over thirty years old.

'Evenin',' says Terry, nodding to Owen and leaning on the bar while pasty weakling Joe sits down at the table nearest the fire. 'We'll have two pints of your finest IPA please Tina, when you're ready.'

'Be right with you,' says Tina.

'We've been watching the news,' Terry goes on. 'Seen they've convicted Tommy with the little lad's murder. I can't believe he'd do that, I can't truly. He loved the bones of that child, really he did.'

'Ah, but he was jealous.' Owen drinks the foam off his pint. 'There's nothing a man won't do when he's jealous. Makes a man mad.'

'*Crime passionnel*, they call it in France,' Joe puts in, in his strange, high voice. 'If you kill your missus because you've caught her with another bloke, they don't treat it the same as normal murder.'

Karen and Les Lacey are coming in the door.

'Evening, all,' says Les.

'What's a normal murder, then?' asks Tina, pouring the first of Terry and Joe's pints. 'Murder's an abomination, whatever the reason behind it.'

'We've just been watching it on the news,' says Karen, and there's a touch of excitement in her voice. 'I heard from Joan he didn't go quietly. They had a right job getting him in the van. Four of them it took, or was it five, Les?'

'It's a brave man who'd try putting Tommy in a van,' says Tina. 'Karen, what're you drinking?'

'I'll have a G and T. Joan said Lizzie's absolutely beside herself. She collapsed in the car park apparently, so they had to call an ambulance. I can't imagine how she's feeling. I'd be out of my mind if one of our boys went to jail.'

'They've taken her over to Dawn's,' says Joe, 'out of the way.'

'He never did it,' says Les. 'I'll have a pint of Spitfire, please, Tina. There's a lot of bluff in Tommy, more bark than bite.'

'You're talking bollocks, lad,' says Terry. 'He did it and probably thought nothing of it. He's a cold, cold heart, has that one.'

The door opens again. Two couples come in, closely followed by the vicar and his wife.

'How do, everybody, how do. Pint of Stella and a large rosé, Tina, if you'd be so kind.'

'We're just talking about this Tommy business, Reverend,' says Terry. 'Whether he's capable of such a bad thing, or whether he's not.'

'Well, apparently he is, according to the due process of law,' says the vicar. 'I shall be saying a few words about it on Sunday. We must stand ready to support both Gail and Lizzie if they need us. Neither of them have done anything wrong, after all. And ours is not to judge.'

'Very true, Reverend, very true,' says Owen, holding up his glass to be refilled. 'And it must be said, in fairness, our boys in blue generally know what they're doing. It isn't very often that they get it wrong.'

In his shared cell, Tommy lies on the lower bunk with his hands behind his head, thinking. His mind's still racing from the jury's decision, and there's no question of sleep. He has two things on his mind. The first, of course, is getting out of this hell hole. And after that, he's planning his visits to the bastards who put him here.

Sitting in her daughter's living room, Lizzie's turned off the TV and is staring at the blank black screen. Dawn and Jake went up to bed hours ago, and Lizzie promised not to be far behind, but shock and grief have her locked in place, unable to believe what's happened. Tommy never hurt that child – she knows it. He might be many things, but she'll never for one moment believe that he's a killer.

In the darkness of her bedroom, Gail lies alone. On the bedside table, both the wine bottle and her glass are empty.

A wailing wind blows, and the long branches of a sycamore tree are tapping on the window.

Almost as if someone left outside might be asking to come in.

PART TWO
Ten Years After

February 2023

THIRTY-THREE

Some places hold on to memories. They just refuse to let them go.

Canfield was certain at Druid's Well he'd find traces of emotion, disturbances of the ether.

After all that pain and sadness, shouldn't there be ghosts?

Yet in the place where Adam lay, there's no sense of him at all.

Canfield has followed the same path he took when the boy was first found, grateful – as he was then – for the mat of fallen leaves saving his shoes from the mud. A return to the scene of a crime – especially after so much time has gone by – is a rarity for him, and he can't claim he was in the neighbourhood; he's driven a long way with no logical reason to do so. He's here out of compulsion, responding to an overwhelming unease, the dread of a catastrophic unravelling and an almighty fall. Everything he's ever worked for – his reputation, especially – is on the line.

And all of it is beyond his control.

If he's honest, he's come here searching for proof that he wasn't wrong.

The wood is eerily quiet, a place where imagination might easily lead to fear: the snap of a twig on which no foot has stepped; the breathing of no one you can see at your side. On that long-ago morning they searched under a clinging shroud of fog, and the thought's occurred to him since that maybe the mist did hide – as Tommy had insisted – someone they never saw, formed a cloak of invisibility around an unseen voyeur. If they'd kept very still, they'd never have been noticed.

He wanders back to his car. The trees at the wood's lower boundary still loom over Risedale's uppermost houses, including Blacksmith's Cottage. As he drives down Main Street, he glances along the narrow drive and wonders if Gail Henthorn still lives there, how her life has been.

Main Street appears little changed. Smoke from the chimneys of the grey granite cottages hangs in the damp air. Near the crossroads by the village green, the allotments behind the post office are bare but for a few stalks of Brussels sprouts and the bent tops of parsnips and swedes.

The door of the Mason's Arms stands open. Canfield's not normally a lunchtime drinker, but on a day like this, who'd blame him for breaking his own rules?

Inside, there have been small changes: the wine-red leatherette that used to cover the bench seats has been replaced by black; additions have been made to the collection of annual photos of the Risedale cricket team.

But as before, a welcoming fire burns in the grate, and the woman behind the bar – Tina, was it? – he thinks could be the same, though she's gained weight and lost some of her outgoing affability. Canfield doesn't blame her for that. Almost a decade of life's reverses and losses might render anyone less buoyant, as he has excellent cause to know.

As she's pulling him a half of Doom Bar, she asks, 'Don't I know you?'

'I don't know,' says Canfield. 'Do you?' His prickliness is uncalled for; events have put him out of sorts. If she does indeed remember him, her memory for faces is admirable. Last time he was here, he was in his thirties and wearing a suit, shirt and tie that screamed *copper*. Now he's in his forties and in jeans, jumper and jacket, sporting the carefully trimmed beard he grew as a gesture to a new him when he and Irene finally went their separate ways. Naïvely, he thought a beard would release him from the daily chore of shaving. Instead, keeping it tidy has become a new obsession.

In a friendlier tone, he asks for a sandwich.

She picks up tongs, and lifts the plastic dome covering a plate of homemade rolls. 'Roast beef or ham and mustard?'

'Beef.'

She's sliding it onto a plate, adding a knife and a paper napkin when she says, 'I do know you. Inspector Canfield.'

He smiles. 'Bang to rights. I'm flattered you remember me, though actually it's Chief Inspector now. What do I owe you?'

She gives him a price and takes his card. The sandwich is expensive for what it is, but it can't be easy making a living in a place like this. Or maybe she's added on a percentage for his earlier rudeness.

As he takes the first sip of his Doom Bar, she says, 'To be truthful, I've a good memory, but even I can't remember everyone who walks through the door. I saw a video clip of you on the breakfast news this morning, from when Tommy was convicted. I remembered you when I saw that, and here you are.'

'Like a bad penny.'

'I suppose he's what's brought you back to Risedale?'

'I was in the neighbourhood. How have you been keeping? Tina, isn't it?'

'Oh, same old same old.' Tina manages a dispirited smile. 'You know how it is. Nothing much happens in life, does it? Well, except when it does. When all that business was going on, we were the busiest we've ever been. People came from all over to – Actually, I don't exactly know why they came. People love misery, don't they? Even a couple of years after they were still coming, purely out of morbid curiosity, to be part of something awful, take pictures of themselves at Druid's Well. Ghouls, I'd call them. At one point, I gave serious thought to selling souvenir Mason's Arms mugs and tea towels.'

Canfield shrugs. 'I wouldn't blame you if you had. And I'd be surprised if you don't see another up-tick. Whichever way it goes.'

The beer is smooth and mellow, and Canfield regrets having the car, not having the option of spending a long afternoon here with a couple of pints more, in the quiet by the fire.

The door opens, and Owen Luck comes in, very elderly now and leaning on a stick, a tweed jacket over his twill trousers. As he's hanging his cap on the corner coat stand, Tina's already pulling his pint.

'Good day, all.' Owen settles on his habitual stool at the end of the bar, close to where Canfield is standing. 'I'll have a ham roll to go with that, please, Tina.'

He studies Canfield, trying to place him.

'You remember Chief Inspector Canfield, don't you, Owen?' Tina prompts him. 'From the police?'

As Tina puts his pint and sandwich in front of him, Owen asks, 'Have they let him go, then? Are you here looking for new suspects?'

'Ah, today's the actual decision day,' says Tina. 'That's why you're here.'

'Shouldn't you be in London trying to keep him inside?' Owen goes on. 'Never a man more guilty than he was. They should have thrown away the key the moment he was locked up.'

Canfield raises his hands. 'Nothing to do with me any more. I'm on different cases these days.'

'Haven't they called you, though?' asks Tina. 'To give evidence or something?'

'I gave evidence at the original trial. They're saying I got it wrong.'

'Well, did you?' asks Owen.

'I don't believe so. We built a case against him, which the jury accepted at the time.'

'So why aren't they accepting it now? What's changed?'

Canfield shrugs. 'To be honest, I don't know. They say new evidence and now you know as much as I do.'

'It's those bloody do-gooder charities,' says Owen, and he downs a third of his pint, as if he's been two days short of a drink. 'Saying there's been a miscarriage of justice. Folk here won't be very happy if they let the bugger out. Everyone round here knows he did it. He was a wrong 'un from the day he was born, and you can tell your chief constable I said so.'

'It's poor Gail I feel sorry for,' says Tina. 'She's been through so much already, poor soul. The last thing she needs is for all this "who did it" stuff to start up again. We'd all drawn a line, moved on. If they say it wasn't Tommy, then who was it? We'll all be pointing fingers again, quaking in our beds.'

'I suppose he'll be wanting to claim compensation, if he gets out,' says Owen. 'Bloody ridiculous if you ask me.'

'How is Gail?' asks Canfield.

'Oh, good days and bad days, I suppose,' says Tina. 'She had another baby very soon after but the little soul couldn't seem to fill the gap Adam left. She's a lovely lass, but Gail's been a bit neglectful of her. Well, you can't blame her, can you? A shock like that, and the child's own father . . . I don't think you'd ever get over it, would you?'

'What if he turns up here?' asks Owen. 'I'll run him out of the village myself. What he did to that little lad makes my blood run hot. He'd better look out for himself if he comes back to Risedale.'

Canfield has no appetite for pointing out the punishments that vigilante justice would attract, or the fact that if new evidence has proven Tommy not guilty, his welcome should surely be warm. But Owen's all talk, like a million others who'll threaten violence in someone's absence and wish them good morning to their face. Even so, he suspects Tommy won't get the warmest of welcomes if he does come back to the village, and it's not out of the question that someone younger and fitter than Owen will decide to do what they see as the right thing. Hopefully Tommy will realise that and stay well away. And yet, Tommy was born and bred here, never lived anywhere else except the years he's spent in jail. It would be a daunting prospect for anyone with his background to start again elsewhere.

Canfield picks up his glass and sandwich and heads from the bar to a table by the window. As he sits, a BBC Radio Derby outside-broadcast car drives slowly up the road, obviously come to report on the announcement. He doesn't want to be caught by them revisiting the scene, and certainly doesn't want to give an interview. Anyway, what does it matter what he thinks? The world turns, and this time round he's an irrelevance.

The snug door opens again, and two men come in, a stocky, muscled youth and an older man, wiry and weather-beaten. Both of them wear hi-vis vests and boots splattered with slurry, giveaways that they're workers at the quarry.

The older one offers the room a general hello, but before he can get properly inside the bar, Tina speaks.

'Eh, you two, wipe your boots! Don't come in here dropping your dirt on my clean floors.'

Smiling, the older man ignores her and reaches the bar, while the younger one, more obedient, does as he's told.

Owen nods a downbeat greeting to the older man. 'All right, John?'

'Not so bad. Two pints of your finest shandy, please, Tina. Got any sausage rolls?'

'I might be able to find a couple, seeing as it's you. Russ?' She calls to the young man. 'Are you wanting a sausage roll?'

'Not for me, thanks, I'll have a ham sandwich. And a packet of salt and vinegar.'

Pints are pulled, plates are put before the men.

'You lads are early,' observes Owen. 'Half day for you, is it?'

'Nah,' says the older man. 'They've got a problem with the saw, been waiting for an engineer all morning. So we told Stan we'd take an early lunch.'

'Well, you can stand up to eat it,' says Tina. 'I don't want you sitting on my chairs in those filthy trousers.'

Russ turns round, trying to get a view of his own backside. 'They're not dirty,' he says. 'Clean on this morning.'

'Clean on, my arse,' says Tina. 'If you took them off, they'd stand up all by themselves.'

John takes a long draw on his pint. 'What do you think about Tommy, then?'

There's a beat of silence, as if a tableau has frozen. Tina stops polishing the glass she's holding. Owen's pint remains mid-air on its way to his mouth. At his table, Canfield stops chewing his mouthful of sandwich.

'What do you mean?' asks Tina.

'He's out. A free man. As of eleven o'clock this morning.'

'Where did you hear that?' demands Owen. 'One o'clock, they said. They're making a statement at 1pm.'

'We heard it on the news on the way down,' says Russ. 'They made a special announcement. They brought it forward for Tommy's safety, is what they said. Giving him a head start from a lynch mob, I suppose.'

Tina's gone pale. 'Well, I never. I never thought they'd do it. I'll be damned.'

'New evidence come to light,' says John. 'Casting doubt on his guilt. The judge has ruled his conviction unsafe.'

'Unsafe – what does that mean?' asks Russ. 'Didn't they prove him guilty beyond all doubt? Else what did they bang him up for in the first place? Makes no sense to me.'

'He was guilty then and he's guilty now,' insists Owen. 'The only miscarriage of justice is that he didn't hang by the neck.'

'Good job he didn't, isn't it, if he didn't do it?' suggests Tina. 'What on earth's poor Gail going to say?'

The snug door clicks shut. Tina glances over, and sees Canfield's empty glass and plate on the table.

Canfield himself is gone.

He remembers the way to the cemetery, a short walk down the lane opposite the church. He feels compelled to come here. Apologies must be made, and Adam is first on his list.

He let the child down.

The last time Canfield came here was for Adam's funeral. Inevitable public interest made the occasion difficult, turning what should have been a dignified ceremony into a morbid circus of press, gawpers and even social-media 'personalities' blocking access to actual friends and acquaintances of the stricken family.

Today, there's only him. A few sheep have been put on the grass to graze; when they hear the squeal of the rusting gate, their heads come up and they trot away to the far wall, under the trees.

Canfield makes his way across the sodden grass, passing between the oldest graves marked by great gritstone slabs, some so weathered their inscriptions can barely be made out. But one name catches his eye: *Samuel Henthorn, 1746–1794*. Some ancestor of Tommy's, no doubt. Undeniably, Tommy's Risedale roots ran deep, but prison changes people, and he won't be the same man he was when he went inside.

Wrongful imprisonment. What he should say to Tommy will be the most difficult apology of all.

Adam's grave is easy to find, marked by a stone of white

Italian marble that shines among the dour grey and black granite around him. Under less tragic circumstances, it might be viewed as a celebrity memorial, paid for as it was by a well-known TV presenter and erected with a special dispensation from the parochial church council.

But there's nothing to celebrate here, only a stark reminder of a young life shockingly ended. In front of the stone lie a few long-dead roses, too weather-beaten to determine their original colour. Canfield crouches to read a cellophane-wrapped card pinned to one of the stems: *To a little angel, never forgotten. RIP from the Stour family, Leeds.* Can this sentiment be genuine? he wonders. Why is Adam's fate still drawing people from such distances to pay their respects?

Because, like him, people care.

He got it wrong, and now he can name that unfamiliar feeling that's been dogging him for days.

He is ashamed.

THIRTY-FOUR

Lorna needs a minute.

Hiding in the ladies' toilets isn't a mature way to behave, but the pressure of these past few days has been immense: poor sleep, snatched meals on the go, above all the stress of her first time leading a team in a case of national interest.

And the national interest is here, waiting outside.

Yet now her big moment has arrived, she's overcome by huge misgivings.

Searching in her bag for lipstick and powder, she peers in the mirror and touches up her lips, dabs the shine from her nose. Everyone she knows will be watching. Her mum will have told everyone that it's happening, and Jess said if she could get time off work she might even come down in person.

Lorna's ambition has never been in doubt, and the time and effort she's put into climbing a steep and crowded career path – from the CPS to a well-known criminal law practice, from there into charity work, acting on behalf of victims of miscarriages of justice – has paid off, both financially and in terms of reputation. Professionally, she's at the top of her game.

Then Fate dealt her a twist: she was offered the Tommy Henthorn appeal.

She could have said no, legitimately claiming a personal interest.

But she didn't do that.

The door to the ladies' swings open, and Angie totters in on her high heels, as usual not a hair out of place, her security pass dangling from a lanyard round her neck.

Seeing Lorna, she lets out a sigh of relief. 'Lorna, thank God, there you are. I've been looking everywhere for you.'

Lorna puts the cap back on her lipstick, wondering whether the shade she's used is too dark. Too late now. 'Sorry. I was just freshening up.'

'They're ready for you downstairs.' Angie holds out a typed piece of paper. 'Your statement's here, so just read straight from that. I've put it in a press release and they've all got a copy already. You reading is just for the audio and video really. Up to you if you want to take questions, but I think it would be good if you could. If you need rescuing, just give me a nod and I'll wrap it up. OK?'

The butterflies in Lorna's stomach all take flight. Following Angie along the corridor and down the winding courthouse stairs, she has a horrible feeling she might throw up. As they approach the front doors, she can see the assembled crowd through the glass, the cameras and the microphones waiting for her.

This is it.

Payback, Ryan Canfield. You screwed up.

They say revenge is a dish best served cold. What remains to be seen is, will it taste sweet, or bitter?

* * *

Driving home, though he's told himself he wouldn't listen, Canfield can't resist the pull of the radio news. At five minutes to the hour, he pulls into a lay-by and drums his fingers impatiently on the steering wheel through the end of an interview of no interest to him and the announcements on what's coming up after the bulletin.

As the familiar news intro finally plays, he finds he's dreading what will be said. Is he going to be named and – far worse – shamed?

Here it is: the second item. A reporter does a very brief recap on Adam's murder, and summarises the court's decision that Thomas Henthorn's conviction was unsafe. 'Following the judge's ruling, Mr Henthorn's legal representative Lorna Winrow made a statement on his behalf.'

A woman begins to speak. To Canfield, the voice is familiar. 'Of course Mr Henthorn is over the moon and extremely relieved after a decade-long battle he should never have had to fight. He's spent the last ten years imprisoned for a crime he didn't commit, vilified for the murder of his own son, and I think the best possible way for him to re-start his life as a free man would be with a full and unqualified apology from Derbyshire Police. Although he will be entitled to financial compensation, no amount of money can make up for the time he has lost, nor for the damage to his reputation. Grave errors have been made, and I call on the chief constable to explain what actions he'll be taking to ensure such miscarriages of justice never happen again.'

The statement ends, and the announcer says, 'Lorna Winrow there speaking on behalf of the prisoners' rights charity Inside Out.'

Lorna. Could it possibly be her? The surname is different but she might easily be married. Could the author of his disgrace be his Lorna, the woman he's never managed to forget?

THIRTY-FIVE

After years of kicking his heels and praying, of giving up and having his hopes resurrected, of imagining many times a day how it will be, the one thing Tommy dreaded about his eventual freedom was loneliness.

And here it is.

In the end, it all happened so fast. He wasn't allowed to be in court to hear the appeal – that was down to London lawyers – but the night before, he tossed and turned on his narrow bunk, nauseous with excitement and worry, flipping minute by minute from believing he'd be a free man in the morning to certainty he'd never get out of there. At breakfast – for which he had no appetite, but ate anyway out of ingrained habit – he went through all the usual routine thinking: *Could be the last time I'll stand in this queue, the last time I'll drink this shit tea, the last time that little runt of a snitch is going to try and take the piss out of me.*

Then back to his bunk and the usual monotony, trying to read a book to the soundtrack from the cell next door, where his mate Micky is melting his brains with daytime TV.

Until two prison officers arrive, all joshing and smiles.

'Come on, then, Tommy, get your stuff together. You're on your way, mate.'

Tommy regards them stupidly, not daring to believe what he thinks he's hearing.

'Am I moving cells again? Because . . .'

One of the screws laughs. 'No, mate, you're moving out, as in out the front door. You're famous! You won your appeal.'

For the first time Tommy can remember, the officer touches him – not to put on cuffs or do a body search, but to clap him on the back in congratulation, signalling to Tommy that the barriers have fallen. He's these men's equal. They no longer have power over him. He's a free man.

The officers watch him gather up all that's been his in this constrained life. Tommy takes down his photos of Adam, of his mum and of Buster and Nell. On his bed, he makes a pile of what he wants to donate to his mates: the little chess set Dawn sent him; the remains of a jar of instant coffee and a packet of biscuits; his shower gel and shampoo; a couple of DVDs he's watched a million and one times. And then, at the last moment, he decides to keep the chess set. Maybe he and Dawn can have a game. She deserves to know what a sanity-saver it's been.

When he's ready, he asks if he can say goodbye to Micky. The officers shrug and agree, and unlock the cell next door.

The dismay of abandonment shows in Micky's face. Not everyone gets on with Micky. Tommy's seen men come at him for no better reason than that they're wound up and needing to let off steam, taking Micky's tattoos and bald ugliness as meaning he'd be good in a fight. But Tommy knows better. Micky can handle himself because he's had to, but to Tommy, he's been a good friend.

Tommy holds out his impromptu gifts.

'Hey, mate,' he says. 'They're letting me out. I thought you might be able to use this stuff.'

Micky takes the gifts and drops them on his bed. Grabbing Tommy's hand, he squeezes it hard.

'Good for you, my friend,' he says, in his Brummie accent. 'You really didn't do it, eh? Fucking good on ya, mate. Fucking brilliant, eh?'

Unexpectedly, now the time's come to leave, Tommy finds himself unwilling to go. Besides Micky, there are others he'll miss in here: Scab and Riley and Jacks and Tolly; Benny and Doggo and Shanks. They've been a band of brothers who've kept each other going through the never-ending cycle of bad news inside: declined paroles, absconding wives and girlfriends, refused appeals. Except Tommy's team have pulled off a rare miracle, and got him out. Most likely he'll never see his friends again. Tommy will do the usual vanishing trick, just disappear like they all do.

'I'm to go right this minute,' he says. 'No time for . . . You know. Will you do me a favour, say goodbye to the lads for me? Tell them to stay out of trouble.'

'Ah, but you'll not miss this place, will ya?' asks Micky with a wink. 'You'll not miss these fellas here.' He nods in the direction of the two officers, who seem to be actually pleased to be liberating a man who doesn't deserve to be there. 'You'll have a pint for me, won't you? And you know what, have a curry for me as well, hot as you like, a chicken vindaloo. I'd kill for a curry, I would. Man, you're a lucky bastard, Tommy. Absolutely brilliant, that is, good for you.'

* * *

Tommy's sudden departure is out of the ordinary, and no preparations have been made.

At the desk where he only vaguely remembers being checked in, they give him back what he had with him on the day of his conviction, objects Tommy barely recalls. His desperately outdated mobile phone. The grey suit he wore for his trial – now too big for him – along with black dress shoes, which would look ridiculous with his scruffy prison clothes. His watch, his wedding ring, his wallet containing his driving licence and several out-of-date credit cards.

A volunteer – a kindly woman who introduces herself as May – beckons him into a side room, and invites him to choose some clothes from a pile of what look like jumble-sale leftovers. She advises him to take an extra sweater. He might be glad of it at night.

Sorting through the cast-offs for something in his size, he finds only clothes he wouldn't have been seen dead in on the outside. Old men's sweaters. Teenagers' jeans.

Beggars, though, can't be choosers.

Barry, the officer on desk duty, has always been fair with Tommy, one of the good guys. Standing in front of him, Tommy feels oddly nervous, bursting with petty questions and some not so inconsequential.

Like where he will sleep tonight.

'Here's your form to say you're in receipt of your discharge pack.' Barry pushes a form across the desk. 'Eighty-two pounds in cash, your travel voucher and your form for claiming benefits. Sign here, and here, and here.'

Handing back the ballpoint pen, Tommy asks, 'Where should I go?'

An expression Tommy hates to think might be pity crosses Barry's face. 'You got family somewhere? Friends?'

'Only my sister.'

'Best go to her, then, to begin with, take it from there. In your situation, you'll get a decent lump for compensation. You just have to hang in there until then.'

'I'm not exactly sure where my sister's living. They were getting a lot of aggro after I came inside, so they sold up and moved. I never needed the address. All I know is they went somewhere in Derby.'

'Use your travel voucher and get yourself to Derby, then,' says Barry. 'Call her when you get there.'

'My phone's dead. Been dead for years.'

'You need to get yourself a charger. Supermarkets are your best bet. Find yourself one of the big stores, you'll be laughing.'

'What if I can't contact her? Where should I stay?'

Barry stands up and slips the pen back into the pocket of his uniform shirt, and Tommy's overcome by the cold realisation that he's dismissed, out of the system, no longer the responsibility of Barry or any of his colleagues.

And now he has his freedom it feels terrifying.

'You'll do all right,' says Barry, tidying away the paperwork from the desk. 'When that money comes, you'll be just fine.'

'How will they know where to send it?' asks Tommy, but Barry is heading for the back office, and appears not to hear.

Though it seems unreal, impossible, the prison gate stands open.

Tommy walks out into the car park.

The wind is in his face, the iron tang of rain is in the air. The sky is grey and it's all beautiful.

At the station, Tommy exchanges his travel voucher for a one-way ticket to Derby and the information that the next train leaves from platform six in twenty-five minutes.

On platform six he finds a buffet, and deciding to celebrate a little, he treats himself to a strong, hot coffee and an amazingly tasty chicken pasty, with a super-sized Mars bar for dessert.

For the moment, life is good.

THIRTY-SIX

Time passes, and leaves some people unchanged.

But Gail Henthorn is one of those for whom the opposite is true. When the door to Blacksmith's Cottage is opened – only a crack – the BBC Derby reporter thinks he's got the wrong house. The woman he wants to interview is in her forties, and the pictures he's seen of her – taken at her son's funeral ten years before – show a woman beautiful even in the depths of grief. The face he can see – cheeks and eye-sockets hollowed out, sallow-skinned and emaciated, grey hair in a long, greasy ponytail – must surely be a much older sister or her mother.

'Mrs Henthorn?' asks the reporter, uncertainly. 'Gail Henthorn?'

'Yes.'

The reporter stifles a look of surprise. 'I'm from the BBC. We'd like to have a word if we may about today's decision to release Adam's father from prison.'

Gail doesn't answer, only stares at him with uncomprehending eyes.

'So would it be possible to maybe do a short interview with yourself?'

'Piss off,' says Gail dispassionately, and she closes the door in his face.

The reporter isn't fazed; he's used to such rejection. Plan B is already in place, and he and his team make their way to the agreed spot outside the church for him to do a piece to camera.

When the set-up is ready, the production assistant offers the reporter a mirror to check his hair and tie. When he's happy, the director counts him in.

'This quiet backwater of a village is today reeling under the shock of a court decision taken many miles away in London,' he begins. 'Tommy Henthorn, convicted a decade ago of the murder of his four-year-old son Adam, is today a free man, confounding many local people who have long believed him guilty of Adam's death. With that conviction overturned, Tommy himself will be in line for a significant pay-out for his years of what must now be called wrongful imprisonment. And while some here are reluctant to admit they got it wrong, for others Tommy's release signals the beginning of a new and disturbing mystery. If Tommy isn't guilty and the trail's gone stone cold, is it even possible for the police to pick up the threads for a new investigation? And how will people here sleep soundly in their beds, knowing that all this time, a child-killer may have been living undetected in their midst?'

THIRTY-SEVEN

Derby's a town Tommy used to know well, but everything's changed.

As dusk falls, the glare of streetlamps is reflected on the wet roads. Beyond the station, the traffic is heavier than he remembers and faster-moving. Crossing the street will be challenging, even hazardous. Were car headlights always so blindingly bright?

And everyone's in a hurry. He sees people peering at mobile-phone screens, even texting as they walk, and their absorption is disconcerting. Why aren't they watching where they're going?

Unsure what to do, Tommy does his best to make himself inconspicuous. Finding himself a place out of everyone's way, he feigns casual interest in the taxis coming and going as if he might be waiting for someone.

'All right, pal?'

Tommy doesn't at first know who's called out to him, but then notices a man sitting on the pavement with his back against a wall. The man's huddled in a blanket, a bedroll and overstuffed backpack beside him, a black-and-white terrier lying at his feet.

Tommy walks over to him. 'How are you doing?'

'I saw the luggage.' The man points to the white plastic bag holding Tommy's belongings. 'You just released?'

Sensing a member of his tribe, Tommy crouches down and ruffles the dog's head.

'This morning.'

The man holds out a grimy hand, which Tommy takes. 'I'm Brian.'

'Tommy.'

'Congratulations. No idea why they have to give us those bags. Couldn't shout ex-con any louder if it tried.'

'What about you?' asks Tommy. 'How long have you been out?'

Brian waves a hand to signify vagueness. 'Couple of months, I suppose.'

'And you're living rough?'

'I wasn't, in the beginning. They found me a B'n'B so I had an address at least. But there was a cock-up in my benefits payments so I got thrown out. Then I was of no fixed address so I couldn't get benefits. Vicious circle, you know what I mean? What about you? They must have found you somewhere to go?'

'Long story,' says Tommy. 'I'm trying to get to my sister's, but I've got no battery on my phone. Be glad to buy you a cup of tea if you can help me out.' The dog whines. 'Might even run to a can of dog food.'

'Cup Cake café,' says Brian, 'behind the market. It's a fair walk, but they let you plug in your phone if you buy something. I could show you, if you want.' His face falls. 'It's getting late, though. They're probably closed.'

'Right. Well, thanks anyway.'

'Give us a pound and you can borrow my phone. Have to be quick, though. Just a couple of minutes.'

'That'd be brilliant. Thanks.'

Brian hunts in his backpack and puts a phone in Tommy's hand. A cheap phone, but working and unrestricted, which is a luxury to Tommy.

'Can you remember your sister's number?' asks Brian.

'Course I can. I've been calling her nearly every week.'

'These days, mate, you'd be surprised. Nobody bothers to remember anything. They all put their trust in digital.'

Tommy smiles as he dials, believing Dawn will be excited to hear from him.

But she doesn't pick up. At the beep, Tommy leaves a message. 'Dawn? It's me, it's Tommy. They let me out at last. I'm an actual free man. Maybe you already know, maybe it's been on the news. Anyway, I'm in Derby and I'm hoping you can come and get me since I've no place to go and no money. The state of me, eh? Anyway, can you call me back? This bloke's lent me his phone so if you could ring me straight back, I'd really appreciate it. OK, that's it. Soon as you get this, right?'

'Good luck with it,' says Brian despondently, as Tommy hands back his phone. 'Call from a random mobile, she'll probably block it.'

Half an hour goes by, and full darkness falls. Tommy buys tea and sits down next to Brian, and for a while they talk of how their lives have been.

'Doesn't look like your sister got the message,' says Brian

eventually. 'And I have to find me a place to bunk down before the best spots all get taken.'

Tommy nods. But as they're getting to their feet, Brian's phone rings and he hands it to Tommy.

'Dawn? Am I pleased to hear from you. Yeah, still in Derby, outside the station. Can you come and get me? I would so appreciate it. OK, that's great. No worries, I can wait. I'm out front, near the taxis. I'll see you soon.'

'Saved by the bell.' Brian is hauling his pack and bedroll onto his back. 'Hope it works out for you.'

'So do I, mate. And all the best to you.' Tommy presses four pounds of his discharge grant into Brian's hand. 'Thanks so much for your help.'

'No worries.' Brian pats his thigh to let the dog know they're on the move again. 'Us outcasts have to stick together.'

Tommy finds Dawn's hug warmer than any other he can remember, even counting wedding days and Dad's funeral.

She stands back to look at him. 'You look well.'

Tommy shakes his head. 'No, I don't. I look like shit. I've barely seen the sun for ten years and I'm wearing somebody else's cast-offs.'

'What do you want to do? Are you tired?'

'Are you kidding? No, I'm not tired. You know what I want to do? I want to eat the biggest, juiciest steak and drink the longest, coldest pint this town can offer.'

'All right,' says Dawn, climbing back into the car. 'I know the very place.'

'You know I've barely got a penny to my name, don't you?'

asks Tommy, as Dawn starts the engine. 'Eighty-two quid they gave me, and a train ticket home.'

'Don't worry about it,' says Dawn. 'It's a celebration, and it's on me.'

THIRTY-EIGHT

A long, exhausting day at the end of a gruelling battle.

The euphoria of victory – and, if Lorna's honest, revenge – didn't linger long.

As she makes her way down the crowded carriages looking for an empty seat, her threatening headache – triggered by the celebratory fizz cracked open in the office after the announcement was made – is growing worse. Probably she's dehydrated. What she'd really like is to be already home, hands round a fresh-brewed mug of tea, but there's an hour and a half to get through on this train followed by a twenty-minute drive from the station. She's messaged Ed to ask him to let Max and Dottie stay up until she gets home, even though she knows that's not fair on him, that he'll already have had enough and be all too keen to see them fast asleep in bed.

But she sees too little of them. Missing them is a nagging ache in her heart.

She hears a whistle from the platform, and the train lurches forward. In the carriage before the buffet, a young guy deliberately zoned out with eyes closed and headphones in has taken a seat for his bag. Lorna's not in the mood for social niceties.

Leaning forward so he can't pretend he hasn't heard her, she asks, 'Is this seat taken?'

His eyes snap open so fast, she knows he probably knew she was there. He doesn't speak, but huffily hauls his bag onto his lap.

'I can put it up on the rack for you if you like,' she says, but he's already turned his face to the window, where the ghostly images of the carriage interior are imprinted on the station buildings receding outside. She was lucky to catch this train; another ten minutes rehashing their success and she'd have been on the slower 18.10. Then there'd have been no chance at all of seeing her children.

She flops down in the vacated seat, realising as soon as she sits how much her feet hurt and how tight her calf muscles are. The guard begins his announcements, but she knows them all off by heart and doesn't listen. The young man beside her is drumming his fingers on his bag, tuned into music she can't hear. What happened to the days when train travel was sociable, when you might chat to your fellow passenger, pass the time of day?

For God's sake. That's like something her father would say.

Maybe a glass of wine would be better than that cup of tea.

As she turns into the avenue two hours later, the lights in the downstairs windows and the glow of Max's hedgehog night-light behind his bedroom curtains bring a flutter of gladness to her heart. This commonplace house – a three-bed detached, small garden at the back – is the dream home for which she and Ed resolved to work. Mostly, it feels like a huge achievement. Only sometimes does the mortgage feel like a noose around her neck.

She tries to be quiet as she unlocks the front door to let herself in, disappointed that no little whirlwinds come running to meet her. As she shrugs off her coat and hangs it up in the hallway, she catches a whiff of bubble-bath wafting down from the bathroom. She doesn't call out to Ed; Dottie's a notoriously light sleeper, and since she's evidently already in bed, better to have an hour or so of tiptoeing and whispering to make sure she won't wake.

She finds Ed in the kitchen, leaning on the counter, grinning. He's in his old jeans and socks, and there's fingerpaint on his T-shirt. He looks like he didn't find time to shave today, and his eyes are puffy with fatigue. By the kettle he's put out her favourite mug – the one with *WINNER* written in bold capitals, and the handle formed in a gold trophy. He knows her so well, and takes such good care of her. Of all of them.

She loves him very dearly. Yet when he opens his arms to her, she crosses the floor and gives him the briefest hug, a light peck on the lips, then steps away, switches on the kettle, noticing he's already put a teabag in the mug. He folds his arms, as if to hug himself instead, and his smile fades.

'So how was it, superstar?'

She wants to tell him everything, but she's too wired or tired or both.

'Yeah, it was good. Well, we got the result, so . . . You put the kids to bed. I thought you were going to let them wait up?'

Now his smile's all gone. 'I can't just decide that on their behalf, Lorna. Max was crashed out by seven and by the time I'd got him in bed, Dottie was in her pyjamas waiting for her story. They've had a busy day too, in their own way. We all have.'

Lorna looks at him, really looks at him. 'I'm sorry.' She goes back to him, hugs him, lays her head on his shoulder. 'I'm ridiculous, I know. I miss you guys, that's all.'

'Take a less demanding job, then. Be here more. We could cope with less money. We could both work part-time.'

It's a proposal she's heard a dozen times before, but she doesn't believe he means it.

The kettle's boiled. She goes to the fridge for milk, and finds a bowl of pasta Bolognese, plated up and ready for her.

'You cooked.'

Ed gives her a look. 'I always cook. In case you hadn't noticed. Do you want me to warm it up?'

'You're such an angel – that would be brilliant. All I've had today is a Pret sandwich. And Ben brought in celebratory doughnuts. Too much sugar for me.'

She passes him the pasta, and he carries it to the microwave while she prods the teabag in the hot water, getting the brew as dark as she can make it before she adds the milk. Probably it's too much caffeine at this time of the evening, but she's hoping it'll help her headache.

He switches on the microwave and says, 'You were on BBC news. You should be able to get it on iPlayer.'

She can't deny she's tempted to watch. 'Maybe I will. It's not every day I'm on TV.'

'You did good, lady.'

As she eats, he talks about his day, and Lorna's pleased for a while to wind down into how Max is learning – or mis-learning – new words and Dottie had a fall today at playgroup and wanted to show Lorna the plaster on the tiny cut on her knee.

'You'd better be sympathetic,' he says. 'She misses you, you know.'

'I miss you guys too,' says Lorna, and means it. Is she missing too much as the months of their short lives whizz by?

Ed's itching to get to his darts match at the pub. Darts night is what he calls his adult playtime, and she understands his need to go.

When he's left, the house's silence is soothing. She sits for a while, contemplating an early bed and a long night's sleep undisturbed by wakeful worry over what needs to be done in the morning.

Upstairs, unable to resist, she peeps round the doors of Max's and Dottie's rooms. Max is sound asleep, the huge blue teddy he's loved from when he first began to walk tucked in beside him. Dottie is in her strawberry-patterned pyjamas, her blankets all thrown off as usual. Lorna carefully covers her, knowing that by morning the blankets will be back in a rejected heap.

There are paracetamol capsules in the bathroom cabinet and she takes two. In her and Ed's bedroom, she's tempted to crawl under the duvet and stay there, but instead she removes her work clothes (is it her imagination that they reek of city grime?), swapping them for vanilla-scented jogging pants and a cosy top from her wardrobe. Padding back downstairs, she thinks what an angel Ed is with the laundry. Wine would be an unnecessary unkindness to her body, which craves cool water and rehydration, so instead she pours herself a glass of chilled San Pellegrino from a bottle in the fridge, taking a long drink before she curls up on the sofa. Something is digging into her thigh: one of the kids' toys is stuck between the cushions, a plastic cow from the farm set with which Max is currently infatuated. She places the cow on the glass-topped coffee table, and picks up the remote, scrolling through the channels until she finds this evening's BBC *News at Six* on catch-up. She's right – it is quite a thing to be on there, sharing the billing with presidents and billionaires and reports of national and international importance.

OK, she's near the end, but even so . . .

The item is announced, and there's a picture of Tommy ten years before, a photo of Adam, and – a video fragment of Ryan Canfield, speaking outside Derby Crown Court on the day of Tommy's conviction. Unexpectedly, her heart lurches, and she's grateful Ed isn't here. The segment moves on, and here she is outside the Court of Appeal, looking as authoritative and in control as Ryan did then, saying – as he did – what a great day it is for British justice.

How is Ryan feeling now? she wonders. Adam's murder was his biggest case, the one that put him on the policing map, gained him a promotion.

Now she's helped to prove he messed it all up.

Does he even remember her?

Well, if he'd forgotten her, today has been a sledgehammer of a reminder.

THIRTY-NINE

So many things Tommy has forgotten, and some he never knew. The world has been transformed while he's been locked away. People pay for everything with mobile phones and watches, and the prices are sky high. No wonder the pub is emptier than he expected.

As they wait for their food order, Tommy takes the first long drink of the pint of ale he's been dreaming of for years, and finds himself underwhelmed.

He holds up his glass to the overhead light.

'Have they changed the way they make this?'

'Not that I'm aware of,' says Dawn.

'Tastes different.'

'You'll learn to love it again.'

But his food – a medium-rare rump, a shovel-load of chips, grilled mushrooms and battered onion rings – are all he was hoping for. He chews on the first mouthful of steak for a long time.

'They never gave us red meat, not proper meat like this. When we had shepherd's pie, you never knew what was in it, cat meat probably, or horse.'

A waitress is passing by. Tommy pushes away his beer and asks her for a Coke.

'How was it in there, really?' asks Dawn. 'I thought about you a lot. Wondered how you were getting on. I worried about you.'

Tommy shrugs. 'You get used to it, up to a point. And it was difficult, at times. But you have a lot of time to think, too much time. At first, I thought a lot about payback, what I'd do when I got out. But after a while, that left me. I just kept my head down, accepted the situation. Bided my time. I'll tell you when it was bad, the worst – when Mum died. It drove me mad that they wouldn't let me see her before she went. Half a day for the funeral, and that was it.'

Dawn remembers that time well. She's long believed Tommy's guilty verdict killed their mother, who was diagnosed with cancer eighteen months after Tommy's conviction and died only six months later. She remembers the funeral, the embarrassment in front of friends and family of Tommy being led into the chapel in handcuffs, the men they sent to guard him standing at the back, silent sentinels reminding everyone of what they'd much rather forget. And the moment the service was over, Tommy was led away, not allowed to speak to anyone, not even to touch Mum's coffin, no chance at all for a proper goodbye.

'I'll take you to the cemetery, first chance we get. We'll take her some flowers.'

'And Buster and Nell,' Tommy goes on. 'Is anyone ever going to tell me what really happened to them? How must they have felt when I abandoned them? They kept me sane, those dogs did, when Gail and I . . . When things were getting hard. Best dogs I ever had, and she gave them to a shelter, didn't she? Mum said Gail told her she'd found a good home on some farm, but I know that lying sow. She'll have taken the easiest option she could find, like she always did. They might have gone to anybody, somebody who didn't love them, but she wouldn't care. Doesn't matter now, though, does it? They'll be long dead, buried who knows where.'

Tommy's right. Dawn felt bad about the dogs at the time, but Gail had already handed them over before she could intervene. She was quite keen to take the dogs on herself, but of course Jake wouldn't hear of it.

'I thought about things too,' admits Dawn. 'I didn't want to believe you'd done it, but I assumed the police were right. You don't like to think they might have got it wrong, do you? Because if they screwed up your case, how many others have they got wrong? And the big question is, now we know for sure you didn't do it, who the hell did?'

'You've no idea how much time I've spent thinking about that,' says Tommy. 'While I was locked away, someone on the outside was laughing at me, and that was hard to stomach. But what was a sight worse was knowing they thought they'd got away with it, with killing my little boy. And you know what was hardest of all? Thinking that whoever it was might die before I got to them. Well, I'm back. If they're not dead yet, they soon might be. And I've got some ideas. I will find out who did it, believe me, and then . . .'

Dawn reaches across the table and squeezes his hand. 'Don't talk like that. They'll put you away again.'

'You know what? If I've got justice for my boy, honestly, I won't care.'

Dawn's phone rings. 'That's Jake. I'd better see what he wants.'

With an apologetic smile, she leaves the table. Through the window, Tommy can see her outside, frowning as she talks, her hand on her forehead as if she's hearing bad news.

'All good?' asks Tommy, as Dawn sits back down and picks up her fork.

'Yeah, nothing to worry about. He's just bothered that we don't really have room for you, so he's booked you into the Premier Inn. It's all paid for. You'll be comfortable there. Lap of luxury it'll be, after what you've been used to.'

Tommy feels a pain in his heart. Dawn won't meet his eyes.

'He doesn't want me at your house.'

Dawn sighs, puts her fork down again. 'It isn't that. He's just – concerned. Give him a few days to get used to the idea.'

'I thought me and Jake were solid.'

'You are solid. But you have to understand, we've had a hard time of it. People wouldn't speak to us. We had to move here for a fresh start.'

Tommy leans forward across the table, and speaks low.

'*You've* had a hard time? You and him? In case you hadn't noticed, I've been locked up for the last ten years for something I didn't do. I lost my son, my life's blood. So don't you dare tell me you two have had a hard time. For fuck's sake.'

'Tommy, listen . . .'

'No, you listen. I'm not some dirty little secret you can hide at the Premier Inn. I'm your brother, Dawn, your own flesh and blood. I'm at rock bottom, absolute rock bottom and through no fault of my own. If I can't rely on you, who can I rely on?'

'I'm not saying you can't rely on me. Just he needs a bit of time to . . .'

'To what? Square it with the neighbours that your ex-con brother's coming to stay for a few days? You know what that is? It's pathetic. He lords it over you and always has. Pathetic.'

Across the remains of their celebratory meal, to Dawn's dismay she sees tears in Tommy's eyes.

'Just stay at the hotel tonight, Tommy. Please. Give me time to talk to him. It's come as a shock, you know?'

'So much for the welcome home party, eh?'

Tommy pushes away his plate. Half his food is uneaten, the bloody juices from the much-anticipated steak seeping into the cold chips. In the old days, he'd have made a dramatic exit, left Dawn sitting at the table and walked out with his head held high, marching across the moral high ground.

He's not that stupid any more. A cold, wet night in Derby is no time to be turning his nose up at a warm and comfortable bed.

'Where is this place?' he asks.

'Not far away, just across from the new Sainsbury's. I'll drive you, of course.'

But there are some gestures that can still be made.

'Don't trouble yourself,' says Tommy. 'I can find my own way there.'

Lying on the sofa, Lorna must have dozed, because she's woken by the ping of an incoming message on her phone. She's no idea how long she's been asleep. The TV is still on, but it's not showing the programme she was watching. Dazed, she glances at the phone, seeing a mobile number with no name attached to it.

Through the curtains she sees the flash of headlights and hears the car pulling up on the drive. Ed's home.

She opens the message.

Can we talk? R

Who's R? She thinks for a couple of minutes before realisation dawns: R for Ryan. So he does remember her. He even still has her mobile number.

And she finds – irrationally – she's pleased.

Then unbidden, unwanted, a memory comes to mind: a moment of her and Ryan together at that poky flat she had on Armitage Street, candles burning low and the bed all rumpled, her completely happy just to be with him, him holding her close because he didn't want to leave.

But he did leave. He left her for good.

Ed's key is turning in the front-door lock.

Lorna switches off her phone, deciding she'll take her time making up her mind whether she should reply to Ryan's message.

Or whether she should simply delete it.

FORTY

Tommy can't deny his night at the Premier Inn is a marvellous luxury.

Putting down his meagre luggage, he locks his room door, then opens it again and steps out into the corridor to make sure he can, to relish the freedom of being in control. Then he locks himself in again, and wetting a small piece of toilet paper, sticks the sodden blob into the peep-hole in the door. He's had enough of prying eyes spying on him.

Stripping off the clothes on which he senses the smell of prison still clings, he spends a full twenty minutes in the shower, keeping the water as hot as he can stand.

Then he lies down on the wide and splendid bed – crisp white sheets and a soft, supportive mattress, with two plump pillows under his head – and in his mind thanks Fate for bringing him to this place.

For the freedom to put right what's been wrong for far too long.

The triple glazing muffles all noise from the car park and beyond, and for the moment there are no voices or trundling suitcase wheels in the corridor outside his room. Tommy takes a few minutes to appreciate the silence, because the place he's come from was so rarely quiet. Even after lock-up there was always something to disturb your rest: the tramp of warders' boots; rattling keys and slamming doors; the cries of the deranged, the enraged and despairing. What he really missed, what he never heard, were the soothing sounds of home: the sough of the wind, the bleating of sheep, the patter of rain. Home wasn't silent, but it was peaceful, alive with the energising sounds of nature, sounds you could walk out into and be part of as the wind ruffled your hair and tugged at your clothes, and freshening rain fell on your face. With his eyes closed, he's carried back there on a cold December morning, with the cold pinching his fingers and his breath frozen into mist, the dogs running ahead, keen and glad as him to be out. He was a lucky man then, much luckier than he knew; best above all, he was father to a boy who loved him perhaps as much as he was loved in return. Him and Adam holding hands as they crossed the fields, Adam stopping from time to time to pick fluffy heads of dandelions and blow the seed parachutes into the air: rare and precious moments he didn't appreciate enough, not like he would now, when they've been lost to him for so long.

The fantasy of returning to that old life was what's kept him going, but it's a fairy tale that won't come true. Nothing will ever be the same. How can it be?

His innocence has been proven, and he's a free man. The world knows he didn't harm his son, and maybe that's enough.

Maybe it would be better for everyone if for him, it all ended here, tonight.

Except he's no intention of leaving Adam's death unpunished.

FORTY-ONE

In their king-sized bed, Tessa and Peter Rains lie as far apart as they can, both mentally wide awake, both closed-eyed and dissembling sleep, or pretending to be drifting in that direction.

But when Peter hears the hall clock chime one, he turns over onto his back and switches on the bedside lamp.

Blinking, Tessa rolls over to look at him. His grey hair is ruffled, his face is sallow in the yellow lamplight. The last few years have made him an old man. 'Are you OK?'

'How can I be OK? We have to make a decision, decide what we should do.'

'I thought we'd already decided you'll stick to your story. Say you made an honest mistake.'

Wearily, defeated, he rubs his hands over his face, mussing his hair even further. 'But I didn't, did I? I lied on oath. God, I wish I'd never done it. I must have been mad.'

Tessa touches his arm. 'We've been through this a million times. You did it for Simon.'

'And look where that got us. Absolutely nowhere. I don't think I've got any choice but to tell the truth, tell them I lied.'

'You can't do that. You'll be arrested.'

'As I deserve to be.'

'You were just doing what any father would have done.'

'Was I? Not any father, surely? Not everyone's the father of someone like Simon, are they? Not everyone carries that burden.'

'Do you think they'll start asking questions about him again?' Tessa's voice is small, her fears for her son always at the front of her mind. 'They'll be going back to square one, won't they?'

'I'm damn sure they will. And from here onwards, we could get that knock at the door any time.'

'But they know where Simon is, surely? They know he's not here.'

'The police will know, but what about Tommy? He sat in court and heard me lie. I think it's a stone-cold certainty he'll be here before long.'

'Oh, Peter. We talked about this. How could he find us?'

'If he has access to the internet, I imagine it'll be quite easy.'

'Please, stop worrying. You'll make yourself ill again. I'll go and make us some tea.'

She has one leg out of the bed, but he stops her. 'For God's sake, Tess, you can't cure everything with tea. We have to go away somewhere, at least for a while. And the sooner the better.'

'But where will we go?'

'I'll find an Airbnb, Scotland maybe, or Wales. We'll get a good rate this time of year.'

'Are you mad? What about work, what about my job?'

'Tell them you've been called away, a sick relative. Ask for compassionate leave. Anything.'

'But I don't want to leave here. We're settled, we have friends.'

'You stay, then, but I'm going. I'm not just going to wait around for Tommy to come and beat the living daylights out of me.'

'Won't he be on parole or something? Tagged, maybe?'

'Parole from what? His sentence has been quashed. He's a man who's spent ten years of his life behind bars, and I helped put him there. If I were him, I'd be top of his list of people he wants to talk to.'

'Do you really think he'd hurt you?'

'I think he'd kill me. He's had ten years to stoke his anger, and if I were him revenge would be the only thing on my mind.'

FORTY-TWO

The hotel reception area lacks couches or chairs which might encourage people to linger, so Dawn is standing near the vending machines, waiting.

As the lift door opens, Tommy sees her brighten and begin to smile before her expression becomes uncertain. As well it might. Tommy's still angry after last night, yet he can't deny he's pleased to see her. Even a place like Derby feels intimidating when you've nowhere to go and have no friends.

'What brings you here?' he asks. 'Shouldn't you be at work?'

Dawn looks like she hasn't slept. 'I told them I'm not coming in. I was hoping I'd catch you. I thought you might have been up and off at crack of dawn, like you used to be.'

'Up and off where?' asks Tommy, but Dawn pretends she hasn't heard. 'Why didn't you have them call upstairs? I'd have come down.'

'Apparently they don't have telephones in the rooms any more,' says Dawn. 'Everyone's got mobile phones.'

'Everyone except me.'

'I asked her to let me go up and knock on your door, but apparently that's against security rules. So I just had to wait.

I'm sorry about last night. I want to make it up to you. Fancy a bite of breakfast? I'm starving, and I'm gasping for a coffee.'

As they're shown to a table in the restaurant, Dawn glances down at the large white plastic carrier bag Tommy's still carrying around. 'We've got some errands to run this morning, and the first is to get you a decent bag to put your stuff in.'

'Is here all right?' asks the host. 'Help yourself to the hot buffet. Juices, tea and coffee are over there. Enjoy your meals.'

Tommy drops his bag on the seat of a chair. 'At least I don't have to worry about anyone nicking my stuff. And now I'm going to grab me the biggest plate of bacon and sausages you've ever seen.'

When breakfast is eaten, Dawn fetches them both another mug of coffee. The place is emptying, and the buffet is being cleared away. Now there's no one nearby, there's space for them to talk.

'We'll get you some of your money from the bank,' says Dawn. 'I've been looking after it properly. I've kept all the receipts.'

'How much is there?'

'About eleven thousand. Most of that's what Mum left you, but I put what I got for that old Land Rover in there, plus those other few bits you wanted me to sell. And there were expenses to pay out, but not many. Anyway, it's something.'

'It's enough to buy a car.'

'Not anything fancy.'

'I don't need anything fancy. I need a phone, though. And some new clothes.'

'Argos for the phone, Asda for the clothes. And when we're

done there we'll call in at the solicitors and tell them you want to revoke the power of attorney you gave me.'

'Thanks for doing all that.'

Dawn shrugs. 'You'd have done the same for me. And we'll ask them about the procedure for claiming compensation. You could get a pile for that, couldn't you? You'll be set for life.'

Tommy looks away. Since he lost Adam, there is no life.

'Where do you think you'll stay, short-term?' asks Dawn.

'Short-term, long-term, it's all the same. I'll go and live at Mum's.'

'You're not serious?'

'Why not? The house is empty, isn't it?'

'Yes, but it's in a bit of a state, to be honest. No one's lived there since she died, and the damp's got a real hold in places. Really, we should have sold it.'

'I didn't want to sell it. Not without saying a proper goodbye.'

'I get that. But when you've said your goodbyes, you need to find a new place. You don't want to stay there, Tommy. It's not fit to live in. It'll make a fair bit, these days. Folks are all over country cottages in places like Risedale. We'll split the money like Mum said in her will and you can get yourself a flat.'

'A flat? What would I do in a flat? If it was good enough for her, it's good enough for me. Ted and Joan still next door?'

'Ted died, and Joan's in a home. Dementia. Their cottage got bought by a couple from Surrey. They're not there very much. Sometimes they rent it out on Airbnb.'

'But the electric's still connected, isn't it, and the water?' Dawn nods. 'Well, then. I'll light the fire, get it aired, be right as rain in a few days.'

'Come on, brother. That's not really a good idea, is it?'

'Why not? I got mates there.'

'Have you? You used to have mates there, same as I did. But the people in that village, you don't know what they've been like.'

'You don't think they'll welcome me back with open arms? Why wouldn't they? I'm an innocent man. His Majesty's officials say so.'

'But those old bigots and stick-in-the-muds, once they've formed an opinion, they don't easily change it. Me and Jake, we've said it's the best thing we've ever done, getting away from Risedale. And there's Gail . . .'

Tommy bristles. 'What about Gail?'

'Well, don't you think it'll be awkward, living so close by?'

'Why? Do you think I don't know she's got another man?'

'She had one. I heard he's long gone. But she had . . . I just think you should go somewhere else, make a fresh start.'

'She had what?'

Dawn sighs. 'Do you really want to know? She's got another child now, a daughter.'

'Has she? How old?'

'I don't know. Eight or nine, maybe.'

'The grass didn't grow under her feet, then, did it?'

'I hope you're not harbouring any ideas of a reunion?'

'Nah. That ship sailed long ago. But there's one or two people there I want a word with.'

'You be careful, Tommy. Don't go stirring things up.'

Tommy gives a slow smile. 'When the pool's stagnant, a good stir is what's needed to see what's down there at the bottom.'

'I mean it, Tommy. Don't you go making trouble.'
'I won't. Not for anyone who doesn't deserve it.'

By the time Dawn's helped Tommy do everything needed to begin his reintegration into modern life, daylight is beginning to fade. Tommy's finding it like being in the Twilight Zone anyway, zapped forward to a future place that's similar yet not the same, where everything's automated and scanned, where in many places of business – banks and shops – human contact has been minimalised or completely removed. He's finding this hardest of all; despite the countless downsides of being in jail, he was living at the heart of a community, constantly in direct contact with his fellow prisoners and their guards, so there was always banter and barter, eating, working, everything was done together. Tommy is – or was – a sociable man, and he found the enforced closeness easier than many. He misses a bit of chat at the checkouts.

'Better get used to it,' says Dawn.

Tommy's new car is anything but new, and nothing like a vehicle he'd like to own. Dawn found it scrolling on Autotrader on her phone, a fifteen-year-old low-mileage Toyota Yaris, a private sale in a city suburb by the son of an elderly woman recently deceased. But it runs well and has a long MOT, will be cheap on fuel, anonymous, and will get him from A to B. With the keys in his hand, for the first time since his release, Tommy feels something like truly free.

And yet he's nervous. It's been a long, long time since he drove. He used to consider himself a king of the road, fearless and afraid of no one, not traffic, not storm or snow. In a Yaris, people will expect nothing of him, and perhaps that's just as well. He can drive like the old lady who was its previous owner, and no one will bother him or care.

All day, he's looked forward to the journey home, but now the moment's here, he finds his mood blue. As Dawn waves goodbye and walks away to her own car, Tommy's beginning to realise Dawn's probably right, that Risedale isn't the place he should be planning on staying. Well, if he doesn't like it – if it doesn't like him – he can leave. He's no ties to keep him where he's not wanted.

Crawling from one set of traffic lights to another, he makes his way out of the city, heading for the open road at its perimeter. From there, he follows the tail lights of the car in front, passing through familiar places until he sees the first sign to his home village and makes the turn.

The lane is narrow and dark, and the Yaris's lights are inadequate, even on full beam.

In Risedale, no one sees him arrive.

The place where he always used to park is occupied by a family saloon. Tommy drives further up the road and finds a space outside the church, where Adam lies in the nearby cemetery.

Tommy blows an affectionate kiss into the dark. 'I'll be coming to see you tomorrow, mate. You and Grandma.'

The keys to his mother's house are in his pocket. As he approaches the cottage, he has the strangest feeling of a slippage in time: the place is the same as he remembers, and yet not. Never before has Lizzie not been here to welcome him when he's been away. He misses her, immensely.

The passage to the back door is pitch black. As he turns the key, a dog begins to bark next door, and a light comes on in what he remembers as Ted and Joan's kitchen.

The neighbour's door opens, silhouetting a sharp-featured woman in her late thirties.

'Can I help you?' Her voice is high, and Tommy realises she's afraid, that she thinks he's breaking in.

He steps into the light. 'I'm Tommy Henthorn.' He expects her to know his name, to say a word of welcome, but when she says nothing, he adds, 'The bloke who didn't kill his son.'

'Oh. I see.'

'I'll be staying here a while.'

'You're staying here?' She sounds displeased. 'Your sister said she was going to be selling the cottage. We've friends who might be interested.'

'Well, circumstances have changed, as you've no doubt seen on the news. Sorry, I didn't catch your name?'

'I'm Alicia.'

'Nice to meet you, Alicia. Maybe when I get settled in, you could come round for a brew.'

'Oh. Well, we're very busy, a lot of the time. But I suppose so, sometime, yes.'

'Is that your car parked over there?' Tommy nods at the family saloon across the road.

'Yes, it is.'

'Well, anyone round here will tell you that's my spot. Always been my spot, since I got my first bike longer ago than I care to remember. So if you wouldn't mind.'

'Wouldn't mind what?'

'Wouldn't mind not parking there.'

Alicia pulls a face. 'It's a free country,' she says, without irony. 'First come, first served.'

'Right you are,' says Tommy, apparently cordially. 'Sounds like you've got a dog. What kind is it?'

'It's a miniature dachshund. My mother breeds them.'

'I'm thinking of getting a dog, but I prefer something bigger, something that makes a racket when there are bad people around.'

Behind Alicia, a man's voice is asking what's going on. 'Nothing,' she says. 'Everything's fine.'

'Tell your husband I said hello,' says Tommy. 'What's his name?'

'Nick.'

'I'll remember that. Nice talking to you, Alicia.'

He pushes open the door to his old home, and switches on the light. The kitchen smells damp, of dust and dry rot, all markers of a building in decay, and his regret at his insistence on staying here increases.

When those uniformed bullies rough-handled him from this house, it was a warm and welcoming home. A sanctuary.

Yet now – as if he's slipped through some dark looking-glass – he finds himself in a blighted, abandoned hovel. The cottage is bone-bitingly cold, in the way of places that haven't been heated for years. In the kitchen, a lampshade Tommy remembers putting up when his mother first brought it home is draped in cobwebs, and the light from the bulb beneath seems tinted with sulphurous yellow, so everything around is jaundiced. The table where they all used to eat is lacking a cloth, though his mother was always particular about laying a clean one for every meal, and so had quite a collection; opening a drawer he finds them still there, folded and ironed, the patterns all nostalgically familiar. The mugs he drank from still hang on their hooks on the wall; the kettle's there waiting to be filled, with the tea caddy alongside, but empty. On the shelf above the window stands a line of empty jars waiting for summer jams of raspberries and moorland bilberries – whole days they would spend up there when he was a boy, Mum and Grandma doing the picking, him and Dawn not much help but happy making dens among the bracken.

He dumps his bag of groceries on the table, pulls out a can of beer, and popping the top wanders through the hallway into the lounge.

Here is more confirmation of time's cruelty. Nothing is the same.

He sits where Lizzie used to sit, and sees no brightly coloured knitting on the sofa, no reading glasses on the coffee table, no carefully tended pot plants on the windowsill. What he used teasingly to call his mother's tat – twee ornaments, souvenirs of seaside visits and Christmas gifts of pottery cats – has vanished from the mantelpiece.

The room's so cold, his breath smokes on the air. Dawn advised him not to use the heating until he's checked there's oil in the tank, but he could fetch logs from the shed and light a fire.

Or he could leave that for tomorrow.

Maybe things will look better in the morning.

A man on foot is going by the window. His voice is loud, a one-sided conversation as he talks into a phone.

Tommy knows that voice: his old mate Alan Griffin. Tommy and Alan go way back. At school they were an inseparable pair of terrors, always in some kind of trouble.

Grinning, Tommy runs across the room and bangs on the window.

Startled, Alan – older, balding, running to fat – stops and peers in. Tommy smiles, beckons, and gestures downing a drink as an invitation. They've a lot to talk about, him and Alan. Alan will fill him in on what's been happening while he's been gone.

Alan squints, unsure of who he's seeing, but realising it's Tommy, he gives an unconvincing smile, taps his wrist to signal there's somewhere he has to be and walks on by, continuing his call.

Not even a 'Good to see you'. Not even a 'Welcome home'.

Tommy can't deny the snub, and it hurts. Aren't he and Alan mates? At least, they used to be.

Realisation is dawning, that Tommy has been a fly petrifed in amber, his life in freeze-frame.

Meanwhile, everyone else has moved on.

He needs to put that aside.

Tommy's back in Risedale for a reason.

Welcome or not, there's a job he has to do.

FORTY-THREE

Of course, Canfield knew the call was coming.

He passed a restless night rehearsing what he might say, then was up extra early, paying close attention to his shave, giving his shoes a thorough polish, even though it's way too late in his career to rely on making a good physical impression.

Heading into the Kenton Road offices, he does his best to appear relaxed: head up, shoulders back, a cheery 'Good morning' for everyone he meets. In reality, his embarrassment at this disaster kept him in his car for a full five minutes after he parked, putting off the awful moment when the world must be faced. Once in his office, he resists the urge to close the door and shut out his team, because that would be out of character. But none of them trouble him anyway. The stink of the pariah is already on him.

For over an hour and a half he waits. Time ticks slowly by; deliberations are apparently prolonged. But just when he's thinking he might risk a quick trip to the gents', his desk phone rings with an internal extension in the display.

He lets it ring four times before picking up.
A female voice tells him he is wanted upstairs.

Canfield has known Deputy Chief Constable Darren Lomas ever since he was a probationer. Somehow Lomas has always stayed two or even three steps ahead of Canfield as they climbed the professional ladder, in Canfield's view more likely due to Lomas's dedication to the local masonic lodge than to his natural abilities. On the grapevine he's heard Lomas is tipped to go all the way to the top in the not-too-distant future – in sharp contrast to Canfield, whose star is suddenly and disastrously descending. Just how far he's going to fall, he'll find out in the next few minutes.

Reading anything into Lomas's expression is impossible. He's sitting behind his desk leaning on his forearms in an almost presidential pose, his white shirt holding its ironed-in creases, his face still pink and shining from that morning's shave. His wiry build is unusual for one who spends so much time sitting on his backside, but Lomas is a marathon runner, always has been, and it pains Canfield to acknowledge how good Lomas looks on it.

As he declines coffee and takes the offered seat, Canfield thinks if he's going to have spare time on his hands, he might do worse than follow Lomas's example.

Oddly, Lomas doesn't immediately speak, but leans further forward on his forearms to look intently into Canfield's face. The silence becomes uncomfortable, until Canfield wonders if he's supposed to break with protocol and start the conversation himself.

But then Lomas asks, 'How long has it been, Ryan?'

Canfield tries to keep his face composed, despite not understanding the question. Happily, Lomas gives him a clue.

'Since you joined us? Must be going on twenty years.'

'Soon be twenty-three,' says Canfield. 'I joined in the millennium year.'

Like Canfield's terrifying old headmaster mulling over punishment, Lomas slowly nods. 'And for the most part, you've had a stellar career, outstanding.' A pause. 'But this, I can't describe in any other terms than as an unprecedented catastrophe. It is without doubt the most monumental screw-up anyone here can recall.'

Canfield feels his innards sink, and an embarrassingly bright blush spread across his face.

'The thing is, sir—'

Again channelling that headmaster, Lomas holds up a warning finger. 'Let me finish.'

'Sorry, sir.'

'Obviously we've got egg on our face, but that's not the worst of it. This outcome, this reversal, throws into doubt any number of other convictions over the past decade, maybe even further back than that. Plainly we were incompetent, but there are those who would take great delight in suggesting it was something worse, that Henthorn was framed. But I'm sure you're going to assure me that wasn't the case?'

Before he can control his reaction, Canfield's face shows his anger. 'I resent that.'

'The question is a valid one. And if it comes to light there was anything irregular in Henthorn's conviction – any convenient solutions, anyone aiming for a quick result – the consequences are going to be severe.'

Without thinking about it, Canfield finds himself on his feet. 'That's a bloody insult. I haven't given over twenty years to this job to be accused of being bent. And if that's what you think of me, I'll leave right now.'

Lomas holds up a placatory hand. 'Sit down, Ryan. Sit down.'

Reluctantly, Canfield does so.

'You were lead on the case – you're going to take some flak. And of course we're in a position now where heads are going to have to roll.'

'I presume that means me.'

Lomas sighs, as if he might feel genuine regret. 'You know how it goes.'

'Demotion? Or retirement?'

'Remains to be seen. There'll be an internal inquiry, of course.'

'And in the meantime?'

Lomas's smile is sad. 'Have you had a decent holiday recently?'

'Don't tell me. Now's my chance.'

'My hands are tied. It's not a local matter. This will be of national interest.'

'Can I say my piece now?' asks Canfield. 'If my team screwed up – and I suppose we must have done – then I think I deserve to have another look at the evidence, see where we went wrong.'

'I believe new evidence came to light.'

'What new evidence?'

'In view of your current position, I can't share that with you, but it will be passed to the Cold Case team leader when the case comes up for review.'

'That could be years away. Why not give me a couple of weeks to have a look at it, see what I can do? If I'm on paid leave, you might as well use me. I know the people involved, I know the background. Look, it was my screw-up. If I can work a miracle and get to the right answer, our honour is saved.'

Lomas shakes his head. 'You know that's not how things are done.'

'Let's set a precedent.'

'Precedents are dangerous.'

'Doing nothing is worse. What if I can get a result? We'll at least have the right person in custody, and the world will move on.'

For a long moment, Lomas considers, and Canfield knows he's thinking of himself, of the stain on his own record that the Henthorn case could leave.

'Two weeks,' Lomas says at last. 'You'd have to be totally unofficial and under the radar. The press release that's being drafted will say you've been relieved of all duties with immediate effect. I'd have to have your assurance you wouldn't do anything to make anyone think that wasn't the case.'

'I'll need some time to review the files to get me started.'

Lomas looks doubtful. 'A day. Half a day.'

Lomas glances at his watch. 'The time now is 10.48am, and I will be leaving the office this afternoon at 5pm sharp. At some point before then, I want you to come back here and hand me your warrant card.'

'That's long enough,' says Canfield. 'I can do a hell of a lot of reading in six hours.'

FORTY-FOUR

Tommy walks down to Risedale's cemetery.

On the face of it, little has changed. A few more headstones have appeared to fill some of the empty spaces in the row of new graves, and the ash tree that stands at the corner diagonally opposite the gate has grown taller and spread. And, he notices now, a second bench with a plaque screwed onto its back has appeared by the wall where there used to be only one. As he passes, he reads the few engraved words – *In memory of Betsy Cranford, 1936–2020* – and feels a pang of sadness. Mrs Cranford taught Tommy at the little village school. She was kind and patient, and with her patience Tommy – though he struggled – learned to read. What must she have thought of him when he was arrested for his own son's murder? The loss of her good opinion is yet another offence he has no choice but to bear.

His father's grave is little changed, the ground appearing undisturbed. But those few new words carved on the grey headstone carry momentous weight. The dates his father was born and died are now followed by an inscription he can hardly bear to read: *Also Elizabeth (Lizzie) Henthorn née Taylor, much loved wife and mother . . .*

Close by, Adam's white headstone is bright against the dour granite memorials which surround him. Tommy reads the message on the dead flowers left by strangers on his son's grave, and walks over to drop them on the compost heap by the ash tree. Adam is his boy and his alone, now properly in his care.

And his killer has still not faced justice. Eight years have passed since his mother died, and this is the first time he's been able to visit her burial place.

Wrongs must be righted.

He's brought them both flowers, of course. For Adam, a simple wreath of creamy white roses, and a packet of chocolate buttons; for Lizzie, the most vibrant blooms in the florist's shop, in all the colours she used to love.

As he lays his gifts on the sodden grass, he apologises to each in turn for his neglect.

'I'm here now though,' he tells Adam, before he walks away. *'And those who are guilty are going to pay.'*

FORTY-FIVE

Canfield doesn't see much of Manny Pearson these days.

Pearson left the service shortly after Tommy Henthorn's trial, citing stress and a growing aversion to spending most of his waking life dealing with misery. In a raucous city-centre pub shortly before his departure, when Pearson had downed significantly more than his usual abstemious pint, at one point in the evening he'd stood, slightly swaying, in front of Canfield – himself a long way from sober – and said some words the exact form of which, given the circumstances, Canfield can't remember, but the gist was straightforward. Pearson said too much bad energy was eating his soul. The kind of people they were dealing with, day upon day – the drug dealers and the people-traffickers, the wife-beaters and child-molesters – were infecting him with their corruption, and no amount of soap and hot water could wash him clean. *'I want to go over to the other side,'* he'd said. *'I want to do something that will purify me.'*

To an extent, Canfield understood what Pearson meant. Life spent among perpetrators of serious wrongdoing takes its toll, making you jaded and cynical, as Irene had told him many times. But Canfield's ethos is rooted in stubbornness, a refusal to give in, an immovable sense of duty that makes him continue to hold the line. Because if all of them throw in the towel, like Pearson, what is going to be left but anarchy and chaos, and inevitably more crime?

Given Pearson's stated aspirations, Canfield was almost expecting him to enter holy orders, or at least join the congregation of some religion. Instead, the next he heard Pearson was managing a downtown gym, a job that Canfield knew for someone like Pearson could only present a troubling daily battle with the sins of the flesh.

Time has gone by — maybe three or four years — since they've been in touch. But Canfield feels a nagging wish to speak with his old colleague, to rehash the decisions they made, the conclusions they drew. To try and figure out — as far as possible, at this distant remove — where they went wrong with Tommy Henthorn.

When he calls the gym, a young woman answers. Canfield asks to speak to Manny Pearson, and there's a short pause.

'Sorry, I'm new here,' she says. 'Let me just ask someone.'

Canfield hears her talking to someone close by, asking about Danny Pearson.

A man comes on the line.

'Can I help you?'

'Yes, I hope so. I'm looking for a mate of mine, Manny Pearson.'

'Oh yeah, Manny. He doesn't work here any more, not since before Covid.'

Before Covid. The new BC.

'Any idea where he went?'

The man considers. 'I did know. Give me a minute to think. People got scattered all over the place, know what I mean? But I reckon Manny said he was going into security, supermarkets and that. I think he went to that place on Ridgeway Road, where they have all the red-and-white vans outside, what do they call that place? Safelink, Securilink, something like that? I expect you'd find it on Google. Maybe try there.'

'Thanks for your help.'

'No worries. When you find him, tell him Rob says hi.'

Canfield knows the place. Not being pressed for time – given his circumstances – he drives the few miles to Ridgeway Road and the fenced compound of Securitylink. Several of the red-and-white vans Rob mentioned are parked in a regimentally straight row to one side of a single-storey office block with aluminium-screened windows. The vans make Canfield optimistic he's in the right place – neat and tidy was a Pearson trademark – but this seems an odd place to find a man wanting to spend his time away from lowlifes.

He feels the prick of curiosity, wonders if Pearson's been OK, what road his life has taken.

A buzzer sounds as he pushes open the office door. He's expecting the pleasure of recognition and a warm handshake, but though the man behind the desk is of similar age to Pearson, he's flabbily overweight and tired-looking, with heavy bags under his eyes and a couple of days unshaven growth on his jaw. Nothing at all like Pearson used to be, except for the suit.

And then the man says, 'Ryan Canfield.' Grinning, he hauls himself from his chair.

Canfield holds out his hand. 'Manny, is that you?'

'Large as life and twice as ugly.' Pearson grabs the offered hand and shakes it. 'Great to see you, mate, great to see you. What brings you to this hell-hole? Grab a chair, sit yourself down.'

Canfield sees no hell-hole in the surroundings, only the tediousness of a hopeless dead end. The three other desks in the office are empty, suggesting lay-offs or roles too underpaid to attract staff. The plastic plants dotted around are dusty, the water-cooler is dry. A month-to-month calendar pinned on the wall behind Pearson's chair has no entries at all except for a long black line through two weeks in June, with *Annual Leave* handwritten above.

'I was looking for you,' says Canfield. 'Thought we might have a bit of a catch-up.'

Something flickers in Pearson's eyes. 'Not much to catch up on at my end. Same old same old, day in, day out. Still, it pays the bills. How about you? You been seeing anyone? How are the kids?'

'Oh, they're thriving. Caitlin's hit the stroppy teenage phase, so there's that to contend with. Annabelle's still pony-mad and asking Dad why she can't have one of her own, but on my salary, there's no way.'

'Kids are a big expense.'

'You said it.'

'Before you know it, you'll have grandkids too.'

'I suppose so. How about you, Manny? How are you doing? You still living with – sorry, what was her name?'

Pearson waves a dismissive hand. 'That was all over years ago, didn't even last a year. You know me – I'm not the living-with kind. Play the field, that's my mantra.'

Canfield finds it hard to believe Pearson finds many women to date, the way he looks now. The transformation from the fit and handsome guy he remembers is shocking.

'So what happened to the gym? I thought you really enjoyed it there? Rob says hi, by the way.'

'Ah, so that's how you found me. To be honest, I was ready for a change some time back. There's more to life than lifting weights, you know? Then the gym closed down for Covid, and I was stuck at home. Got a bit depressed by my ownsome. You know how it goes.'

'You should have called me.'

'Well, I was a classic case. Ate and drank a bit too much, as we all did. By the time the gym opened up again, I wasn't really fit for it. Tried to get into the old tracksuits and there was no way. If I'm honest, I'd got lazy. Gotta love that short commute from bed to couch. Then even I got a bit sick of my own company, so I started looking around for office work, and I found this. With my police background, they were glad to have me.'

Canfield thinks they'd be glad to have anyone. 'What is it that you do, exactly?'

'We provide teams for security patrols, night-time, daytime, whenever.'

'Supermarkets, stuff like that?'

'Not supermarkets so much. The big guys, Lidl and B&M, they have their national contracts. We're more factories, office blocks. Anybody who's got anything worth nicking, really. What about you? How's things at the old place? I heard you made chief inspector.'

'So you probably also heard I got suspended.'

Pearson frowns. 'You? What for?'

'For screwing up on the Tommy Henthorn case.'

'You know what, let's have a coffee.' Pearson slaps both hands on the desk. 'I've got all sorts in the back. Cappuccino, latte, Americano. Take your pick.'

'Not for me, thanks. I'm cutting down, trying to reverse my caffeine addiction. You did know about the Henthorn judgment?'

Pearson's getting out of his chair. 'You know me these days, couldn't give a monkey's about all that.'

'Even so. It's been all over the news.'

'What has?'

'He's out, Henthorn's been released. The conviction was ruled unsafe.'

'First I've heard of it. I don't watch the news any more. Too depressing.'

'I was hoping you and I . . .'

Canfield's interrupted by the door opening. A young man breezes in, looking far more like the old Pearson than Pearson himself, lithe and smartly dressed in jeans and an overcoat, razor-barbered and confident.

'Afternoon,' he says.

'What's up, Wayne?' asks Pearson.

'I don't want to interrupt,' says Wayne. 'Not if you're with a client.'

'I'm not a client,' says Canfield. 'Manny and I are old mates. We used to work together.'

Wayne looks Canfield up and down. 'You're police, aren't you?'

'Is it so obvious?'

'Fraid so. Plus, no offence, you don't look like a gym nut. Process of elimination.'

'What is it, Wayne?' asks Pearson again.

Wayne ignores him. 'You've just let that bloke go, haven't you?' he asks Canfield. 'That guy from Risedale?'

'Not me personally,' says Canfield, apprehensive of what might come next. Tommy's arrest was big news across this district, and people have a right to ask questions about his release, but with no information forthcoming from Lomas on the new evidence that's been uncovered, Canfield might have to shamefacedly admit he doesn't actually know why the conviction was ruled unsafe. 'But he's been released, yes.'

'My mum knows his wife. She comes from Derby, doesn't she? She and my mum were at school together.'

'Wayne, what is it you want?' interrupts Pearson. 'The chief inspector and I are talking.'

'Oh, right, sorry. Can I change my next week's schedule? You've got me down for weekend shifts and I have to have Saturday off. It's life and death, mate, honest.'

'Only if you do Sanderson's tonight,' says Pearson. 'I've got someone called in sick.'

'I'm doing Sanderson's tomorrow, and I hate it up there. It's colder than the Arctic.'

'Better put your long-johns on, then. And this is the last time. You have to take your share of weekends, same as everyone else.'

'It's not like the old timers have anything lined up on weekends, though, is it?' Wayne gives Canfield a wink. 'Some of us have lives.'

'Cheeky sod,' says Pearson. 'Go on, piss off.'

When Wayne's left, Pearson says, 'I'm having coffee anyway. Sure you don't want anything?'

'Really, I'm fine.'

Pearson goes through a door behind his desk into a small kitchen.

Canfield hears the rattle of cups, the click of a button and the whirr of a machine beginning its work. He, too, stands, and goes to lean on the open doorway.

'I wanted to ask you if you and I could talk about the Henthorn case. You know, have a bit of a brainstorm.'

'No.'

Pearson's blunt answer is surprising. 'Why not?'

Pearson has his back to Canfield, decanting the contents of a pack of own-brand Jaffa Cakes onto a plate. He pops one in his mouth, and his voice is thick with sticky chocolate when he says, 'Because what's the point, Ryan? You're off the case. It's nothing to do with either of us. I left the job years ago. What could I possibly contribute?'

'Lomas gave me a few days to look into it again.'

Pearson turns round, and his smile is disparaging. 'Oh, I'll bet he did. They don't change, do they? Why not give you a few days to look into it, just in case you can get him a quick result on the cheap, save him a fortune on his budget down the line when it's full-on case-review time. You know what your trouble is, Ryan?'

'I have a feeling you're about to tell me.'

'For a seasoned copper, you're naïve. People take advantage of you, and you don't even see it.'

'What, like that young lad just now took advantage of you?'

'There's a world of difference between giving a lad a break

so he can get his leg over and being stitched up for a week of unpaid overtime. The minute Lomas suspended you, you should have told him where to shove it. With your record and your service, the prick should have stood solid behind you, told the world he's got continued faith in you, lessons will be learned and all that bollocks. You weren't on your own in that incident room, were you? There were dozens of us in that investigation, detectives and CPS and barristers and twelve good men and true on the jury. But somehow it's all your fault and he makes you chief scapegoat, even though he's the management where the buck should stop. You alone will pay the price. They make me sick.'

'So that's definitely a no, then.'

'It's a big, fat no, yes. Do yourself a favour, why don't you? Forget all about it, and take yourself off somewhere. Have a week in Bournemouth, or Benidorm. Consider your future. Because I'll bet you're never going to be back on that team. Early retirement, that's where you're headed. Goes without saying, when it happens, there's a job here for you if you want it.'

'Thanks a lot.'

Canfield turns and heads for the door.

Pearson calls after him. 'Ryan?'

'What?'

'Don't be a stranger, all right?'

FORTY-SIX

The offices Tommy's lawyer occupies – in a Georgian building overlooking the marketplace – have seen better days. Tommy and Dawn climb to the top floor, their way lit by a skylight around whose perimeter pigeons coo, every step of the wooden stairs creaking under a carpet that has long ago lost its plush.

At reception, a pleasant-looking young woman stands up from behind her desk and leads them down a low-ceilinged corridor – ex-servant's quarters, thinks Dawn – to a door bearing the name Simon Macclesfield.

The young woman knocks, and without waiting for a reply opens the door, announces, 'Your eleven o'clock, Mr Macclesfield,' and with a bright smile for Dawn and Tommy, she departs.

Dawn leads the way in, and Tommy follows. Macclesfield is standing behind an old-fashioned desk topped with embossed green leather, the desk positioned to give him the optimum view of the busy market-place below. The opposite wall is given over entirely to shelves filled with books, collections of matched volumes bound in black, red and blue, which look to Tommy as if they've never been read.

Macclesfield himself is a man Tommy would pick out of any crowd as a lawyer: three piece suit with the waistcoat buttoned, smooth shave and cropped hair, a flashy tie to suggest he's a more interesting person than he will ever really be. Tommy might even have bumped into him, somewhere along the path he's trodden. One brief gets to look very much like another.

Smiling ingratiatingly, Macclesfield stretches out his hand for both of them to shake and indicates the two chairs in front of his desk.

'Good to meet you at last,' he says, sitting down himself. 'I believe you met with my colleague, David Sharp, last time you were here, and of course David's given me the run-down of what we're all about.' He folds his hands together on the desk and leans forward wearing an expression of sincerity. 'You've had quite a time of it, I hear, Mr Henthorn. How are you coping? Are you managing to find your feet back in civilian life?'

'Just about,' says Tommy. 'Things have changed.'

'Ah, the world's a fast-moving place these days, that's for sure.' Macclesfield reaches for a folder near his right hand and opens it. 'So. I have begun preparing the paperwork for your compensation filing for wrongful incarceration. This compensation will be calculated by an independent assessor to include damage to your reputation and your mental health, loss of past and future earnings, loss of freedom and any legal bills you have incurred. I've checked the dates, and the elapsed time you were actually incarcerated post-arrest comes to a little under ten years. I don't expect you to see it in that light, but it's a shame you didn't quite hit the ten-year mark. If you had, you could be looking at a million pounds in compensation.'

'I'd have stuck around a few more days if I'd known,' says Tommy, despondently.

'Indeed. But as it is, I think you should still get close to the maximum amount allowed in the lower bracket, somewhere in the region of five hundred thousand.'

'Wow,' says Dawn. 'Tommy, that's great.'

Tommy glowers. 'Nothing about this is great. It's the absolute least they can do.' He looks at Macclesfield. 'Do I get an apology to go with it?'

'I'm afraid I doubt that,' says Macclesfield. 'And I do have to advise you the five hundred thousand is a top-line figure. There will be deductions.'

'Deductions?' asks Dawn. 'What deductions?'

Macclesfield appears uncomfortable. 'Under a recommendation published in 2006, in cases like yours – where the conviction is overturned – the prison service is allowed to make a charge for your stay with them.'

Tommy shakes his head. 'I don't understand.'

'They're entitled to charge you board and lodging. A per-diem amount calculated on the number of nights you were imprisoned. It's what they term saved living expenses, the minimum amount you would have had to spend to live day to day in the outside world.'

Tommy's face is growing red with anger. 'That's bullshit. They can't do that.'

'Sadly they can,' says Macclesfield, awkwardly. 'There's no way I can defend it to you, but basically they're entitled to present you with a bill for your stay at His or Her Majesty's pleasure.'

'That can't be right,' objects Dawn. 'He was a victim of

wrongful imprisonment. How can they charge him as if they're some kind of hotel?'

'And they don't charge the guilty?' asks Tommy, bitterly. 'Only the innocent?'

Unable to answer, Macclesfield shrugs. 'I'm so sorry, Mr Henthorn. Even in government there is a sense of unfairness about the charge, and there's much talk of the guidance being changed, but since it hasn't yet done so, I'm afraid it will make a dent in what you receive.'

'How big a dent?' Tommy demands.

Macclesfield hesitates. 'I suspect it could be somewhere in the region of a hundred and twenty thousand pounds.'

Tommy begins tapping his wrist in what Dawn recognises as an NLP technique. Anger management.

'If you wish, we can look at suing for damages to recover some of those costs,' suggests Macclesfield. 'I believe you have a good case.'

'This is all bollocks,' mutters Tommy. 'Those absolute bastards. Total bollocks.'

He stands up, and without another word, walks out of the office.

Dawn proceeds in logical fashion round all the pubs in the immediate vicinity, eventually finding Tommy in the bar of the Frog and Parrot.

He glances up at her but doesn't speak. The pint glass on the table in front of him is almost empty. She takes a seat beside him.

'I'm sorry,' she says.

'What for?'

Dawn shakes her head. 'That everything's been so hard for you.'

'I've got the reverse Midas touch,' says Tommy. 'Everything I touch turns to ratshit.'

'Don't think that way.' Dawn squeezes his hand. 'You're going to get through this.'

'How do you know?' Tommy's voice is low and controlled, but every word is supercharged with rage. 'How do you know I even want to? I've no mates, no job, and now those bastards are going to rob me of my rightful compensation. And that's despite the fact they're totally to blame for the mess they made over my son's death. My Adam's murder. Someone killed him, they've never found out who, and all they do is try and claw back money that's rightfully mine.' He shakes his head. 'Honestly, I can't even tell you how angry I am right now. I could jump over that bar and smash every bottle behind it, throw every table and chair in here through that window.'

'Please don't do that. You'll get arrested.'

Tommy gives an odd smile. 'You're right. I don't want to get arrested. When I get re-arrested, it's going to be for something worthwhile.'

Dawn doesn't like the expression on Tommy's face, a frank brutality she's never seen before. Is this what prison's done for him? 'What do you mean?'

Tommy drains his pint, and taps the side of his nose. 'That's for me to know.' He stands up. 'Anyway, love you and leave you.'

'Where are you going?'

'To do a bit of shopping.'

'I'll come with you.'

'Nah, don't bother. The way I feel right now, I'm not fit company for anyone but myself.'

FORTY-SEVEN

Lorna's conscience is pricking.

She hasn't exactly lied to anyone: not to Ed when she told him as she left the house this morning that she was meeting someone previously involved in the Henthorn case; nor to her office colleagues when she told them the same thing. All she did was fail to mention – especially to Ed – that she and this man were previously involved, and in her case, actually in love. Any of her colleagues would call that a conflict of interests. By any standards, there's an element of deception, but if she were to give a name to her subterfuge, she'd call it a mere sin of omission.

Who are you kidding? Her conscience asks the question repeatedly as she's taking extra care in straightening her hair, choosing what to wear, telling Ed she doesn't have time for breakfast when in fact her stomach's too full of butterflies to countenance food.

She still hasn't spoken to Ryan. Their meeting's been arranged in a series of curt texts – day, time, place – with nothing in them that could possibly arouse any suspicions. So why has she been so careful to keep the messages out of Ed's way?

Lorna chose the location thinking it would be convenient, but there was an ulterior motive too: she'd be unlikely to be seen. Motorway services are for people passing through. Less danger of being spotted by anyone she knows.

But the M1 service station is a poor choice for a meeting. She anticipated that early on a Tuesday afternoon it wouldn't be busy, but it turns out to be a peak time at Leicester Forest East.

She's arrived a few minutes early. As she leaves the car, drizzle is starting to fall, the kind of drizzle that looks harmless hanging in the air in front of you, but somehow manages to elude the protection you expect from your outer garments and transpose its chill into your bones. Even under her long overcoat – the navy-blue greatcoat that Ed calls her court coat – she shivers, not sure if it's from cold or nerves.

Inside, the atrium is damply warm, the air thick with the smell of fast food. She buys herself a vastly overpriced coffee, and finds a table on the perimeter of the communal seating area as far away as she can get from other people. But her relative isolation doesn't last. This is a quick-turnover place, people coming and going every minute, and the table which was quiet when she sat down is suddenly surrounded by astonishingly noisy teenagers, part of some school trip.

Lorna has no hesitation in switching seats, but there she's soon joined by two men in suits, who set up spreadsheets on a laptop and patch in a remote colleague on a loud video call.

She picks up her coffee and wanders back through the main doors to wait outside.

In the far corner of the car park, a woman in a faux-fur jacket is trying to persuade a shivering Yorkshire terrier to toilet on the grass. A huge truck bearing the livery of a Spanish company is heading out of the lorry park. For a moment, Lorna is seriously tempted to run over and beg the driver to take her with him, drive her south to a new life in the sun.

But she'd miss Ed and the kids so much.

Wouldn't she?

Then she sees him, the man who broke her heart: Ryan Canfield, older, greyer, in so many details not how she remembers him at all. Yet undeniably he's evolved into something of a silver fox, still tall and looking good even in unfashionably cut jeans and a red wind-cheater. He spots her, and smiles the way she can't help but remember, a smile full of warmth and – she knows she's not mistaken – pleasure at seeing her. And despite her promise to herself to be cool, her heart betrays her with what her gran would have called a flutter, and she finds herself smiling back.

At least she manages to compose herself, and cuts the smile short.

Standing awkwardly a little distance apart at the busy entrance, neither of them knows what they should do next. Shake hands? Air-kiss, hug? In the end, Lorna shoves her hands deep in her overcoat pockets, determined to keep them there.

'Hello, stranger,' says Ryan, still smiling, and Lorna notices the new crinkles round his eyes, how well they suit him. 'How have you been?'

'I'm good,' she says, coolly. 'You?'

He gives a little laugh. 'Well, I'm good too. Apart from pretty much getting fired.'

Lorna feels her mouth wanting to open, and an almost irresistible urge to snap, *Well, you shouldn't have screwed up.*

But she's not the naïve girl he used to know, and revealing that her bitterness and anger towards him have never left her can only diminish her in his eyes. This time, she's holding all the cards; she's in the position of power.

'Shall we go inside?' he suggests. 'It's perishing out here.'

She pulls a face. 'My bad. It's bedlam in there, not really somewhere we can talk. I thought it would be quiet mid-afternoon.'

'No problem. I'll grab myself a coffee and we can sit in my car.'

'My car's just there,' she says, unable to resist the temptation to stay in control. She points to her white Range Rover, realising too late she's showing off.

'Nice,' he says, apparently impressed. 'Much better than my old wreck. OK, your car it is.' He points to her coffee. 'Can I get you anything else while I'm in there? Refill?'

'Not for me, thanks.'

Despite Lorna saying she wants nothing, Canfield brings glazed doughnuts from the Krispy Kreme concession. But as he climbs into the passenger seat, she feels more of that conscience-pricking guilt: this car is her and Ed's space, and she's committed an unnecessary betrayal by inviting her ex-lover to invade it. From this day forward, every time she gets in the car, she'll be able to picture Ryan sitting in that seat.

Oblivious, Canfield offers her the bag. 'I got the old-fashioned plain ones. Boring old me, eh?'

Lorna's instinct is to take nothing from him and decline, but with her empty stomach she finds the sugary scent of them hard to resist. Choosing one, she takes a big, satisfying bite.

Canfield takes the lid off his coffee, stirs in sugar and says,

'So, shall we call this meeting to order? There's only one item on the agenda. Tommy Henthorn.'

'No surprise there. But with respect, I don't see he's anything to do with either of us now. We both did our jobs. Our involvement is over, and if you'll forgive me for saying, your professional interest ended a long time ago.'

'That's taking a very detached view.'

'Isn't that the nature of the job? You win some, you lose some. Look, I get that it's hard to know you made a mistake, but it happens to us all. Forget about it, leave it in the past where it belongs, get on with your life.'

'I didn't think it was a mistake at the time, Lorna. I thought we got it right. The same as you do now – you think you've done the right thing and you can leave it at that. But just getting him out isn't the end of the matter. He's had ten years of his life taken away, he's probably got nothing to go back to, and because he's not on probation or of any further interest to the legal establishment he'll have been cut loose. Where is he now?'

Lorna shrugs. 'I've no idea.'

'No, you haven't, and apart from educated guesses neither has anyone else. You know how it works. When lifers are released under normal circumstances, they go to confirmed addresses, they have meetings with probation officers. The police know where they are, what they're up to. They're supported to find work, find a way back into the community – at least in principle they are – and where the state falls down, there are charities who'll step in, do their best to make sure ex-cons don't end up sleeping on the streets. Tommy doesn't have access to any of that. He's a free and apparently innocent man whose friends likely deserted him years ago. His mother's dead – he was allowed out very briefly to attend her funeral a couple of years after he was jailed. It's not much of a stretch to suggest her life was shortened by his incarceration and her belief her son had killed her grandson. That must have further fuelled his anger. Because I've no doubt he's a man brimming over with rage, despite all those anger-management sessions they'll have put him through inside to teach him to keep a lid on it. All that does in my opinion is let it fester, heat it up until it's glowing hot.'

'I feel like you're criticising me for getting him out. I'm sorry if your ego is damaged, Ryan, but I was just doing my job.'

He's finished one doughnut, and offers her the bag before helping himself to the last one, in a blokeish, don't-care-about-the-calories way she envies.

He takes a bite, swallows and says, 'I know you won't have considered that you doing your job might have consequences for me. Why should you?'

Lorna frowns. 'What consequences?'

'Come on. Switch off the dispassionate lawyer persona for a minute and put yourself in Tommy's shoes. You've been proven right after years of being called a liar and a murderer. You were telling the truth all along, but no one believed you. What would you do now? What might you have fantasised about non-stop for the last decade?'

'I dread to think.'

'Please, Lorna, don't play the fool. Payback. Don't you see that? The guy's likely to be bent on revenge. And who was in charge of putting him – wrongly, as it turned out – behind bars?'

'Ah.'

'Ah indeed. If Tommy doesn't comes looking for me, I'll be very surprised. He's off everyone's radar, no tag, no probation check-ins. And I don't suppose it'll take him long to find out where I live.'

'I think you're being a bit over-dramatic.'

'Do you?' He puts the last of the doughnut in his mouth, scrunching up the paper bag along with his napkin as he chews, and she notices the gold wedding ring he used to wear is no longer there. 'There's something else, equally as important. If Tommy didn't kill Adam, who did?'

'Well, of course I've wondered about that, but again, I have to say, not my remit. Not yours either, I'm sure. I doubt they'll let you anywhere near the case again. Will they?'

'In case you haven't read it in the press, I've been suspended.'

'I'm sorry.' Actually, she finds she is. Revenge isn't tasting as good as she thought it would.

'That's how it goes. Though I was granted a concession on the quiet before I handed over my warrant card. The thing is, whatever you think of me, my motivation for investigating any crime is to get the bastard that did it. And in a child murder, that's doubly important. Now we have a black hole where Adam's killer used to be. Think how that is for his mum and dad, for Gail and Tommy. A murder like that wrecks lives, and now they're going to get wrecked all over again, because they're left knowing that whoever killed their son is still free.'

'There'll be a new investigation.'

'In due course, yes. When Adam's turn comes up on the Cold Case list – and that could be a dozen years from now, possibly longer – they'll assign a specialist team for six months to see if they can dredge up anything new from the evidence that's been mouldering in some basement. Witnesses will have to be tracked down. Some will have died. With every day that goes by, the chances of getting justice for Adam become fainter and fainter.'

Lorna looks away from him, towards the windows of the main building, where Easter has already made its premature entrance. Pastel-coloured eggs and a huge, long-eared bunny: Dottie's old enough this year to enjoy all the playgroup activities, and Max will love all the fuss and excitement, even if he doesn't understand what it's all about. What would she do if she lost either of them? How hard must these seasonal events be for those who've lost a child? For the first time, she wonders what freedom will mean for Tommy. How could she not have considered it before? Has she become a total ice queen?

'Why are we talking about this, Ryan? Since you're on suspension and you won't be involved?'

'But I am involved, I'll always be involved.' He taps his head with his forefinger. 'It's all still up here. The deputy chief constable gave me access to the files before they ran me out of the building. Highly irregular, but I had half a day for the fastest-ever case refresher, so I took a few photos on my phone when no one was looking. Don't for God's sake tell anyone. The point is, the decision to charge Tommy was made on the evidence available at the time, and on witness statements people made. The DCC said you got him released on new evidence. If you'll tell me what that was, what changed and what got corrected, I believe I can put the case back together, make sure the right offender gets charged and put away.'

'You're very confident.'

Canfield shakes his head. 'No, I'm absolutely not. I just want a chance to put right what I got so wrong. To help Gail and Tommy.'

'You're asking me to share confidential case notes.'

'Yes.'

'I can't do that.'

'Because it's against the rules.'

'Yes.'

'Sometimes the right thing is to bend the rules,' says Canfield. 'This should be about justice, not protocol. If you'll help me, I promise no one will ever know.'

'So how will you introduce new evidence, if you can't know what it is?'

'I'll work it backwards. You tell me what you know, I'll go out into the world knowing what to look for. Please.'

Lorna shakes her head, uncertain. 'I don't know. I'll be compromised.'

'No one will know.'

'I'll know.'

'You'll know you helped put the right guy away, as well as getting the wrong guy out. Two gold stars.'

'Are you making fun of me?'

'Not remotely. I'm begging you to help me do the right thing this time.'

'I'll have to think about it.'

A silence falls between them. 'Well.' Canfield looks down at his lap. 'Am I allowed to ask how you're doing? If you're happy?'

Somewhere deep inside, she's touched that he wants to know, but ice queen Lorna gives a conventional glib answer.

'Great. Married.' She holds up her hand so he can see her rings.

'Congratulations. Kids?'

She smiles. 'Two, a boy and a girl, two and four.'

'Ah, that's great. Those are lovely ages. But a lot of work.'

'Mostly not down to me. Ed's a stay-at-home dad.'

Canfield nods thoughtfully, and Lorna has the sense there's more he'd like to ask, if he dared. But she doesn't want to be questioned, and so she heads him off. 'You? I see the ring is gone.'

He holds up his own hand in confirmation. 'We divorced a while ago now, eight, nine years. The cracks were already showing when you and I . . . Back then. The kids were upset at the time, but they're over it now. At least I think they are. They're growing up, starting to show some independence. You spend all that time worrying yourself sick over them, and then it turns out they can just about look after themselves, after all.'

'I hope so.'

'Can I say something?'

She senses danger, a change in mood. 'Depends what it is.'

'You look fabulous.' Something between satisfaction and elation makes her blush. She should be mad at him for taking such a liberty, and yet she finds she's not. 'And now I should go.'

'Thanks for the doughnut.'

'Ring me. Please. I really need your help.'

'I promise I'll give it some thought.'

FORTY-EIGHT

Without his dogs, Tommy's walks are not the same. Before, his eyes were always on them as they trotted along, keen and alert. Solitary walking gives him headspace, time to think.

He's reluctant to go through Raymond's Wood. Part of him is disturbed by the place, thinking how he found Adam there, and occasionally he's even troubled by the morbid fear that the boy might in some awful form still linger, lost and wandering, crying to him for help. Only sometimes, when the sun is bright, does he think that maybe one day soon he'll go and see if there's anything of Adam at Druid's Well. Maybe when the bluebells are in bloom, he might hear his laughter, or a voice calling to him to follow as he used to do: *Come on, Daddy, catch me! Faster, faster!*

But today is overcast, shadowless and at the same time all in shade. He walks up the road with purpose, but doesn't go as far as the path into the wood. Instead, he stops a few metres short of his old home, and stands at the roadside, considering. A car goes by, a woman he knows at the wheel, who for certain knows him; before he was taken away, she was secretary to the parish council, and may still be so for all he knows. He raises his hand, but he might as well be invisible. She drives past pretending she hasn't seen him, eyes fixed straight ahead.

The woman's attitude gives him no reason to expect an enthusiastic welcome where he's going. Nothing ventured, though, nothing gained.

The gate of the house next door to Blacksmith's Cottage squeals on its hinges as he closes it behind him. Walking up the path to the front door, he recalls a day many years ago – how old would he have been, four or five? – when his mother brought him here to visit, and he remembers too his excitement as he gripped his mother's hand, because she had told him they would see some kittens. Sure enough, there they were, soft and precious, tucked up in a wicker basket in front of the living-room fire, guarded by a tabby cat called Lily. And when Tommy knelt awestruck by the basket and asked his mother if they could have one, she had said yes, and allowed him to pick one out, and the choice was next to impossible. But in the end he chose the only black one in the litter, and what seemed like months later – time passed slower in those days – they came to take the kitten home. That was Gatsby, a cat with guts and character, a champion mouser and fearless fighter. He lived to be fifteen. Even so, he was long dead now.

He knocks at the door, and it opens with such speed he knows she must have seen him coming up the path.

'Hello, Barbara,' he says.

Barbara Derwent has aged, of course, but she's still sprightly. Skinny though she is, she hugs him tight enough for him to feel her clavicle and ribs, so hard he's afraid at her age, something might break. Then she stands back and holds him at arms' length.

'It does my heart good to see you, boy,' she says. 'Truly it does. Come in, for heaven's sake. Come in.'

Inside, the house is the same but different in that disorientating way Tommy's finding almost everywhere: new wallpaper, new three-piece suite, same pictures on the walls. And the cat rubbing round his legs is different. He bends down to pet her.

'Who's this?'

'That's Elsa,' says Barbara, switching on the kettle. 'My granddaughter chose the name. It's from that film they're all mad about, what do they call it, *Frozen*?'

'I don't know anything about that.'

'You've not missed much there. Sit yourself down. I've been wondering when you'd be coming to see me. I'd made up my mind if you didn't come soon I'd come to you, but here you are. I'm not going to lie to you, you don't look well, too thin and since when have you been so pale? I hope you're getting yourself out in the fresh air? And are you getting enough to eat? You can always come to me for your dinner – you know you'd be welcome. It's as easy to cook for two as it is for one.'

Under her caring and concern, a lump forms in Tommy's throat. If he could let himself cry, Barbara would understand.

Instead, he says, 'I'm all right. But thanks.'

'Well, the offer stands. Any time you want a hot meal and a bit of company, you come to me. Least I can do, for your sake and your mum's. Do you want sugar in your tea?'

'Two, please.'

'And you've come on the right day. I was baking yesterday.

Even though Eric's been gone five years now, old habits die hard. I still bake once a week. I made shortbread, and there's flapjack.' She places a tin covered in a picture of deer foraging on a snowy hillside on the table, and a plate in front of him, and the buttery sweetness coming off the tin's contents makes him want to cry again. Simple tastes of home. 'Eat plenty, Tommy. Otherwise there's only me and it'll all go for the birds.'

Gratefully, Tommy helps himself to a piece of flapjack and takes a bite.

'Reminds me of school days, this does,' he says. 'Mum used to make flapjack for me and Dawn so it'd be ready when we came in from the bus. To fill us up, she said it was, so we wouldn't be mithering her about when tea would be ready.'

Barbara brings their cups, and sits herself down with a square of shortbread.

Tommy sips his tea. 'That's so good. You don't get a cuppa like that anywhere else.'

Barbara smiles. 'Pure Risedale water straight off the hillside, that's the secret ingredient. No other place has that. Now you're here, I don't know where to start. I want to know everything and yet I don't. Was it really bad in there?'

'Sometimes.'

'But mostly did they treat you all right?'

'Mostly. I made some good mates, actually. Some of them I was sad to leave behind.'

'And I dare say they're not treating you so well in this village, are they?'

Tommy shrugs. 'Not especially, no. I suppose I can't blame them. If I didn't kill Adam, who did? Until they've got someone else for it, they're always going to believe it was me.'

'Course they are. More fool them.'

She motions him to try the shortbread, and he obliges.

'And Gail?' He has to ask; he can't resist it. 'How's she doing?'

Barbara gives a short laugh. 'Not as good as you, by a long chalk. She started drinking the day Adam died and she's never stopped since, as far as I can tell.'

'She liked a drink before then,' says Tommy. 'A nightmare she was, when she'd had a couple of glasses.'

'Well, it's been the ruin of her. I tell you, you could meet her in the street and I doubt you'd know her. She had another child, not long after you went away. A little girl. Sabrina, they call her, but Gail in her state wasn't up to the care of her, poor lass. Last I heard social services were getting involved, worried about her not showing up for school. I haven't seen her for a while now. Maybe she's in foster care, who knows?'

'Who was the father?' asks Tommy. 'Because it damn sure wasn't me.'

'I suppose it was that fancy man she had prowling round before Adam died.'

'I always knew there was someone. Who was he?'

'A very dark horse, a very dark horse indeed. I never got plain sight of him, just a glimpse through the hedge sometimes as he was coming or going. You never saw them in public together, and I certainly never had the feeling she was lining him up to be husband number two or anything, or if she was, he wasn't having any of it. Made me wonder if he might already be married. Then one day it occurred to me I hadn't heard or seen anything of him for a while, and he was gone.'

'Did the police know about him?'

'Yes, because I told them about him myself, when they came round asking questions, and they said they'd look into it. So I suppose they ruled him out. Which leaves of course only the one possible, doesn't it?'

'Are we thinking of the same person?'

'Probably.'

'Simon Rains?'

Barbara gives a confirmatory nod. 'Sure as eggs are eggs. That boy wasn't right in the head, not from the first day they came here. Always hanging about in those woods, he was. He had every opportunity to grab Adam and whisk him away. He was young and strong, so he could easily have done it. He should be right at the top of their list, now. And they won't have far to go to find him.'

'What do you mean?'

'They got him for something else, not two years later. He interfered with a young girl in some park somewhere, lured her into the bushes and did God knows what to her. His mum and dad – Peter, they called him, and she was Tessa. You probably remember?'

'I remember.'

'Well, they would have done anything to protect that boy. Even when it was plain as the nose on your face he was guilty, they worked night and day to get him proven not fit to stand trial – in other words, he was ruled a nutcase – and he got sent to some special hospital – Northumberland, I think – where as far as I know he is to this day.'

'You mean he's locked up?'

'I hope so. If he isn't, he should be.'

'And what about the family, his mum and dad?'

'They were on the move again pretty soon after, as you can imagine. No choice, really, and actually I felt rather sorry for them, actually. They hadn't been here five minutes before Adam was taken from us. After Simon was put away, the shame must have damn near killed them. What else could they do but up sticks and move on?'

'Where did they go?'

Barbara frowns as she thinks. 'Where did they go? Brierley? Abbersworth? Yes, it was Abbersworth, just over the border into Cheshire. They bought a property next to the pub which used to belong to a friend of my father's, years ago. We visited sometimes as children. She wasn't looking forward to going, starting over again, poor woman. Simon put years on her, on both of them, in fact.'

'And they're still there, are they?'

'I've no idea. This was seven or eight years ago, after all. But never mind them, it's Simon they should be going after. I never understood why they looked at you over him anyway.'

Silence. The cat sits by Tommy's feet and begins to wash her back legs.

'Can I ask you a question?' Tommy asks eventually.

'Of course you can.'

'But I want you to be honest. I have to know. Did Mum think I was guilty?'

Barbara drains her cup. 'Well, you deserve an honest answer, and I'll give you one. Sometimes she believed it, and then she used to get upset, wondering how you'd gone so wrong. But mostly she was bemused. She was as sure as I always was you couldn't have done it. She knew how you loved that child. Dawn was the same. We all loved Adam, didn't we? He was a ray of light in all our lives, God rest him. And then your mum used to say, "He never harmed him, not my Tommy. He never could have done such a wicked, wicked thing."'

Now Tommy's properly ready to cry. Barbara presents him with a box of tissues, then pretends not to see.

'I never got to say goodbye,' he says. 'How could she ever forgive me for that?'

Barbara leans across to squeeze his hand. 'Do you think she didn't know you'd have been there if you could? Wild horses wouldn't have kept you away if you were a free man – she knew that. There's nothing to forgive you for, boy. Others, though, are a very different story.'

FORTY-NINE

'Penny for them?'

Lorna is staring out of the kitchen window, watching the dimpled patterns of raindrops in the puddles on the terrace. Aware that Ed has spoken, she finds a smile and turns round.

'Miles away, sorry.'

'I said, penny for them. As in, what's on your mind?'

Lorna shakes her head. 'Nothing, really.'

'So relax.'

The house, for once, is quiet, a Sunday morning with nowhere special to go and nothing particular to do. Ed's mum and dad have bravely volunteered to have the children overnight, so Ed and Lorna can have what Ed's mother calls married people's time. And they spent a pleasant evening with close-by friends: adult chat and drinks, a whole different vibe to bath-time and bedtime stories. More and more, Lorna finds herself craving times like that. But before long the in-laws and the kids will be here for Sunday lunch. Lorna daren't even acknowledge to herself that she's dreading it.

Ed comes up behind her and puts his arms round her waist.

'I know there's something on your mind. Why won't you talk to me? You used to tell me everything. Are you afraid us house-husbands aren't capable of complex thought?'

'Never that.' She turns to face him. 'Are you sure you want to know? Even if it involves work?'

He gives a sigh. 'You could just forget it for today. Just be my wife.'

'It isn't that easy, though, is it?'

'All right, let's hear it.'

'I had a couple of messages about the Tommy Henthorn case.' So far, so true. 'One of the detectives who worked on the original case wanted to talk to me about it.' Also true.

'What does he want, exactly?'

That's a question Lorna is only prepared to answer in part. 'He wants to know what the new information was that got Henthorn released.'

'So why did he ask you for it? Can't he get it through the proper channels?'

'There's a difficulty. He's not supposed to be involved in the case any more. He's been suspended.'

'So why is he asking for information?'

'I told him I can't help him. But he makes some valid points. I thought we'd scored a great victory in setting Tommy free, but actually we've opened up a whole new can of worms. Because we've got justice for Tommy in one way, but now no one knows who killed his son. In fact, it's taken the case right back to square one, needing a fresh investigation, but that may not happen for years. According to this guy.'

'Years? Why not?'

'Because it's a cold case, and cold-case reviews are rare things. Adam will have to wait his turn. Also, Tommy's situation is actually worse than it was before. He's been liberated into a world where many will still believe him guilty. Chances are he'll live his life as a pariah – until whoever actually killed Adam has been found. Because if Tommy didn't kill Adam, who did?'

'Not your problem.'

'Maybe not. But this guy wants to make it *his* problem, on the quiet. He's got a real interest because he knows he got it wrong the first time, and a huge incentive to get it right this time. If he doesn't do it, who else will?'

'Again, not your problem.'

'But I feel like it is. If I give this guy what he's asking for, it might be the key to catching the actual killer.'

'That's a bit of a leap, isn't it?'

'I just think morally I should help him.'

'Legally you can't.'

'But when does morally trump legally?'

'That's a question people have been asking for millennia.'

'I think I should give him some pointers, give him something to run with, at least. But if I get found out, I could be disciplined, even struck off for breach of confidentiality. Even though I would be acting for the best.'

'Whose best, Lorna?'

Good question.

'I feel like I want to help him.'

'OK, well, help him. Only not today. Today, please be here with me. Be here at home with your family.'

She gives him a smile, hiding a treacherous secret.

Now Ed's given her the green light, what she won't be telling him is that she intends to deliver the information in person.

Because though she hates to admit it even to herself, she has a strengthening urge to see Ryan Canfield again.

FIFTY

The village of Abbersworth is high up on the windy moorlands, popular in summer with hikers on the more challenging pathways that criss-cross that area of the Peak District.

Tommy came here once with Gail, before Adam was even thought of. He brought her on the motorbike he had back then, a temperamental BMW. Gail didn't like motorbikes, though she'd never admit it. She liked the image of wild freedom, but she hated wearing a helmet because it messed up her hair. And she was afraid. She never said so – she was too much of a bullshitter for that – but Tommy knew it from the way her arms tensed round his waist every time they leaned over for a sharp bend. He loved her enough back then to take pity on her, and traded the bike for more stable four-wheeled transport not long afterwards.

Today, the village appears all but deserted: a few houses and cottages arranged around what was once the market square; a post office and a pub; a primary school and a recreation ground. Tommy isn't trying to hide and he doesn't care who sees him, so he parks in an empty space near the school.

According to Barbara, the house he's looking for is next

to the pub. Could be the cottage on the left, or the more substantial place to the right. Based on what he knows of the people he's looking for, he'll try the larger house first.

A lion's-head knocker on the front door strikes him as a nice period detail, but he doesn't recognise the device screwed to the doorframe: a Ring doorbell.

He raps at the door, and waits.

Someone is there, behind the door; he's sure of it. He raps again.

'Are you there, Rains?' he shouts. 'Open the door, then we won't have a scene in front of your neighbours.'

A key turns in the cast-iron lock, and a bolt is drawn.

The door opens. Peter Rains is standing there, Tessa hovering nervously behind him.

'Hello, Tommy,' says Peter.

Tommy punches him hard in the face.

Peter staggers back, holding his nose. When he checks his hand, it's full of blood, and Tessa begins to scream.

Tommy steps calmly across the threshold, closing the door behind him.

'What do you think to that, you prick?' His face is red with rage. 'You lying piece of shit.'

'Tommy, leave him!' begs Tessa. 'Please, leave him alone.'

'Leave him alone? I haven't even started.'

'The doorbell's recorded your being here,' says Tessa, desperately.

Tommy's eyebrows raise. 'What doorbell?'

'The doorbell's connected to the internet. It records everyone who comes to the door.'

Tommy smiles. 'Does it? Clever idea.' He opens the door,

looks briefly at the doorbell, studies how it's attached and sees it's with Velcro. He pulls it from the door, studies it again, takes the back off it and removes the batteries, slipping both gadget and batteries into his pocket. 'Not very secure, is it?'

'I'll call the police,' threatens Tessa, looking round for both a phone and an object she can use as a weapon.

Peter raises his bloodied hand. 'Wait a minute, Tess. Please, Tommy. I don't care what you do – I deserve it, God knows. But before you hit me again, just listen. We might have information that'll help you put Adam's real killer away.'

'You would say that, wouldn't you, you lying bastard. Why should I listen to anything you say?' But Tommy's hungry for information, thirsting for justice, and a part of him wants to hear what Rains is offering. If it turns out to be nothing of value, he can always beat him to a pulp later.

'Let him speak, Tommy,' pleads Tessa. 'Just hear him out.'

'All right, I'll give you two minutes. You tell me what you know, and I'll decide if it's worth hearing.'

'I know you think it was Simon who hurt Adam,' begins Peter. 'In all honesty, we thought it was possible too. Sometimes he strays across boundaries, he struggles to tell right from wrong. That's why we said what we did. We were only trying to protect our son. Wouldn't you have done the same?'

'Not if it cost someone else's freedom,' says Tommy, fiercely. 'Jesus. What kind of people are you?'

'At the time we were desperate,' Peter goes on. 'A policeman came and said Simon was a suspect, but that they were looking at you, too. He made us think there was a real danger Simon would be arrested. But Simon was like a child. How would he have coped with being locked up? We honestly thought we were only adding fuel to a fire that was already lit under you, underlining their suspicions. I said I'd seen you in the village that afternoon, but I didn't know my evidence would be so crucial. I thought they'd have more to go on, eventually. I only said it to take the heat off Simon. When they'd got their other evidence, I was going to withdraw my statement, say I'd made a mistake.'

'And yet you never did. Why not?'

Peter hangs his head. 'Because I was a coward. What I'd done was perjury. I could have gone to jail for it myself, and I was afraid. I'm truly sorry, Tommy. You have to believe that.'

'Not sorry enough to speak up and get me out of there.'

'We talked about it,' says Tessa. 'When we found out there was no chance . . .'

Peter turns sharply round to stop Tessa saying more.

'What?' demands Tommy. 'What were you going to say?'

Peter shakes his head. 'Go on, you might as well tell him.'

Tommy recognises the look in Tessa's eyes, the emptiness of loss. 'Everything we did was for nothing. Simon was arrested a couple of years after you went inside for an assault on a young girl. There was nothing we could do to help him that time. He was guilty and that was that. Of course, that made us think we'd made a terrible mistake protecting him in Adam's case, and we became pretty certain he was guilty of that too. So we discussed with the lawyer representing him what it would mean for Simon if he asked for Adam's case to be taken into consideration.'

'Don't tell me your consciences were pricking,' says Tommy.

'Believe me, they were,' says Peter. 'But the lawyer came back to us after he'd made some enquiries and told us we could put our minds at rest in regard to Adam. The police ruled Simon out before your trial took place. There was nothing found anywhere to match his DNA.'

Tommy appears stunned. 'You're saying Simon couldn't have killed my son.'

'He couldn't have, Tommy,' says Tessa, earnestly. 'One hundred per cent not. There's no way he was involved.'

'So then,' continues Peter, 'we thought you must have been guilty and the police had got it right after all. We breathed a huge sigh of relief thinking we were off the hook and got on with our lives.'

'It hasn't been much of a life with Simon locked up,' says Tessa, sadly.

'Wait a minute,' says Tommy. 'If Simon didn't kill Adam and I most certainly didn't, who does that leave?'

'That's what we want to tell you,' says Peter. 'What we did was wrong. So if we can do anything to help you get answers, we will.'

'And how would you do that, exactly?' asks Tommy.

'Maybe we have a lead for you,' says Tessa, 'though you need to be careful how you use it.'

'Go on.'

'I hope it isn't news to you,' says Peter. 'But Gail had a boyfriend after you and she split up.'

'I knew that.' Tommy dismisses Peter with his hand. 'The world and his wife knew that.'

'He was careful not to be seen though,' Peter goes on. 'I always thought it must be because it was someone we knew, you know, someone from the village, though we couldn't think who it might be.'

'We thought it must be someone married,' puts in Tessa, 'to be so secretive.'

'After you were . . . gone, only a month or two later, Tessa saw his face. It was late afternoon, falling dusk, and she was driving down the lane. He was coming out of your old driveway, and in the headlights she got a really clear view of him.'

'I was really, truly shocked,' says Tessa. 'But I knew him. And there's no doubt whatever in my mind who it was.'

FIFTY-ONE

'I'm glad you got in touch.' Canfield is sitting opposite Lorna in a country pub, holding himself back from saying how beautiful she looks, how he likes her hair longer, trying not to remember the way it used to feel. There isn't room for any of that in their relationship this time around, and anyway, this isn't a relationship. This is all business, all about cleaning up the mess he's made on his side. If he can go back to Lomas with a quick result – a really quick result, as the days are slipping by – there's a chance he might get to keep his job long-term. A slender chance, admittedly, but if he goes back with nothing, he's no chance at all. 'To be honest, I didn't think I'd hear from you again.'

Lorna's got a white wine and soda in front of her she hasn't yet touched, and Canfield wonders if she's regretting her choice, if she wishes she'd opted for something non-alcoholic as he did, out of long-term habit regarding lunchtime drinking.

She seems surprised. 'Really? Do you think I'd be that petty, to spoil the chance of finding a new suspect in the case because of my history with you?'

He shakes his head. 'No, of course I know you wouldn't do that. I'm sorry. I just meant—'

'I know what you meant. Don't worry, we're on the same team. For the time being at least.'

He decides to change the subject. 'What are you going to eat?'

'Just a sandwich, the chicken pesto, I think. You?'

'Same, but the roast beef. Let me go and order, and then we can talk.'

While he's at the bar, Lorna takes out her phone. No messages. She has a sudden feeling of being somehow adrift, cut loose from her usual safe harbour, and wants to call Ed, ask after the children, ask him to put them on video so she can see their cheery faces, hear their prattle. The urge to connect with them all is strong, as if their connection is somehow threatened.

She glances over to the bar where Canfield's taking out his wallet, passing a card over the contactless machine. He's still an attractive man. The danger she senses is real.

She takes a large gulp of her drink.

'So.' He sits back down. 'We agree, I assume, that this is all off the record. What happens in the White Swan, stays in the White Swan.'

'Agreed.'

'What I don't have access to is the new information that got Tommy released, the info which wrecked our original case.'

Now the moment's here, she hesitates. 'Between us, right?'

'Absolutely.'

'Someone gave him an alibi.'

Not at all what Canfield expected. 'An alibi? But Tommy

never claimed any alibi. He was always straight up that he didn't have one.'

'Well, he did.'

'So? Don't keep me in suspense.'

But Lorna isn't quick to tell what she knows. 'I can trust you, can't I, Ryan? Because without wanting to go over old ground, your track record on honesty with me isn't good.'

He lets out a sigh, and hangs his head. 'I've no right to ask you to trust me, I know. But you can. I'm not the man I was . . . back then. A lot of water's flowed under the bridge. And if you want a better reason, Deputy Chief Constable Lomas will have me publicly flogged if anyone finds out I've been talking to you. I'm not supposed to be anywhere near this case. So I'm hardly likely to be sharing this conversation, am I?'

'OK.' She takes a drink. 'There was a guy in Morton Hall prison.'

'Over Lincoln way.'

'Yes. He was coming to the end of a long sentence, but in an unfortunate twist of fate, just when he was about to get his life back, he was diagnosed with terminal cancer, weeks to live. On the point of meeting his maker, he presumably wanted to try and clear his slate, because he decided to share a few things he'd heard during his time inside, which probably helped your lot's detection rate massively. Anyway, Tommy's name came up. This guy swore Tommy couldn't have killed Adam, because he had an alibi. He was with this guy and a couple of others most of that day.'

Canfield's unconvinced. 'What made anyone think he was telling the truth? The statement of a career criminal, not exactly hard evidence, is it? He might have been a friend or even a relative of Tommy's, or even just someone who owed him a favour.'

'True enough,' says Lorna. 'But he named other names, other people who were there. And one of those people he named decided he was prepared to back him up. All self-interest, of course, to be taken into account when they were up for parole. But two witnesses swearing blind Tommy couldn't have been in Risedale when Adam went missing was something that deserved to be taken seriously.'

Their sandwiches arrive. As he's salting his chips and Lorna's taking a first hungry bite, Canfield asks, 'Where did they say they were?'

'Looking at real estate with a view to buying. Here, there and everywhere, driving round the Dales. It wasn't all good news for Tommy, of course. They weren't the kind of company he should have been keeping. But if they say he was with them, the evidence must be accepted. Tommy was in shock to begin with – to say the least – but in the end he agreed they were telling the truth, that he was with them that day.'

'So why in God's name didn't he say so at the time?'

'Well, best guess has to be that they were up to something nefarious, doesn't it? That he was involved in criminal activity, just not the criminal activity of which he was accused. From what I've read on the case, a decent chunk of the evidence against him was circumstantial. Maybe his brief told him he'd get off without having to mention he was keeping bad company.'

'But he still never said anything at his early appeal. Surely whatever he was up to, it can't have been worse than murder?'

'You're the detective.'

'Probably not for much longer.'

Lorna stops eating and looks at him. 'That would be a shame. You've done some great work, I know. Made the streets safer for my children.'

'And mine. There's always a bit of self-interest, as you say.'

'What will you do if they let you go?'

'Since I only know one job, probably get a licence to be a private investigator.'

'What, more of the same? Isn't there anything else you've always wanted to do? No big dreams prodding you to head off into the wild blue yonder?'

'Not really. Nothing I'd want to do on my own. How about you? What would you be doing if you weren't fighting the good fight for charity?'

Lorna shrugs. 'I don't know. It's not easy to go after your dreams with two small kids in tow.'

Canfield's expression is thoughtful. 'So here we both are, destined to be permanent workaholics.'

'Nothing lasts forever.'

They eat in awkward silence for a while, until Lorna's had enough and pushes her plate to one side. 'What will you do with what I told you?'

'That's a good question. If I still had a warrant card, my next step would be obvious – pay a visit to Tommy.'

'So why don't you do that?'

'Well, firstly, I don't expect him to be pleased to see me, so I'd better not be going without back-up. And secondly, see my above comment about Lomas. He'd probably call it interfering with a witness.'

'But that's not what you're doing, is it?'

'Not in my mind. In the eyes of the law, probably.'

'I still think you should go. Come on, where's the hungry-for-justice copper of yesteryear?'

'He's had the stuffing knocked out of him by protocol and political correctness. We do everything by the book, and the book's got a hell of a lot more pages in it than it used to have.'

'Come on, Ryan. If they're going to fire you, so what?'

'Not firing, hopefully, retiring.'

'You're way too young for that.'

'You know, you're right. But it still wouldn't be right for me to speak to Tommy. I might damage any future legal proceedings. Interfering with witnesses isn't a good look for the police.'

'I'll go for you, then.'

'What? Are you mad?'

'Why shouldn't I? He knows me. Knows of me, anyway. You give me a list of what you want to know, I'll get your answers. I can be pretty persuasive, you know.'

'I know you can.'

'Anyway, I'm interested to talk to him face to face. I don't very often get to talk to the people I help.'

'I'll think about it. Can I get you a coffee?'

Lorna shakes her head. 'I have to go.' Maybe the wine has let her guard down, because she adds, 'It's been good to see you.'

Canfield looks serious. 'You too.'

'Listen, I've got a present for you outside.'

Canfield's eyebrows raise.

'Don't get too excited.' Lorna smiles. 'It's a work-related present.'

FIFTY-TWO

That evening, Canfield makes himself a strong black coffee to keep his brain firing, and settles down in his spare-room office to study the papers Lorna has given him.

Their order is unhelpfully random, and he guesses Lorna has done no more than hurriedly grab anything accessible she thinks might be of value. Some are print-outs of emails between her and her colleagues and other legal professionals involved in the case: opinions and suggestions, references to the original case, including some mentioning him by name. Others are police forms; others still are official statements made at the time and – of real interest to him – in the past twelve months. Everywhere he looks, he sees names he recognises, members of his team as it was back then.

To make his job easier, he decides to begin by sorting what he's got into logical order, numbering each document and listing them in a notebook. When that's done, what remains is to read everything through and highlight anything of interest. Thorough and careful reading is going to be a daunting task, but his hope is to get it done in one evening. Working into the night when necessary has always

'Then I'll walk you to your car.'

Lorna picks up her coat, and as she moves to put it on, Canfield takes it from her and holds it up, resting his hands on her shoulders for a moment as she settles into it. He's standing close behind her, and she's afraid of what will happen if she turns round and they're face to face. To break the mood, she steps away, and pretends to be searching her handbag for her keys.

Outside in the car park, she opens the rear door of her car. On the back seat is a grey box file, which she picks up and hands to him.

'Wow, it's heavy,' he says. 'What's in here?'

'You didn't get them from me. I couldn't see how you were going to work from photos on your phone, so I pulled out some of the key documents from our case and had somebody copy them for you. But tell no one, OK? I'm putting all my trust in you.'

'I don't know what to say,' says Canfield. 'I don't deserve this.'

'No, you absolutely do not. Let me know what you find.'

'I will.'

She climbs into the driver's seat, pulls the door closed and winds down the window. 'Bye then, officer.'

'Bye. Thanks for coming.'

'My pleasure,' says Lorna, realising as she drives away that those words are true.

been part of his job. When he starts to flag, there's plenty more coffee in the kitchen.

One of his favourite mantras has always been *Start with what's difficult and proceed to what is easy*, but looking at the papers in front of him and thinking he would benefit from more space on the table, he decides he'll tackle the official forms first, since they are quick reading, and statements of essential facts. And they are few.

At his level of seniority, he's never normally concerned with data at this level in an investigation. Collecting these from their source – the call-centre database – and filing them electronically and in hard copy in the case files is a junior job, for a detective constable or even a trainee.

The first form he looks at is from the call centre, a 999 call dated several months before Adam's murder. It's a report of domestic abuse from Blacksmith's Cottage, Risedale, and a request for immediate assistance. There are two names on the report, Tommy and Gail Henthorn.

He's mildly surprised to see a name and signature he knows on the document's official date stamp, but thinks little of it.

The next document he looks at has the same sign-off when it was brought into the case files. That's logical, if they were retrieved at the same time. The rest of the information is similar to the previous form, though the date is different: another call for immediate service to Blacksmith's Cottage, Risedale, a domestic incident naming Tommy and Gail Henthorn.

These forms, as he remembers – or at least the knowledge that these forms existed – were accepted by him and his team as corroboration from local intelligence gathered door to door that, before they separated, Tommy was violent towards his wife. The call-outs were mentioned in the outline case presented to the CPS as evidence of Tommy's predisposition to violence and that he could be capable of killing, and were included as part of the package when the CPS ruled the prosecution was viable.

Yet as Canfield now recalls, this evidence wasn't mentioned in court, even though he seems to remember they had a witness from the village lined up to confirm that the police had visited Blacksmith's Cottage on more than one occasion.

Maybe the prosecution decided the evidence wasn't needed after all.

He's about to put the forms to one side when something strikes him about the first form, a detail his assumption-making brain has missed. Something's not right. Probably it's a clerical error: Tommy and Gail's names have been reversed.

No big deal. Mistakes get made.

Except that the second form is the same, with Tommy listed as the caller who asked for assistance.

Two similar errors on different dates seems improbable.

Canfield frowns. What was actually going on here?

The people to ask would be the local beat officers who attended those incidents. He can track them down easily enough. They'd be working out of Bakewell or Matlock. He remembers one of them quite well, a bloke recently transferred up from the Met, keen to get his young family away from London's high crime rates. The guy was very tall, which gave him a problem with the low doorways in the old rural cottages, so he was always complaining about banging his head. Phil someone.

Someone in the local nick will know.

And someone else who'll know is Tommy.

Maybe asking Lorna to speak to Tommy is a good idea after all.

He glances at his watch. It's getting late, but surely not too late to send a message?

Lorna and Ed are watching TV when Lorna's phone pings.

A text from Ryan.

When Ed asks who's messaging at this hour, for some reason she lies.

'Just the bank,' she says. 'We've gone into overdraft on the current account. I'll sort it out in the morning.'

She drops her phone back on the sofa, deciding she'd prefer to read and reply to the message when she's alone.

FIFTY-THREE

Of course, it's a coincidence Canfield has chosen a time to visit Bakewell's Community Policing team when Lorna will most likely be in the area.

At least that's what he tells himself.

There's also the fact that he knows the schedules on which the county's few remaining outlying stations operate. Between 8.30am and 9am, he's got the best chance of finding a beat officer like Phil Dewar in person, in the office, preparing to head out for the day.

The town centre is quiet, and Canfield finds a convenient parking spot outside the Co-op. Overnight rain has pooled in puddles on the pitted tarmac. A straggler schoolboy, tie askew, dodges between the slow-moving traffic to jump aboard the bus he's almost missed, his friends laughing and jeering at him from the windows of the upper deck. On the roof ridge of the nearby branch of the NatWest bank – a splendidly ornate example of late-Victorian architecture, whose doors recently closed to the bank's customers for the last time – a row of moth-grey pigeons huddle together against a chill breeze.

The police station is also quaintly Victorian, and could take a role in a period drama – except for the way it's been fortified against the British public, with windows barred and all doors but one bricked up and sealed. Outside, a notice board announces the hours of opening: Monday to Friday 9–5, Saturday 9–2. Outside these hours, those in need of urgent assistance are instructed to call 999, though no phone is provided for them to do so. In Canfield's eyes, modern policing has in some regards completely lost its way. Maybe it will be a blessing if his time is up.

He presses the buzzer at the door, and waits what he regards as too long for an answer, sensing himself being scanned by the eye of an unseen camera before the door clicks and he pushes it open.

Inside, a man in a crisp white shirt and perfectly knotted uniform tie sits behind a Plexiglass screen. He looks sternly at Canfield, then grins and stands up.

'All right, Ryan?' he asks, approaching the screen. 'Good to see you, mate. What brings you out our way?'

Canfield is smiling back. Geoff Toft was station sergeant at one of his earliest postings, when he was first in uniform. Toft was firm but fair, a guiding hand through sometimes overwhelming protocols and procedures.

'All right, Geoff? Can't believe you're still around. I thought you'd have had the sense to pack it in and take your pension years ago.'

'Cheeky sod. I'm not that old, you know. Though I am here past my sell-by date. The money comes in handy, doesn't it? You're still with us too, then?'

'Hanging on by my fingernails.'

Toft nods sagely. 'I saw that. Talk of the town round here, of course. I can't believe they let him out.'

'That's why I'm here, actually,' says Canfield. 'Sort of on my own initiative, if you know what I mean. I'm looking for Phil Dewar, if he's still based here.'

'Oh aye, he's still here, is Phil. If you're quick, you'll just catch him. He's in the lunchroom making coffee. Just to the left at the end of the corridor. I'll buzz you through.'

The lunchroom is a poky space that barely accommodates a kitchenette with the basic services of a sink, a fridge and a microwave. The stripes of iron bars spoil a nice view of the river from the window, and Canfield thinks not for the first time that something's gone horribly wrong when the authorities – though such paternalistic vocabulary is not allowed these days – are barricaded in against those they're supposed to be protecting.

Because of his height, Phil Dewar manages to make the room appear even smaller than it is. He's balder than Canfield recalls, but otherwise much the same, seated at a table with his uniform jacket slung round the back of his chair, a half-drunk coffee and a sausage roll in front of him, scrolling on his phone. He glances round at Canfield, then turns properly, ready to get up, unnerved by a stranger in this space, but Canfield puts him at ease by holding out his hand.

'Remember me, Phil? DCI Ryan Canfield, from Derby. We met during the Tommy Henthorn case.'

Dewar nods, and shakes Canfield's hand. 'I remember. How's things?'

Canfield raises his eyebrows. 'Honestly? Not great.'

'Win some, lose some,' says Dewar. 'Want a coffee?'

'Black and one, thanks.'

Dewar gets up to fill the kettle while Canfield takes a seat at the table. 'Actually, Phil, it's you I've come to see. An off-the-record chat, if you've got a couple of minutes. Management don't want me involved in the Henthorn case after what's happened, but I've got a two-week under-the-radar pass to see if I can work some kind of miracle. Which is getting less and less likely, given that most of my allotted time has already passed.'

Dewar's spooning Nescafé into a mug. 'Good luck with that.'

'I know. But I've been having a go-through of some of the old call logs, and I've come across something of an anomaly.'

The kettle's boiled. Dewar pours water, adds sugar to the mug, places it on the table in front of Canfield and sits back down before he says, 'What kind of anomaly?'

'Just a small thing that doesn't quite add up.'

Dewar takes a large bite of his sausage roll and chews, waiting.

'Back before Adam's death, there were a couple of call-outs to the Henthorn house. Probably logs, judging by the domestics. No charges pressed. There were two, quite close together. Do you remember those?'

Dewar appears to be thinking. 'I remember one. I attended with – who the hell was it? Must have been Sandra.'

'Can you remember what had happened?'

Dewar shrugs. 'Henthorn's missus had belted him a right one across the face. She hadn't broken his nose, but still there'd been plenty of blood. Then she'd gone after him with a bag of potatoes of all things, whacking him about the head, all across his back. And she'd done him some damage. There were plenty of bruises. At the time I felt quite sorry for the bloke, actually.'

Canfield is conscious of a strange ringing in his ears, a reaction to the about-to-drop bombshell that he really did screw up. 'Wait a minute. *She* assaulted *him*?'

'Yep.'

'So who made the call? Who fetched you out?'

Dewar shrugs. 'Well, I don't know, but I assume he did. What does it say in the logs?'

'It says exactly that,' admits Canfield, reluctantly.

Dewar shrugs again. 'There you go, then.'

'But part of the case against Tommy was built on those incidents of domestic violence,' says Canfield. 'That he had form. Are you saying he didn't?'

'I'm not saying that, no. I'm saying in the incident I attended, it was vice versa – she'd had a pop at him. Maybe that's how it was just on that one occasion.' Dewar takes a slug of coffee. 'But actually I don't think so, because now I think of it, I spoke to Sandra after she went there the second time, and she said the same thing had happened, or pretty similar. The second time, his missus had actually broken his nose.'

'Jesus.'

'Isn't all this in your case files? Presumably someone looked into it at the time?'

But Canfield has a horrible feeling no one did. Is it possible they all fell into the trap of making assumptions, that Tommy as the male in the relationship must be the aggressor?

Maybe he should speak to Emma about it. She's still at Kenton Road.

Then a thought strikes him. Thinking aloud, he says, 'But why wouldn't Tommy have spoken up? When we were saying he was prone to violence, he never said a word to defend himself.'

'Embarrassed,' says Dewar, as if it were totally obvious. 'You see that a lot. Female on male domestics, much more common than you think these days, but the blokes don't want to admit it. Not very manly, is it, getting beaten black and blue by the wife? They're worried what their mates will say. If you ask me, there should be a government campaign, encourage blokes to speak out.'

Canfield recalls again that ultimately, the call-outs were omitted from the proceedings, suggesting Tommy asked his defence team not to use them. 'But it might have changed the jury's whole view of him if he'd let the truth come out in court. Surely he'd have risked being embarrassed to save himself fifteen years inside?'

'You'd have thought so, wouldn't you?' Dewar drains his mug. 'I'd have taken any amount of ribbing from my mates if that was the alternative. He must have had other reasons for keeping quiet, maybe nothing to do with the fact his missus was prone to violence.'

'Other reasons like what?'

'No offence,' says Dewar, 'but you're the detective, last I heard.'

'What about the little boy, Adam?' asks Canfield. 'Did you see him while you were there?'

'Never saw him, no,' says Dewar. 'Not until they found him in that wood.' A look comes across his face, a distressing memory quickly pushed away. 'It was a bad business, that.'

'It's still a bad business,' says Canfield, grimly. 'Thanks for your help, Phil. Do me a favour, will you? Don't tell anyone I was here.'

Back in his car, Canfield sits a few minutes, thinking over what Phil Dewar's said. He can't help but feel a total idiot. The incidents should have been treated as what they were, not what the investigating team – with their prejudices – had assumed them to be.

But who in the team had actually seen the call-out sheets? He hadn't, because logging in paperwork was well below his pay grade. Someone had told him about them though, and told him they'd been appropriately filed.

And Canfield remembers exactly who that was.

FIFTY-FOUR

Lorna's made a weak excuse to Ed as to why she's going to work in jeans and trainers, telling him the office is having a dress-down Friday. She feels bad lying, but not half as bad as she does when at the end of the road, she turns left instead of going right, her normal way to the office. Why hasn't she told him the truth? She isn't doing anything wrong.

Except she knows she is. She's spending way too much time thinking about Ryan Canfield.

A woman as smart as she is would surely cut any further ties with him, tell him to do his own legwork. But apart from anything else, this is something out of the ordinary, a break from the norm, and she's surprised how energised she feels playing truant for once, being someone different from conscientious, one hundred per cent reliable Lorna. Maybe that's what Ryan's bringing out in her, a long-quashed need for rebellion.

If only the nagging worry would leave her alone: the guilt of deceiving her husband.

She's driven through Risedale before on the way to other places, but never stopped in the village. She parks close to the pub as Canfield suggested, and follows his instructions, walking up the steep main street, heading for Field Cottage where Canfield believes Tommy is probably staying.

The cottage is easily found, but appears so neglected, Lorna doubts anyone is living here – until she sees the woodsmoke drifting up from the chimney.

She presses the doorbell, but hears no answering ring from inside; then she notices the cracked casing and the loose wires dangling from its base. Instead, she raps on the frosted glass in the door, which rattles, loose in its frame.

She waits a few moments, until behind the glass's distortion she sees a splintered figure moving.

'Tommy? Is that you?' She keeps her voice soft, friendly. No need to spook him, make him feel the threat of officialdom. God knows he'll have had enough of that.

'Tommy, it's Lorna Winrow. I represented you in court for your release appeal.'

Surely that will persuade him she's a friendly face, but she still senses hesitancy.

'Tommy? Have you time to have a word?'

A key turns in the lock, and the door opens a few centimetres. Tommy peers round its edge, checking she's who she says she is.

'I'm on my own,' Lorna reassures him. 'Can we talk?'

'What about?' His voice is loaded with suspicion.

'About your case. There are one or two outstanding questions I'd like to ask, if you don't mind.'

He opens the door a little wider, so he can get a full view of her and anyone else who might be concealed down the passageway.

'I won't take long, I promise.'

Still reluctant, he stands back to allow her inside.

In all the time she was working on his release, Lorna never met Tommy in person. He was a name to her, a case number, and she's surprised to see how far he is from her preconceptions. She heard his reputation as a bully, saw him presented in the paperwork from his original trial as a man who could be handy with his fists. That doesn't square with what she's seeing now, a wiry man with sad eyes, below average height, not what she'd call attractive, wearing khaki and camouflage like some TA recruit.

Lorna doesn't know what she's expecting from a recently released middle-aged man living alone, but it certainly isn't what she sees in the kitchen – the place spotless, the floor damp from mopping, the scent of floor-cleaner strong in the air. The stainless-steel sink sparkles, the kettle stands with its cable wound round its base. This is a level of housekeeping she and Ed have never attained.

'This is nice,' she says, and it is: old-fashioned but cosy, the kind of place your grandma would serve you cake and jam tarts.

'I'm trying to fix it up.' She hears a note of pride in his voice. 'This is my mum and dad's old place, where I grew up. Mum always kept it nice, so I'm trying to follow in her footsteps. Plus when I was inside, you had to keep things tidy. Not much space for your stuff in a two-man cell.'

'I suppose not.'

'You want a cup of tea or something?'

'Tea would be great, thanks.'

As he busies himself with the tea – mugs taken from a

wooden stand, teabags from a regimented line of matching canisters with an eighties vibe, labelled *Coffee*, *Tea*, *Sugar* – she tries to put herself in Canfield's shoes, wondering whether he'd be spending this unobserved time looking round for clues. But in a place so clean and tidy, clues might be hard to come by.

'You don't look or sound like a local,' he says, guardedly. 'Where're you from?'

'Derby.' She sits down on a wooden chair that smells of lavender polish. 'Not too far away.'

'Far enough that you weren't passing through. Not many people are just passing through Risedale. So who sent you, all the way from Derby?'

She should have anticipated the question, and had an answer prepared. Instead, she blurts something like the truth. 'I'm curious. We managed to get you out of there, ten years too late. But our case for doing that was based on something you could have told us yourself. You had an alibi. You could have avoided conviction in the first place.'

The kettle's boiled and he's pouring water into the mugs. 'Maybe.'

'So why didn't you?'

'I had my reasons.'

'They must have been very solid reasons for you to spend ten years locked up.'

'They were. They still are.'

He dabs at the teabags with a spoon, fishes them out of the mugs, adds milk to both and two sugars to his own. 'Sweet tea. That's what kept me going in there. Tea reminded me of home. Whenever things looked bleak, my mum used to say,

"Chin up and kettle on." In the face of all those drugs you could get in there, everything I could have taken to escape the monotony up here –' he taps a finger to his temple – 'it was tea that kept me going. Tea and prayer.'

'Are you religious, Tommy?' He wouldn't be the first; she's met several men who've turned to what serves as the church inside, usually a tucked-away chapel and a weekly visit from a C of E vicar. She wonders what he might have told anyone he spoke with under the label of spiritual guidance. No point in asking. When it comes to discretion and keeping secrets, she's found men of the cloth more faithful to their oath of confidentiality than any lawyer, doctor or policeman.

'Not really. But I prayed for different things at different times. Not that it made any difference. When I was first arrested and put inside, I prayed for justice to be done and to be let free. Didn't happen. Then I prayed for Mum to be kept safe till I got out, but that didn't happen either. I was let down big time on that one. She died when I'd only been inside two years. Then I started praying for retribution, for the guy who killed my Adam to get proper punishment, to die a horrible, painful death. But there was a chaplain I used to talk to, and he made me see things differently. Even though my life had taken a really bad turn, he encouraged me to see the big picture. Where was it all going? He said I didn't need to understand the why and the wherefore, that God has a plan for each and every one of us, and it's only at the end you can see the sense in everything.'

Lorna's sceptical. 'That's a nice theory.'

'It's like expecting some big reveal at the end of a film. Probably bollocks. But I know I'll see Adam again. He'll be waiting for me, when it's my time. Sometimes I think that can't come soon enough.'

The sadness in his eyes has deepened.

'Come on, Tommy. Don't think that way. Now you're free, you've loads to live for, surely?'

'Really? Like what? Want a biscuit?'

He lifts an old Family Favourites tin down from a shelf, removing the lid to show several packets of Jammy Dodgers.

Lorna takes one. 'Not had one of these in years.'

'Boyhood favourite. We used to get those as a treat sometimes, me and my sister. High days and holidays.' He joins her at the table. 'Come on, then, Mrs – what did you say your name was?'

'Lorna, Lorna Winrow.'

'Mrs Winrow. What are you really doing here?'

Lorna studies him, and decides that after all he's been through, he deserves to have the truth. Even if it gets her unceremoniously kicked out.

'A friend of mine,' she begins, though she isn't sure Canfield's a friend, isn't quite sure what they are to each other, these days. Properly, of course, they should be nothing at all. 'He was involved in putting together the original case against you.'

'He's a copper.'

'Yes.'

'Which one?'

'I think it's better if you don't know.'

Tommy nods. 'OK. We'll put that aside for the time being.'

'He wants to know how he got it wrong. If you ask me, he feels guilty.'

'So he should.'

'He does. He wants to try and find Adam's real killer. The problem is, Adam's case will most likely just be marked unsolved for the time being, and go on the list for cold-case review. But that might be years away, even decades.'

'I won't let that happen. My little boy has waited long enough.'

'Apparently that's how it is. But this guy, my friend, he doesn't want to retire without the right guy banged up.'

Tommy nods again, and helps himself to a Jammy Dodger. 'I can relate to that. No loose ends. That's how I feel about everything. I want it all nice and tidy before I go. But I'm not going to lie to you. Whichever one he is, he's part of my clean-up operation. They think they're going to have their little inquiry, offer the senior screw-up early retirement or put him in charge of paperclips. Well, I think he deserves more than that.'

'People make mistakes, Tommy.'

He leans forward, too close, and for the first time she feels fear of the man, understands what he might be capable of.

'Mistakes have to be paid for,' he says, low and menacing. 'He doesn't just get a free pass. My life was ruined beyond repair when I lost Adam, but he did what I thought was impossible and ruined it more. So I don't think he should just be allowed to slink away into a well-funded retirement, do you?'

Reluctantly, Lorna admits she can see his point.

'He'll never go on trial, though, will he?' says Tommy, bleakly. 'He'll never see the inside of the dock.'

Lorna shakes her head. 'I'm sorry, but I agree with you. I don't think he will.'

'So why is that fair? You tell me why that's fair?'

Not for the first time, Lorna finds herself reflecting that the law of the land is – more frequently than you'd expect – unjust. 'I don't know what you can do about that.'

'Oh, things can be done,' says Tommy, darkly. 'Things can definitely be done.'

'But if he helps sort this out, puts the right guy away? That would go some way towards making things right, wouldn't it?'

'Not really. That would be him doing the job he should have done in the first place, and you can tell him that from me. Tell him if he wants to apologise, he knows where to find me, and he can be a man and come and say it to my face.'

Tommy's right, of course. Lorna decides to change tack. But as she's about to speak, he goes on. 'It wasn't totally his fault, though, was it? He was deliberately led astray. By people who were lying.'

'Lying? Who was lying?'

'That shithead Rains and his missus. He lied on oath that he saw me in the village that afternoon, which was an impossibility since I was miles away somewhere else.'

'Which you could have proven if you'd given your alibi.'

'And his missus was as bad, telling everyone how me and Gail were always fighting. It wasn't like that. There were fights, but they weren't what she said they were.'

'In what way?'

'That's for me to know.'

'You're not giving us much to go on.'

'Us? You working with this guy, are you? Why would you do that? You're for the defence, aren't you? So how come you're so keen to be putting someone away?'

Lorna finds herself blushing.

'I get it.' Tommy gives a knowing smile. 'You and he have a thing going. He married as well?'

'What makes you think I'm married?'

'Your wedding ring.'

'OK. But we don't have a "thing going".'

'I think you do. Remind me, what's his name? And if you tell me it's that first-class prick Pearson, this conversation is over.'

'I don't know any Pearson,' says Lorna, but she's afraid to say more for fear of putting Canfield in harm's way. Ryan was right about being vulnerable to reprisals. Stories of ex-prisoners' revenge on the policemen who put them away are not uncommon.

'I don't care if you don't tell me,' Tommy continues. 'I can find out easy enough through the internet, court records and that. They're public, aren't they?'

'Yes, they are,' admits Lorna. 'But the thing is, Tommy, even though we got you released through new evidence, that evidence hasn't taken us any closer to finding Adam's killer. Your alibi is somewhat clarified, but to really move forward, you're going to have to help.'

Tommy becomes thoughtful. 'I get you. I thought for years it was the Rains's boy, Simon. He isn't a boy now, though, he's a full-grown man easily capable of the attempted rape or whatever it was he did to get himself put away. His mum and dad, they knew he was bad all along. That's why they both lied, to keep their precious son out of jail. They didn't care what happened to me. Didn't help them in the end though, did it, because their boy's serving his time anyway, as he should be. But you should be going after his dad for lying in court.'

'If you're right, that's what will happen.'

'You think?' Tommy's sceptical. 'Not going to be top of anyone's list, though, is it, prosecuting a nice couple like them for doing the dirty on someone like me.'

'I'll make it a priority.'

'But my Adam's not a priority, is he? If we have years to wait for a new investigation.'

Lorna sighs. 'Cards on the table. The detective, my friend. His job's on the line.'

'Good. As it should be.'

'He asked for a chance to try and put things right, unofficially, under the radar. It's a long shot, but now you've said you know some people lied under oath, maybe he can do that. Will you help him?'

'I'd rather rip his head off.'

'I understand that. But for Adam's sake? What about your ex-wife – Gail, is it? You have to think of her too, Tommy.'

He laughs. 'I don't give a damn about her, the treacherous whore. She knows plenty about how the police work. Pretty friendly she was with them.'

Lorna feels uncomfortable. What's Tommy referring to? Is there something Canfield's not told her?

But she needs to stay on track.

'For Adam, then. For Adam alone.'

In the silence as she waits for his answer, a clock ticks. She sees him thinking, weighing up what he's going to say.

'I might. It isn't only Adam. There's other things that need to be put straight.'

'What things?'

He shakes his head. 'I can't say – it's not safe for me to say. I need to be sure I'll be looked after before I say any more.'

'What do you mean, looked after?'

'Witness protection. They have to sort me out somewhere far away from here to live, a new name. A new face, even.'

'If it's necessary, if you have information and the circumstances warrant it, of course that can be done. But if you speak to the detective, you have to understand that at this stage, it's unofficial. He wouldn't be in a position to authorise witness protection.'

He looks her straight in the eyes. 'Not even when you tell him I know where there's a body buried?'

'A body?' Lorna's suddenly out of her depth. Is Tommy going to make a confession? If so, what should she do, what should she say? 'Whose body?'

'I won't say anything until I know I'll be safe. It'd be like slitting my own throat. You wouldn't expect me to do that, would you?'

'Of course not.'

'Then tell your friend what I said. I'll give him my whole alibi and tell him where to find the body – I'll tell him everything I know – but they won't get a single word out of me until my safety is guaranteed.'

FIFTY-FIVE

Armed with the number of Tommy's shiny new but cheap mobile phone, Lorna wanders back to her car. There's plenty to think about – more pieces to this puzzle than anyone's so far considered. If Tommy will break his silence on his whereabouts the day Adam died, everything that's been assumed about the circumstances of his death could be overturned.

But something's bothering her. What did Tommy mean about his ex-wife being 'friendly' with the police? She's seen photos of Gail Henthorn from the days of Tommy's trial; she was a very attractive woman, and Lorna has a sick feeling in her stomach that he might have been referring to Canfield. How badly was she played by him, back then? She always thought she was the only one, a serious contender to be the new Mrs Canfield. What if she was no more than one of many casual liaisons, not even worthy to be called a proper affair?

More troubling still, why does she even care? Yet if it turned out Canfield had a thing with Gail, she knows she'd never speak to him again. And that's one hundred per cent proof that she's far from indifferent.

Her best move, she decides, is to go and see Gail Henthorn for herself. If she still lives in Risedale, she's right on the spot.

The best way to find her is obvious.

Lorna climbs out of her car again, and makes her way across the road.

The post office is all she anticipates, stocked with what a village shop would term staples – baked beans, sliced bread, alcohol and chocolate.

The woman behind the counter studies Lorna over the top of her glasses as she enters, and greets her with a 'Good morning' and a taut smile. Hungry after skipping breakfast, Lorna heads for the fridge and chooses a cheddar on wholewheat sandwich and a bottle of water.

At the counter, the woman rings up her purchases without showing any inclination to chat. Lorna decides to be blunt.

Taking out her purse to find her bank card, she says, 'I wonder if you can help me, actually. I'm looking for Gail Henthorn. Does she still live in the village?'

The woman bristles. 'I'm afraid I can't disclose information like that.'

So that's a yes, then.

'Your protection of her privacy is admirable, I totally get it. But I'm not press, I'm a lawyer. I worked on Tommy Henthorn's release.'

Again, the woman peers over her glasses. 'Did you?'

'I spoke outside the court after he was released. I was on the BBC news. You can google it if you like. I just want a word with Gail to clarify some statements Tommy made.'

'Isn't that the police's job?'

Very astute. Lorna thinks quickly. 'It's to do with compensation, whether Gail might be eligible for a share.'

'I don't see why she should be. She and Tommy were separated when he first went to jail.'

Lorna sees her inroad. 'Separated, but not yet divorced. Hence her possible entitlement.'

The woman folds her arms. 'I have to say, not everyone in this village is pleased to see him back.'

Lorna's face shows her surprise. 'Why on earth not? It's a cause for celebration, surely?'

'If he didn't do it, who did?'

'Well, that is the police's job. Look, I just want to speak to Gail very briefly, drop off some forms in case she wants to make a claim.'

The lie comes easily, but whether the woman believes her or not, she's growing tired of being gatekeeper.

Lorna's card pings the card reader.

'You want a bag?' asks the woman. 'They're 10p.'

'No, thanks.'

'Blacksmith's Cottage, right at the top of Main Street,' says the woman, as Lorna picks up her purchases. 'Personally, I think you're wasting your time trying to get any sense out of her, but if she gets a whiff of money, who knows?'

Tommy's house was in need of TLC, but Blacksmith's Cottage looks as if it might best be improved by demolition and rebuilding.

Stepping carefully around the rain-filled potholes in the overgrown drive, she approaches the faded front door and knocks. Moments later, the corner of a grubby net curtain is lifted, and a scowling face peers out. Lorna gives her warmest smile. The face disappears, and the curtain drops back into place.

Nothing else happens.

When she thinks she's waited long enough, Lorna knocks again.

Still nothing. But as she's making up her mind to walk away, a bolt slides back and the door opens to the length of the chain that secures it.

'Yes?'

Lorna can only see the central part of the woman's face, but she appears to be in her sixties, not her forties as she knows Gail Henthorn must be. And the face is very clearly not welcoming.

'Gail?'

'Who wants to know?'

'My name's Lorna. Can I have a word?'

'What about?'

Here, Lorna's on dangerous ground. She considers lying, tempting Gail – assuming this is she – with the possibility of a financial windfall; but that goes against both her personal standards and all the ethics of her profession.

'Look, let me be straight with you,' she says. 'I was involved in getting Tommy released, but I don't have any official reason for being here. I just want to ask you a question, one woman to another.'

She expects the door to be slammed in her face. But Gail considers, until eventually she says, 'At least you're honest.'

The chain rattles, and as the door opens Lorna smells woodsmoke and old cooking oil, along with something oddly unpleasant, both fusty and sour, which Lorna suspects may be from Gail herself. A child's manic scrawling covers the hall walls, but it's faded as if it may have been there some time, perhaps even years.

Still protective of her privacy, Gail blocks the doorway, arms folded across her chest, her hollow cheeks and disturbingly thin hands suggesting that under the several layers of knitwear and the man's outdoor fleece she's wearing, she's not someone who's a regular eater.

'Ask away, then,' she says.

Now Lorna feels foolish. But Gail's plainly some kind of addict or alcoholic, maybe both. Whatever Lorna says is unlikely to be remembered an hour from now.

'I'm trying to get information on someone you might know, Ryan Canfield.' Gail's eyes flicker, and Lorna suspects she's on to something. 'You know him?'

'Name rings a bell.' Gail's expression is sly. 'Maybe.'

For a few moments she's silent, until as Lorna's wondering why she doesn't continue, Gail says, 'You got kids?'

'Two.'

'Expensive little bastards, aren't they? I've got a daughter, she's not cheap to keep. And then with her birthday coming up and all.'

Gail gives Lorna what's supposed to be a winning smile, showing uneven yellow teeth. At the reference to a birthday, Lorna's bemused, until she realises she's being asked for money. She pats her jacket pockets, and hearing the answering jingle of change, digs into both to find a few coins, altogether less than four pounds.

She drops the money into Gail's skeletal hand. 'It's all I've got.'

Gail registers the gleam and weight of cash. She frowns. 'What did you ask me?'

'About Ryan Canfield.'

'You mean Manny's old mate. He came here a couple of times when Adam . . . You're not from round here, are you?'

'I live in Derby.'

Gail nods. 'Well, Manny worked with that Ryan for a while, quite a long while, actually. Apart from that I don't know anything about him. If I did, I've forgotten.'

'Who's Manny?' asks Lorna.

'Is that a different question?'

'I suppose so, yes.'

'If you want to know who Manny is, you can ask your Mr Canfield,' says Gail, and she closes the door.

Back at her car, Lorna calls Ryan. The obvious thing to do is to tell him everything she's learned on the phone, then head into work. There's no need to see him again.

But Canfield – perhaps by coincidence – tells her he isn't far away. There's a pub nearby, he says, where they could have a bite of lunch.

Fighting the loud whisper of her conscience, Lorna agrees they should meet.

When she calls Ed, she lies about where she is, and – feeling more guilty by the minute – asks brightly how his day is going.

FIFTY-SIX

The Jug and Bottle is a quaint, stone-built place, in a sleepy village at least a dozen miles from Risedale. When Lorna arrives, Canfield is waiting in the almost-empty car park.

Watching her as she climbs from her car, he smiles as she walks towards him.

And she smiles back.

Careful.

He holds the main entrance door open for her, letting her lead the way as he says, 'I didn't call ahead. I hope they have a table.'

She walks into an all-but-empty bar, and turns to find him smiling at the joke.

While she settles at a corner table, slipping off her jacket and hanging it over the back of her chair, he goes to get drinks. A vase of coppery chrysanthemums stands on the sill of a lead-paned window; beyond the window is a field of sheep, and beyond that the open uplands. Lorna and Ed used to walk in this area, spend whole days in the hills, stopping at places like this – including this very pub – to eat and rest their sore feet. She can't remember the last time they went walking alone together – before Dottie was born, for certain. Those were good years; she and Ed were happy back then. Her conscience is whispering louder. She shouldn't be here.

Canfield brings her a local mineral water and a tonic for himself, and hands her a laminated menu printed on plain A4 paper.

'It's not the most exciting choice,' he says. 'Chips with everything.'

'Chips are good, once in a while.' Lorna reads, and keen to talk about Tommy, makes a quick choice. 'In fact, I'll have chips, nothing else.'

'Well, you're a cheap date.' As soon as he's said it, Canfield's embarrassed, and manages to make it worse by apologising. 'Not that this is a date, obviously. Chips it is.'

He returns to the bar to order and retakes his seat. 'So, come on, let's hear it. How did you get on?'

Lorna smiles. 'You should pay me a retainer. I think I did pretty well.'

'I'd love to pay you a retainer, but at the moment I'm barely retained myself. You spoke to him, then?'

'Yes, I did. He wasn't very keen at first, and it was definitely the right decision for you not to go. He's spoiling for a fight with you guys, for sure.'

Canfield pulls a face, and thinks of what he's had confirmed about the call-logs by Phil Dewar. 'Can't blame him for that.'

'He's angry and out for revenge. And also bamboozled to have discovered that the guy he was certain should have been banged up in his place couldn't have killed Adam.'

'Who was he thinking?'

'Someone called Simon Rains?'

Canfield sighs. 'I knew he'd be thinking that. At the beginning, Rains seemed the obvious suspect. Only young at the time – fourteen, fifteen – but he was an odd character for sure, and I couldn't swear he wasn't taking an interest in Adam. When we arrested Tommy, he went on and on about Rains, telling us we should speak to him. But we had spoken to him, more than once, and Rains willingly gave us DNA samples which proved beyond any doubt he hadn't touched Adam. That ruled him out very early on.'

'I see. But Tommy was never told that?'

'It's not policy to share details of an ongoing investigation with a suspect. As I'm sure you're aware.'

'Well, somehow he's found out all by himself. According to Tommy, Rains is now in a secure unit for attempted rape or something.'

'So I've heard.'

'And he says Rains's father lied on oath to get him convicted, that his statement was false.'

'Which, bearing in mind Tommy's new alibi, could be true.' Canfield bows his head, beginning to realise the possible extent of the errors made in Tommy's prosecution. 'So now we might have perjury charges to bring. What a mess.'

'I'm sorry, Ryan,' says Lorna, 'but it might be even worse than that.'

'Go on.'

'He says he knows where there's a body.'

Canfield is shocked. 'You're kidding me. Whose body?'

Lorna shakes her head. 'I don't know, and he's not prepared to say unless he gets witness protection. New identity, new home, the lot.'

'He's out of his mind.'

'I don't think so, honestly. He's emotional, of course, but I think he was telling the truth. What he said makes sense, if he never came up with an alibi because he was in fear for his safety. But circumstances have moved on, haven't they? He's prepared to tell you what he knows, but it's a two-way street. Think about it. He had ten years to produce this alibi and – assuming it's solid – get out of jail free. But he never did that, until now. He must have been vulnerable in prison. You know, bad people? Are you OK?'

Canfield's bent forward in an attitude of despair, his face in his hands. Sitting up straight, he forces a smile. 'Just processing what could turn out to be one of the biggest fuck-ups in Derbyshire policing history. If he's telling the truth, not only did we lock up the wrong man, we took false witness statements into court and potentially missed a connected second murder case. My career is one hundred per cent over. Apart from that, I'm great.'

'It's a bit early to assume it's that bad. Isn't it?'

'Well, it is until we see a second body. I think the false witness statement is looking increasingly likely. If I were Tommy, I'd be ready to kill me.'

'If it's any comfort, he mentioned someone on your team I think he hates even more than you – somebody Pearson?'

'He mentioned Pearson by name?'

'He said if I was anything to do with Pearson, he wouldn't speak to me. So at least you're only second on the list. But you'd better watch your back, and maybe tip Pearson off.'

'But who could Tommy have been so afraid of?'

'You're the detective.'

'That's the second time I've been told that recently. And actually, I'm having serious doubts.'

The landlady bustles over carrying a tray with two plates of chips, sauces and vinegar. When she's left them, Lorna says, 'Ryan, I'm sorry.'

Canfield squeezes ketchup onto the side of his plate. 'What have you got to be sorry for?'

'I got you into this mess.'

He shakes his head. 'No, I got myself into this mess. I screwed up. We screwed up. I'm only beginning to realise how badly.'

'But I'm sorry I acted for Tommy. I'm sure you know it didn't have to be me.'

Canfield gives her a sad smile. 'I kind of suspected you weren't the only lawyer they had.'

'I was . . . you know . . . angry.'

'You stayed angry a long time, then. Listen.' He leans forward, speaks in a low voice so only she will hear, even though there's no one nearby. 'I'm sorry too. I didn't want to end things between us, but I had to make a choice. When you have kids . . .'

'I understand that now.'

'Anyway.' He reaches across the table and squeezes her hand. 'What's done is done. I'm glad I got to spend some time with you, put things right between us. We're OK, aren't we?'

Lorna smiles. 'Yes, we're OK.'

In silence, they begin to eat, until Canfield says, 'Question is, how do I pass on the intel that Tommy might have information of serious interest? I can't exactly announce I encouraged you to go and speak to him.'

Lorna hesitates before she responds. 'There's something else. Who's Manny?'

'Manny?' Canfield looks at her. 'What have you heard about Manny?'

'Time for a confession. I went to see Gail Henthorn too.'

Canfield sits back in his chair, eyebrows raised. 'Wow. You have been busy. If I had my warrant card, I'd be handing it over to you. You'd be better at my job than I am.'

'I was curious about her.'

'Curious? Why?'

Lorna blushes. 'No. That wasn't it. I was curious about you. Tommy mentioned Gail's new boyfriend at the time was a policeman, and – this is so embarrassing – I thought it might have been you.'

'And that bothered you?'

'Yes, actually, it did. So I went to ask her, get it from the horse's mouth. And she only remembered you vaguely, but she said you worked with Manny.'

Canfield puts down his fork. 'She used that name, Manny?'

Lorna tries to recall the conversation exactly as it was. 'She said you and Manny worked together, and if I wanted to know more I should ask you. To be honest, she was shot away, completely messed up. Alcohol, I assume, but maybe some kind of drugs. She said she has another child now. I hope for her sake social services are taking an interest, because she didn't look like a fit mother to me.'

'Some kids get a rough deal.'

Lorna glances at her watch. 'Listen, I have to go soon.'

She sees something – could it be regret? – in Canfield's eyes.

'I should get on too,' he concedes. 'It's been good talking

to you, Lorna. I really appreciate your help in trying to dig me out of this pit I find myself in.'

'You make me feel so bad for putting you there.'

'I suppose at least it makes us even.'

Unsure whether it's appropriate or not, Canfield walks Lorna to her car, then waits awkwardly as she hunts in her handbag for her keys.

A group of cyclists – all men in Lycra and pointed helmets – roll into the car park and dismount, chatting and laughing as they discuss the challenges of the last few miles of road.

Lorna finds her keys. 'Well. See you around.'

Canfield can't help himself. He bends towards her.

Lorna knows he's going to kiss her, and she wants him to. She's closing her eyes . . .

'Lorna?' One of the cyclists, blond hair damp from sweat, has come up behind her, his expression one of smiling surprise. 'I thought that was you.' He extends a hand to Canfield. 'Hi, I'm Harry. I was at school with Lorna's husband.'

Lorna blushes furious red. 'Harry, hi! This is DCI Canfield, an old friend of mine from Derby CID. We were just catching up on old times.'

'Well, don't let me interrupt,' says Harry. 'I just thought I'd say hello. Tell Ed I'll see him at darts on Thursday.'

As Harry rejoins his companions, Canfield apologises. 'I didn't mean to get you into trouble.'

'There's no trouble,' insists Lorna. 'But I really do have to go.'

Driving away, though, she feels sick with apprehension. Of course Harry will mention to Ed that he saw her. How she's ever going to plausibly explain what she was doing, she doesn't know.

Worse than that is how she feels about Canfield.

How disappointed she is that they didn't actually kiss.

On his way home, something's nibbling at the edges of Canfield's consciousness, a memory from the time around Adam's murder, something connected to what Lorna said about buried bodies. But so much water has flowed under the bridge, so many faces and cases have intervened. It's hardly surprising that he can't quite join the dots.

In the end, he puts in a call to Emma Goodwin, recently back in the office after her second maternity leave.

'Derby CID.'

He doesn't use his rank to announce himself. 'Hi Emma, Ryan Canfield.'

'Oh, hello, boss. How's it going?'

'Could be better, if I'm honest,' admits Canfield. 'Listen, I'm not sure how best to address this, so we might call it an anonymous tip. A little bird's told me Tommy Henthorn has information regarding a buried body.'

Emma sounds sceptical. 'What do you mean? Buried by him?'

'I don't know, but I don't think so. Sounds like it's information he's been sitting on for God knows how long, but he's saying he's afraid for his safety. I'm thinking it might be in your interests to have somebody have a word with him, see if there's anything in it.'

'OK. I'll put it out there at tomorrow's team meeting.'

'If I were someone who wanted to impress people at that

meeting,' Canfield goes on, 'I might be inclined to have to hand a list of missing persons from around the time Tommy was arrested. Maybe from the previous six months?'

'Good idea,' says Emma, 'as long as I can find the time. Things are pretty hectic round here in your absence. When are you coming back?'

'I think you know that's not up to me.'

'Well, we miss you. Sorry, I'd better go.'

'Em, this intel didn't come from me, OK?'

'We never spoke. See you soon, I hope. Naming no names but certain people have got their eyes on your office.'

'Somewhat over-optimistic at this stage,' says Canfield.

FIFTY-SEVEN

Canfield knows Stapleton's scrapyard all too well, by reputation at least. Hidden away at the back of an industrial estate, it's been used for years by the criminal community to dispose of vehicles that might harbour incriminating DNA. Stripped and crushed into shiny steel cubes, dropped by crane onto a small mountain of twisted scrap metal, the ruined hopes of hundreds of convictions form an ugly landmark blighting that side of the city.

At 11pm, Canfield parks his car outside the compound. By day, Stapleton's is loud with trucks bringing in scrap from all over the county and the constant working of forklifts and cranes. By night, he discovers, the place is eerily quiet, the poorly lit yard a certain playground for rats, the slipping, settling metal behind the office buildings creaking like a sinking ship.

The main gates are padlocked shut. The personnel gate alongside is locked too, but there's a buzzer there and a two-way speaker. Canfield presses the buzzer, and waits.

'Hello?' The voice through the microphone is distorted.

'I'm looking for Wayne?'

'Who's asking?'

'DCI Canfield, Derbyshire Police. We met in Manny's office.'

There's no immediate reply, and Canfield's not surprised. If he were going to rob a property, his first move would be to announce himself as the police.

But then the microphone fires up again. 'I'll come down.'

Moments later, the rectangular light of an open door shines from the offices, then goes out again as it closes. He hears boots on concrete, and sees the bright flash of a torch pointed in his direction as a figure walks towards him, attempting a swagger of self-confidence.

In the light of the streetlamp behind him, Canfield can see that it's Wayne, dressed in the anonymous dark trousers of a uniform and a heavy hi-vis jacket with the Securitylink logo on his chest. A black beanie hat is pulled down over his head. As he draws closer, he shines the full blinding beam of the torch in Canfield's face.

Canfield covers his eyes with his forearm. 'Give me a break. Wayne, it's me, really. We met at your offices a few days ago, remember?'

Wayne lowers the torch. 'You're out late. What are you doing here?'

Canfield can hear the relief in Wayne's voice.

'Sorry if I gave you a fright. I wanted to talk to you.'

'No worries. But I can't let you in, it's against regulations. They'll see it on the CCTV.'

'I don't need to come in. And I'll only be quick. Here, I brought you a present.' He holds out the paper-wrapped parcel he's carrying, offering it through the railings. 'Hope you like kebabs.'

Wayne steps forward and takes the barely warm package. 'Thanks, mate. Life saver.'

'I just wanted to ask where I can find your mum. I want to ask her about Tommy Henthorn's wife.'

'Gail?'

'Gail, that's her. Now Tommy's gone free, we're ramping up enquiries again, talking to old witnesses and looking for new ones. Did your mum speak to the police before?'

'Not that I know of.'

'Do you think she'd speak to me now?'

'Probably. She likes a bit of drama. But you'd have to ask her yourself.'

'Could you give me her mobile?'

In reply, Wayne reels off a number. Canfield asks him to slow down, pulls out his own phone, and keys the repeated number into his contacts.

'Thanks very much. You can tell her I'll be in touch.'

'Not this time of night. She goes to bed at nine. Why you asking me this stuff now, anyway? You could have asked me when I saw you in the office. Or got my number from Manny.'

'It was just something I thought of while I was passing. In the area, anyway.'

'Yeah, right.'

'OK, look, full disclosure. It's better if Manny doesn't know I spoke to you. Because mistakes were made, some of the work he did is under review. He's a good mate of mine, and I don't want him worrying that he messed up. So between us, right?'

'Fair dos. I'll tell Mum you'll be in touch. But don't expect her to keep anything quiet. She couldn't keep a secret to save her life.'

'Thanks for the heads up.'

'Thanks for the kebab.'

Wayne's already walking back to the office when Canfield makes up his mind to gamble, to ask the question he really isn't sure about. Still. Fortune favours the bold.

So he calls after Wayne's retreating back.

'One other thing. I've a memory like a sieve, and I don't want to let on to him I've forgotten. Manny's daughter, what's her name?'

'Sabrina,' calls Wayne, and he disappears into the dark.

FIFTY-EIGHT

Back at home, not yet ready for sleep, Canfield sits down at his laptop to go through his emails, and finds amongst all the usual junk and nonsense one from Emma's official police address to his own.

The tone of her communication is formal, asking him to review the attached document, which is part of an ongoing inquiry, requesting that he get back to her if he sees anything that could relate to the Tommy Henthorn case.

The attachment, when he opens it, is the list of missing persons he suggested she download. Clever Emma. All traceable and above board.

The list of the long-term missing is lengthy for a small area of the UK, and holds the names of people of all ages from young children and teenagers to the very elderly. Canfield has often wondered where Britain's missing go. If you take out a percentage as voluntary runaways and – happily – a much larger percentage for those eventually found safe and reasonably well, still the number of people in the UK who simply disappear every year is disconcertingly large. If Tommy's telling the truth and he knows where one of them is buried, that could mean essential closure for the family of someone on this list.

He scrolls down the screen with his mouse.

And stops.

Here's a name that jolts his memory.

He remembers a woman with a small boy, who came to Kenton Road and hassled and hassled him. A woman whose husband was missing, who was determined she and her young son hadn't been deliberately abandoned.

Is it possible she was right?

His name is here.

Faizan Jutt.

Canfield feels the buzz of jigsaw pieces rearranging themselves, falling into new places. He wants to share with Lorna what he's found.

But it's way too late to message her. Anyway, he shouldn't. Should he?

Lorna, oh, Lorna.

His eagerness to reconnect with her is clouding his judgement. He's a single man, but it wouldn't be fair to her.

But then, when is life ever fair?

FIFTY-NINE

All evening, since Ed left for his weekly darts night, Lorna's been on tenterhooks.

In the days following her lunch with Ryan, she's struggled to be her normal self at home, veering from being too upbeat and manically cheerful to moody and withdrawn, snapping at the kids and being short whenever Ed's spoken to her.

Her mind is full of what she'll say if Ed discovers she's lied to him about being with Ryan, what possible reason she can give for not telling the truth. She'd love a glass of wine to settle her nerves, but doesn't pour one. If Harry's mentioned seeing her, she's going to need a very clear head indeed.

The hands of the clock on the living room wall move past the time Ed usually returns home. No big deal, she tries to persuade herself. He's having a good time, no doubt deep in some lads' conversation about bikes or politics or beer. Another half hour goes by. No sense in waiting up any longer; she has to be in the office early tomorrow. She goes upstairs, checks on the kids, gets into bed.

Though sleep won't come.

One hour and fifteen minutes later, she hears the car pull

up in the driveway, the front door opening and closing, the chink of his keys dropped in the bowl on the hall windowsill. He goes into the kitchen, and she thinks maybe he's making tea, but there's no sound of running water, not even of the light being switched on.

For a few minutes she listens to the silence. Maybe he's looking at stuff on his phone, reading messages and emails he's missed while he was out.

But yet again, her guilty conscience pricks.

Pulling on her dressing gown, she heads downstairs.

He's sitting at the kitchen table, in the dark. Seeing her standing in the doorway, he glances at her, then away.

She asks if he's OK.

He raises his eyebrows, gives a sardonic smile. 'Am I OK? Well, it's very good of you to ask.'

'You're very late.'

'I went for a drive.'

'A drive? Where to?'

'Oh, round and round, here and there.'

'Why haven't you come up to bed?'

'Why haven't I come to bed? Because I'm not sure it's me you want in there with you.'

Lorna feels her head becoming light, the same feeling she used to have sometimes in pregnancy when her blood pressure was too low. She puts a hand on the doorframe to keep herself steady.

'What on earth do you mean?'

Now he sneers. 'Oh, come on, Lorna. Show me a little respect at least. Don't take me for a complete idiot. That guy Harry saw you with, who was he?'

'I told Harry. He's a policeman.'

'Does he have a name?'

'Canfield. Ryan Canfield. He was involved . . .'

'Don't tell me. He was involved in the Tommy Henthorn case. You mentioned his name once or twice.'

'Did I?'

'Yes, you did. So often, in fact, I did wonder if there was something personal in your quest to get Henthorn out of jail. Now I gather it's so personal, it involves meeting him in remote country pubs even after the case is over. And it involves *lying*.'

He slams his hand on the table, making Lorna jump.

An instinct for self-preservation puts weasel words in her mouth.

'Where was the lie?' The question is unreasonable and she knows it, knows such defensiveness can only make things worse. 'I don't tell you every meeting I have in my diary.'

'You told me it was dress-down day. At the office. Have they moved your office?'

'No, of course not. Look, I'm sorry. It was . . . The situation's complicated.'

'It's not complicated.' Ed gets up from his chair. 'I'm the mug who's the boring stay-at-home dad, and you're the straying wife. It doesn't get any simpler than that.' He pushes past her to head upstairs. 'Why don't you sleep on the sofa tonight? Somehow I don't feel I want your company.'

SIXTY

Wayne's mother, Julie Petit, lives in a modest semi-detached home in one of Derby's outer suburbs.

Canfield finds space to park on the road outside, and walks up the drive past a Ford Ka and a tarpaulin-covered motorhome. While he and Irene were still together and Caitlin and Annabelle were small, he went through a phase where he hankered after owning a motorhome, thinking it would be perfect for family holidays, the four of them together and the freedom of the open road. Then he did some research, and discovered that – in England at least – the reality was not so much freedom and adventure as crowded campsites and long hours stuck in traffic.

But the urge to travel with no particular place to go took hold and has never left him, and with his future uncertain, the covered vehicle makes him wish he were elsewhere and far away, or at least had plans to be. He's always wanted to visit Ireland, where his grandmother was born: wild seas and hidden beaches, pints of Guinness and fresh-caught seafood, the starched whiteness of hotel sheets . . .

He pushes Lorna from his mind. Again.

Mrs Petit – with henna-red hair and freshly done nails – insists he calls her Julie, ushers him into a comfortable lounge and offers him coffee, which he – recognising a woman who'll talk all afternoon if given the opportunity – declines.

Sitting down opposite him, she announces her unashamed curiosity as to why he's there.

'Wayne didn't say much, except it was about Gail Henthorn. Gail Stuckey, she was, when I knew her at school. She lived on the same road as we did so I knew her from us being kiddies growing up. Back in those days it wasn't like it is now, all the kids stuck in their bedrooms on their phones. We used to get outside and play, come rain or shine. Life was better then.'

Canfield finds himself agreeing, then thinking what a dinosaur he's become.

'The thing about Gail was,' Julie's going on, 'she was a real beauty. A lot of girls are pretty when they're young, but Gail was more than that, the kind that could stop traffic. To be honest, it was just as well she was a looker, because she didn't have much else going for her. Nobody liked her dad. He was a regular bully, from old mining stock, but that generation of men who lost their way when the pits all closed down. Her grandad was a miner and his dad before him, but Gail's dad – Keith, they called him – he was only down the pit a couple of years before the strike and then wallop – like so many of them, he was unemployed and a fish out of water. Never settled at another job, he didn't. Bricklayer, carpet salesman, you name it, he tried it. Even had a stall on the market at one time, selling bits of what he called antiques he picked up at auctions and junk shops.

Money was always short for that family, and that leads to bad tempers, doesn't it? And did Keith Stuckey ever have a bad temper. He punched my own dad once for – well, I don't even know what it was for. I just remember a lot of shouting and screaming and my dad's shirt being covered in blood and the police coming round to find out what had gone on. They all took a few poundings in that house, Gail and her sister and her mum. She divorced him in the end, but he still wouldn't leave them alone. He used to come round late at night after the pubs had shut, stand in the front garden yelling at her to let him in.'

Canfield thinks of a quote posted on the whiteboard of a training course he attended back in his days of Neighbourhood Policing: *Happy families are all alike; every unhappy family is unhappy in its own way.* Down the years, that's turned out, in his experience, to be largely true, even if the roots of unhappiness – too often the lack of money – remain the same.

'How did that affect Gail?' he asks. 'Did she have problems at school?'

Julie considers. 'Not as such. She wasn't the brightest button, but looking the way she did, she didn't need to be. But you couldn't say she was happy. Always serious, she was. And nothing fazed her. The teachers could be telling her off for not doing her homework or being late or smoking on school premises, give her detention for whole weeks at a time, she didn't care. It was like she'd switched off from the world. All she bothered about was how she looked. And she met her alter-ego in that department. Eamon Pearson. He was a good-looking lad – no doubt about it, a very good-looking lad – and when those two got together, it was a match made in heaven. They acted like a pair of film stars, preening and posturing. These days it'd make me laugh, but we were no more than children. All us girls wanted to be like Gail. She used to trawl the vintage shops, and she had this knack of finding things – dresses and blouses and jewellery, all sorts that you'd think was old rubbish on the hangers – that she made look amazing. And Manny was always such a snappy dresser, shirt pressed, shoes all shiny – I never saw Manny in a pair of trainers outside a PE lesson. All the girls had their eyes on Manny. I suppose that was a big part of the problem.'

'They didn't stay together, obviously?' puts in Canfield.

Julie shakes her head. 'Love's young dream came to an abrupt end one night when she caught him out the back of some pub with a girl from out of town. Well, by all accounts Gail went wild, screaming at this girl, scratching her face, pulling her hair. She got her on the ground in the end and started kicking her, until Manny pulled her off. Not long after that, they broke up. Whether that was Gail deciding Manny couldn't be trusted – which I don't believe he could – or whether he thought she might be the bunny-boiler type, I don't know. Anyway, next I heard, she'd married Tommy Henthorn and was living in Risedale. That's all I know.'

'What do you know about Manny after that?'

Julie shrugs. 'Not much, really. I saw him around from time to time. I knew he'd joined your lot, which didn't surprise me much. I expect he thought he'd look good in a uniform, which of course he did.'

'No more serious romances?'

'Not that I'm aware of. I'm sure it's not news to you, but

Manny was too busy playing the field to really think of settling down. Though I think he always carried a candle for Gail, and she for him too. Don't we all have one big love in our lives that never really lets you go?'

SIXTY-ONE

Right up until the last minute, Lorna's been in two minds whether she should honour her arrangement to meet up for drinks with her sister Jess, whether it's worth the aggravation.

Since their row over her lunch with Ryan, Ed has veered between frosty politeness – mostly in front of the children – and glowering suspicion every time Lorna's phone pings with incoming texts, social-media alerts or emails, so much so that she feels the need to sing out an explanation for almost every one, and even show him to his face anything which might be of passing interest. Certainly, she's made sure he's seen the message thread between herself and Jess – the discussion over where they should go, what time they should meet, and of key importance, confirmation that Jess's always-affable husband will pick them up and give Lorna a lift home, as long as it's not after 11pm.

Yet still she feels she shouldn't go. Not that there's anything wrong in a night out with Jess; drinks together is something they've always done, from time to time. But in her heart of hearts, Lorna knows what her priority topic of conversation will be. She wants Jess's advice on what she should do about Ryan Canfield.

Because craftily, deceitfully, among all those phone communications she's shared openly with Ed, two have slipped by him. The first was a message signed with a single kiss asking her to have lunch, the date a few days from now, the place a small boutique hotel well known for the excellence of its restaurant's food.

Lorna typed her furtive reply – *OK but don't message me again*, followed by an echo of the single kiss – while stirring spaghetti for dinner, praying Ed was totally occupied with Max's current tantrum, and when Ryan responded to her reply with a red heart, she deleted the stream.

She and Jess have plenty to talk about. She'll risk Ed's sulks and interrogations, and go.

Despite being what she herself calls an old married lady, Jess still keeps abreast of what places in town are what she calls (doing bunny-ear quotes with her fingers) hot and happening. Usually they're loud and crowded, with a crush at the bar and a significant risk of bumping into a professional footballer or two on the way there. But the place she's chosen this evening has a different vibe, relaxed and comfortable with chilled music, and smiling service from waiters moving smoothly between the low glass tables.

'A place we can talk,' Jess says as they check in their coats at the red-lit cloakroom.

Maybe her sister knows her better than she thinks.

Settled into deep, soft sofas – Lorna remarks that if they have too much to drink, they'll struggle to get up with anything approaching decorum – they study the drinks menu. The stylish surroundings come at a high price.

'First round's on me,' says Jess. 'I got a rise at work.'

While they wait for their drinks and a mixed platter of tapas, they talk about what's going on with Jess's job, how much she loves the work, how she struggles to like her unimaginative boss.

Then, after the first sips of their elaborate cocktails and initial tastes of the tapas, Jess puts down her drink, turns to Lorna and says, 'So tell me what's going on with you.'

And from nowhere, Lorna – ambushed by a sudden wave of intense sadness – finds she's crying.

'Oh my God, what did I say?' Jess hands Lorna a napkin, her face a picture of concern. 'Sweetie, what's wrong? Here, drink more, drink more.'

With half her glass quickly emptied, Lorna begins to feel the weight of melancholy floating away.

'I'm so sorry. I've no idea where that came from.'

'I think you have,' says Jess shrewdly. 'Spill the beans, right now.'

'I can't tell you. You'll be cross.'

'Maybe, maybe not. Try me.' Jess's eyes narrow. 'Or let me guess. This is about that policeman, isn't it?'

Lorna fakes indignation. 'What makes you say that?'

'Because when you were having your proud, career-defining moment on the BBC recently, they showed him on an old video clip, didn't they? Preening, he was, over getting the guy you got released put away. I thought his name was familiar and then it came to me – he was the bastard who broke your heart. And I wondered then why you'd got involved, because surely you haven't given that man another thought since you and Ed met? Please tell me you haven't?'

'Revenge is a dish best served cold,' says Lorna, defensively.

'You have to be kidding me. Don't you know what the opposite of love is? It's indifference, in genuinely not giving a shit. Not sitting quietly in the shadows like some demented lunatic waiting to strike. What were you thinking? You should have been a million miles away from that case, and you know it. Hell, I know absolutely nothing about legal protocols and all that stuff, but I know what a conflict of interests is, and, lady, you had one big time.'

'I won the case, didn't I?'

'Yes, you did. So what happened next?'

'He asked to speak to me.'

'And you agreed?'

'Yes.'

'Why?'

'I suppose I wanted to gloat.'

'Because you didn't have anything better to do, did you? Like another case you could have been working on? Or being home a couple of hours earlier so you could spend extra time with your husband and kids? No, you chose to go and rub salt in that has-been's wounds.'

'He's not a has-been.'

'He is now. You saw to that. I read online that he's been suspended from the police. So your revenge is complete. Or is it?'

Lorna doesn't answer. She sips at her drink, almost emptying the glass. 'These are good. I'm going to have another. You want one?'

'Yes, I do,' says Jess, 'and I also want you to answer my question. Have you seen him again?'

'Kind of.' Lorna stops a passing waitress and asks her to bring two more of the same.

'"Kind of" meaning . . . ?' Jess persists.

'I said I'd help him with something. They gave him the chance to look at the case again, to see if he could come up with a new suspect. Unofficially.'

'And what did that have to do with you?'

'He asked me to go and talk to Tommy Henthorn.'

'Oh. My. God.' Lorna's unnerved by Jess's reaction; she appears genuinely disturbed. 'Lorna, you didn't?'

'Why not?'

'That is so out of order. You could get struck off for something like that.'

'Why? I went as a civilian. The only problem was, after I'd been, Ryan and I met to talk about what Henthorn had said, and a friend of Ed's saw us together.'

'Saw you together what?'

'Just together.'

'Lorna?'

'At a pub. I think he was going to kiss me.'

The waitress arrives with their next drinks, and spends a few moments tidying the table while Jess waits impatiently for her to leave.

When the waitress is gone, Jess says, 'I think you have finally taken leave of your senses.'

The alcohol is softening Lorna's brain, removing the inhibitions that might have stopped her from telling the truth, just like that time before, ten years ago, when Jess told her she was mad to be dating a married man.

'I think I might still be in love with him, Jess. And I think he loves me.'

Jess shakes her head in frustration. 'You're not in love with him – you don't even know him. You have this idea of him, this romantic ideal we can all form when life seems hard and dull. You're a married woman with young kids. The days of Acapulco holidays and long Sunday-morning love-ins are in the past for now. But it's a rite of passage, part of growing up. And you have to grow up, Lorna. Your focus should be all on Ed and Max and Dottie, not on some ageing copper who wants you to do his dirty work and then bed you. Ed's a lovely man, and you don't value him enough. If you're not careful, he'll be walking out on you, and then you'll really have your hands full.'

'Ed wouldn't walk out on me.'

'Why wouldn't he? While you're having your little flirtation, what's he doing? He's at home wiping noses and bums, cooking your dinner and hoping you're not too grumpy when you finally get home.'

'I'm never grumpy.'

Jess laughs. 'Listen to you. Everyone knows you're grumpy after your so-called hard days in the office. You know something? I never call you on an office day. Have you never noticed that?'

'No.'

'Think about it. You should cherish Ed. He's a very cherishable man.' Jess picks up her glass. 'Here's to Ed, salt of the earth, great father and long-suffering husband.'

'Ryan's asked me to have lunch with him.'

'Lunch? Where?'

'The Florentine.'

'That's not a restaurant – it's a hotel. With rooms.'

'I know.'

'Lorna, listen to me. Please don't go. There's so much at stake. Think about losing the kids. You'd regret it forever and ever.'

'I don't want to lose him again.'

'You never had him, and he's got no business putting you in this situation. Did he mess up his marriage, leave his wife for you?'

'No.'

'And you know why? Because even though I hate him for breaking your heart, actually he did the right thing. He chose his family, and that's what you have to do, too. If you go and sleep with that man, you'll poison your bond of trust with Ed. That's permanent, and you'll never put it right. Something between you will always be broken.'

'It's only lunch. I could at least talk to him, explain.'

'What did he do when he broke up with you?'

'He sent me a text.'

'There you are, then. Right back at him. Send him a text, job done.'

Lorna takes a big slug of her fresh drink. She's beginning to feel liberated, adventurous, daring. 'You're so melodramatic,' she says to Jess. 'I really don't think it would hurt if we just have lunch.'

SIXTY-TWO

Canfield has given in to a craving that has been nagging him for days.

When his phone rings, he's about to take the first bite of a still-warm Gregg's steak bake. His phone's in his pocket, and he almost decides to ignore it until he's indulged in his guilty pleasure, but then it occurs to him there's an outside chance – a million to one shot, but even so – that it could be Lorna.

Returning the toothsome pastry to its bag, he checks who's calling. Not Lorna, but someone he knows wouldn't call him for a casual chat.

'Ryan Canfield.'

'Hey, Ryan, Tate Fritchley. How's things?' Canfield hasn't heard from Fritchley in a long time. Fritchley's work in Serious Crime keeps him out in the field most of the time; he's not someone you bump into in the Kenton Road cafeteria. 'Is now a good time?'

Canfield glances wistfully at his pie. 'Of course. What's up?'

'You busy right at this moment?'

'Not excessively. You probably heard I got suspended.'

'I did hear that. But I got Lomas's permission to speak to

you, so we're all above board. Can you spare me a few minutes? Might you drop by? Not Kenton Road, my other office.'

'Be my pleasure,' says Canfield.

Canfield's been to Fritchley's unofficial office once before, and it's only a short drive away.

The tired-looking houses on the street where Canfield parks might boast a view of open hills, if it weren't for the all-but-derelict factories built in front of them. But between the backs of the houses and the abandoned relics of lost industries, somehow the residents have held on to a small and valuable part of their past: the Bishop Street allotments.

Tate Fritchley doesn't live on Bishop Street. Canfield has no idea how he's secured himself a piece of this land, which used to be a necessity to the working families who lived here, a place where they could grow fruit and vegetables to supply themselves with low or zero-cost fresh food. Probably he's simply gone to the council and asked, and maybe the council were glad to have him. A significant number of the allotments are abandoned and overgrown, sad contrasts to those under cultivation.

Like Fritchley's. His is tidy, with rows of leeks and sprouts, the unused ground weed-free and raked, ready when the time comes for spring planting.

When Canfield was last here, he asked Fritchley why he had this place; it seemed an odd sort of a pastime for a man with a reputation for hard drinking and a known passion for motorbikes. Fritchley's answer was short: '*I come here to be washed clean.*'

There was no need for clarification or elaboration. Canfield understood him perfectly.

Canfield picks his way up the muddy path, noticing that after last night's rain, the allotments smell refreshingly rural. From a distance, he can see Fritchley smoking a cigarette, surveying his bit of land like his own grandfather might have done. It's comforting to know some things remain the same.

As Canfield draws closer, like a deer alerted by some windborne scent Fritchley looks around, waving to Canfield when he spots him. It's impossible to get close to Fritchley without him noticing. Like creatures in the wild, his survival instincts are well honed, a necessity for a man who's earned more than his fair share of enemies.

Fritchley goes inside the allotment's wooden shed. By the time Canfield joins him, he's spooning coffee into two enamelled metal mugs, while a kettle set on a camping gas burner is coming to the boil.

'Come in, come in.' Fritchley nods in the direction of a canvas picnic chair. 'Grab a seat. Milk, sugar?'

'Yes to both,' says Canfield, remembering Fritchley's coffee is alarmingly strong. 'Two sugars.'

Fritchley doesn't speak again until the coffees are made, but Canfield doesn't mind the quiet. The view across the allotments is revitalising, a vista of what people can create when they invest their energies in worthwhile projects.

Fritchley hands him his coffee and settles in the chair beside him.

'Thanks for coming,' he says. 'Sorry to hear you've been declared official scapegoat.'

'Someone had to do it.'

'Have you ever noticed, though, it's never anyone above our rank? When can you remember anyone at senior level falling on their sword? Never, that's when. Reminds me of that old Bruce Hornsby song. That's just the way it is.'

'Lomas has given me a chance to go back over the old ground, effectively undercover. Redeem myself.'

'That's big of him. No impact on his budget, then. Think you might have come up trumps, though.'

'Really?'

Fritchley nods. 'That sergeant of yours, what's her name, Emma somebody?'

'Emma Goodwin. She's bright. Reliable.'

'I've been wondering who gave her the idea to look at the long-term missing persons lists.'

'Couldn't possibly comment.'

'And I remember you and I had a conversation around the time Tommy Henthorn was arrested, didn't we, way back when?'

'Yes, we did. About Faizan Jutt.'

'You've a good memory for names.'

'I've been doing a bit of revision.'

'Thought so. Your sergeant might be bright, but nobody's so bright they can pull the right name out of a hat ten years later.'

'You think it's the right name?'

Fritchley puts down his coffee and lights a cigarette. 'Here's the thing. With the media interest, Lomas can't sweep under the carpet this new information that Tommy reckons he knows where there's a body buried. Of course, he could be bullshitting, but I don't see why he would. What's he got to gain? Actually, he'd be better off keeping his mouth shut, waiting for his compensation and then riding off into the sunset. That's what I'd do. So you have to ask yourself, why's he stirring the pot?'

'Guilty conscience?'

Fritchley nods. 'I think this could actually be one of those very rare cases. He wants to come clean, get it off his chest, even though doing so could bring clouds of wrath down on his head. I've been doing a spot of homework on my own account, and it seems Faizan Jutt was a man of some ambition, and enough of a chancer to try and muscle in on that psycho Steven Bull's operations. You remember Steven Bull? Him of people-trafficking, drug-running, illegal-gambling fame?'

'Who could ever forget? As I recall, there weren't many pies he didn't have a finger in. Haven't heard anything of him for a while, though. What happened to him?'

'I'm delighted to say he got what was coming to him a couple of years ago. He was doing a short stretch for money laundering – like Teflon, he's always been, always got an alibi when one's needed, so we never got him on the big stuff. Anyway, they put him in a Cat C prison. Well, you and I know he shouldn't have been anywhere but Cat A, but sometimes you have to count your blessings. Security works both ways, doesn't it? There was a nasty incident in the prison kitchens involving a pan of boiling chip oil, which I'm sorry to say Bull didn't survive.'

'He's dead?'

'As the proverbial, and his little gang of faithful followers dispersed to the four winds. So when Tommy heard that . . .'

'Wait a minute. Have you spoken to him?'

'I have. I thought I'd pay him a personal visit, put his mind at rest about witness protection and all that bollocks. Then we got talking about this body of his, and he provided a rock-solid alibi why he couldn't have been in Risedale killing his son, because he was at Birdmoor burying a corpse for Steven Bull, under threat of a serious beating or worse if he didn't comply and under permanent threat of punishment if he ever spoke out. They told him they'd go after his family, and lo and behold, when he got back to Risedale and found Adam missing, he believed there was a possibility they'd made good on their threat regardless. He was very close to his mother, so he was worried sick for her. And after she died, he was – not unsurprisingly – looking out for himself.'

'Poor Tommy.'

'Poor Tommy indeed. Anyway, he's co-operating fully now. Keen to do what he can to get the man he was made to bury home to his family.'

'But does he know who it was?'

'He didn't at the time, no. But asked for a description, he can only be talking about one or two people on our missing-persons list. The deceased was of Asian appearance, he said. Which to my mind makes the most likely candidate . . .'

'Faizan Jutt,' says Canfield. The image comes again to his mind, that determined but desperate woman who demanded to see him, and her young son who was already fatherless, though he didn't yet know it. Maybe she knew it, though, or suspected it. Perhaps she felt her husband's loss somewhere inside, in her heart and in her bones. He's sorry now he didn't pay more attention. At the time, he thought himself too busy investigating the murder of Adam Henthorn, while in fact he was being presented with a crucial piece of evidence in that case. There's a lesson to be learned there. When things happen concurrently, never assume they're not connected. If Laila Jutt had been properly listened to at the time, if Faizan hadn't been written off as a worthless scrote or an errant husband, the outcome could have been different. Tommy would have had an alibi for his son's killing. Steven Bull could have been arrested for murder and taken off the streets once and for all. Canfield himself wouldn't be facing the sudden and embarrassing end of what had been a distinguished career. Him not listening to Laila had cost a lot of people very dear.

He feels overcome by a crushing weariness, overwhelmed by the magnitude of his terrible errors. Lorna had been right to come after him. If he'd paid more attention, got to the right answer, Adam's real killer would still be in jail.

'You OK, mate?' asks Fritchley.

'Not really.' Canfield shakes his head. 'I can't believe how badly I dropped the ball. Jutt's wife came to see me, not once but twice. She was certain something bad had happened to him, and she asked me to help her, but I was too busy going down the wrong path to listen. Is Tommy saying some of the witnesses lied?'

'Yes.'

'What a God-awful cock-up.'

Fritchley stands and crosses to the little stove and strikes a match to relight the gas. Canfield is silent while Fritchley makes more coffee, this time adding a generous nip of cheap corner-shop whisky to both mugs.

Canfield takes a comforting sip. 'What happens now?'

'Well, to begin with, we don't jump the gun. Tommy says he'll take us to where the body's buried, but maybe he doesn't remember as well as he thinks he does, or maybe he's talking crap. If we find anything, there's recovery to go through, forensics, identification. You know how it goes. Nothing will happen fast. You've still got time.'

'Time for what?'

'To get the right answer.'

'I think I have the right answer. Maybe.'

'There you are, then. That's what happens next.'

'I think it might be time for me to give you what I've got and walk away.'

'Come on, Ryan. You're better than that. We've all had failures. God knows I've had too many to count, some bad ones, too. If you want to pack it in, fine, but not until this job is done. If you think you're close, get back out there and bring back the proof. We'll make a deal. I'll go with Tommy and find Faizan Jutt. You go and get whoever it was who killed Adam Henthorn.'

SIXTY-THREE

The harsh lights of the interview room show dark shadows under Peter Rains's eyes, making him look like a man who hasn't been sleeping well. And maybe he hasn't been sleeping well, but DS Emma Goodwin has seen enough facial injuries to recognise the fading bruises of a broken nose. Alongside him, his solicitor looks bored, as if he has better things to do. Maybe Rains hasn't been completely honest with him about the depths of trouble he could be in. Or maybe Rains himself isn't aware of it, yet.

She sits down opposite him, next to the CID team's latest recruit, DC Jordan Archer. Archer is there primarily as notetaker, and has with him a thin cardboard file, from which he takes three copies of a single document, laying them face down on the desk as he's been taught.

Goodwin gives Archer the nod, and he switches on the recording equipment.

Peter Rains looks uncomfortable.

'Good morning, Mr Rains.' Goodwin's voice is cheerful and upbeat as she introduces herself and Archer. 'As was explained in the letter you received, this is an interview under caution.

You do not have to say anything, but it may harm your defence if you do not mention something when questioned that you later rely on in court. Anything you do say may be given in evidence. All clear?'

'Absolutely,' says Rains.

'May I call you Peter? What happened to your face, Peter?'

Rains touches the bridge of his nose. 'Such a stupid thing. I walked into a cupboard door.'

Goodwin lets it pass, and reaching for the face-down papers, turns them over and pushes copies across the desk to both Rains and the solicitor, keeping the last one for herself. 'Do you recognise this document, Peter?'

Rains makes a performance of taking a glasses case from the pocket of his jacket, opening it to remove a pair of gold-rimmed glasses, putting them on and adjusting them on his nose. Through the glasses, he peers at the document as if he still can't see it clearly.

'Yes, I do,' he says, at last.

'Can you tell me what it is?'

'It's a statement.'

'For the recording,' says Goodwin, 'the statement is dated 28th November, 2013. Is that your signature at the bottom?'

Again, Rains goes through the pantomime of adjusting his glasses. 'I believe so.'

'Could you read through the statement, please, Peter. Take your time. We'll wait.'

Goodwin watches him as he reads, seeing his eyes travel quickly down the single page and stay there as he plays for time, thinking.

Eventually, he looks up and gives an uncertain smile.

'Do you wish to say anything about this statement that you made?'

'You do not have to answer,' says the solicitor.

'I'd like to answer,' says Rains, removing his glasses. 'I believe it's possible I got the day wrong. That is to say, the wrong date.'

The solicitor sighs, giving an almost imperceptible shake of his head.

'You swore in a court of law that you were certain of what you saw on that date.'

'It's easy to get mixed up, though, isn't it?' says Rains. 'To make an honest mistake?'

'Is that what you're saying you did? Made a mistake?'

'You're not obliged to answer,' says the solicitor, more emphatically.

'Peter?' asks Goodwin.

But Rains has picked up on the solicitor's tone, and only says, 'No comment.'

SIXTY-FOUR

On the hills above Edale, across the moorland heather an icy wind is blowing.

Canfield used to come here sometimes when his marriage was failing, finding a level of comfort in the wild emptiness, in its unchanging magnificence, its permanence when everything around him seemed to be falling apart. Sometimes, he cried; sometimes, he was just plain angry, at cruel things Irene had said, at her vindictiveness over their settlement; sometimes he was afraid of a solitary future, that his relationship with his girls wouldn't be the same. But he got through it. It took time, but everything worked out, in the end.

Now here he is, facing another crisis. His conversation with Tate Fritchley has made him realise he's more to blame than he first believed for Tommy's wrongful conviction. And Fritchley's right. To walk away and leave it to others to clear up the mess is not the honourable way. If he wants to live with himself and be able to tell himself he did his best to make amends, he needs to act on what he knows.

Even if that means betraying someone he used to call a friend.

* * *

At the Securitylink offices, the neat line of vans parked in the compound is shorter than it was last time Canfield was here. Business must be booming.

Inside, Pearson's desk is occupied by a stranger, a young woman with her hair coloured an old-lady grey.

Canfield asks for Manny Pearson.

'He's working from home today,' says the young woman. 'Anything I can help you with?'

'It's a personal visit. I'm an old friend, just thought I'd drop in and say hello. Does he live far away?'

'Somewhere in Allestree, I think. Are you by any chance a policeman?'

'What makes you say that?'

The woman shrugs. 'You have that look about you. Manny's the same.'

'Once a copper, always a copper,' says Canfield. 'Don't suppose you could let me have his address? I was hoping to surprise him.'

'If you're police, I suppose I can,' says the woman, tapping on a keyboard. 'Give me a minute and I'll find the file.'

When they were working together, there were times when Pearson used to share his hopes for the future, things that he hoped to achieve, places he was going to go. He had an interest in architecture, and talked about night-school classes; sometimes he showed Canfield amazing landscape photos he'd taken on his days off, blazing sunsets and moody, overcast skies. But none of those dreams resembled anything like what Canfield finds at the Allestree address: a small 1950s semi on a respectable suburban road, the car in the driveway not even half as nice as the Audi parked next door. Pearson's house looks conformist, beige curtains at the windows and the scrap of front garden of uninspired design. If he pursued any of his creative dreams, the outcomes aren't obvious here.

At the front door, Canfield hesitates, contemplating the irrevocability of the step he's about to take. What he's intending to say can't be unsaid, and if he's got it wrong – again – he'll have destroyed the remnants of a long-term partnership and a relationship of trust, of which he had only good memories. Equally, though, how can he unknow what he's recently discovered? Pearson has some explaining to do. The policeman in him will understand that.

Canfield rings the doorbell. Almost immediately, he hears footsteps approaching the door, which is opened wide by a smiling Pearson. At first, Canfield thinks Pearson must have seen him through the window and that the smile is a welcome for him, but on seeing him, Pearson's smile changes to an expression of mild surprise.

'Oh,' he says. 'Hello.'

Canfield can see Pearson's disappointed he's not someone else, someone expected, but it's not his business to ask who that person might be. Whether it might become his business is another matter.

'Is now a good time?' Canfield asks.

'No offence, mate,' says Pearson, affably enough. 'A good time for what?'

'I thought you and I might have a word about a couple of questions I've got over the Henthorn case.'

'You still running with that?' Pearson's tone is dismissive. 'Not your job, Ryan. They've told you that. Let it go.'

'These questions are specifically for you,' says Canfield. 'If you'd rather I sent someone else round, I can do that.'

Pearson sighs. 'I suppose I've got a few minutes. Come on in.'

Inside, the house is welcomingly clean and tidy, with the fresh smell of ironed laundry in the air.

But Pearson suggests they go outside.

'It's not a bad day, is it? We can talk on the terrace. You can admire my gardening skills, such as they are. I don't do a lot, but I've got a few things in pots.'

Canfield recognises distraction chatter when he hears it, and wonders what he's meant to miss. Pearson too casually pulls shut the dining room door as he leads Canfield past, but Canfield has already noticed the ironing board draped with a pink duvet cover. They pass through the kitchen – no offer is made of a drink – and out of a rear door to a French café style table and chairs, where Pearson invites him to have a seat.

He waves his arm to take in a garden empty of interest except for evergreen shrubs, garden-centre staples providing colour here and there, surrounded by high fencing that allows some degree of privacy from neighbours who are really too close. 'All my own work.'

'Nice,' says Canfield, increasingly curious as to why they're out here in the cold, what Pearson is so keen to hide inside the house. 'Manny, I'm going to cut to the chase.'

Pearson pulls a puzzled face. 'What chase?'

'Let's start with you and Gail Henthorn. You knew her, didn't you? You and she, you were an item.'

'We went to the same school, if that's what you mean. I

thought I mentioned that. What's it got to do with anything anyway? That was years ago.'

'You were together for quite a while, though, weren't you?'

'It was just a teenage thing.'

'Was it? Come on, Manny. This is me you're talking to. Was something going on between you and Gail Henthorn close to or at the time of Adam's disappearance?'

'This is starting to be a proper grilling. Maybe you should read me my rights.'

'I'm not ready to do that. But, for old times' sake, just tell me the truth.'

Pearson sits back in his chair. 'OK, so I was screwing Gail. So what?'

Canfield isn't expecting so blunt an admission. With those few words, the mishandling of Tommy's case ratchets up to a whole new level.

Blindsided and lied to by a colleague he thought of as a friend, Canfield's angry. 'You're not serious? Why didn't you say so, and recuse yourself? So now we're really in the shit, right up to our eyeballs. What in God's name were you thinking?'

'Honestly? I wanted to help her.'

'Help her in what way? By falsifying evidence?'

'That's serious stuff, mate. You'd better have solid grounds for accusing me of that.'

Through the open back door, Canfield hears the kind of no-hurry, sauntering footsteps he hears so often when Caitlin and Annabelle are staying with him.

A young girl appears in the doorway, a very pretty child of nine or ten, her coat unzipped over her end-of-day rumpled school uniform, her long hair coming loose from a clip.

'Hi, Dad,' she says. 'What you doing out here?'

'Just talking, sweetheart. You have a good day?'

'Not bad.'

'Give me a few minutes and you can tell me all about it. Put the telly on for a bit if you want.'

'Hello,' says Canfield to the girl. 'It's Sabrina, isn't it?'

The girl nods.

'Go on inside,' says Pearson, more firmly. 'I'm nearly finished talking. I'll see you in a minute.'

When she's gone, Pearson's look is of defiance.

'Sabrina Henthorn is your daughter,' says Canfield. 'You can deny it if you like, but a DNA test would prove it. And you ask me why you shouldn't have recused yourself.'

'Gail wasn't even pregnant at the time.'

'So your relationship continued both during and after the investigation?'

'I'm telling you, it wasn't relevant.'

'Just give it up, Manny,' says Canfield, tiredly. 'We both know that it was. Anyway, you don't have to tell me anything. It's time for this to go through official channels.'

He moves to stand, but Pearson stops him. 'Wait a minute, wait a minute. What are you on about, official channels? Come on, Ryan, this is me you're talking to. Water under bridges and all that? We're talking a long, long time ago. It wasn't relevant then and it's not relevant now, and you know it.'

'But I don't know it. It's new information, and it should be logged for the new investigation. Especially as I think it explains something else I found.'

'What else?'

'The calls for assistance in the months before Adam's

murder, the ones we took as proof of Tommy's predisposition to violence.'

'What about them?'

'You logged the call-out sheets into the investigation files without telling anyone it was Gail who attacked Tommy, not the other way round.'

Unable to repress the subconscious sign that gives him away, Pearson double blinks, and Canfield knows he's hit a nerve. Pearson's going to lie.

'That's news to me. Wow. Well, that is new information.'

'No, it's old information which was misreported to the team. By you.'

'If it was misreported, it wasn't maliciously done. Come on, you know I wouldn't do that. Why would I? I suppose I saw what I expected to see. I have to say, though, I wouldn't have had Gail down for that.'

'Based on your personal knowledge of her.'

Pearson blinks again. 'Well, yes.'

'Hence why you should have recused yourself. Come on, Manny, you knew the rules. Why didn't you?'

Pearson spreads his hands. 'I'm not going to lie to you. It was a big case – I thought it was open and shut. I thought we'd get a quick result and it would look good on my CV. I was ambitious back then, remember.'

'I remember believing you were ambitious until you handed in your notice straight after Tommy was convicted. Actually you went from being ambitious enough to conceal information about your relationship with Gail Henthorn – which you knew went against all protocols – to deciding you'd had enough of the job and quitting in under a year. Something doesn't add up here. And Sabrina, where does she come into the picture? How come you never mentioned her before? Quite an omission, wasn't she?'

Pearson shrugs. 'We were talking about other things. She's only been living here a couple of years. I stepped in when I was contacted by social services.'

'Why were they involved?'

'Gail has a lot of problems these days. Why wouldn't she, after losing a child like she did? Unfortunately she was taking things out on Sabrina, so I said she could come and live with me for a while. Best thing I ever did, as it happens. Family comes first, doesn't it?'

'It should,' agrees Canfield.

'If I wasn't here, I don't know where she'd be. In care, most likely, maybe in one of those hell-hole council homes where bad things happen to kids like her. You don't need me to elaborate on that one, do you?'

'You saved her from that, then.'

'It was my job to. I'm her dad. You're a dad too. You understand.'

Pearson's expression is closed, hard to read, but Canfield understands exactly what Pearson's doing, how he's being manipulated. He has no doubts now that Pearson knows more than he's saying about what happened to Adam Henthorn, but if he brings Pearson's name officially into play, who knows where it might lead? Has Pearson withheld enough, dissembled enough, to be liable for prosecution? Only he knows; but obviously he thinks it's worth asking Canfield to keep his mouth shut to secure his daughter's stable future.

Here's a sizeable moral dilemma.

If Pearson's relationship with Gail really did have no bearing on the investigation, wouldn't it be best for everyone for Canfield to keep quiet?

Yet his gut is telling him he's at last got hold of the end of a golden thread – a thread that could lead him to the truth.

He stands up. 'I'll see you soon, Manny.'

Pearson doesn't get up. 'Sometimes you have to think about the bigger picture, Ryan,' he says. 'No need to stir the pot for no good reason.'

Canfield gets in his car and sits for a few minutes, thinking over what Pearson has said.

There seems to be no black and white. The whole situation is unsettlingly grey.

When eventually he drives away, he's so preoccupied he doesn't notice a red Toyota Yaris parked a little way beyond Pearson's house.

As Canfield goes by, the man seated behind the steering wheel hides his face.

SIXTY-FIVE

A new sign echoing Billy Challiner's old threat is nailed to the gate of Hagg Side Farm: *Trespassers will be shot.*

Time has not been kind to the place since Tommy was last here. Back then, on that awful day when Adam died, the place felt as if it were waiting for someone to pick up the reins old Billy could no longer manage, to make the place useful again, put the land back to productive work.

Whoever has owned the farm in the meantime has done none of that. All Tommy can see is decline and decay, the machinery seized up and rusting, the outbuildings and the barn collapsing in disrepair, the fields all lost to rampant weeds. The farmhouse does at least look habitable, though with no sign that anyone's been actually living there since Billy's death.

Tommy feels the burble of butterflies in his stomach, but he's no need to worry. Back then, he was alone, defenceless in the harrowing situation he stumbled into. Today, he's flanked by a small army of police, forensics specialists, Homicide officers. Walking at their head alongside Tommy is Tate Fritchley.

'I used to come here as a lad,' Tommy says to Tate, as they

walk up the overgrown track. 'The old boy who had this place used to give me a couple of quid to help him out on the weekends and school holidays. It was hard work, but I loved it. Always thought I might like to own a farm myself, but I never had the money.'

In the farmyard, the group halts. Fritchley turns to Tommy.

'Over to you, then,' he says. 'Can you remember where it was?'

Tommy can remember perfectly: the scene still haunts his dreams. They made him help carry the body – an Asian man in a three-piece suit and a shirt which had been white, before all the blood, who might have been handsome until Bull went to work on his face. His injuries were nauseating. On one of his hands, the fingers were missing their nails. Tommy had wanted to do him a last service by closing his eyes, but he was too afraid to do so, too fearful of similar treatment if he got up Bull's nose.

'This way,' he says. 'The field behind the barn.'

There are no sheep in the field now, the grazing ruined by ragwort and thistles and, close to the walls, by great spreads of nettles. But Tommy can pick out the spot. In preparation for this moment, knowing it was all he could do for the poor soul they were burying, when they were bored and left watching him for a while for the relative warmth of the barn, he risked pacing it out, making a rhyme of it in his mind to repeat as he was shovelling: *Twenty-three paces to the bottom wall, eighteen paces to the left.*

At the time, with the dead man and his smashed face lying nearby, Tommy had thought it easily the worst day of his life. Sometimes he had to stop to wipe away tears of anguish and despair with hands almost too cold to wield the shovel, not realising that he was blessed, still in the time of Adam being alive. But as he was playing undertaker to that cruelly tortured man, a far, far worse thing was happening at home: the murder of his beautiful son.

In his green wellingtons – considerably better footwear for the job than the trainers he ruined and binned that day – he runs through that rhyme again, pacing it out.

The place where he ends up appears unremarkable, except for an undulation where the land around is better described as flat.

'Here,' he says. 'He's buried here.'

'All right,' Fritchley calls to the team, 'let's get started.'

People begin to move, erecting a grid with poles and tape over the area Tommy's indicated, putting in markers, taking photographs.

Fritchley puts a hand on Tommy's shoulder. 'You can leave it to us now. They're setting up refreshments in the yard. Go and get yourself a coffee, and I'll call you if we need you.'

But Tommy shakes his head. 'I'm staying here. I put him in there, and I want to see him come out. I owe it to him and his family.'

'You can't stay, Tommy. This is a potential crime scene.'

'Make me leave and I'm saying nothing more.'

Fritchley sighs. 'OK, but stay out of the way. I'll see if we can find you a chair.'

A fingertip search is made of the area before a turf cutter is brought in and the gridded area is scalped. A tarpaulin is spread, and using trowels and sieves, two forensics officers begin to sift the soil from the site, dumping the spoil on the tarpaulin.

Hours pass. Tommy leans on the wall, watching. Eventually, Fritchley brings him a plastic crate to sit on, along with a heavily sweetened coffee and a bacon roll.

As he warms his hands on the mug, Tommy says, 'I can't forgive myself. I'll never forgive myself. Why didn't I tell you about him years ago? Why did I never speak up? I deserved to do time for that, for being a coward. His face kept coming back to me, but I was scared to death I'd end up just like him.'

'No one blames you for that, Tommy.'

'Don't they? You'd better ask his wife. I'll bet she blames me. I want to say sorry to her, I really do, but I'll never find the words.'

Fritchley claps him on the back and leaves him alone.

Ten minutes later, a shout goes up.

One of the forensics officers is holding up an object: a rotting rag of navy-blue cloth with a white thread barely visible.

Most likely a fragment from a man's pinstripe suit.

SIXTY-SIX

The day after he spoke to Pearson, Canfield is awake early after a disturbed night. Before he even tried to sleep, he decided his decision regarding Pearson – to declare the information he has to Lomas, or to say nothing – has waited so long that it can wait another twenty-four hours.

But he's nervous and excited, conflicted and uncertain. One thing Pearson said has stayed with him above all else: *family comes first*. What gives Canfield the right to upset another family's equilibrium? Because that's what he has planned.

Today's the day he's having lunch with Lorna.

As he showers and shaves and decides what to wear, the muted voice of his conscience whispers he should call it off. He isn't listening. He really wants to see her, and pretends to himself it's only to update her on how the case is going, even though the restaurant he's booked is wholly inappropriate for that.

Not for the first time with her, his rational mind has been abducted. But as he steps through the gilded doors of the Florentine, into the plush, other-worldly cocoon of oversized sofas, low lighting and deferential service, his self-delusion falls away. He is here to seduce and steal her, take her from the father of her children. Is that the man he wants to be? Should he really be doing this?

A waiter with polished Italian style leads him into the dining room. The space is small and intimate, the tables set apart to allow discreet talk between couples, the windows draped with voluminous velvet curtains carefully arranged so diners are hidden from passers-by on the street outside. The waiter pulls out a chair, and Canfield sits down at a table laid for two with white linen and blue glass.

The waiter hands him a menu. 'May I bring you something to drink, sir?'

Today, for once, Canfield's not planning to drive. 'I'll have a dirty martini. And a bottle of sparkling water.'

The waiter bows his head, and leaves.

Canfield checks his watch. He's a few minutes early; restlessness got the better of him, and he left the house earlier than he needed to, concerned traffic might be heavy or parking difficult. His stomach is roiling. Crazy to be so nervous. It's just a . . . what? A date? Hard to call it that, but the appropriate word – assignation – makes it seem sordid and underhand. But this meeting is underhand, at least for her. Guaranteed she's lied about where she's going to be this afternoon.

When his dirty martini arrives, he takes the first nerve-steadying drink and tries to focus on the menu.

Lorna has indeed lied to her colleagues about where she'll be from 12.30pm onwards, telling them she'll be attending a medical appointment so no questions are asked. When she put the entry in the online team diary, she reasoned that since she and Ed are not on the best of terms he's unlikely to call, but if he did he'd ring her mobile.

All morning at the office, she can focus on nothing. Initially, she feels a bubbling impatience in anticipation of seeing Ryan. But as the morning wears on, she becomes nauseous with guilt and worry, which telling herself this lunch is no more than a business meeting fails to neutralise.

Even she doesn't believe that attempted self-deception. This is a catalyst, a red-line moment, a possible step into a full-blown affair. She recalls how it was before: the delectations of the stolen hours, the piquancy of goodbyes said too soon. All of that, she wants to recapture.

But Jess's common-sense words have gone deeper than she thought. As the time to leave the office approaches, Lorna's 'it's just lunch' defence has failed drastically even for her, and she's thinking less of Ryan and more of Dottie and Max, how much she'd miss them if they weren't part of her daily life. And, to her surprise, she's thinking too of Ed, of how good things used to be between them and of how they might be fixed, if they only talked more, listened to each other instead of too often retreating into sullen silences.

So she won't have an affair. Immediately the decision is – apparently – made, she feels better, and able to justify meeting Ryan to tell him her decision face to face. They can be friends, can't they? Their bond is undeniable, and the thought of never seeing him again is painful, as bad as it was ten years ago.

They have history, a karmic connection. A couple of hours over lunch is the least they deserve.

She leaves the office at the time she planned, having done no work all morning.

But on the short walk from her office to the Florentine her steps are slow, and the eager anticipation she was feeling earlier is gone. Two streets away, she stops and takes out her phone, seeing she's already five minutes late. He must be wondering where she is.

She keys in a message: *So sorry, I can't do this. I need time to think. Don't be mad at me x*

For two whole minutes she stares at the screen, deciding whether to choose the nuclear option or walk the last two blocks to where he's waiting.

She presses send.

Canfield is thinking about ordering a second martini when his phone pings.

Intuition tells him before he's even looked what it must be, and he feels his heart deflate.

He reads her message, and without really thinking, keys a reply: *Is this your final revenge?*

Her response is fast. *No! Please don't think that!*

Then I think you're doing the right thing

You'll be my one who got away

As you have always been mine. Can we still be friends?

Always. Stay in touch x

I will x

She's gone.

For Canfield, the afternoon is empty, nothing to do and no one to share it with, the possibilities of a brighter future he was daring to imagine all vanished.

What to do now?

The waiter's back at his elbow, the menu lying closed on the table.

'I won't be eating lunch after all,' says Canfield. 'Can you please just bring me the bill?'

SIXTY-SEVEN

Now that the decision's been made, Lorna's emotions are mixed. She can't deny a crushing despair and an almost irresistible urge to take back what she's said to Ryan. Maybe it isn't too late.

But she keeps walking towards where she's parked her car, finding that the more distance and minutes she puts between them, the more she's able to look forward to where her time this afternoon will now be spent. She's proven herself trustworthy – faithful – and relaxes knowing she can face Ed with her conscience clear. Her life as it is can be happy, she's sure. She and Ed love each other, in their way. She'll make an effort to reseduce him, to rekindle the way they used to be, make time for date nights and romance. And she'll spend more time with the kids; they'll do more together, as a family. Starting this afternoon. Dottie will be home from playgroup. They could go to that soft-play place both the kids enjoy, afterwards get a pizza.

Yet beneath her optimism, her heart is betraying her. With every step, a part of her hopes her phone will ping, that Ryan will beg her to reconsider. He doesn't. As she drives the familiar route home, the craving for him is still strong, and though she persuades herself of how delighted Ed will be to see her, how pleased he'll be when she lies about taking the afternoon off so they can spend time together, she realises she's going to have to work to sound authentic. Not too upbeat. Don't overdo it.

Ed's car is in the drive, and to her surprise, a Volkswagen she doesn't recognise is parked behind it, leaving no room for Lorna. Annoyed, she parks at the kerbside.

Opening the front door, she hears Max's laughter, that delightful giggling he does when he's being tickled or chased, and that makes her smile.

This is what's important, she thinks. *I have so much I almost lost.*

But in the lounge, a woman she doesn't know – younger than Lorna, in tight jeans and a clinging top, dark-haired and very attractive in a southern Mediterranean way – is chasing Max around an armchair. And Max is loving it, shrieking so loudly that at first neither Max nor Ed – who's lying very relaxed on the carpet, grinning as he watches them play – notice that she's there. The three of them look relaxed together. They look like a family.

Max spots Lorna first, and runs into her legs, gripping them tight. 'Mama!'

He at least is pleased to see her. Ed appears flustered. The woman she doesn't know blushes bright red.

'Lorna.' Ed gets awkwardly to his feet. 'What are you doing here?'

'I live here, remember? Are you going to introduce me?'

But it's Max who makes the introductions. Leaving his

mother, he runs to the strange woman as if he might prefer her and announces her name. 'Rosa.'

Rosa has hurriedly left. Ed has taken a stance of reasonable indifference, telling Lorna Rosa's someone he knows from Dottie's playgroup, that if Lorna ever went there she'd know her too. Sometimes, apparently, Rosa drops in for coffee. Sometimes, after dropping Dottie off, he goes over to hers.

'What, with no one else there?' demands Lorna.

'Not no one, no,' says Ed, reasonably. 'Max comes too. Don't you, Maxie? It's nice to have company sometimes. When you're working, the days can get lonely.'

Lonely? If there's one thing she's never considered, it's that Ed might be feeling isolated. But then she's never thought of herself as the jealous type, and yet here she is.

The family afternoon of soft play and pizza is not going to materialise. Ed says he'll go and pick Dottie up while Lorna does a Sainsbury's shop, but Lorna insists she'll go with him.

'That makes no sense,' he says. 'You go and get Dottie, then, and I'll do Sainsbury's.'

'Why don't you want to be with me?' she asks, and to her surprise he whips round, his expression one of anger.

'Don't you dare, Lorna,' he hisses. 'Me, not want to be with you? Take a look at yourself in the mirror.'

'I don't want you to see her again.'

'Don't you? Well, first of all I'm not "seeing" anyone like you mean, and I resent you thinking that I would. And second of all, I think your detachment from our relationship has been going on for so long now, you've forfeited the right to any say in anything I do. I'm going to continue getting through my days the best way I can, and if you don't like it, feel free to go and live somewhere else.'

He seems then appalled at his own words, as if he'd no idea they were going to fall out of his mouth and end up where they are now, tumbling into the abyss between them.

As if she's been slapped, Lorna's shocked and afraid. This is new territory. A terrifying line has been crossed.

'You don't mean that. Do you?' Her voice is small and hurt, the voice of the girl she used to be when she first knew Ryan. 'Ed?'

When he buries his face in his hands, she knows she's in serious trouble. 'To be honest, yes, I do. I'm sorry, but things aren't good for us any more, are they? I think we need to talk about where we go from here.'

'But I love you,' insists Lorna.

Ed shakes his head. 'No, you don't. We're just an old habit that's going to be hard to break. But I want to break it. I don't want the prime of my life to go by in a blur of making the best of the status quo. Neither of us is who we used to be. You're all busy and important and I'm – nobody, just some guy who wipes noses and packs lunch boxes and cooks the dinners you mostly don't bother to eat. I've had enough of us. Simple as.'

'But we can talk about it, surely? We can fix things, change things. There's the kids to think of. They come first, don't they? Maybe you could go back to work. I could go part-time, job share. I know things need to change. We'd be more of an equal partnership.'

He shakes his head again. 'No. I'm ready to move on. I

want a different life, a fresh start. I can't even think right now what that might be, but I know I want to do it by myself.'

Lorna can't believe how she's hurting inside. 'You don't love me any more.'

Ed's attitude softens. 'I care for you. Of course I do. We've been together a long time. But that's not enough for me, and obviously it's not enough for you either. It's time we faced the facts. The light's gone out of us, and it's never coming back.'

SIXTY-EIGHT

On his way to work, Pearson calls in at a local petrol station to buy fuel. He's running late and normally would use Pay at Pump to speed through the transaction, but feeling peckish he decides he's time to pick up a sandwich from inside the kiosk.

The cashiers aren't busy, and he's soon ambling back to his car, opening the wrapping on his chicken Caesar wrap as he does so. Finding his key in his trouser pocket, he slides into the driver's seat and starts the engine, barely aware as he does so of a figure passing close by the rear of his car.

The passenger door opens, and someone slips into the seat beside him.

Pearson is taken aback, so surprised he's not even afraid, assuming for those first seconds that someone has made an honest and amusing mistake and got into the wrong car.

Until something prods his ribs.

Looking down, he sees the steel blade of a knife.

Believing he's being robbed, his instinct is to get out of the car and shout for help, but the knife point is pressing harder into his side.

'Remember me? You and me are going for a little talk.'

Tommy Henthorn. Despite the inevitable changes in Tommy's face, Pearson knows him. In truth, from the moment he heard of Tommy's release, he's been preparing himself for the possibility of this meeting, keeping a tyre-iron as a makeshift weapon behind the coat-stand in the hall.

What he didn't plan for was an ambush in full public view.

He needs to think fast, because disturbingly, Tommy has a plan.

'Just drive on nice and calm,' he says, 'and I'll tell you where we're going.'

Pearson's heart is beating hard enough to break a rib. No question Tommy's been watching him for a while – his timing and location are well chosen, a busy and anonymous place where no one's likely to have noticed anything out of the ordinary. In his mind, Pearson runs through what he can recall of his abduction situation training.

Page one, rule one: stay calm and establish a connection.

Tommy directs him away from the city centre, and Pearson asks, 'Where are we headed, exactly?'

Tommy responds only with further directions. No doubt he has a place picked out: the more remote, the better for concealing bodies and the worse for Pearson.

But Tommy doesn't direct him to any of the roads that would take them to open country. Instead, they drive to an industrial estate not far from the Securitylink offices, where they weave among functional grey business units anonymous but for the signage at the gates. There are, Pearson notices, a number of vacant units, where the last occupant's signage is covered by estate agents' boards. Tommy knows where he's going; obviously he's thought his plan through.

Pearson's training isn't enough to subdue the panic breaking through his calm veneer. In the past, he himself has attended long-dead corpses, all of them indoors, shut away from the public eye. In open countryside, in woodland or even on waste ground, dog walkers are everywhere, so if Tommy despatches him outdoors his remains should be discovered pretty quickly. But inside one of these disused warehouses, months might go by before he's found. He'll simply disappear, and what will Sabrina do then?

'In here.' Tommy directs him into the fenced yard of a unit with the hallmarks of long-term vacancy: tufts of grass appearing between cracks in the concrete forecourt, the estate agent's *To Let* sign in a state of faded dilapidation.

Against all his better judgement, prodded by the blade, Pearson does as he's told, following Tommy's instructions to drive round the back of the building. There, in a dead-end space between the high boundary fence and the windowless rear of the building, Pearson can go no further. Beyond the fence rises the steep, weed-ridden slope of a railway embankment. They're hidden from all sides in a place no one has any reason ever to go.

Tommy has chosen well.

'You can turn the engine off,' he says.

Afraid he might throw up, Pearson does so.

'Look, Tommy. I realise . . .'

He winces at a hard prod of the knife. 'Shut up and listen. I know what you are, you filthy piece of shit. You're the shitbag who was shagging my wife. Worse than that, you're a lying, worthless copper, the one who put me away for all those years and never said a word about it, went about your daily business like nothing was going on, while the world thought I'd killed my Adam. But I didn't kill him, did I? I didn't kill him, because you did, you rotten, stinking bastard.'

Tommy emphasises his last words with three sharp stabs.

'I didn't kill him, Tommy. I swear it.' Pearson dares to look across at Tommy, and sees a face twisted with hatred.

'Here's the thing, copper,' hisses Tommy through clenched teeth. 'See, I don't give a single shit if you live or die. It makes no difference to me if I kill you or if I don't, because I know the worst they can do is send me back to prison, and that doesn't bother me. I got friends there, and I got nothing to live for out here, so I might as well go back. Then my sister can sell the house – she'll be happy. Only one who won't be happy is your little girl. What do they call her? Sabrina? Pretty little thing, isn't she? Social services will send her to one of those council-run homes, and just imagine how they'll love her in there. You hear some terrible stories about those places, don't you, all those Jimmy Saville types running the show? You took my boy from me, so that's fair exchange, wouldn't you say? Tit for tat, an eye for an eye. The difference is, your little girl won't actually be dead, will she? She'll only be wishing that she was.'

Pearson tries to keep his voice reasonable. 'I didn't kill Adam, Tommy. I swear I didn't.'

Tommy gives a slow smile. 'Well, you would say that, wouldn't you? Under the circumstances, you'd be mad to say anything else. So excuse me when I say I don't believe you.'

'I didn't kill him, honest to God I didn't do it. It was Gail. It's true. At least give me a chance to tell you what happened.'

'I already know what happened. You lost your temper with

my son for whatever reason and you dunked him, thinking you'd teach him a lesson. Didn't you?'

Another painful jab with the knife makes Pearson yelp. 'No! I swear it wasn't me, on my daughter's life!'

'So why have you kept quiet all this time? If you knew who it was, why didn't you do what you were paid to do and speak up? And you're talking crap anyway. A skinny piece like Gail could never have carried Adam all that way.'

Pearson closes his eyes. He's getting that feeling he's so often heard described of his life passing before his eyes, vignettes of himself as a boy playing football with his dad, opening presents with his brother on a faraway Christmas morning. Carrying Adam's body through the woods.

It's time for the truth.

'I did that, I admit. I carried him to the well and laid him on that bench. But I swear he was already dead. Gail killed him.'

'How could she have drowned him, you prick? She didn't have the strength.'

'Please, listen to me. I'll tell you everything, but you have to give me a chance to explain. You can kill me if you like, but you'd be mad to do it before you know what happened. It wasn't me, I swear. It was her. Truly.'

There's no lessening of the knife point's pressure, but Pearson senses Tommy settle a little, ready to listen. The possibility is suddenly there that he might survive, suffer only a beating, if Tommy can be persuaded of how that dreadful day actually was.

He takes a deep breath. 'Me and Gail. You might think you know everything, but you don't. She and I went back a long way. We were just teenagers when we were first together.

She was the most beautiful girl I'd ever seen, and I thought I was the luckiest guy alive, having her. Probably you felt the same, at one time. But we weren't together too long. She had big issues, family stuff. The way her old man was, he was brutal. None of it was her fault, but she couldn't get past it. I don't need to tell you all this – you've been there. You know how she was, volatile, crazy even, mad with jealousy even though there was no need. I loved her heart and soul, I worshipped the ground she walked on, but in the end, I'd had enough. I thought if she was going to make a scene everywhere we went, I might as well be guilty as charged. Things got bad – she went for me with a bottle – and we split up. I couldn't see any other way. But she was my first love. I never forgot her.

'I heard she'd married and we lost contact for a long time, years. Then after you and she separated, she called me out of the blue, said she wanted us to try again. She promised me there'd be none of the old fighting and jealousy. I didn't believe her, but when I saw her she was still . . . Well, you know. She was so hard to resist. I'd have to have been a saint to say no, and I'm not that. But I didn't feel that old spark, and I didn't want what she wanted. She wanted to rekindle the big romance and for us to be a little family, but that's not me. You might say I was using her and maybe I was, but not the way that she used me . . .'

Pearson risks a sideways look at Tommy. He's staring straight ahead, apparently watching the long-stemmed grasses on the railway embankment blowing in the wind, but Pearson isn't fooled. Tommy's processing what he's hearing, deciding whether if, on balance, it's truth or lies.

Pearson goes on. 'That day, you might blame me for being the trigger. I told her I didn't want to see her any more, that we were done. She was upset, angry and hurt. I left her, drove away, but not long after she called me, begging me to go back. She said something had happened and she needed my help.

'If I had my time over, I'd never have taken that call. I should have just kept on driving and never gone back, because as soon as I walked into the house, I was either going to be complicit in her crime or damn her to a life in jail.'

'So you damned me instead,' says Tommy, quietly.

'I was wrong. I know I was wrong. But everything was so fucked-up. She told me what happened. Adam had come in all dirty. He'd been playing in some plaster-dust or something in the shed, and she dumped him in the bath to get him clean, still in his clothes and his little shoes. And he cried and cried – of course he did, he was terrified of her, with good reason. But she got sick of his noise, and she grabbed his ankles and pulled his head under the water and held him there until . . . By the time I got there it was obvious he was dead. It broke my heart to see him, but when she asked me to help her – 'Save me, Manny,' she said – that's what I did. At the time – God help me – it seemed an easy choice. I couldn't help him, but I could help her. I thought about that water butt outside or better yet that big trough in the woods, and I took him there. I knew the forensics and the pathology would check out because of the Risedale water, it being the same water in the taps as it is at the spring, piped direct to the houses, no purification or anything. So I put on your coat and carried him over there and I laid him on that bench where he was found. And I'm so sorry, Tommy. I'm so very, very sorry.'

Pearson begins to cry.

'Are you telling me she killed him because he got his clothes dirty?'

'Yes.'

For a time which seems to go on forever – Pearson crying and praying, waiting for the knife's plunge – Tommy stays silent. When Pearson dares to look, tears are streaming down Tommy's face, too.

'You were the police,' Tommy manages to say, eventually. 'You were supposed to protect him. But you laid him out there in the cold and wet, and you never said anything while I was searching and he was all alone in the dark. All that night, you could have spoken up and let me bring him home. My son. My beautiful boy.'

'You have to believe how sorry I am. I know it was wrong, but he was already dead. I had to try and help Gail. She was my first love. I loved her like I've never loved anyone else.'

Tommy rubs his eyes dry, gathers himself. 'I loved her too, but that woman's a curse. Now you have to decide if you want to save your own life.'

Pearson wipes his running nose on his sleeve, and nods emphatically.

'So I'm going to give you a chance to do that, and do you know why?'

'Why?'

'Because, based on my lengthy experience, I think in your case a few years banged up might be better payment for Adam than a knife between the ribs here and now. Bent coppers get a lot of attention inside. We'll drive down to the nick, you tell them what you've told me, we'll get you arrested and put in a cell, same as I was. Do we have a deal?'

'Yes. Thank you.'

'OK, then,' says Tommy. 'Let's go and make a start.'

SIXTY-NINE

In the tenth year after Adam Henthorn's murder, in an echo of the events of that time, a police car arrives at Blacksmith's Cottage.

Two uniformed female officers climb from the car, walk through the rain to the front door and knock loudly.

Gail answers the door in a state of alcoholic intoxication, swaying as she stands in her stained pyjamas and grubby bare feet, looking from one policewoman to the other, asking them what they want.

'Is it about my daughter?' she asks. 'She's nothing to do with me any more.'

One of the policewomen steps forward, positioning her foot to prevent Gail from closing the door. 'We need you to come with us to the police station for a chat, Gail. You're to be questioned under caution.'

'Me? Why?' Gail seems genuinely confused, but she's confused about so many things these days.

'It's about Adam.'

Gail waves a dismissive hand. 'That's all done and dusted. They got Tommy for it years ago.'

'Now they want to talk to you.'

'What for?'

'Why don't you find your coat and shoes?'

'I can't go now. I've only just woken up.'

'You have to come with us, Gail. It's the law.'

'Is Manny with you?' asks Gail, trying to see behind the women. 'I want to speak to Manny.'

'There's no Manny here,' says the policewoman. 'Only us. Go and get your coat. Better not keep them waiting at the station.'

SEVENTY

'Come in, Ryan, come in.'

Canfield can tell by the way Lomas won't quite meet his eye that the news isn't going to be good. He takes a seat in front of Lomas's desk, finding a little residual warmth in the chair seat. So the woman from HR who was leaving as he came in had been sitting here a while. That also may not bode well.

'I've organised coffee,' says Lomas. 'First of all, how have you been? I hope you've managed to relax, have a think about things?'

'I have done plenty of thinking, yes,' says Canfield.

'Excellent, good. Well, let me begin by updating you on the Henthorn case. We've had what I can only describe as some extraordinary developments. You'll no doubt be as shocked as I was to learn our own Manny Pearson was marched in here by Tommy Henthorn and all but confessed to Adam Henthorn's murder.'

'Really?' Canfield is surprised, and yet not. After his own conversation with Pearson, he finds it quite plausible that Manny was in deeper than he said. Murder, though? He would never have thought that.

But Lomas is going on. 'Henthorn had Manny's alleged confession recorded on his phone. We gave it a listen, of course, and to be frank, it was a plausible story, suggesting Gail Henthorn killed the boy and Manny disposed of the body. Henthorn is adamant there was a long-running relationship between his wife and Manny, but we interviewed Gail under caution and she and Manny both denied it. Anyway, the recording was obviously inadmissible, given it was obtained under duress. Henthorn threatened Manny with a knife, but he's decided not to press charges, which I think was the right thing to do. Personally, I think Henthorn's slightly deranged. Some historic involvement with a Vice-related murder has come to light, which certainly won't have helped his mental health. Anyway, long story short, Henthorn's accusations have unfortunately taken us no further forward in solving Adam's case. Unless you've come up with anything that might be useful?'

Canfield knows he has nothing to lose. 'Faizan Jutt.'

Lomas raises his eyebrows. 'You know about that?'

'I knew about it ten years ago – I just didn't see the connection. I think you might have jumped the gun slightly, letting Pearson off the hook.'

Canfield's challenge brings an expression of disapproval to Lomas's face. 'Manny was a long-serving officer with an exemplary record, Ryan. I'm surprised to hear you suggest he might be a person of interest.'

'I decided he was a person of interest when I discovered he and Gail Henthorn have a daughter together. Sabrina. Pretty girl. I've met her. Didn't Manny mention her?'

Canfield sees a flash of anger in Lomas's eyes. 'No, he did not.'

'Well, I'd say she's firm proof of an intimate relationship between him and Gail Henthorn, which meant he should have recused himself from Adam's case, rather than leave himself in a position where he could mislead me and the rest of the team and point us all in the wrong direction. I'm not saying I'm not to blame for the investigation's failings, because I am. The buck stopped with me. But Manny was involved in Adam's death, take it from me. I'd bet that confession was the truth, but we'll have to find other ways to prove it.'

'I think after all this time, we'd struggle to find proof,' objects Lomas. 'Manny and Gail Henthorn back each other up, no other witnesses. The CPS wouldn't even glance at it.'

'Then it's our job to give them something they will take notice of isn't it? At the very least, let's look at Manny for a Misconduct in Public Office charge, see what we can make stick and take it from there. Not exactly accessory to murder, I realise, but God knows he shouldn't just walk away.'

'All right, we can consider that. I'll get someone to bring him back in. You're sounding very confident about what needs to be done. It's a shame that same clear sense of direction wasn't evident in the original investigation.'

Canfield's heart sinks. Here it comes.

'I'm not going to sugarcoat this, Ryan. The whole investigation was sloppy from beginning to end.'

Canfield sighs, recalling Tate Fritchley's words regarding scapegoats. So be it. 'I think we were misdirected, sir. But yes.'

'So having discussed the matter at the highest level, I'm sorry to say we have no option but to let you go. I've spoken to HR, and I think we can call it a redundancy. There'll be a generous package for you. You've done some excellent work in your time.'

Even though he's lain awake for more hours than he could count worrying about this moment, now it's here, Canfield finds he doesn't care. There are other roads he can take, other paths he's keen to follow.

'I understand.'

Having delivered the blow, Lomas appears uncomfortable, as if he might be feeling a level of regret. 'What do you think you'll do? Any ideas?'

'Nothing solid, as yet,' says Canfield. 'I'll take some time to consider my options. I might do a bit of travelling. I've always wanted to visit Ireland. One thing, though, before I go. What will you do about Gail Henthorn?'

'What do you mean?'

'You said Manny's alleged confession was plausible. So what if it's true? I don't know whether I'm more embarrassed or ashamed of the way we've treated Tommy. We convicted him – a bereaved father – of the worst possible crime and cost him ten years of his life. Now I suspect he's done our job for us and delivered us the actual perpetrators on a plate – literally walked one of them right through our front door – and we've thrown our hands up, declared there's no chance of a conviction and let them both go. To be honest, I'm glad to be leaving, if that's how it's going to be, because that sounds like desperately inadequate policing to me. I realise it's nothing to do with me any more, but, the way I see it, don't you think you might be handing Tommy an open invitation to take matters into his own hands?'

EPILOGUE
The Life That Is Waiting

SEVENTY-ONE

All this time, Tommy's kept a key to Blacksmith's Cottage.

When he and Gail split, he left it on his keyring out of desperate hope, always thinking they'd be back together, him and her and Adam as a family.

That wasn't to be.

When he first went into prison, his keyring was taken from him along with all his other personal belongings and locked away, somehow following him around, he supposes, as they sent him here and there: the first three years in Wakefield, then a spell in Hull and finally to Durham.

When he came out, the keyring of course was given back to him with everything else he owned, and then he left that key on there as a reminder of better times, which – if not, in retrospect, what you'd call happy – at least had Adam in them.

But when it became apparent that bitch was going to pay no price for what she did – to Adam and to him – the key began calling his name.

Maybe Gail had changed the locks, but why would she? A quiet backwater like Risedale, no crime to speak of, not much need of locks to begin with. Anyway, the key's usefulness was easily tested. A visit in the dead of night to do no more than slip the key into the lock and see if it turned.

It did.

The rest was straightforward. In the mornings, so Barbara said, Gail drank, sleeping it off from mid-afternoon. In an alcoholic's stupor, she'd be hard to wake. Even if she did wake, she'd be too dazed and out of it to react or to remember seeing him.

Yesterday, Tommy had good news. Emma from Derbyshire Police called to say they were charging ex-DS Eamon Pearson with several offences relating to his actions during and following the investigation into Adam's death.

She was apologetic. As she said, it's not accessory to murder and any sentence will – though quite likely custodial – probably not be as long as Tommy might think is deserved.

But Tommy doesn't care how short Pearson's time in prison turns out to be. The longer the better, of course, but even a few days would suffice. Tommy's got his mates inside, and Pearson is that absolute pariah, a copper gone bad. No doubt at all, in the end Manny Pearson will get all he deserves, and plenty more.

The afternoon is cold but still. Tommy walks up in the direction of the cottage, not caring if he's seen, because him walking about Risedale is a common enough sight. Reaching Blacksmith's Cottage, he marches along the driveway as if he has all the business in the world being there.

Adam used to love pedalling his tricycle around this cobbled yard. It's all neglected now, nowhere for a child to play.

Keeping quiet as he can, he approaches the front door,

takes off his boots and puts on latex gloves. His key turns quietly in the lock, and in he goes, leaving the door ajar to minimise noise.

As expected, Gail is in the lounge, all but comatose on the sofa, the raddled, ugly wreck of the woman once his wife and the mother of his child. Did he ever love her? Oh yes, absolutely yes, but loving her has been the ruin of his life, and he feels nothing towards her now except blind rage. Let him do what needs to be done to put the world back in balance.

In his mind's eye, he pictures the room as it was while he was still living here: fresh paint, new carpet. Through Adam's first weeks of life, Tommy nursed him in that chair, utterly besotted with his fragile, perfect baby. Sometimes, if Adam was restless, Tommy would sing him the lullabies Lizzie used to sing to him, songs he didn't even know he knew that came from somewhere deep inside. And as Adam grew, the two of them built Lego edifices on that floor, using every brick they could find for maximum height, Adam giggling in delight when they finally toppled over.

When Gail told Tommy she wanted him out, those precious times were fewer.

Until – because of what she did – there were no more.

The wood-burner has been lit but is burning low, a layer of glowing ashes in its base. On the floor beside the sofa is a weekly TV guide, open at last night's pages. All he does is lay it on the embers, close the damper and leave the burner's door ajar.

On such a bed of ashes, the paper will smoulder for some time. And it will billow smoke. The first choking wisps of it are already catching in Tommy's throat.

He checks the windows are all firmly closed and leaves her, locking the door behind himself as he goes.

No regrets. No looking back.

Five days go by before he has a call from Barbara.

'Bad news, Tommy, I'm afraid,' she says. 'I hope you won't be upset, but Gail has passed away. The police broke in to get to her, and an ambulance was called, but she'd been dead a while, they think maybe several days. The paramedics said from the colour of her, almost certainly it was carbon monoxide poisoning. I always said she should get that rotten old stove looked at.'

Tommy puts his keys in his pocket and walks up the village, taking the path through Raymond's Wood as far as Druid's Well.

The bench where he found Adam is still there.

Now he has his compensation, he could buy a second bench. A place to come and sit, to be with his son.

Removing the key to Blacksmith's Cottage from his keyring, he holds it for a moment, then drops it in the water.

With barely a ripple, it's gone.

If he's guilty of any crime, his sentence is already served.

All debts are paid.

SEVENTY-TWO

Jess assured Lorna that a big night out was just what she needed, but for once in life it appears she was wrong.

In fairness to her sister, Lorna can't blame the choice of venue – a lively wine bar, where they've found comfortable seats and been served an excellent bottle of Portuguese Alvarinho.

'It's a great place to meet new people,' Jess said, 'your kind of people. You know, after-work professionals.'

But Lorna's finding the crowd around the bar too noisy, and the women with their office-black dresses and polished make-up appear too desperate to win the men's attention. So many of them look like lawyers. Is it that easy to pick her profession out in a crowd?

Jess refills their glasses, emptying the bottle. 'Drink up. I've got somewhere else I want us to go after this.'

Lorna decides to be honest. 'You know what, Jess, I'm just not feeling this. I might make it an early night.'

Jess is disappointed. 'You're kidding me! We're just getting started. The town's your oyster now you're a singleton again.'

'I'm not a voluntary singleton, though, am I? Everyone

seems so . . . manic. I miss the days when I had a home to go to.'

'You've got a home now, a place entirely of your own. I remember a time when you'd have killed for a place with peace and quiet.'

'You can have too much peace and quiet,' admits Lorna. 'I want a home that has people in it I love.'

For a few minutes, the two of them sit in silence, both aware of how different this evening is to their usual nights out. Near the bar, a woman around Lorna's age is listening to a man with an over-full glass of red recount some anecdote. Lorna notices the woman stifle a yawn.

'It's impossibly awful being back on the circuit again,' says Lorna. 'I'm not meant to be dating at my time of life.'

'You could just cut to the chase,' suggests Jess.

'What does that mean?'

'Your policeman. You could always give him a call.'

Lorna scowls. 'What, you mean the guy you described as an old loser?'

'Yes, him.'

'I expect that ship sailed long ago. Anyway, you've changed your tune.'

'Not really. I always thought there might be something special there. You used to light up when you talked about him.'

Lorna stares, incredulous. 'You total hypocrite. After everything you said, putting him down, telling me what a mug I was being. Now you're saying we were made for each other.'

Jess raises her hands. 'Whoa, don't go putting words into my mouth. I wouldn't quite go that far. I've no idea how you two would get on in the real world, and neither have you, actually. All I'm saying is, you might spare yourself hours of boredom listening to characters like the guy at the bar if you start with someone you know you at least have chemistry with. So rule him out first. Simple logic, wouldn't you say?'

'I wouldn't know what to say to him.'

'Why on earth not?'

'He's probably got someone else by now.'

'Only one way to find out. Call him.'

Lorna feels something bubbling up inside, pushing through the grey mass of melancholy which has been her default setting for many months. If she had to give the bubbles a name, she'd call them hope.

'Maybe I will.'

Jess grins. 'Well, go on, then.'

'What, now?'

'Yes, now. Find a quiet spot and ring him. Hurry back, though, or I'm going to drink your wine.'

Over the past weeks and months, Lorna has thought many times about calling Ryan, but the collapse of her relationship with Ed has sown seeds of doubt around every facet of herself. Who would take on a mother-of-two reject? If she's not attractive any more, will any man ever want her again? But Jess's encouragement – and a glass or two of Alvarinho – prods her to find his number. Without giving herself a second to think about it, she presses call.

Unknown to Lorna, Canfield is close by, in an Indian restaurant three streets away on a fourth date with a woman called Jenni.

Jenni's nice, and she's attractive, and Canfield's hoping that by sticking with her, he'll come to feel something that might help him make some kind of commitment. So far, though, the *give it time* approach has failed.

When his phone rings, Jenni's telling him about a funny thing that happened at the badminton club. Without checking who's calling, Canfield excuses himself, and goes outside to take the call.

'Hello?'

'Ryan? Is that you? It's Lorna.'

Taken by surprise, for a few seconds Canfield doesn't speak and, thinking she's made a mistake, Lorna's ready to hang up.

But then he says, 'Lorna. How wonderful. I'm so glad you've called.'

More bubbles of hope rise through Lorna's hopeless mood. 'It's been a while, and I've no business, really, out of the blue. Is now a good time?'

Through the restaurant window, Canfield can see Jenni sitting at their table, a pleasant, vacuous expression on her face.

He desperately wants to speak to Lorna, but that wouldn't be fair.

'I'm sorry, but actually I'm in the middle of something. Can I call you tomorrow?'

'Tomorrow, yes,' says Lorna. 'Can you make it after six?'

'I can make it any time at all,' says Canfield. 'But after six, of course. I'll speak to you then. And I'll look forward to it.'

Back at the table, Lorna sits down and picks up her almost-empty glass.

Jess is keen to hear what happened. 'Did he sound pleased to hear from you? Are you going to see him?'

'Mind your own business,' says Lorna, firmly. 'Aren't you going to order us more wine?'

SEVENTY-THREE

Sometimes the beginning is also the end.

Their first two beginnings were no better than long endings. Canfield is hoping this time with Lorna will be third time lucky.

County Galway is undeniably beautiful, but the Irish weather is unforgivingly wet.

Caught in a downpour on Silverstrand beach, Canfield has driven Lorna to a café in a nearby village, where they've eaten bacon rolls and drunk mugs of tannin-rich tea.

Apart from them, the café has emptied.

Canfield looks across at Lorna with her damp, wind-trashed hair and her fragilely pale skin the rain has stripped of make-up, and thinks how beautiful she is.

'Sorry,' he says.

She shakes her head, not understanding his apology.

'For this.' He indicates the room around them: the cheap chairs, the lack of tablecloths, the plastic flowers on the counter. 'I thought it would be more romantic. Dodging the rain and bacon sandwiches wasn't quite what I had in mind.'

Lorna laughs. 'Truly, no apology needed. Welcome to real life. Besides, the hotel is very romantic.'

Avoiding the bottles of brown sauce and ketchup, he reaches across the table for her hand. 'I wanted to impress you. We should have gone somewhere hot. Marbella. Or California.'

'You don't have to impress me – you know that. And I don't think I'm a Marbella kind of a girl. But California – wouldn't that be fabulous?'

Canfield's phone pings, and he withdraws his hand. 'Do you mind?'

'Be my guest.'

He reads the message quickly, turns off his phone and puts it away. 'Manny Pearson's sentencing. I asked Emma to let me know what happened.'

'And?'

'Two years.'

Lorna's eyebrows lift. 'OK. What do you think?'

'It sounds light to me, and he'll probably only do eighteen months. But in his position, it'll be tough. The worst thing for him will be knowing his daughter's being put into care.'

'That's hard.'

'Very. Though Tommy might disagree.'

'Do you think so? The girl's innocent.'

'The sins of the fathers, as they say . . .'

'Forget about that. Time to put it behind us and get on with our lives. Do you have any madly romantic plans for us this afternoon?'

Canfield turns to the window behind him. Outside, the rain is coming down hard.

'I was thinking about exploring the town, then on to Coffey's for a few oysters and a pint of Guinness.'

Lorna bites her lip apologetically. 'To be honest, I'm not that keen on oysters. And Guinness isn't my favourite, either. Sorry.'

Canfield laughs. 'No, I'm sorry. That was stupid. I should have asked. There's a lot about each other we still don't know.'

'No big rush,' says Lorna. 'We've plenty of time. And I really liked that wine we had with dinner last night. Why don't we go back to our lovely hotel and order a bottle on room service?'

Canfield squeezes her hand. 'Sounds like a perfect plan to me.'

SEVENTY-FOUR

When she answers the knock on her door, Barbara is delighted to see Tommy on the doorstep.

'Well, aren't you a sight for sore eyes?' she says. 'Come in, boy, come in. It's been a while since you've been to see me. Come on in.'

But Tommy hangs back. 'I brought a friend. If she's not welcome, she won't mind waiting outside.'

At Tommy's feet, Barbara sees a young fox terrier, looking up at her with intelligent eyes.

'Oh,' says Barbara. 'She's a pretty thing. Who's this?'

'This is Meg. They rang me from the rescue centre at Derby to say they'd got a black Labrador come in. When I got there, the Labrador was spoken for, but this young lady was lying all miserable in a corner. She didn't want to be behind bars. She's for the outdoors, like me. Anyway, she's no trouble, but if you don't want her in the house, I'll leave her out here.'

'Don't be soft,' says Barbara. 'Bring her in.'

Barbara serves Tommy coffee at the kitchen table and, though he tries to decline, makes him a thick sandwich of cheese and homemade apple chutney.

'You've got way too thin,' she tells him as he eats. 'I've said to you, you can always have your lunch with me.'

'I have been losing weight,' admits Tommy, 'because I've been working. The cottage is all fixed up now, damp-proofed, new bathroom and kitchen, the lot. You won't recognise the place. Getting it ready to sell.'

'Really?' Barbara tries to hide her dismay. 'I thought you'd decided to stay put.'

Tommy slips Meg a crust of bread under the table. 'That was my plan when I first got out. But my face doesn't fit, does it? Things aren't the same for me here, and never will be. I shan't go far. I won't leave Mum and Adam. I've found a cottage I want to buy, over the hill at Sledwell, just a shell, really, and not even a proper roof, but I've got ideas. It's only one bedroom but I'm going to add to it, and make something of the garden. Dawn wants her share of the money from the sale of the old place – that's only fair.' He pauses, looking down at his almost-empty plate. 'Risedale was my home, but it's not been good to me, in the end. I know where I stand. Time to part company.'

Barbara feels sad; an era is passing. 'You'll come and see me, though, won't you? I shall be sorry to see your old place sold. We had some good times there, didn't we?'

Tommy reaches across and squeezes her bony hand. 'Course I'll be seeing you. Mum would kill me if I didn't take care of you. Anyway, I'll be about the district. I've bought myself a van, so I can set up doing a bit of walling. I learned all the tricks from old Billy Challiner, so I reckon I'll do all right.'

'It's a lonely job, is walling,' says Barbara. 'Why don't you do regular building, extensions and that?'

'I won't be lonely,' says Tommy, reaching down to stroke the dog's head. 'I've got Miss Meg here.'

'I'll cut you a piece of cake,' says Barbara, standing to go to the cupboard. While she has her back to him she asks, 'Any news of that policeman? You know the one I mean.'

Tommy doesn't immediately answer, and she turns round to see if he's heard.

'Tommy?'

'There's news, yes,' he says. 'They've got him in solitary confinement, where they think he's out of harm's way. Two years they gave him – that's all. Two years, after what he did to Adam.'

'He'll get his just desserts – don't you worry about that.' Barbara puts a large slice of seed cake on the table in front of him. 'Life has a way of doing that.'

'Is that what I've got, then? What I deserve?'

Barbara looks at him. She can see nothing of tragedy in his face, nor hear any bitterness in his voice; in fact, his expression is neutral, his question that of a man accepting yet wholly bewildered by the unfairness of his fate. But something about him – something you couldn't put your finger on – declares his ongoing suffering, almost completely concealed by his remarkable stoicism.

On one side, she thinks, *the policeman locked away in his solitary cell; on the other, Tommy alone up there on the hills, stone by stone fixing those broken-down walls.*

She sighs. 'You've a hard furrow to plough, much tougher than most, there's no denying that. But, you know, your mum would despair to think of you always unhappy. If she thought that was all your future, her poor heart would break in two all over again. There's no one in this world can explain to you why these things happen, but if you'll take an old woman's advice, I'll propose you a road to follow. As best you can, you forget about those that hurt you. They don't deserve any more of your time. You put them behind you, and you keep on going, one foot before the other, day after day. You press on through these dark times, you make your plans, you get up every morning and you do what needs to be done. You work hard, and you rebuild your walls and you fix up your house, for Adam's sake and your mum's, but mostly for your own. And I promise you, if you can do that, you'll wake up one day – maybe sooner and maybe later, who knows when it will be – and you'll see that life's beginning to taste sweeter.

'The sun will shine on you again, Tommy my boy. I promise you on my own life, one day it will.'

ACKNOWLEDGEMENTS

My especial thanks go to my insightful and inspiring editor Toby Jones, whose careful guidance – as always – transformed a rough manuscript into a novel worthy of publication. And to all the Headline team, thank you once again for all your talents, and for turning my words into a beautiful book I am truly proud of.

To ex-Detective Sergeant Terry Parry, a huge thank you for your patience in answering my long lists of questions so thoroughly – your input made the story what it became.

To Ken Fishwick, very grateful thanks for your painstaking research and your attention to those details I had missed – I couldn't have done it without you.

And to my wonderful husband Andy, thank you as ever for your wise words, your encouragement and all those cups of tea.

Discover more from Erin Kinsley . . .

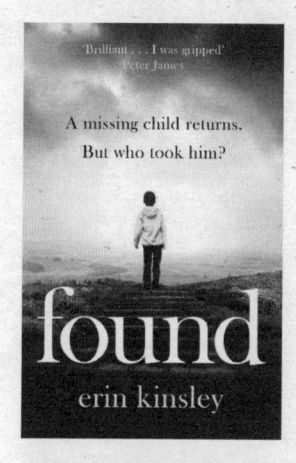

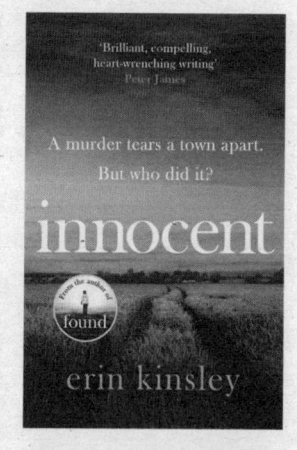

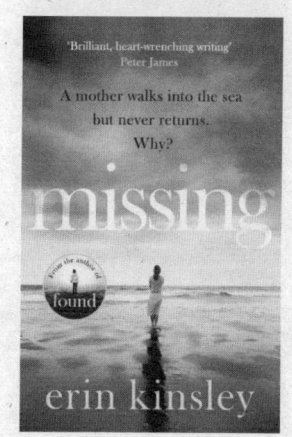

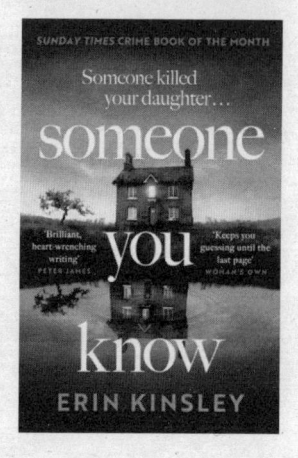

Available to order